WHISPERING
PINES

TALES FROM
A NORTHWOODS CABIN

ELLIOTT FOSTER

For Keith,
all the best,
Elliott Foster

WISE Ink
CREATIVE + PUBLISHING

This is a work of fiction. Other than references to Lake Dunbar, various towns and landmarks, Mona Bell Hill, Helen Bryan, and the Leino's General Store, the places and characters in this novel are the creation of the author, and not intended to represent any real person or place.

ISBN 13: 978-1-940014-54-8
eISBN: 978-1-940014-53-1

Library of Congress Catalog Number: 2015932955
Printed in the United States of America
First Printing: 2015

19 18 17 16 15   5 4 3 2 1

Cover and interior design by Ryan Scheife / Mayfly Design

Wise Ink Creative Publishing
222 N 2nd St., Suite 220
Minneapolis, MN 55401
www.wiseinkpub.com

To order, visit www.itascabooks.com.
Reseller discounts available.

"In Whispering Pines, Foster unearths some of the greatest treasures of Minnesota—her wilderness, history, icons of time and place, and the characters depicted within generations of the Travis family. In this soulful journey, you travel like a ghost, never having to go very far, yet intimately entering the landscape of memories, folklore, and understated Midwestern culture. As a love that comes softly and grows in its magnitude and scope, this vacation place in the Northland beckons stewardship and preservation from all its partakers, readers included."

— CAROLYN BIZIEN, THE RURAL AMERICA WRITERS CENTER

"If Henry David Thoreau made an American icon of the cabin in the Walden Pond woods where he stayed off and on for about two years, Elliott Foster's cabin is a grittier place in Minnesota's Northwoods enjoyed by a family for several generations. In writing that is as fresh and clear as the cabin's lake waters, Foster recalls the simple pleasures and setbacks that make the experience in his beloved "Whispering Pines" getaway not only memorable, but vital to the family's identity, unity, and durability."

— EMILIO DEGRAZIA, MINNESOTA BOOK AWARD WINNER

"Elliott Foster paints a detailed picture of cabin life as experienced by three generations of the Travis family. You'll feel like you are one of the family."

— TERESA THOMAS, AUTHOR OF HOW TO TAP INTO
THE POWER OF WIN/WIN CONNECTIONS

*This story is dedicated to all those lucky people
who have owned a cabin "at the lake,"
and to all those who ever wanted one.
And to the Binder family.*

We shall not cease from exploration
And the end of all our exploring
Will be to arrive where we started
And know the place for the first time.

– T.S. ELIOT, *FOUR QUARTETS*

INTRODUCTION
THE BEGINNING AND THE END

Our story begins and ends on September 15, 1993, in Cannon Falls, Minnesota, a bustling midwestern town of two thousand inhabitants, hugging the banks of the Cannon River halfway between Rochester to the south and the Twin Cities of Minneapolis and St. Paul to the north. Outside of town along U.S. Highway 52 sits The Edgewood. This renowned local supper club is nestled in a growth of tall pine and mighty oaks—the remnants of a great hardwood forest that once swept the fertile plains from the Mississippi to the Missouri rivers. The Edgewood is a respectable establishment with well-dressed patrons. It's a place to order typical midwestern fare like New York strip steaks, broasted chicken, and batter-fried shrimp. And, a baked potato accompanies every meal, as do fresh-brewed coffee and unlimited trips to the salad bar. All for $9.95 per person.

From Minneapolis, two cars sped toward The Edgewood. They quickly passed through the towns of Hampton, Coates, and Vermillion. From the south came two more, bearing down on the Cannon Falls city limits, passing through the hamlets of Pine Island, Zumbro Falls, and Harwood Corners. By 7:30, all had arrived, and the most important was Isabelle. Each had journeyed to The Edgewood this particular evening for a special celebration: Isabelle's eightieth birthday party.

Our family has been known to transform birthdays into raucous celebrations filled with culinary delights, youthful enthusiasm, and passionate laughter. At Jack's fortieth birthday party, he was ruthlessly roasted by family and friends alike, culminating with his wife's

1

affectionate toast: "Here's to Jack, raise your glass. Here's to Jack, he's a horse's ass!" At Ruth's fiftieth birthday extravaganza, hotel security was summoned as she proudly rode her cherished birthday present, a restored maroon 1948 Roadmaster Luxury Liner bicycle, around the tenth-floor balcony of the Embassy Suites Hotel to the cheers and laughter of those in attendance. When other guests summoned hotel security to investigate, all the guard could do was suppress his own laughter, and assist the birthday girl in re-attaching her loosened bicycle chain halfway through her route around the hotel's top floor.

Isabelle's eightieth birthday party was different. Not that the family avoided laughter on this potentially solemn occasion, for they roasted and teased her thoroughly. In fact, between dinner and cake, each family member took turns at a podium telling "Grandma Stories." With eighty years of material to work with, we continued until well past closing time. Isabelle, after all, had been the matriarch of our family for sixty years. Her strong will, fiery determination, and sense of family were legendary.

As the storytelling progressed, everyone quickly realized most of the stories revolved around our individual and shared experience with Isabelle at the Travis family cabin on Lake Dunbar in northern Minnesota. Our experience is the quintessential northern-Minnesota cabin experience. This is where we began fishing in the 1920s, built a cabin in the 1950s, and lived out our lake country dreams for more than half a century. This too is where we encountered both the famous and infamous of northern Minnesota, including Mona Bell Hill, Helen Bryan, Herb Beer, Dusty Lane & Fiddlin' Russ, and of course the unforgettable Screamer from Squaw Lake.

The Travis family's rich story on the shores of Lake Dunbar, as told through the memories of those attending Isabelle's eightieth birthday party on a cool autumn night in 1993, is a tale of natural beauty set in the heart of one of our nation's last vast forests. Ours is a story of joys and triumphs echoing across the generations, as well as a story with sorrows and tragedies that molded the will and strength of this family.

It is indeed a blessed gift to experience life amidst the power of the trees and rivers, with the freshness of the wind always in your presence, and the limitless freedom of the wilderness. Such is the foundation for this sacred place that shaped the lives of the Travis family for four generations, and counting. By the end of the September night in Cannon Falls so many years ago, those assembled had re-told tales of comedy, tragedy, and triumph, virtually the entire story of the family's shared journey through time, and with our neighbors along the shores of Lake Dunbar. That story, as told in three parts by Grandma Isabelle, her daughter Ruth, and her grandson Eddie, went something like this.

PART I

ISABELLE

Footprints Under the Whispering Pines

I WAS SIXTEEN YEARS OLD THE DAY I FIRST HEARD THE NAME Dunbar. Those two rapscallion uncles of mine were visiting my parents' home outside of Greenwood in southern Minnesota, and were spinning a long yarn about their latest adventure. Louie and Frank frequently regaled family and friends alike, telling stories of Herculean battles with dangerous forest beasts and mammoth-sized fish lying deep in our state's abundant waters. Of course, my uncles always won the battles. For some reason, they did not bring home the actual fish from their latest excursion. They proffered reasons, such as neither brother particularly liked to eat fish, so their plentiful catch was either given away or thrown back into the lake. "Catch and release," they called it. "Embellish and exaggerate" may have been more accurate.

It was the summer of 1929, and my second-to-last summer living at home on the farm. It seemed like such an exciting time in the world. Hoover had just succeeded President Coolidge, those crazy Germans built and flew a Zeppelin dirigible around the world in twenty-one days, and a new fizzy beverage called "7-Up" was now on the shelves at the grocery store on Main Street. Along with Mom, Dad, and a few too many annoying brothers and sisters, we had a house full of constant activity to keep me from getting bored. Our favorite family activity was to gather 'round the tall wooden radio in the front parlor on Saturday nights to play mah-jongg, work crossword puzzles, and listen in on the Grand Ole Opry being broadcast all the way from Nashville, Tennessee. I'm not one to brag, but we were one of the few rural farm families to have a radio just like all the folks in town.

All was good, yet from as early as I can remember, I yearned to leave this farmstead and see the wider world. Those may have been the silly musings of a sheltered young country girl, but these dreams remained with me as I stood on the threshold of becoming a woman. Perhaps this is why I was so enthralled with my uncles Louie and Frank, listening with rapt attention to their frequent tales of travel and adventure. Second-generation Americans whose agrarian grandparents emigrated from northern Germany, Frank and Louie fought for our country in World War I eleven years earlier, and remained restless for the next adventure. My uncles were instinctively drawn to far-off places, and fully enjoyed sharing tales of their discoveries with all who would listen, especially their favorite niece—me, Isabelle.

We all had larger-than-life dreams at the end of the 1920s, after all, still living high in the so-called Roaring Twenties, unaware of all the heartache that would follow in the two decades to come. Everything seemed possible and promising in 1929. Women now had the right to vote, Pope Pius emerged from the Vatican for the first time in sixty years, and there were rumblings of ending the terrible idea of Prohibition. Back then, I was always excited to make the trip into town where I'd meet my school friends and pay a few cents to watch talkies at the Bijou. I couldn't believe my eyes when I saw the movie *On With The Show*, completely in color. The world seemed unconquerable, the possibilities endless. I was enraptured by all of the days' music, which spoke of faraway places. "Carolina On My Mind," "Way Down Yonder in New Orleans," and "Alabamy Bound," just to name a few. Al Jolson's "California Here I Come" really piqued my imagination, though. Everything about the far-western coast of the U.S. fed my dreams of exotic travel. After all, all of the new movie stars lived there, and California was seemingly the nation's future.

In this unprecedented year of financial turmoil with the stock market crash, my uncles took off in the early spring seeking fishing nirvana. Louie and Frank planned to travel more than three hundred miles from our small southern Minnesota town as far north as Grand Rapids, a booming lumber mill town poised at the entry point to northern Minnesota's immense lake country. Following in their explorer heritage, I suppose it was only natural Louie and Frank discovered the secret of Lake Dunbar. My uncles fit in naturally with the great northern forests and their waterways. They were big boned, tall, and powerful men who would not have been out of place or mistaken as latter-day descendants of the great Paul Bunyan himself. By divine inspiration, a happenstance recommendation, or simple dumb luck, they landed in the don't-blink-or-you'll-miss-it village of Deer River, in the heart of the Leech Lake Indian Reservation. Using this town as a base, Louie and Frank spent several days trying their luck fishing on a variety of nearby lakes. Dixon, Cass, Winibigoshish, Island, Squaw, and Dunbar. My uncles seemingly found their favorite spot, for they made the three-hundred-mile journey back to Dunbar twice more the same year.

Perhaps this tranquil spot turned out to be the fishing Valhalla my uncle Frank had originally sought, because Dunbar was the last sport-fishing spot he ever visited in Minnesota. Frank may well have decided he'd reached the pinnacle of what the generous Land of Ten Thousand Lakes had to offer. Or perhaps it was his unquenchable yearning to explore new boundaries, or the hope to rid himself of the effects from the oncoming Great Depression. The following year, Frank moved west to the Golden State of California. He was living my dream, and I didn't know whether to be envious or excited at the prospect that I might someday be able to visit him. In the meantime, I would work hard on the farm and at school, looking for every opportunity to turn the fantastic visions of my childhood, from Lake Dunbar to California, into the firm realities of an adult. Yes, I was sixteen years old the day I first heard of Lake Dunbar, and its images would remain in my heart for the rest of my very long life.

Ninety miles from the Canadian border, the waters of Lake Dunbar splash against soft, muddy shores surrounded by a vast virgin forest. While Dunbar is but one of the thousands of medium-sized lakes in Minnesota's flat northern landscape, it exudes a character all its own. A small creek fills Dunbar's depths with cold, spring-fed water. Tall shoots of wild rice surround its shores. And towering pines protect the creatures depending on this lake for sustenance. Simply put, Lake Dunbar is beautiful.

In contrast to most of the accounts I can tell you about Lake Dunbar, the actual beginning of my tale is difficult to know for certain. The story of Dunbar's origin is not based upon any records or recollections. No pictures, no writings, and no certainties exist. However, people have many theories as to how and when Lake Dunbar came to be. Some contend the rocks, trees, water, and wildlife sprouted here following the Big Bang, or maybe on the third day of God's creation. Others suggest the land was originally flat, later to be carved and cut by glaciers depositing large chunks of melting ice left behind to form lakes, with evolution filling in the remaining gaps of wildlife and topography. I choose, however, to believe the truth lies within the Minnesotan legend of Paul Bunyan and his companion, Babe the Blue Ox. Paul, according to legend, was a towering lumberjack who stood one hundred feet tall, weighed approximately two thousand pounds, and as near as anyone can recall, strode through the upper midwest creating lakes wherever he stepped. As for rivers, we can thank the gigantic oxen, Babe. While accompanying Paul on his journeys surveying the north woods, Babe's dragging tail created the St. Croix, the Red, and the mighty Mississippi rivers. Oddly enough, Lake Dunbar is shaped like a long foot, with wide arch and rotund heel. Judging from the surrounding landscape, Babe was nearby when Paul Bunyan's huge foot formed Lake Dunbar. The headwaters of the Mississippi River at Lake Itasca lie just a few miles to the southwest. The story of Dunbar's creation is perhaps not all that important. Yet, the creator of this stunning body of water deserves all the kudos credited to any timeless artist.

The history of people in and around Lake Dunbar is somewhat better documented, from what I've read. Native Americans were the first to fish, hunt, and live among the half-million acres of the Chippewa National Forest. Historians and archaeologists estimate humans first set foot in Minnesota around five thousand years B.C. However, the first chronicled inhabitants in the area were part of what is now called the Laurel Culture, a society of hunters and gatherers living here from 500 B.C. to 800 A.D. This tribe prospered along Minnesota's vast lakes and rivers, using the waterways for transportation, trade, fishing, and warfare. The descendants of the Laurels, known today as the Blackduck Culture, populated Minnesota's woodlands for the following six centuries, flourishing in apparent peaceful coexistence with nature and wildlife. Much is known about the Blackduck people from the artifacts, pictorial history, and their descendants. In fact, many an adventurer has discovered an earthen clay pot, an arrowhead spear, or a burial mound on this land. Native American pictographs still cover many rocks on the shores of northern Minnesota lakes, and to this day Native American people populate a vast area of northern Minnesota woodlands and communities.

The history of European men and women in the north woods of Minnesota is more recent, of course. In the 1600s, French voyageurs tramped all through these forests and across Minnesota's lakes and rivers. Daniel Greysolon, Sieur du Lhut, the namesake of northern Minnesota's largest city, headed the first official French expedition to the area. In 1679, they explored lands a few hundred miles to the west of Lake Superior, and as far south as Mille Lacs Lake. In the 1730s, Pierre Gaultier de Varennes, Sieur de La Vierendrye, and his sons explored the territories farther north along the Rainy River and Lake of the Woods, the present-day boundary between Minnesota and Ontario. Certainly, one or both of these adventurers passed through the Chippewa National Forest, perhaps even across the shores of Lake Dunbar. As they penetrated the lands throughout northern and central Minnesota, the French explorers encountered the successors to the Blackduck Culture, the Dakota (Sioux) and Ojibwe (Chippewa) tribes. The French made swift alliance with the Ojibwe, and forced their way into a profitable trade: furs for guns. Armed with newly acquired French weaponry, the Ojibwe drove the Dakota tribes out of the northern forests and onto the plains to the south. Following another armed conflict, the French and Indian War, the English wrested control of the region in 1763, and carried on the booming fur trade.

After procuring this land in 1803 as part of the mammoth Louisiana Purchase, the United States government sent its own explorers to the northern woodland frontier. Captain Zebulon Pike, the namesake for northern Minnesota's feisty lake fish, led a mission in 1805 to build a fort on the upper Mississippi, near Little Falls, and to win the allegiance of the Indians. Some years later, Henry Schoolcraft sought and located the headwaters of the Mississippi River with the essential help of Ozawindib, an Ojibwe guide. Following these explorers, there arrived an influx of white settlers seeking opportunity and exploitation of the Ojibwe homeland. The increasing interaction between European and Native American cultures would change this land forever. First, the Ojibwe were forced to surrender vast swaths of land in the treaties of 1837 and 1854. Upon the discovery of iron ore in some of the remaining Indian Territory, further grants of land were taken from the Ojibwe in 1866, about the time my own great-grandparents immigrated to America from Germany. These treaties led to the establishment Ojibwe reservations, which exist to the present day. In fact, the shores of Lake Dunbar are now within the Leech Lake Indian Reservation.

Having secured massive areas of land, the European-American interests turned in the mid-1800s from the indiscriminate trapping of animals to a pillaging of one of the area's other great natural resources, the trees. Up until the mid-1800s, centuries-old virgin white and red pine trees blanketed northern Minnesota. These towering giants stood hundreds of feet tall, and were anywhere from twenty-two to forty-eight inches in diameter. Although similar in stature, subtle differences exist between white and red pines. Soft-to-the-touch needles, five in a cluster, protrude from the branches of the white pine. Its bark is gray and porous. The red pine's bark is reddish and scale-like, while the branches have long, stiff needles, growing two in a bunch. The white pine's straight trunk and large size also made it the perfect lumber for manufacturing English ship masts.

By the end of the nineteenth century, nearly all of the giant white and red pines of Minnesota had vanished. Luckily, a forty-acre plot of land still covered with these ancient giants lies just a few miles from Lake Dunbar. The Lost Forty, now a National Forest Preserve, stands as a living monument to the greatness of these towering white and red pines. In 1882, as loggers scoured the northern Minnesota forests, cutting down the great pines, a federal surveyor named Josiah King and his crew stayed somewhat ahead of the loggers, surveying and marking the land where the lumbermen would cut next. Fortunately for Minnesota, King's crew made a surveying error, sparing this lonely forty-acre patch of pine trees. Standing beneath the giant white and red pines in the Lost Forty on a breezy day, you can almost hear the pines whispering in unison, "Thank you, Josiah, thank you."

Along with the trees, myriad wildlife still inhabits these forests. Red squirrels are among the most common animals of these coniferous woodlands. I've often heard a lone red squirrel as it eats pine seeds, and cackles to announce the approach of a moose, black bear, or pack of timber wolves. The Chippewa National Forest also shelters numerous species of birds, including pelicans, egrets, loons, and more bald eagles than anywhere else in the lower forty-eight states. These birds thrive in the lakes, woodlands, and marshes of a remote wilderness. While only 20 percent of original wetlands remain in the rest of the state, the Chippewa National Forest stands alone in the world as having the very same wetlands today as it did one hundred years ago.

To view an eagle as it swoops down from a high nest in an old, dead tree, and snatches prey hundreds of yards away with precision, is to watch nature's most perfect hunter in action. To spot an absolutely tranquil egret as it stands motionless in the reeds of a marsh awaiting an unsuspecting fish, is to be in awe of nature's most patient being. To hear the cry of a loon as it spreads his five-foot wingspan, and focuses its blood-red eyes on a mate, is to enjoy nature's most haunting cry of love. Not to be outdone by these woodland creatures, the shores of Dunbar and other nearby northern lakes teem with beauty. Flowers, plants, and berries fill the hillsides and forest floors more densely and colorfully than any painting. Lake Dunbar is indeed a natural paradise, a refuge.

I would not actually see Dunbar's shores for another twenty-five years after first hearing about the lake from uncles Louie and Frank. In the meantime, reminders were plentiful, especially when Uncle Frank visited us from California. He left for the western United States in the early thirties looking for new opportunity, just like thousands of others who had been disillusioned by the devastating effects of the

Great Depression. Frank packed his few belongings and headed west across unknown roads and byways in a Model T truck.

Oh, how I wanted to join Uncle Frank in California, but I still had responsibilities back on the farm. As the eldest of eight children, I was given plenty of chores. My escape was in the books I read voraciously, and radio broadcasts from all over America. I was a decent student, when I applied myself, but my interests veered more toward the arts and adventure travel than to math and science. Perhaps that is why I was attracted to a local boy named Sam Travis who excelled in the subjects about which I cared a bit less. Our town had very few people, but it is still actually a wonder we ever met. Sam had to drop out of school at age fifteen to help his parents on their farm east of Greenwood, so I never saw him in the halls of Greenwood's schoolhouse. More importantly, Sam and his family were strict Lutherans, while we were devout Catholics, so I never saw him at church gatherings either.

Sam's strikingly handsome figure first caught my attention during the 1930 Harvest Days barn dance, an annual Greenwood celebration. Given my mother's vehement opposition, I was actually lucky to have attended this year's dance. She was strongly suspicious of the upbeat jazz music and stylish dancing of my era. "The devil's music," she called it, "full of depravity and vulgarity." I just thought it was fun and exciting, with body movements that made me feel more alive. My friends and I tapped our toes and clapped our hands to the tunes of Eddie Lang and Joe Venuti, while waiting with anticipation for the young local boys to ask us out on the floor for the Charleston, Black Bottom, and Flea Hop dances.

Looking across the makeshift dance hall, assembled inside a barn on the farm nearest to town, I saw him. His firm, dark features and naturally shy demeanor seemed a complimentary fit to my outgoing, gregarious personality. I asked one of my Protestant school friends who he was, and she explained the intriguing circumstances surrounding this mysterious, good-looking young man. I decided to embrace the proverbial "new-woman" approach of our era, and asked him to dance. In hindsight, I'm not sure he actually said yes when I suggested he join me in a shimmy to Fats Waller's "Ain't Misbehavin'," but nevertheless he followed me out on the parquet floor. While I can't say he was the most graceful dancer in the crowd, we did get through "Tiptoe through the Tulips" and "Am I Blue" before he made a beeline for the chairs when the band began to play "Makin' Whoopee." I thought his embarrassment at this crazy song was rather charming, but I was unable to convince him to come back out for another dance the rest of the evening. I was instantly and deeply drawn to Sam Travis—perhaps because he was so unsuitable: a Lutheran, three years older, and without a high school diploma. Because of his good looks, he could have had the pick of the lot when it came to dating the young women of our town. However, Sam wisely chose me, and we wed in 1931. I was only eighteen and never thought I'd be married so quickly after high school, but I said "I do" without regret, either then or ever. It was without a doubt the finest decision of my life to join forces with Sam Travis. Together we planned to conquer our small town, and eventually the world.

We began rather modestly, living and working on a farm just down the road from Sam's parents' farm between Greenwood and Beaver. Though we spent nearly a decade on the lovely farm, with its gentle rolling terrain and limitless views off to each horizon, agricultural life was not our destiny, and together we plotted our next move. Sam was the one who first sensed the transportation need for the many farm kids who yearned to attend school in town, rather than in the rudimentary country schoolhouses dotting the landscape of rural Minnesota. He purchased an old van, cut out a few windows, added seating, and began hauling kids to and from the Greenwood schools under the banner of Travis Bus Service, Inc.

Knowing his talents were in the art of engineering more than agriculture, my husband spent his days working hard at farming and school busing while studying at night via a correspondence course, eventually earning his degree in engineering and electronics by mail. With his new degree, and the money steadfastly saved throughout the difficult 1930s, we sold the farm and moved to Greenwood. Sam and I continued driving the school bus, and opened up a shop on Main Street where he repaired electronics of every kind. Soon after, Sam offered new and used goods for sale, including radios, generators, and all varieties of household engineering essentials of the day. To these trades, my husband added vehicle repair, and ultimately opened a Chrysler Plymouth Dodge dealership. In the span of little more than a decade, our ingenuity and hard work brought our family more success and enjoyment than even I had expected back at the time of our marriage. We believed life would only continue to improve.

Sam Travis was a profoundly honest man who assumed the best in others. Before my uncle moved west to California, Sam would listen to Frank's fishing reports with wide eyes and boyish wonder. Unfortunately, there was no opportunity at this time for us to explore the forested wonderland of Lake Dunbar my uncle had described. We were busy with a new house, our own start-up businesses, a newborn child, and another on the way. We had too many responsibilities to allow for a long trek northward to enjoy a few days of fishing. Instead, we contented ourselves with frequent local trout fishing in the Whitewater River Valley, one of the many excellent trout streams in southern Minnesota's endless hill country. Sam would also sneak away for an afternoon on his own now and then for some real fishing in the backwaters of the Mississippi River, a mere dozen miles from our home. But with each cast in the great river, I knew his thoughts wandered to the images generated by my uncles' stories. He imagined doing some real fishing in the depths of a remote northern lake. He dreamed of the day when he too would find himself angling along the shores of Lake Dunbar.

Sam, like my uncle Frank, was a keen businessman and explorer at heart. He dreamed and read of far-off places, secretly yearning to make the long drive to Alaska one day. During the 1940 and 1950s, Sam and I accomplished the first leg of his dream by driving the entire family to visit my California uncle on two different occasions. The journey was challenging, as all of our children, as well as my parents, were in very cramped quarters. We arrived at Frank and his wife's stately home just above downtown Hollywood. Hollywood was in its prime, unequalled in the world. Uncle Frank and Aunt Ruby's hilltop manor was nestled among the homes of many Hollywood stars of the 1950s including Jeanne Crane, Tyrone Power, and Ozzie and Harriet Nelson who lived directly across the street. Frank and Ruby's mansion was an incredible sight with huge rooms, abundant guest quarters, and thirteen bathrooms. (I counted them!)

Uncle Frank welcomed us warmly, and was eager to talk with us about Minnesota, and fishing in particular. Frank listened with disappointment as Sam explained why we had not yet explored the area around Lake Dunbar. Frank, who had purchased two lots on the upper end of the lake, asked us to investigate Lake Dunbar and check on his property since he could not go himself. Sam promised to do so, and I knew we would soon visit the fabled Lake Dunbar. After all, my husband was a man who kept his word.

In his book, *A Sand County Almanac*, Aldo Leopold wrote, "there are some who can live without wild things, and some who cannot." Our family should be counted among those who cannot. Although it had been years since first hearing of Lake Dunbar, Sam and I finally headed north in the summer of 1952 with our four children. We had kept our word to my uncle, and journeyed north to investigate the mystical lake Frank and Louie had described for us so vividly. Sam and I sat up front, while Eleanor, Jack, Ruth, and Stella were squished in the back.

The five and one-half hour drive seemed endless. The chatter, bickering, and exasperated pleas from the backseat to "move over" nearly drove us parents through the roof. After two hours, we stopped in Mora for lunch at the Sportsman's Café. Sportsman's was a classic greasy spoon treasure. Several red vinyl-wrapped booths were set between Formica-topped tables adorned with sugar dispensers, plastic squeezable ketchup containers, and mismatched salt and-pepper shakers. The miniature-sized jukebox in each booth played an assortment of fifty songs for five cents apiece. Separating the kitchen from the booths was one long, continuous countertop with faded maroon swivel chairs on one side and storage for the café supplies on the other. The cooks and waitresses looked as if they had worked in the café for years, most likely a product of long days and back-to-back shifts in this northern Minnesota tourist town. After our family had scoffed down six servings of hot beef sandwiches, accompanied by mashed potatoes and gravy, we were back on the road once again, heading north.

The next two hours of driving and bickering slowly crawled past. As our '52 Dodge pulled into the Grand Rapids city limits, smiles enveloped Sam's face and mine, listening to the sound of deep, sleepy breaths from the backseat. As we passed through the town's main drag, Sam pointed out various landmarks he recognized from my uncles' many stories, like the new county courthouse, the paper mill, and the old brick schoolhouse where Frances Gumm received her elementary education before changing her name to Judy Garland and moving on to Hollywood fame.

"Sam, look at the tall wooden Indian over there next to the drug store."

"Wow. Someone put a lot of hard work into carving the old boy."

"It reminds me of a Marty Robbins song. What's it called? Oh yes, 'Calijah the Indian.'" Suddenly, I had an idea. The ride had been too uneventful and void of good cheer. I decided it was time to wake my sleeping children with song. Mind you, despite my enthusiasm for song and laughter, I must admit I'm no Marty Robbins and no Judy Garland. No matter. I belted out those lyrics, singing of the old wooden Indian, his love for a maiden, and his stubbornness when it came to love. "Come on, everybody. Sing with me. Sam and Jack, that means you guys too," I joyfully announced.

"Ma, we're tired," was the unanimous response from the backseat. True, they were tired from the long drive. "And we don't know the words." Untrue, they had all heard the song before.

"Then just join in on the Calijaaahhh part," I commanded before continuing with my song.

Hearing no one join me when I got to the chorus, I threw a stern look toward the backseat. The enthusiasm I had hoped for was simply not present. The children, in turn, looked at each other with concern. Without saying a word they finally chimed in, perhaps hoping I just might leave them alone after one or two verses. They waited for their next cue as I began yet another verse. As I watched from the corner of my eye, the backseat singers put forth with booming voices.

"Calijaaaaaaaaaaaaahhhhhhhhh!

Too stubborn to ever show a sign
Because his heart was made of knotty pine."

For years to come, whenever we'd spot the old wooden Indian on the streets of downtown Grand Rapids, the entire family would enthusiastically burst into song.

Forty-five minutes later, everyone in the backseat was asleep again as the Dodge rolled through the towns of Cohasset and Deer River. We were now at the gateway to the Chippewa National Forest and Leech Lake Indian Reservation. Like a cruise ship on windless waters, the solid metal Dodge sailed smoothly along Minnesota's northern highways. Thirty more minutes of driving found us passing excitedly through the Avenue of Pines and over the Laurentian Divide, where waterways on one side flow north to Hudson Bay, and on the other, to the Mississippi River before winding south to the Gulf of Mexico. We were getting close, which was a good thing. Six people, including our three girls and Jack, confined to one car for several hours left us all longing for fresh air and a chance to stretch our legs.

When we passed through the small town of Squaw Lake, I squinted to decipher the faded penciled map sketched by Uncle Frank. Five miles out of town we were instructed to turn onto the first of several rough gravel roads, intermittently supported with old logs to prevent washouts. Soon we passed one of the map's landmarks, the Hinck Farm. It was here old man Hinck apparently met an untimely demise, having been gored to death by his own bull. After a series of turns on dusty dirt roads, seventeen-year-old Jack shouted, "I see a lake! Over there to the left, across the meadow."

Sure enough, beyond the small white chapel, which served as the Good Hope Township Hall, and before, as the one-room Dunbar Schoolhouse, appeared a barely visible patch of blue water. On subsequent trips, we always knew we'd arrived at Lake Dunbar when someone yelled, "I see the lake!" Following a few more turns, our car came to rest in the driveway at Earl's Place, a small resort on the lake run by a crafty guy named Earl Ritter. Although the resort's cabins were in full use for the weekend, Earl offered to show us around. From the end of Earl's dock, we surveyed Dunbar's seemingly endless lakeshore. Earl explained that the entire eastern perimeter of the lake was owned by the federal government, and would forever remain undeveloped.

From Earl's Place, we set out on a long hike around the western side of Lake Dunbar. The first section of lakeshore rested in a marshy swamp, too much of a quagmire through which to navigate, so we followed the township road. We walked to the northern end of the lake where it opened up into the main body of Dunbar's waters. Everyone stood in quiet amazement at the beauty of tall pines in the backdrop of the sun glistening on the water. We continued to hike throughout the afternoon, and then returned to our car and headed into Squaw Lake to find lodging since Earl's place was fully booked. Thankfully, one large rental cabin was left at a resort just outside of town on Round Lake. For my son, Jack, our sojourn at the Round Lake Resort was sweet revenge on his sisters for years of inconvenience. Although Jack and the girls still had to share but one bathroom at the resort as they did at home, this bathroom was outdoors. For some reason, the amount of time the Travis girls occupied the outhouse was much shorter than their normal routines in the modern facilities back home.

We stayed at the Mallard Resort near town, returning to Dunbar's shores early the next morning, re-examining and scrutinizing the lakeshore properties. After traipsing through the thick woods, and the children losing three shoes in a muddy swamp, Sam and I brought the family to a gently sloping hillside near a small cove on the lake's western shore. With great pride, my husband announced, "Listen up, everybody. Your mom and I discussed it at lunch, and we've decided to buy all of the lakeshore property in this cove. Starting next summer, we'll come up here as often as we can to build ourselves a cabin."

The children erupted with immediate shouts of joy. They ran excitedly through the property that would soon and forever be their own. After exchanging hugs, kisses, and self-congratulations, my daughter Ruth posed an important question. "Dad, what will we call the cabin?"

"What will we call it?" Sam inquired.

"Yes, Dad, our cabin will need a name."

For a few moments, everyone was quiet, each child hoping to

come up with the best name. As they each stared out toward the lake and surveyed the heavily wooded land, a brisk breeze swept through the tall trees and across their pondering faces. Looking up, a smile came to my husband's face. I knew instantly he had an inspiration. He had heard the name for our cabin.

"We'll call it Whispering Pines, children. On the shores of Lake Dunbar, the Travis family will build a cabin called Whispering Pines."

COULD HEAVEN BE ANY NICER?

UNCLE FRANK'S WIFE, RUBY, FREQUENTLY POSED THIS QUES-
tion to us whenever we visited southern California during her later
years in life: "Could heaven be any nicer than this?" "This" usually
referred to the beautiful, sunny southern California skies and Ruby's
immaculate backyard gardens. Yet Ruby, who also grew up in the
fine-looking hill country of southeastern Minnesota like I did, would
probably have echoed the same sentiment and posed the same question had she ever been along with Frank and Louie on their discovery
of Lake Dunbar. Indeed, could heaven be any nicer than that?

Surveying the heavens from Lake Dunbar's shores reveals a
sweeping spectacle. Located almost three hundred miles in any direction from the lights of a major city, the nighttime sky explodes with
stars and other celestial objects. Lying face-up on the end of the dock
in front of the cabin, our children and many others have enjoyed the
beauty of heaven's living portrait. The familiar players always appear:
Orion and his two dogs, Canis major and Canis minor; the big and little dippers; the glow of the Milky Way galaxy; and Polaris, the North
Star. Sitting this far north, an observer from Lake Dunbar's shores
is most fortunate to have one of the best possible seats for heaven's
grand performance. Aurora Borealis, the Northern Lights, regale
the lucky sky-gazers with streams of blue, green, and red light that
streaks through the sky in motions so subtle they can be missed with
the blink of an untrained eye. The dancing lights will entertain for
hours, and never disappoint the keen observer. The Dunbar sky has
other worthy things to observe, like falling stars, or meteors, shooting through the Earth's atmosphere in one final blaze of glory before
disintegrating into nothing. And the patient observer might spot the

occasional satellite moving swiftly across the northern sky, reflecting the light of the sun.

The first member of our family to witness a Dunbar summer night was our son Jack in 1953. In the summer of his eighteenth year, when his friends were traveling, working to save money, or chasing young women, Jack dedicated three months to building the family's dream cabin. Jack lived on Dunbar's shores all summer in a small tent. Unless it was raining, he spent his nights in a sleeping bag under the stars. Each weekend, some combination of us would drive north to help Jack. Everyone played a role in the creation of the Whispering Pines cabin. Even my seven-year-old daughter Stella did her share of the "work." In fact, Stella was overjoyed to tag along with her beloved older brother Jack on one of the first construction trips to Lake Dunbar. On their first night of sleeping under the stars, Jack, the decorated Boy Scout, tucked Stella into her sleeping bag and zipped her all the way in so that no mosquitos would bite her. The next morning, all bright-eyed and bushy-tailed, Stella awoke to a living painting.

As she told me later, Stella remembered that trip as breathtaking. "The sky was pitch black except for the moon and stars. Only the hooting owls, crying loons, croaking frogs, and splashing fish broke the night's silence. The sun rose to give us a wonderful day. Nothing there but woods, and it was beautiful."

The family had plenty of work to do in order to transform this wooded lot into the Travis family cabin, and everyone worked hard. Trees were cleared, lumber purchased, and exact plans prepared, mostly by Jack and Sam, with help from the rest of the family. The arduous work continued week after week for three successive summers, 'til 1955. One of the first required tasks, after the land was cleared and leveled, entailed pouring the foundation. Foregoing teenage fun with his friends back home, Jack even remained at Lake Dunbar on the long Fourth of July weekend in '54, hoping to get the foundation done. He would have finished it too, except for a torrential downpour that lasted the entire weekend. With the exception of a few breaks in the weather, Jack spent the weekend in one of Earl's rental cabins, dejectedly looking out over the stormy lake. From where he stood, Jack could barely make out the spot where the

Travis cabin would eventually sit. He could also see the only cabins thus far on the lake: a small green shack in a meadow, which would be torn down several years later; another one across the bay from Earl's Place; a farm down by the power lines running across the lower section of the lake; and a fourth cabin on the far eastern shore. Since the weather spoiled Jack's plans, we decided to hire a local mason to do the job for the outrageous price of sixty dollars.

The next step was building the frame with sturdy 2x8 cuts of wood, constructing the outer walls, and covering the roof with plywood and shingles. Sam and my uncle Louie came up one weekend to help Jack build the roof for Whispering Pines. Sam and Louie made their way across the thirty-foot-long cabin, one row at a time, attaching the plywood sheets and nailing on asphalt shingles. Jack, in addition to his other work, spent a fair amount of time keeping after his father and great uncle so they would actually get some work done, and not just slack off exchanging tall tales. One evening, as he emerged from the woods dragging some large fallen branches for a fire, Jack saw Sam and Louie standing up on the roof, talking, and pointing off toward the lake. "They're worse than kids," Jack thought.

"Uh, Dad. Are you guys done with the shingles already?"

"Jack, we heard some screams from across the lake and got up to see what's going on."

Sure enough, all three men heard more screaming and hollering, but could only decipher one word: "Bear!" Before the Travis men could move toward the pickup truck to go investigate or offer help, they heard a gunshot—and the screams ceased. Soon they saw people walking calmly around the yard across the lake. With Jack's prompting, Sam and Louie returned to roofing. Eventually the body of the cabin was complete, and then the interior decorating began. As a luxury (the women members said it was a necessity), we opted for digging a well and installing a pump for running water. In the absence of such convenience, we had thus far made frequent trips into the nearby town of Squaw Lake to fill our two-, three-, and ten-gallon milk cans with fresh water.

In order to determine where the well should be dug, an experienced local Native American man, known as a diviner, was summoned to the Travis property upon resort owner Earl Ritter's recommendation. The man emerged from his rundown auto and, following a simple non-verbal nod of hello, started by moving slowly around the property. He held a homemade divining rod crafted from a forked willow branch, one hand on each part of the Y section, the straight branch toward the ground. He watched his rod closely, and when it dipped down a little, without any movement from him, he stopped. Curious, Sam and Jack were walking with him—and then they saw it dip too. A mere five feet from our newly constructed cabin, he declared, "Dig here, forty-five feet down." After Sam paid him his meager fee, he got back into his car and drove away.

We wanted to believe in his ability, but still skeptical, Sam and I looked at each other wondering what folly we had just watched. How could this fellow possibly know water existed forty-five feet below this certain spot? Was his expert opinion based solely on a hunch from the alleged divining rod? Was it a joke or for real? So as not to be considered complete skeptics, Sam and Jack began digging at the promised spot. Four feet down. Nothing. Six feet down, drier nothing. Ten feet down, nothing but solid clay. Had we been taken, was this guy a joke, a mediocre actor? Was Earl Ritter a greedy middleman set to receive a cut of the action at our expense? Yes, we did get a second opinion, this one much more high-tech than a willow stick. They showed us the location of water on our land. Then we tried digging for a well the rest of the summer. Ultimately, a well was excavated in the summer of '55. Would you believe it—it was on *the very spot* the diviner originally indicated, forty-four and one-half feet below the surface of the earth.

As for the other necessities of life, we constructed an outhouse several yards from the cabin toward the woods. While eventually opting for indoor plumbing, some in the family still preferred the natural experience. The outhouse was nothing fancy, just a raised wooden platform with an appropriately sized opening. The lone danger in using the outhouse came neither from the potential for falling through the hole, nor from the gargantuan spiders on all four walls. Rather, anyone using this outhouse feared Jack, who was always on patrol. Firecracker patrol. Whenever anyone used the facilities, especially newcomers, my prankster son inevitably set off firecrackers right next to the outhouse and scared the, well, crap out of any unsuspecting occupant.

As one might expect, with the construction of the Whispering Pines cabin mostly complete, the family turned again more fully to their passion of fishing in 1956. A wide variety of gilled creatures filled the deep waters of Lake Dunbar, including bass, sunfish, and walleye pike, to name but a few. Jack was the first to take advantage of Dunbar's fishing opportunities, the honor his rightly so, given his hard work on building Whispering Pines. Jack meticulously planned for this first fishing adventure all during the summer as he worked on the cabin, including hours of reading on the art of fishing. Jack also had bragging rights for his fancy rod and reel for this first adventure, one of those expensive South Bend anti-backlash reels everyone was talking about, affixed to a brand new wooden rod.

Jack practically jumped into our new wooden boat, undecided about where to venture first. It reminded me of his first trip to the Greenwood candy store as a kid, looking around in pure wonderment, not knowing which treat to choose. Jack steered the small motorboat toward a good-sized cove opposite our cabin. The weeds in the large bay stretched out fifty yards from shore. Jack had read big northern pike prefer to hang out deep in the weedy areas where they can hide from unsuspecting small minnows as the pike slithers through the murky waters to catch its dinner. Being his first time out, Jack wasn't sure of the best place to anchor his boat. He ended up coasting a little too close to the weeds, and the motor killed after the propeller became tangled in some strong lily pads. Jack spent fifteen minutes removing weeds from the engine's blades and working on the over-heated motor—instead of fishing. He eventually reignited the engine, although his hands and arms were now covered in grease.

Finally, everything was perfect. The boat in position, the sunlight and breeze just right for catching fish, Jack knew he would be suc-cessful with his top-of-the-line rod and reel. He held the rod firmly, pushed the release, gently tossed the rod backward above his head, and snapped his wrist forward to cast the line as far as possible. Spying on him with my binoculars from the cabin, it was pleasing to watch his fishing line fly twenty yards from the boat. Regrettably, his expensive rod and reel flew with it. Jack's hands were so slick from working on the greasy engine his pole slipped from his grip. Jack was stunned, but he could do nothing as the pole disappeared below the surface in a matter of seconds.

Jack went out later with a hook and sinker hoping to snag the rod and reel from the bottom of the lake, but never found it. The way people around the lake tell it, fishing on Lake Dunbar was never quite the same. The fish in the northern end just never seemed to bite again quite the way they used to. Rumor has it the fish in that part of the lake use Jack's submerged pole in their "How Not to Get Caught" classes, classes only taught in schools, of course.

Because the better part of Jack's summer was consumed by building the cabin, fishing would have to wait until the following year. In late September, we put our finishing touches on the cabin, winter proofing it to prevent damage from the bitter Minnesota temperatures, and expected mounds of snow. As we drove away from Lake Dunbar on a lovely, crisp fall day, each of us looked back as long as possible until our redwood-colored cabin was completely out of sight. We hoped and prayed when we returned in seven months' time the cabin would still be there.

Sam and I pondered the possibility of making a winter trip to Dunbar's icy shores after the first of the year, but decided against it. The cabin would be too cold to sleep in overnight, so we chose to wait through the long and difficult winter of 1956. As I would discover many years later, those who brave a northern Minnesota winter, even for a few days, enjoy the peace and quiet of nature at her strongest. What astounds people most about Lake Dunbar in January is *the absolute quiet*. The lake is covered with a blanket of white, interrupted only by snowshoers, snowmobilers, deer, or moose. Snowshoeing is no easy task on the lake because of the deep snow and no groomed trails. Such rigorous activity is certainly not meant for the faint of heart, or those with minimal survival abilities. During the long winter of 1956, two young kids from the lower end of the lake, the Murdoch boys, tested their own survival skills against that of a Dunbar winter. We met the Murdoch family earlier in summer, and once meeting them, we could confirm the boys' reputation as the premier adolescent instigators of fun in Good Hope Township. Anyway, as those boys headed out for some mid-winter fun, it was a bright, clear day, quite warm for northern Minnesota. A perfect day for ice skating. The boys were out on the lake early seeking excitement. Bundled up warmly so as to please their mother, the Murdoch kids set to work clearing off enough ice in the middle of the lake to do some real skating. Not just kids' stuff, but the real thing, or the closest they could muster with their limited training.

The Murdoch boys reportedly had the center of the lake as their stage, and they skated with enthusiasm and the full vigor of youth. They were indeed free. What a wonderful feeling to skate, ski, or snowshoe on a bright sunny day in the depths of winter. The cool breeze and warm sun leaves the children with rosy cheeks. Those who live on Lake Dunbar still picture the Murdoch boys the same way—young, bundled up, clumsily striding across the ice, and laughing through their scarves around their face—the last picture one would ever have of the Murdoch boys. As they made one last stride through the softening ice, it soon gave way, dropping the boys gently into Dunbar's frigid waters. Their brief struggle for life was assuredly valiant, but the lake was not kind that day in 1956. It was not kind at all. Their suffering was over, but for their family, it lasted forever.

One of the eternal joys of fishing on Lake Dunbar is the opportunity to get away for peace and solitude. Even if twenty people were staying at the Travis cabin, fishing took place in shifts of only two or three people at a time. Group fishing simply didn't work. This philosophy was confirmed in the summer of 1957 during our first (and last) time the entire family had an outing on the lake at one time. I should have known better than to go out fishing together, and Sam probably warned me as much. The children had been bickering all morning about who would wash dishes or who could next use the bathroom, and other minor details to annoy any sane parent. I must confess it was my suggestion that an hour out on the lake together might do them all some good, and calm everybody down. Sam, Jack, and Eleanor climbed into one of the green wooden boats while Stella, Ruth, and I used the other. At first, the group fishing concept seemed to work well. The two boats stayed close together as we rowed and fished around the northern bay. Inevitably, though, a stowaway named "bickering" reared its ugly head.

"Can we go back now?" asked seven-year-old Stella. "I'm tired of fishing."

"Me too," said sister Ruth, almost fifteen.

"Good thing we brought two boats. I just knew the girls wouldn't be able to stay out very long," Jack observed, perhaps a bit too caustically.

"Jack, you just be quiet," Stella added.

During all of the squabbling that filled the air for the next long five minutes, my husband remained calm. A good fisherman doesn't let himself become distracted by quarreling companions, I guess. He simply blocked them all out. While I too consider myself to be a good fisherwoman, my motherly ears didn't miss a word. Eventually, I had enough. I really wanted the girls to toughen up; however, I started instead on Jack.

"Jack, leave your sisters alone. If they want to go in, then fine. I'll take 'em in."

"Maybe throwing them in would be a better idea," Jack jabbed, perhaps regretting saying it—but it was too late.

"Don't you sass me, young man." I was quite stern. I never did take kindly to my kids' backtalk. In his defense, I must note Jack was neither a troublemaker nor a fighter. Yet, something had struck a nerve in him, and he clearly chose to launch a verbal counterattack. At twenty, Jack was becoming a man now, and presumably thought he didn't have to take such rebukes from his mother. Rather than backing down, it was time for Jack to stand tall, despite the consequences. Of course, he had the comfort of knowing I was in the other boat, and could not reach him.

"Don't sass you? Well sass, sass, up your ass!" And there it was, a moment of newfound bravado to strike a balance with the past as a dutiful son. No one rightly recalls who moved faster—me in order to bring my boat closer to Jack, or Jack trying to get farther away. Words flew back and forth as loudly as the splashing water. I never did reach the other boat, and eventually warned my brave son, "Jack, I'll see you back at the cabin." Sam continued to act oblivious to the whole situation. No sense in him getting involved now since he would inevitably end up on the losing side. Mostly I suspect, although he did not condone the sassing of one's mother, he avoided looking at me because it simply took all his strength to keep from laughing.

Despite this frustrating episode years ago, I of course loved my son dearly, as I love all of my kids. Equally, I was proud of who they were as children, and even more so of how each became a successful, caring person into adulthood. However, this didn't mean I couldn't be hard on them, mind you. If I didn't push them, who would? I remember a couple years later how a dinner guest, trying to make small talk, asked me about Jack, who was by then away at college in Chicago.

"Isabelle, I understand your son is away at college." I was in the middle of cooking a beef roast, admittedly a bit distracted, and grunted some indiscernible response. Oblivious, the guest continued. "Gee, this must make you very proud. What is your son going to be when he gets out of college?"

To this I tersely replied, "An old man!" Hopefully people understand my sometimes-gruff exterior is just a facade. I have always been extremely proud of all my son has achieved, just as I have been proud of my three daughters. While Jack's talents were most noticeable in his woodwork creations, and in his innate ability to fix almost anything, my daughters' forte at this age was music. Lord only knows where they inherited such a gift. Neither Sam nor I had a musical bone in our bodies. All of our girls were masters at the accordion, and became quite well known in our area of the state from their school concerts and performances. In fact, two of my daughters (Ruth and Stella) joined forces with three other girls from our town to form the only quintet of female accordion players in the entire state of Minnesota.

Ultimately, the group caught the attention of producer David Stone in Minneapolis who broadcast the famous *Sunset Valley Barn Dance* every Saturday night on KSTP radio. The *Barn Dance* show was a classic, and we all gathered 'round the radio on Saturday nights in the 1940s and 50s just to hear the wonderful mix of folk music, fiddle tunes, songs of hearth and home, and even a bit of comedy to the delight of KSTP's broad listening audience. I especially loved tuning in to hear Andy Walsh sing, as he strummed his guitar like magic. On this show, he was followed by a pair of fantastic fiddle players, Dusty Lane and Fiddlin' Russ. Perhaps sensing their listening audience yearned for something more, something a bit eclectic, the *Sunset Valley Barn Dance* producers expanded their format in the mid-1950s to include a segment called "County Road 5" where they featured music and entertainment from visiting rural families. Our daughters caught their big break after being invited on the show to promote the centennial anniversary of our hometown, Greenwood. Their performance was a tremendous hit all across the state.

The year 1957 also brought new neighbors to Lake Dunbar. Across the public access on land next to Whispering Pines, Leland Jensen constructed a small weekend cabin. We met Leland in '56 over at Earl's Place, and were impressed with the stories of his expertise as a premier carpenter. Perhaps that explains why Sam and I stood in amazement as we emerged from our car upon arrival at Lake Dunbar in the spring of '57. Not one window or door on the Jensen cabin was the same size, and the structure was painted bright yellow. I cringed, as did everyone else. As it turned out, the external appearance of the Jensen cabin was only the beginning of a fateful turn of events. The Jensens had a notably different concept of recreation, vacation, and celebration. They were quiet, demure people and we most certainly were not. Whether it was the Fourth of July or the twelfth of September, fireworks were to be lit whenever my family was on the lake, and lots of laughter was always emerging from our little redwood cabin until the wee hours of the morning. It was ultimately all too much for the Jensens. They continually complained about the loud Travis frolics, and I had no tolerance for their bellyaching. I worked hard to afford my family's time on Dunbar's shores, and by God, *we were going to enjoy ourselves.* A resolution was finally reached two years later. On a cool Indian summer evening, my husband walked down the lake access and up the small hill, reaching the Jensen cabin's slightly unleveled front door. An hour and a pot of coffee later, Sam walked back to Whispering Pines, now the proud owner of two side-by-side cabins on Lake Dunbar. The Jensens moved to the other, more solitary end of the lake. Sam never did tell me how much he paid for the Jensen place, despite my constant prodding. It was probably not one of his better business deals, truth be told. The yellow cabin sat empty for ten years before we finally sold it, probably at a loss. All I do know is we were now able to continue living life on Lake Dunbar to the fullest, loudly, and without protest.

When the Travis family tired of entertaining ourselves at Whispering Pines, we would drive into nearby Squaw Lake for an evening of fun. The general store was known by the name of its owners, the Leino family. Above the general store sat an old wood-floored hall used for town meetings, special gatherings, and Saturday night dances. Not everyone in the Travis family liked to dance, but most enjoyed the music and atmosphere of a Saturday night at Leino's Store. Sam and I swung wildly around the hardwood floors to our big-band favorites while grandson Walt clapped along, sipping a root beer and stealing looks from the local girls. It was especially fun watching our daughters Ruth and Stella show us older folks how to move to the music of Elvis Presley, while also introducing us to the exciting new songs and rhythms in the music of the 1950s and early '60s. I was particularly fond of "Little Darlings" by the Diamonds, "Duke of Earl" by Dean Chandler, and "Runaround Sue" by Dion and the Belmonts. Some of my friends back home questioned this new genre of music, and specifically the grinding and thrusting on the dance floor, which nominally passed for dancing. I embraced it, and encouraged my own kids to enjoy the music and movements of this magical era, for that is what this time in our lives felt like: magic.

Released in 1961, one of those new songs best captured this moment in time for me, not so much in its lyrics but in its iconic melody and inviting, irresistible tune: "The Lion Sleeps Tonight" by the Tokens. Closing my eyes, I can still hear the jukebox in Leino's upper hall bellow forth this wonderful song, and I can't help but want to sing along to its crazy, indecipherable lyrics while feeling the beat of its rhythm and melody deep within my soul. America at this time was really coming into its own, and we all sensed it was a time of limitless possibility. While there were certainly far-off dangers such as the communist evils over in China and the Soviet Union, those fears never touched us here at Lake Dunbar. Standing in the corner of Leino's Dance Hall on a Saturday night, holding a Coca-Cola in one hand and Sam's arm in the other, I tapped my toes and sang along to the old and new music alike, thankful for this magical moment, this magical place. It was an evening of pure joy, a time of celebration. After all, it was the best time of our lives, a time of hope, prosperity, wealth, and family. The Travis family was together and happy on Lake Dunbar. Indeed, could heaven be any nicer?

HUNTING AND GATHERINGS

MINNESOTA WINTERS ARE LEGENDARY THROUGHOUT THE land. Those from out of state often question the sanity of Minnesota's hearty Scandinavian descendants once they hear about blinding snowstorms and frigid temperatures. Yet, most of us survive and even thrive in these conditions. Still, no matter how well one adapts to the snow and the cold, Minnesota inhabitants universally believe winter is just too darn long. Come March, many in the state are yearning for the first sight of spring and the promise of summer. As they often say around here, Minnesota has two seasons. Winter is coming, and winter is here.

Soon, the wait between cabin visits from September to May became too much for my family to bear. During the mild winter of 1957, the Travis men headed north to behold our cabin under cooler conditions. While ice fishing was out of the question because the lake was not yet completely frozen, there was still action to be found as the group ventured out on a new undertaking: hunting. Truth be told, there was actually no hunting to be done by any Travis in 1957. My menfolk merely went north to investigate the winter with my uncle Louie. The three men spent a long November weekend hiking through the Travis property, lightly dusted with frost. They scoured the woods by day, checking out various hunting spots recommended by resort owner Earl Ritter. Occasionally they happened upon a deer stand perfect for their needs. Luckily, it was not yet deer hunting season, or these wandering idiots might have been mistaken for lumbering bucks. Although Whispering Pines was not yet winterized, and thus not suitable for cold-season residents, the Travis men persevered by cooking their meals outside on the fire, and sleeping in the living room near the warmth of a portable Nipco heater. Earlier, Sam had hauled an old wood-burning stove up to the cabin he'd retrieved from his parents' homestead after they had both passed. Following a shivering night with the minimal heat from the tiny Nipco, Sam swore he'd install the wood stove the following summer. We also had no running water in the winter for showers, but the Travis men didn't need such conveniences.

On the second afternoon of their stay, the men drove toward the town of Blackduck which Earl said was prime hunting ground. While they had no trouble locating the right fields, they had inexplicable trouble finding their way back to the cabin. The back roads of Itasca County are not well marked, which is typical. In winter, when most landscapes look the same for miles around, navigating these uncharted byways is challenging. It turned out to be a monumental challenge for Sam, Jack, and Louie. What's more, they couldn't even find a house or cabin where they could stop and ask for directions. All of the places they passed were closed up for the season, with no one in sight. Finally, they happened upon a run-down farmhouse with two men sitting out on the porch. Getting close, Jack thought the men were about sixty years old each, with very long gray beards stretching down to their respective chests.

Jack, Sam, and Louie nervously emerged from their truck, approached the old men, and asked for directions back to Lake Dunbar. The men looked at the Travis men as if they were aliens. After a few uncomfortable moments, a third man with an even longer beard emerged from the cabin. He appeared to be older than the other two, probably in his early eighties. He spoke with the first two men in barely audible voices, yet loud enough for Jack to decipher that they were speaking a foreign language. As my husband and son turned back toward their vehicle, the eldest man spoke at them, in broken English.

"May I help you?"

Sam answered, "Yes, we seem to be lost. We were over in Blackduck, and are trying to get back to Lake Dunbar. Do you know the way?"

"Let's see," said the old man, "I haven't heard of Dunbar. What's it near?"

"It's not too far from Squaw Lake or Alvwood," Sam tentatively replied.

"I'm not familiar with those places either."

Sam, Jack, and Louie were beginning to wonder what time and space warp they had just entered. Sam tried a new approach. "Sir, can you point us in the direction of Blackduck?"

"Oh yes," the Rip Van Winkle lookalike responded as he drew a map in the air for the Travis men to follow. "If you follow that road, you'll run right into town. By the way, you'll have to excuse my sons. They're just here visiting me from Quebec, and they don't speak a word of English. I barely know it myself. Good luck finding your home."

Sam, Jack, and Louie climbed back in the truck and headed toward Blackduck. From there, they decided it was wiser to stay on major roads. Although the highway route took a bit longer, the men returned safely to Lake Dunbar, with no more forays into foreign lands.

Hunting was actually a sensitive subject in our family, and debates raged over the morality of shooting defenseless animals. Sam needed to be convinced the family should engage in or sponsor such activity. While he had no problem with catching and eating the lake's fish, my husband seemed to feel more compassion for the deer of the northern woods. Granted, the first Native American and European settlers in this area were hunters and gatherers who found their food grown by the earth. Always the joker, Sam had no problem with the *gathering* part. In fact, he especially loved a rowdy gathering at the cabin. Yet, Sam had steadfast reservations about hunting and actually killing such magnificent creatures. Finally, in November 1958, he was persuaded to join a winter hunting expedition.

In October, Jack and Sam began searching for the necessary hunting equipment. First, my husband bought a 1907 Winchester 351 automatic rifle from his best friend back home in Greenwood. The Winchester was a heavy, powerful gun with a split stock, now nailed back together. Sam didn't mind purchasing a weapon second-hand. In fact, he advocated the purchase of used or reconditioned items whenever possible. "Why waste money on something brand new?" he often asked me, much to my chagrin. Besides, Sam didn't know if he could bring himself to actually shoot a deer. Next, gear needed to be found for Jack and Ruth. No one else in the family was interested. Eleanor was too delicate for hunting. She contended such activity was too messy, cold, and boring. However, fifteen-year-old Ruth jumped at the chance to go out hunting with her dad and brother. She loved doing things with the boys, and really thrived on competing with them.

Speaking of competition, I remember a particular fall afternoon earlier when Ruth and Jack were helping me in the kitchen at home as I was canning black cherries. When I left to run my afternoon school bus route, I specifically instructed the kids to continue working, which they did, but apparently only until I was out the door and down the driveway. Then, Ruth challenged Jack to a cherry-eating contest. They each devoured the sweet cooked cherries as fast as they could, recording each consumed cherry on a notepad with increasingly purple-stained hands. Although she inhaled nearly fifty of the plump cherries, Ruth lost the contest to Jack who allegedly ingested twice as many. Needless to say, very few cherries were left for canning when I returned home and, as you'd expect, I was not at all pleased. Being a stern, calculating disciplinarian, I devised the perfect punishment. I told Jack and Ruth to finish consuming all of the uneaten cherries before biking down to the market to purchase several more sacks of the ripe fruit (using their own allowance money) so they could start canning all over again. To this day, neither Jack nor Ruth can hardly bear to look at any food containing cherries.

Despite such setbacks, nothing could prevent Ruth from keeping up with her brother and dad. In fact, she could often be found working with her father and brother under an engine at Sam's repair shop after school. A tomboy, perhaps, but others say Ruth just put up with these traditionally masculine activities in order to be closer to Sam and Jack. Maybe that explains why Ruth did not put up a protest when my husband decided they would buy a twenty-two gauge hunting rifle for Jack, and only a forty pound hunting bow for Ruth. She had no need or desire to be equal to her brother in this endeavor; rather, she only wanted to be with him.

Finally, they found all of the required hunting attire at various shops around town, including camouflage-colored hats and trousers, and a big faded red hunting jacket for Sam. Now, they were ready. On the weekend before Thanksgiving 1958, the Travis hunters embarked on their journey to Lake Dunbar. Sam, Jack, Ruth, and eight-year-old grandson Walt anxiously awaited their first family hunting expedition as they sped north toward the cabin. I tagged along, too. Although I wouldn't do any hunting myself, I knew I should accompany them in order to keep them warm, fed, and out of trouble. On the first day, the foursome walked north from the cabin about half a mile to one of Earl Ritter's many deer stands scattered throughout the forests surrounding Dunbar. From sun up to sun down, they sat in their deer stand—and didn't see a thing. Disappointed, they returned to the cabin for the night.

On their second day, the group decided to split up in order to double their chances. Jack and Walt trekked to a deer stand farther up the road while Ruth and Sam returned to the first day's location. For Ruth and her father, it was yet another day of uneventful hunting. The two would take turns rustling through the woods in an attempt to scare up some deer, but there were simply none in the area. Deep down, neither Sam nor Ruth really minded the absence of hunting action. My husband never truly wanted to hunt in the first place, and Ruth simply enjoyed spending the day out in the woods with her father. Jack and Walt were surprisingly luckier on their outing. They returned to the cabin with two good-sized does in the back of their pickup truck. While Jack and Walt shot their respective catches in relatively simple fashion, when the deer unknowingly wandered right up to their elevated stand, Walt (to no one's surprise) gave us a hero's exaggerated account of his victory.

"You wouldn't believe it, Grandma. I was so nervous I shut my eyes as I pulled the trigger with the deer in my scope. Well, I must have moved a little since my shot ended up hitting a big old tree limb. There was so much force in the shot a limb busted right off the tree, falling on the deer and causing it to run headlong into an oak tree, knocking the deer unconscious. I ran right over to the beast and stabbed it with the machete. It was amazing!" While Walt would later become infamous for his ability to spin a yarn, this one had an obvious flaw. The deer had a bullet hole in its head, and no knife wounds to be found anywhere.

As we all sat on Dunbar's western shore looking out over the lake in the evening, I wondered aloud about the strange, solitary cabin on the far side of the lake. The sprawling log cabin was seemingly built in pieces before being mashed together into a single building, though on the outside there was a gently sloping, beautifully manicured lawn. It was the only manmade structure remaining on the east side of the lake. To the north sat the federal lands, to the south the spectacular Norway pine groves of the Ronning Forest. We rarely saw anyone come or go from the unique place, but we always admired the immaculate gardens spreading across the lawns between the cabin and the lakefront. Earl Ritter, the unofficial lake watchman, said the current occupants were the Cox family, but the true story worth telling concerned the cabin's famous prior inhabitant.

At the turn of the twentieth century, railroads were a driving force in the westward expansion of America. The wealthiest and most famous railroad baron of the era was James J. Hill, developer of the Great Northern and Northern Pacific Railroads. Hill owned millions of acres of timberland, wheat fields, and grazing lands across the great northwest and Canada. His holdings stretched from the railheads on the Mississippi River in St. Paul to the far ports of Seattle and Vancouver. Throughout this vast empire, from the lake country of Minnesota to the Rocky Mountains and on to the stunning Pacific shores, there were undoubtedly thousands of special places the prestigious Hill family might have selected as a refuge. Among them was Lake Dunbar.

Mona Bell Hill, a distant member of this great family, and a remarkable true-life character in her own right, spent several anonymous years on the shores of Lake Dunbar. Her relationship to the greater Hill family was a bit complex, but I'll do my best to re-tell it correctly. You see, the famous James J. Hill had an eldest daughter named Mary Francis, who met and wed a prominent Harvard-educated lawyer named Sam Hill (no relation, at least until they were married). She then became known as "Mary Hill Hill," I kid you not! Sam Hill had previously made quite a name and small fortune for himself by suing the Great Northern Railroad. He was so successful, in fact, the wise railroad magnate James J. Hill hired his arch-nemesis Sam Hill to work for Great Northern, if only to have the area's best legal mind fighting for, rather than against, him. Anyway, Sam Hill's legal work for his new father-in-law was ultimately more successful than his marriage to James's daughter. Apparently they were never quite a perfect match, and in fact separated after only a few years of wedlock. Part of the reason for the separation may well have been due to Sam Hill's strong affection for other women, and for producing children with those other women. Given Mary's unshakeable Catholic faith, however, the couple never divorced but merely lived apart for the remainder of their lives.

Sometime early in the second decade of 1900, just before the onset of the Great War, Sam Hill met a young lady thirty-three years his junior, and was immediately smitten. Mona Bell was a legendary force of nature. College educated and an award-winning basketball player at the University of North Dakota, Mona was furthermore an accomplished horse rider and a mean shot with a pistol. For several years after college, she reportedly made a living dressed as a male rodeo rider, performing in the famous Wild West Show of Buffalo Bill Cody himself. Needing a new life challenge, the young Mona Bell then set out to see the world, and to tell folks about it. She became a renowned journalist for various magazines and newspapers, traveling the world and writing about the flora and fauna of Africa, Latin America, and other exotic locations. During the course of her investigative reporting, Mona Bell also found the time and fortitude to swim the Straits of Juan de Fuca. She allegedly greased herself up and swam the eighteen-mile-wide frigid and wavy waterway between the U.S. and Canada leading out to the Pacific Ocean.

Although Mona had two brief marriages early on, one to a doctor and one to a dentist, Sam Hill was clearly the love of her life and they finally had a child together in the summer of 1928. Not wanting to have his child raised by an unwed mother (in those days the child was then called a bastard), and because he himself was in an unbreakable marriage, Sam Hill arranged for Mona to marry his cousin Edgar Hill solely as a matter of convenience. (Didn't I say the family's relationships were complex?) Mona and Edgar never lived together; in fact, she stayed in close proximity to her lover, Sam, first in Oregon and then right here at Lake Dunbar in the years after Sam died.

Mona's parents had purchased seventy-four acres of Lake Dunbar waterfront property back in 1926 and at some point erected an impressive hunting lodge, only the third structure on the entire lake. Sadly, the old hunting lodge burned to the ground shortly after Mona and her son moved to the lake, so they lived temporarily in a caretaker's cabin while building a new one. Reflective of her intensely frugal nature, the new cabin was assembled on the cheap, both from some portion of original construction, and by dragging used shacks from elsewhere on the lake over to her property to be annexed onto their growing home. That certainly explains the strange look of the place. Though I was never inside, Earl told me it was quite comfortable with two bathrooms and generator-powered electricity, and adorned with handsome brass fixtures, crystal doorknobs, and paned windows. What impressed local folks most, however, were Mona's exotic gardens, which they all said reflected her exotic personality. After all, how many people do you know who boil the dirt in their yards? Apparently Mona did, and it worked wonders, seeing as she had the finest patch of lilies anyone on Dunbar has ever seen anywhere.

I only wish I had arrived here on Lake Dunbar back when my uncles Louie and Frank did in the '30s. Who knows, maybe Mona and I would have become fast friends. We certainly shared a zest for life, and the avant-garde notion that a woman could do anything a man could do, and most likely quicker and more successfully. I especially enjoyed hearing Earl Ritter tell me about his first encounter with the famous Mona Bell Hill. Earl apparently stopped there one day in an effort to introduce himself as the lake's new resort owner, but in truth to satisfy his unshakeable curiosity about the cabin's reclusive occupants. Landing his small boat on Mona's property, he waved to the middle-aged woman standing just outside her front stoop with a rifle pointed his way. Earl quickly hit the ground in fear as Mona Bell fixed her scope on a nearby clothesline, and proceeded to shoot a dozen clothes pins off the line at a distance of twenty-five yards. Poor Earl climbed up to his knees, shouting that he was only here for a friendly chat, and to offer an introduction to his hunting buddies down the lake who would be mightily impressed with this woman's marksmanship. Mona Bell apparently summed up the situation for him real quick.

"You tell those boys back at the hunting club there's a woman out here who can shoot—and will!"

He did. From then on, folks knew to approach Mona and her property with care and plenty of verbal warning, lest they get shot first and asked questions later. This and many other stories fed the inevitable rumor mill sweeping through Squaw Lake and the wider Dunbar community. Who was this mysterious woman who had a son, but no husband? How could she live in such a ramshackle old cabin while driving a fancy DeSoto, and wear lavish jewelry on her trips to the local market? And where exactly did she go all winter long when she abandoned Lake Dunbar year in and year out? They also marveled from afar as she tamed a wild deer, and kept him for an entire season as a pet. Slowly, Earl says, Mona emerged from her reclusive nature during her years on Dunbar, and even interacted culturally with the locals. Mona's best friend by far was old man Ronning, her next-door neighbor. Perhaps she respected the fact John Ronning and his family were the very first inhabitants of Lake Dunbar, and did so much for the local community, including establishing and teaching at the Dunbar School across the lake. Or perhaps Mona reveled in the fact John clearly adored her, and helped her out with innumerable tasks and errands over the years until he died.

Eventually, Mona interacted with an ever-wider circle of neighbors near the lake and in town. The Korpalas, Rajalas, Ojannens, and so many other families we've met during our own first decade on Lake Dunbar could still today regale us with stories about the inimitable Mona Bell Hill, and always with a strong mix of admiration and even affection in their tales. They told us how she once invited everyone to Leino's old dance hall to show homemade movies of her safari to Africa. However, most of the locals passed at her invitation to also join her back at Dunbar for a cookout where she was serving up barbecued raccoon. While Mona was legendary for her professed ability to eat virtually anything, the good Scandinavians of Squaw

Lake apparently felt grilled northern rodent was beyond their culinary limit.

For some reason, closures and goodbyes never really went so well for her, especially when it came to leaving the only three homes she ever owned. First, there was her striking turreted castle atop a high bluff with vast vistas up and down the Columbia River Gorge in northern Oregon. Inherited from her lover Sam Hill, the home was gigantic, with more than twenty rooms, and reportedly as fancy as a museum both inside and out. However, only a few years after Sam's death, the U.S. government began proceedings to condemn the property in order to make way for the construction of the Bonneville Dam. And if the government thought Mona would simply take their money and run without a fight, well, they vastly underestimated this formidable woman. There were trials and re-trials over the course of several years, and many angry words in between. Ultimately, the government took possession of Mona's amazing property, but not before paying dearly for it—in fact, triple the amount originally offered. Her angry and hurtful departure from Oregon led Mona back to the calm, quiet shores of Lake Dunbar where she would face no threat of the government taking her land.

The next skirmish took place when Mona eventually left Dunbar in the mid-1950s. She sold the property on a contract for deed to a family named Cox, who we got to know quite well. And although the contract price was fully paid off within two years, Mona Bell apparently took issue with how much timber the Cox family cut down from the property during those two years when Mona technically still owned it. She even allegedly threatened to sue or take other legal action, likely because the hundreds of felled trees, many of them hundreds of years old, opened up the old wounds from Oregon. Twice now, lands Mona had hand-cultivated and spent so much of her blood, sweat, and tears to improve, had been callously ripped apart by the next occupant.

As I said, Mona's presence on Lake Dunbar preceded our arrival on the lake, though we just barely crossed paths. Mona Bell sold her place on our lake in 1954, the very same year we built Whispering Pines. Mona moved on to Riverside, California, where she continued to indulge her passion for gardening, but never returned to these great northern forests again. Oh, how wonderful it would have been to sit around a Dunbar campfire and hear Mona Bell tell me stories of her journeys to India where she reportedly embraced a monster-sized snake for a photograph, or to Kenya where she traded clothing with local women, shot and skinned a cheetah, and was arrested for attempting to hunt big game in the African bush "without a white man." Yes, we would have regaled ourselves with tales both tall and true for hours into the cool Dunbar nights and connected in ways only women truly can. And even though I never met Miss Mona in person, I feel as though I know her from Earl's stories and from the description given by Mona Bell Hill's own daughter-in-law a few years after her death in 1981. They are words I can imagine my own children saying about me and my solo journey in the later years after Sam's passing when I had to become my own woman, forging a new path forward toward adventure in this wonderful world. "Beneath her rough exterior was a soft core. She had such a heart for the underdog. She would get tears in her eyes when she talked about some people and how they lived. She was brilliant. She had a presence. She was a woman alone, and she was okay with that."[1]

But my favorite account of Mona's inability to let go of a beloved home occurred toward the end of her life. Well into her eighties, Mona lived alone in a modest two-bedroom home in Sun City, California. Though she had admittedly increasing challenges with the basics of daily self-care, and an apparent onset of age-related dementia, Mona adamantly refused to move to a senior center or, God forbid, a nursing home. Ultimately, her son had no choice but to try and force Mona into some form of assisted living facility. To do so, however, he would either need her consent, or the doctor's conclusion Mona could not care for herself or mentally make the right decision about her own care. Well, obtaining Mona's consent was about as likely as getting me to give up my morning coffee and town gossip down at the Beanery in Greenwood. I wouldn't do that without a fight, and neither would Mona. The way I heard it, Mona's son and daughter-in-law took her for an alleged routine check-up, but when the doctor started asking questions about her mental state, the old gal must have quickly deduced what was truly going on. Determined not to go without a fight, or at least not without taking her son down with her for this dastardly deed, Mona turned on the charm with guns a-blazing.

"I see you brought some folks with you today," said the doctor as he continued his valiant attempt to build a rapport with the defiant octogenarian.

"Yes, this is my son, S. B. Hill," Mona apparently said with a straight face. "S.B. stands for 'Son of a Bitch.'"

Kind of sums up her temperament.

The more we learned about this formidable woman, the more my daughter Ruth said Mona reminded her *of me*—which may or may not be true. Certainly, I enjoy a good adventure, though I never traveled the world as widely as Miss Mona. I think we did share a kindred love of Lake Dunbar, however, as well as the idea that a strong woman could survive and thrive here on her own. Hopefully I did not share Mona Bell Hill's more strident side, at least according to the stories I heard.

With our first hunting expedition deemed a success, we packed our belongings, closed the cabin for the '58 season, and headed back home to Greenwood. Our hometown in southern Minnesota was a typical small, midwestern agricultural village. As long as anyone can remember, it has had a population of roughly fifteen hundred people. Fifteen hundred white people—Catholic, Lutheran, Methodist, and Presbyterian people. Fifteen hundred hardworking, flag-waving, red-blooded, God-fearing American people. Greenwood is a place where everyone wants to grow up, move away from, and come back to after they realize the rest of the world isn't any better. It is the epitome of Robert Frost's definition of home as a place where, when you get there, they have to take you in. Of course, the big cities in this region, such as Minneapolis and Chicago, have more offerings in the arts, professional sports, and metropolitan glamour. Yet, like other small American towns, Greenwood is simply a great place to live and raise a family. Quiet, safe, and clean, and a place where everybody knows each other, sometimes too well.

In Greenwood, one could set his watch by any number of visible signs. At six o'clock every morning, with the crow of the rooster at sun-up, men and women on all of the farms surrounding Greenwood make the groggy walk from their farmhouses to their barns for the morning milking routine. At seven thirty, businessmen stream into the Heartland Cafe for their morning coffee, breakfast, and an earful of town gossip. At eight, big yellow buses come barreling out of Travis Bus Service, heading for the countryside to pick up the farmers' kids for school, as our bus company has since the 1930s. At nine o'clock, main street bustles with activity as stores open, shopkeepers set up for the day, and housewives peruse the latest offerings. At twelve, everyone checks their watches for accuracy as the fire station blares its daily noon whistle. Shortly thereafter, many workers at the local creamery file into Ralph's Diner for the daily special. At three o'clock, the Travis buses are back in front of the town schoolhouse to take sulking farm kids back home for afternoon chores, as the uptown kids head toward the Greenwood General Store for candy and a chocolate soda, or to play billiards at Tiny's Pool Hall.

By six o'clock in the evening, the streets are again quiet as most people are back home for mealtime. The same thing will happen tomorrow with some variation, but not much. The same people will be at the same tables sipping coffee just as they did the day before. It is a routine, and it is more or less predictable. But if all this sounds boring, then perhaps you just can't appreciate Greenwood. And it would be unfair to describe the town or its people as boring. The Travis family is but one example of the town's adventurous folk, and there are hundreds more. We also live in one of the more beautiful areas of America, in the rolling green landscape above the Mississippi River valley. The numerous hills, valleys, and streams surrounding this piece of God's country provide Greenwood's citizens with a plethora of opportunities for pleasure and trouble: fishing and hunting, bar hopping by snowmobile from town to town, hiking and camping, cow tipping, and thousands of other pranks.

As soon as stories about Lake Dunbar started trickling back to Greenwood, our friends and family members began to subtly seek weekend invitations to Whispering Pines. Being at home in Greenwood to observe the Sabbath in the "proper" church no longer seemed to matter. God would forgive you since it was a mighty drive from Dunbar to any church. At first, the visitors included just our extended family. My parents made a trip in 1958. My sister from California arrived at Lake Dunbar for the Fourth of July 1959. Even Uncle Frank made one last pilgrimage in the summer of '63, more than thirty years after first setting eyes on Dunbar's shores. Frank drove north with his wife, Ruby, and me for a few lazy days of fishing. And fish is exactly what we did. After the first day, we caught enough fish for lunch, dinner, and breakfast the next morning. While fish for breakfast probably doesn't sound very appetizing, for us any meal time was appropriate for fresh white fish from Minnesota's cool waters, pan fried to perfection.

Soon our cabin was open to friends as well as family. Had we been more modest in our descriptions of Lake Dunbar, perhaps we would not have experienced such an influx of visitors in those early years. However, after hearing tales of plentiful fishing, peaceful relaxation, and stunning wooded beauty, everyone wanted to visit Whispering Pines. Guests at our cabin soon came to realize, as did we, the secret of Lake Dunbar. It was not the best fishing lake in Minnesota, or even in the surrounding area. It was simply an oasis of ordinary size, ordinary fishing and hunting, but extraordinary beauty and solitude. And a visit to the Travis cabin made for a relaxing and spirited sojourn as well. Each time we entertained guests at our cabin, visitors signed a guest book, logging their appearance at Whispering Pines for posterity. The guest book was a collection of off-white, thick paper pages bound together with a wooden cover and backing. At first, only people's names were entered into the book, along with the dates of their stays. By 1960, we also began recording our own visits to the cabin. Then in 1961, comments routinely appeared next to the names and dates, such as "good fishing," "cold weather," and "excellent coffee." By 1962, the first hand-drawn pictures of the cabin and its surroundings were also entered in the book. After 1965, it seems as though the written discourse would never end. Full accounts of the groups' trips were given, along with much exaggeration, to be sure.

The cabin's guest book is a permanent reminder and record of my family's presence on Lake Dunbar. It reveals our adventures, our accomplishments, and our tragedies. Most of all, it is proof we shared our good fortune on Lake Dunbar with family, friends, neighbors, and all who would gather with us in God's country. And I think our visitors always knew they were welcome to return to Whispering Pines, time and time again. As it says on the very first page of our guest book:

Welcome to our cabin, and enjoy your stay
Rise with the morning sun, then start fishing for the day
We're delighted to have you right here beside us
Just sit back and relax, 'cause we don't make much fuss.

You can eat the famous sandwiches that Aunt Ellie will make
And end the evening meal with Ruth's delicious chocolate cake
Though our family's jokes, tales, and antics may bring you to tears
We hope you'll enjoy our Whispering Pines cabin and come back
again next year.

LOST HEROES

IT IS DIFFICULT TO SINGLE OUT ONE PERSON AS THE MOST instrumental figure responsible for the Travis presence on Lake Dunbar. Some say the acknowledgement should go to me, if for nothing more than my longevity, but many others contributed to the construction of Whispering Pines, and to the creation of our memories there. Still, if one person's input were greater than any other, it would have been Sam Travis. My husband was a big man, both in stature and in heart. He was also a self-made man. His wisdom came from within, seeing as he had to quit school at the end of the eighth grade to begin working full time on the family farm. Despite his less-than-middle-class upbringing, Sam Travis rose to become a man of great prosperity, owning and operating several small-town businesses, including Dodge and Plymouth car dealerships as well as a Massey-Ferguson farm machinery dealership, Travis Sales and Service, Travis School Bus Service, and the area's first television business, to name a few. We also owned a farm on the outskirts of town. Starting with nothing, Sam's businesses would eventually come to be worth hundreds of thousands of dollars. By the end of the 1950s, Sam and I owned half a block on Main Street in Greenwood. The land and buildings housed the Travis school buses, the dealerships, and the shop. Additionally, Sam Travis was a mid-twentieth-century renaissance man: businessman, husband, sportsman, and father. The eldest son of homesteading farmers, Sam learned to love and respect the land at an early age. It is understandable, then, why he was so captivated by the shores of Lake Dunbar.

It was at the height of our joint personal and business success when the strength of our family's mettle was put to its greatest test.

I vividly remember that calm and peaceful March night when I heard the screams of our eight-year-old daughter Stella, who had just gone to bed with complaints of a stomachache. Our youngest had been in bed for several days with mild tummy troubles. Dr. Burton had been by the house earlier in the week and diagnosed it as the stomach flu. Stella was a very energetic, playful child, and not one to cause problems or complain, so it is no wonder she lay so patiently and quietly despite what turned out to be quite serious. All week, she would eat some chicken soup and gelatin, then spend the day reading in her bedroom on the top floor of our large white house on Water Street. A door in Stella's room led to the attic and a small closet. Nothing too big, mind you, but big enough for a young girl to store clothes, dolls, and other favorite playthings.

Racing to Stella's room in the middle of this horrific night, I immediately noticed bloodstains on the sheets when she fell to the side of the bed. Frantic, I wanted to scream, but held it together as best I could for Stella; then I hollered for Sam to call Dr. Burton again. He did, and was told to take Stella to St. Luke's Hospital as quickly as possible. Seeing the severity of her pain, Sam and I rushed her to the hospital, twenty minutes away. Our youngest daughter underwent emergency surgery, involving cutting her from just under her breasts to the base of her pelvis as the doctors were not exactly sure what to look for. However, as they worked furiously on her weakening body, the surgeons discovered her appendix had ruptured, shooting poison throughout her fragile system. Peritonitis, they called it, when a poison surrounded her intestines, apparently after her appendix had burst.

What an excruciating passage of time as our entire family sat in the hospital waiting area, staring blankly at the walls, and jumping to attention every time a nurse or other hospital staff person passed through the room. I couldn't even look at my other children for fear I'd burst into hysterical tears. Regrettably, in retrospect, each of us sat there dealing with our own personal torment. As long as I live, I will never forget those few moments when the doctors finally came out of surgery looking dejected with heads hung low, unable to make eye contact with us for more than a second. Despite their best efforts,

Stella wasn't going to make it. They assured us every measure was taken to save her life, but the poison was just too strong for her fragile little body, and she never regained consciousness from the surgery. Before she passed, Sam, the children, and I surrounded Stella's bedside, said our incredibly difficult goodbyes, and laid kisses on the forehead of our sweet sister and daughter, the bright light of our family.

As would be expected, Stella's death in March of 1960 hit us all very, very hard. For my other children, all in their teens and twenties, the invincibility of youth was dealt a tragic blow. "How could this happen?" they asked. "How could this happen?!" "Why Stella?!" they demanded, "Why Stella?" For Sam and me, the burden was even greater. The loss of a child at any age, especially one so young, is an indescribable torment unparalleled to other tragedies. Everyone in my family went through a lengthy grieving process: anger, disbelief, shock, hurt, and ultimately acceptance. Each went through these stages at his or her own pace. The funeral was a blur to me, still to this day. Stella's entire third-grade class attended with their teacher, as well as hundreds of people from town. With my husband being such a popular businessman in Greenwood, our customers, friends, and other townsfolk showed us tremendous love and compassion.

However, more than anyone else, Sam seemed to languish in the stages of hurt and shock. My husband was a quiet, gentle man to begin with. To say he was a car salesman was to state an oxymoron. After all, this was rural America. Sam's car-selling success was due to his honesty and integrity, not by slick or disingenuous measures. People always knew they would get a fair deal at the Travis Dodge and Plymouth dealership. Yet, this family tragedy seemingly ravaged the enthusiasm and optimism from my gentle giant of a husband, and everyone knew it. Stella's death had pure and simply broken Sam's heart, and her memory remained in the forefront of his mind for the rest of his life. For my husband, there were no visits to Lake Dunbar in 1960. Instead, he spent more and more time in his workshop at Travis Sales and Service in downtown Greenwood. While various family members and I made a few trips to Whispering Pines that summer, Sam stayed behind. Too much work to do, he would say. I knew better, but didn't push him. On many a late night, I would even awaken to find him gone. On one occasion I went looking for him, only to find Sam sitting beside Stella's gravestone. Anytime he was gone, I knew where to find him. He would have to grieve in his own way, and he did.

By the beginning of 1961, Sam had made great strides toward acceptance of Stella's death. He was helped through this time by the strength and encouragement of his family, especially the growing number of grandkids. Eleanor's two kids, Walt and Rose, were the first, and a few more would follow by the end of the 1960s. Walt was now ten years old and followed his grandpa everywhere. Like Mary and the Little Lamb, wherever Grandpa Travis went, Walt was sure to go. My husband was a big man, over six feet tall and two hundred pounds. He soon became known as "the Man with the Shadow" by his friends who, whenever Walt was in tow, greeted him with, "Hey Sam, the sun must be shining on you again today. I see you have your shadow with you!" In the summer of 1961, I finally convinced Sam it was time for a return trip to Lake Dunbar. I was very happy to see my husband's excitement about returning to Dunbar with his little pal, Walt. Suddenly all the new fishing equipment the girls had given Sam at Christmas became his most prized possessions. Sam Travis was a frugal man who rarely allowed himself new things. If there was money to be spent on the little things of added pleasure, he always wanted it to be for me, or the children. Seeing my husband's excitement as he strung the new poles and polished the leaden lures, I decided to present something to him I'd been thinking about for a while now. In the years since first building the cabin, we had outfitted Whispering Pines mainly with second-hand items. A large part of Sam's business success was built on the fact he knew how to make a deal. In the vernacular of his youth, he was what was known as a natural horse trader. The cabin's stove, the refrigerator, the bunk beds, and dressers were all items he had taken as trade-ins on appliances or televisions. Sam knew how hard rural people worked to make their lives more comfortable. He knew there was more than one way to skin a cat. Though Sam knew quite well how to get a deal done, sometimes I stepped in when an arrangement got dicey. Occasionally people took advantage of my husband's kindness and compassion.

If repossessions had to be made, I took over with my no-nonsense, take-no-prisoners style. Business was business, and it generally took only one visit from me to clean up any problem.

"Sam, I would like to get a new sofa for the cabin to take up on this trip. We sure could use one. In fact, I would like one of those new rollout-bed types. We could get it in memory of Stella, something new and fresh as a special reminder of how much she loved Dunbar. We can put it in front of the picture window in the living room, and look out on the lake." After pausing to check his reaction, I continued. "This would be a special way to remember her every time we're together in a place where she was the happiest."

Sam thought for only a second. I think he realized because he was so consumed by his own grief over the past year, he had often overlooked my needs. I had been grieving for Stella too. It was now time to do something special. "Isabelle, what a wonderful idea. Let's get the kids and go down to Wiedermeyer's Furniture store right now and pick out the one you like."

We tried out every rollout couch in the store. The poor store clerk had never made such an exhausting sale. My grandson Walt was especially excited to see a rollout sofa for the very first time. "Look, Grandma, a trampoline you can hide!"

My husband's strong recovery from our sorrowful loss of Stella held the family together as we entered the tumultuous decade of the 1960s. From my perspective, the '60s changed America perhaps more than any other in my lifetime. Certainly, no one can deny the powerful images brought to one's mind at the mere mention of "the 1960s"— drugs, music, war, riots, leadership, assassination, religion, race, rights, liberation, sex, and youth. The Sixties also remind us of our many lost heroes and leaders like JFK, RFK, and Martin Luther King.

It was only fitting that ten-year-old Walt accompanied us on our first joint trip of this exciting new decade. On the third afternoon of our visit, I went to town for some cooking supplies. Sam and Walt had Lake Dunbar all to themselves. My husband was anxious to try his new pole and lures, so he and Walt fled the distractions of the cabin for the solitude of Dunbar's southern end. No cabins or other man-made improvements were anywhere on this end of the lake. The weeds and lily pads flourished here without being cut down to make way for a dock or an improved view. After the fifteen-minute boat ride, Sam and Walt outfitted their poles with bait, and were ready to catch some fish.

"Grandpa, do you really think there's any fish way down here?"

"Walt, can you keep a secret?"

"Sure, Grandpa. What is it?"

"Right here is the best fishing spot on the whole lake. It is a hiding spot for all the big, wily northerns and walleyes. You see, this is their domain because very few people come down here to bother 'em. That's why we shut the motor off and rowed in the last hundred yards."

"So they wouldn't see us or hear us, right?"

"No, Walt, they know we're here. These old fish are smart. We just came in quietly to show 'em some respect. To let 'em think we're just here to enjoy the scenery."

"Are they really big, Grandpa?"

"Oh yes, but even if you are clever enough to hook one of the really big ones, we won't keep him."

"Why not, Grandpa?"

"Well, it's about respect, like I said before. A fish doesn't get real big unless he's been around for a while, like me. And if he's been around for a while, it means he's outsmarted fishermen for years. It would really be a shame to catch and keep him. So I always let the really big ones go. I just throw 'em back."

Walt was indeed confused. On the previous trip north, his dad told him how they couldn't keep any fish less than thirteen inches or one and one-half pounds. The fish should be given a chance to grow up and be caught when they're big, his father had explained. With a mix of frustration and bewilderment, Walt asked, "If we release the small ones because they need time to grow up and we let the big ones go because they're old, what the heck do we keep?"

"Ones like this," said Sam with a nod toward the water where the tip of his pole was becoming increasingly bent as he battled with something below the surface of Dunbar's murky waters.

"Reel him in, Grandpa. I'll get the net."

With tense shoulders and calm concentration, my husband reeled in a four-pound northern pike, above-average size, and a keeper.

"Grandpa, if you were a fish, would you be a northern or a walleye?"

Sam had never really thought about such an important question, but paused before answering so as to give Walt's inquiry full consideration. "I guess I'd rather be a walleye. The walleye is Minnesota's state fish, and has good-looking crystal-like eyes. They even look mystical. And since they travel in schools, you know they're real smart. Yep, I'd be a walleye."

Walt contemplated this answer, both content and proud that his question had been taken seriously. "Actually, I'd rather be a northern. They're strong and get to swim around all on their own. Besides, I would go crazy having to go to school every day."

From then on, Walt gave up his quest for fishing logic. All he knew was the lake had fish he was going to catch, and keep. After a few hours, Sam and Walt had a stringer full of keepers, an even mix of northerns and walleyes. While they didn't quite have their legal limit of three northerns and six walleyes per person per day, the men had plenty to keep them busy cleaning and filleting into the night.

As my husband recounted for me later in the evening, he and Walt reeled in their lines, pulled the full stringer of fish into the boat, and headed full speed toward the cabin. While Sam drove, Walt pondered the existence of these creatures they had captured. They were cold, razor-toothed, and slimy. In other words, a boy's dream.

Walt joined us on a similar trip north the following summer. This time, though, we had a slightly larger crowd. My daughter Eleanor was there with her husband, Paul, and their two children, Walt and Rose, in addition to my daughter Ruth. At 6 a.m. on the first full morning of the family's stay, Sam and Walt sat patiently and impatiently, respectively, in the small, green wooden boat waiting for Rose and me to join them for an early morning fishing expedition. It took me a few minutes longer than usual to get ready because I was bringing Walt's six-year-old sister, Rose, out for her very first Dunbar fishing expedition.

"Grandpa, I don't know why we just can't go without 'em."

"Listen. We promised Rose we'd take her out for some fishing, Walt. Grandma's rounding her up now."

"Why do girls have to take so dang long to get ready?"

"Oh, they'll be coming. Just sit tight."

"Why are we taking them anyway? Girls don't know nothin' about fishing."

"Walt, remember. We agreed to show Rose how to fish with live bait, with minnows."

"Oh, brother."

"Here they come. Now be polite."

With everyone in the boat, I invoked my usual send-off of "Here we go," and pushed the little craft away from the dock. The group set out for a large marshy bay on the western edge of the lake. This much of a concession Walt was able to extract from his grandpa: they wouldn't take us girls to the boys' secret spot in the southern end. Walt cast his line in the water as soon as the boat slowed to a troll. While racing across the lake, he had fastidiously and gleefully placed a minnow on his hook. He reached into the small white bucket full of small brown sucker minnows, and grabbed the biggest one he could find. With the slippery, wiggling character in hand, Walt pushed the tarnished gold hook through the helpless creature's mouth, out the right gill, and back through the fish's neck. Walt purely and simply loved this ritual. Rose, on the other hand, did not.

"Walt, don't be so mean," said Rose, thinking of the poor minnow.

"It doesn't hurt 'em. Besides, you're gonna have to do the same thing if you expect to catch any real fish."

"No I don't," Rose replied. "I'll get you or Grandpa to do it for me."

"I'll show you how, but you have to put your own minnows on your hook. It's the rule of fishing, right Grandpa?"

"Walt, I think there's an exception for your first time out with live bait."

As it turned out, Walt spoke a bit prematurely about girls and their ability to fish, given the final score. Sam caught and kept one northern, a pretty good tally since he spent most of his time baiting hooks, untangling the kids' lines, and netting fish. I was able to reel in two northerns and a perch while Rose caught three bass. Poor Walt ended the day with only two northerns.

"You see, Walt," said Rose, "girls can catch fish too. Grandma got three and so did I."

"Well, only if you count perch as real fish. I caught two northern pike. Those are the best kind there is!"

"Say, everybody," announced Sam, "get your lines in the boat. It looks like a storm's comin' our way so we'd better head back to the cabin."

The waves on the small lake were twice their normal size, and the wind had picked up to about twenty-five miles per hour, producing whitecaps across the whole lake. My husband poured some gas into the outboard Martin engine, and after three or four tugs on the starter cord, it began to roar and more. It began to spit out fire like a space-age rocket. Then it quit. So there we sat, in a boat without a second oar and an anchor. Sam was able to use the one oar to paddle toward the cabin, but we encountered increasingly strong waves. From far across the lake, we could barely make out a lone figure on the Whispering Pines' dock, but not enough to identify him. We simply began waving our arms wildly in hopes of communicating our distress.

From the dock, our son-in-law Paul could see our boat was in trouble, which meant even more trouble for him. Paul couldn't swim, and even worse, he feared deep water, especially deep and wavy water. Just the year before, he had barely escaped with his life after his truck went off a slippery bridge and into some fairly deep backwaters of the Mississippi River. But Paul had no choice or options. Our two grown daughters Eleanor and Ruth had gone to town for groceries, and Paul was the only one home. With life preserver firmly in hand, he cautiously climbed into the other green Travis boat and motored nervously across the windy waters to the rescue of his in-laws. We were grateful and very relieved to see him, and Paul became an instant family hero. As Walt later recalled, "What a pleasure to see him. He got us home."

For Paul, the requested reward was simple: "Let's get back to shore."

By late afternoon, the old Martin engine was repaired and running like new, thanks to Jack, who drove up late that night to join us at the cabin. Jack was like his father in so many wonderful ways. He was smart, handsome, and a master of all trades. He especially loved to fix and restore things—you name it, like motors, cars, and appliances. Years later, he would become quite accomplished at restoring the vintage cars of his youth, the Chryslers of the 1950s. His special love was the 1957 Plymouth Fury with gold metallic tails.

After repairing the Martin boat engine, Jack and Sam took a ride out on the now-calm Dunbar waters. Sam enjoyed these trips out on the lake with our only son. They fished, talked, and had typical father-son outings. Jack and Sam exchanged endless thoughts about the cabin, the family business, politics, and professional athletics. When it came to sports, the primary focus was always upon Sam's heroes, George Mikan and the Minneapolis Lakers.

"I still can't believe the Lakers went down in four straight to the Celtics," Sam lamented. "They're better than the score indicates."

"They've had a good run, though. Five world championships in the last ten years," Jack noted. "And I think they'll be good for some time yet to come."

"Jack, have you heard the latest? Rumor has it the team is moving out to Los Angeles. Boy, what a loss that would be."

"*Los Angeles?* Are they going to change the team's name then? What I hear from Uncle Frank, there isn't a single lake in the whole dang city!" In fact, the Lakers did leave Minneapolis in the early 1960s. It was a great loss for Sam, Jack, and thousands of others across Minnesota whose basketball heroes would become legends of the game.

Back at the cabin later, Sam headed out to clean and fillet fish for dinner, followed by who else but Walt. At age eleven, Walt was still a bit young to clean the fish himself, but he accompanied his grandpa for moral support, and to keep the mosquitos off of Sam's back and arms. Walt would stand guard over Sam, daring any pesky mosquito to land on his beloved grandpa, doling out punishment to the vexing trespassers in the form of a quick, life-ending slap. Sometimes Sam didn't know which was worse: a tiny mosquito bite or Walt's constant whacking. Upon return to the cabin from these fish-cleaning episodes, Walt would always announce the number of mosquitos killed, and told of the untold agony he had saved his grandpa. But Walt's tales of mosquitos soon became as exaggerated as the fish stories I used to hear from uncles Louie and Frank.

Years later, in reminiscing over some of these exploits, Walt recalled one in particular. "Once I saw a mosquito carrying off one of the smaller grandkids. Luckily I had my pistol BB gun, shot the bug, and saved the kid." When asked for more details to verify the story, Walt simply said, "I don't want to name the child because we are both very shy and private people."

No, Walt, we wouldn't want that.

On this particular day, though, Walt had an important job to do as his grandpa began cleaning the fish. Two of the creatures in their catch were still alive. As I spied from the cabin's kitchen window, Walt carried out his manly duty, and quickly put the fish out of their misery. Walt then watched with big, brown, captivated eyes as Sam laid each fish across an old wood stump, and filleted them with great care. First, a slit was made behind the fish's left gill, down to the spine. Sam then rotated the knife one quarter-turn to the right and cut through flesh and bone, bringing the knife back to the surface just above the tail. The same procedure was used on the fish's right side. Next, holding the skin with a pliers in one hand, Sam meticulously moved the sharp knife gently back and forth, firmly separating meat from the outer scaly skin. After Walt cleaned the fillets in a bucket of fresh water, he rushed them into the kitchen where I pan-fried them in a big black iron skillet, along with onions and potatoes. It was a meal fit for royalty, and the princes and princesses of Lake Dunbar enjoyed every mouth-watering morsel.

In the fall of '62, Sam and I spent a weekend alone together at Whispering Pines. It was the last weekend trip of the season, and time to close the cabin down for the winter. We pulled in the dock from the soon-to-be frozen lake, boarded up the tool shed and outhouse, and drained the pipes between the pump and the water heater so as to avoid rupture of the internal pipes from frozen water. It was a chilly yet sunny autumn weekend at Lake Dunbar. It was a classic, gorgeous day. Before leaving for the long ride home, Sam and I took one last walk through the Travis property, surveying the woods, the lake, and all corners of Whispering Pines. As we walked and talked, Sam and I reminisced about our first eight years on Lake Dunbar. It had been so eventful with construction, improvements, and numerous journeys with the kids and grandkids. The cabin was finally finished, more or less. Something always needed work, but the major projects were done.

"You know, Isabelle, I sure do love this place."

"I know you do. I'm rather fond of it myself," I said with a smile. "It feels like home, as if we always belonged here."

"When I first heard Louie and Frank talk about Dunbar, I didn't believe there could be such a peaceful, beautiful place on this earth. But I'm glad we investigated for ourselves."

"It's been a lot of hard work, but I guess it was all worth it. The grandkids sure enjoy themselves up here, running all over the woods and everywhere."

"Oh, Isabelle, you're just as wild as they are. They're usually running all over the place because you're chasing 'em." We both laughed, independently recalling the many family antics over the years.

After reaching the top of the grassy lane cut through the federal land behind ours, Sam seemed wistful and happy. "We're lucky people, Isabelle, despite all that happened with Stella."

"Sam, I think about her every day, especially up here where she loved to run, play, and just be a little girl. But I'm thankful for what we've been given, and for what we still have."

"Yeah. Our kids are all grown up and having children of their own now. The businesses are doing pretty well. And we have this excellent place for a weekend escape, maybe longer once we retire. The Lord has certainly blessed us."

The last of our children left home when Ruth graduated from Greenwood High in the spring of 1960. During her junior year, Ruth met the love of her life, Ted, a quiet guy who was the second of a dozen children born to a family living on a large dairy farm northeast of Greenwood. Ted and Ruth dated steadily and attended two junior-senior proms together. In the course of their blossoming relationship, Ted of course also met Sam Travis, a man for whom Ted had great admiration and respect. The young man even purchased his first car from us, a 1954 Chevy. My husband was surprised to see seventeen-year-old Ted walk into the Travis dealership early one Saturday morning back in the fall of 1959. "Teddy, good to see ya. If you're looking for Ruth, I think she went over to Rochester with Mrs. Travis."

"No, sir. I've actually come in to see you, sir. To buy a car."

"Well, well. Let's go out and see if there's anything you might like." Before they actually looked at any particular vehicle, Sam and Ted spent forty minutes talking in general about cars, farming, school, our daughter Ruth, and of course, fishing. Ted had apparently not attempted much fishing in his first seventeen years, aside from afternoon trips down to the creek behind his parents' farm for trout. So he listened intently to Sam's stories about Lake Dunbar. Finally, they got down to looking at the cars in the Travis lot. Both Sam and Ted knew which car Ted would choose: the black Chevy. Ted was a star athlete in Greenwood, and this car formerly belonged to the local football and basketball coach. Sam and Ted both knew there would be some obligatory bargaining, but Sam intended to give the young man a break. Sam knew Ted did not come from a wealthy family, but he was a hard worker who understood the value of money. Eventually they settled on a price of three hundred dollars. "Let's go inside, sign the paperwork, and set up a payment schedule for you."

"Oh, Mr. Travis, I don't need a payment schedule. I intend to pay you in cash. Here." Ted took out a wad of bills totaling just over three hundred dollars in hard-earned greenbacks. Sam was stunned. Not many people, especially young men, ever paid him up front in cash. He was also impressed knowing Ted had saved every penny of the three hundred dollars from his summer work at the Lakeside packing plant outside of Greenwood. Ted worked there for ten hours every day all summer long, in addition to his duties back home on the farm. The name Lakeside was obviously the product of mischievous Scandinavian humor since no lakes were within fifteen miles of our town. Sam took the cash from Ted, sending him off with the Chevy. It is difficult to say who was prouder: Ted for his new car, or my husband for his new friend.

At Sam's invitation and Ruth's urging, Ted made his first visit to Lake Dunbar the following summer of 1960. The trip not only confirmed Ted's love for Ruth, but also his relationship with Sam, who had become a friend, a role model, and his hero. Another of Ted's heroes (and mine) was elected president in November. Answering the call of the young, vibrant President John Kennedy, nineteen-year-old Ted left college in 1962 and joined the first class of Peace Corps volunteers to spend two years in the rainforests of South America. On the day Ted was scheduled to leave for South America, Ruth and Sam drove out to the farm where Ted's family lived. The young man had accepted Sam's offer to drive him to the airport in Rochester for the first leg of a very long journey. Ted said goodbye to his parents and many siblings, climbing into the '61 Dodge, and watched out the rear window as the family farm, the only home he'd ever known, soon faded out of sight.

During the thirty-minute ride to the airport, Ted and Ruth held hands and promised each other to write frequently. Telephone calls would be nearly impossible, given the remoteness of Ted's destination. Sam simply drove along without interrupting as the two young lovers enjoyed their last moments together. Finally, they arrived at the terminal, unloaded Ted's sparse belongings, and said their emotional farewells. The exchange between Ted and Ruth was expectedly tearful and difficult for my daughter. At their age, I'm certain two years seemed like an eternity. After letting go of one final hug, Ted stretched out his hand and was met with a firm, loving handshake from Sam.

"You take care of yourself, son."

"I will, sir. Thanks. I'm sure Ruth will fill you in on everything I write. Well, almost everything."

The handshake continued and finally Sam took hold of Ted's shoulder with his other strong hand. "Good luck."

The ride home was very quiet. Ruth was no doubt deep in thought about Teddy, trying to imagine where he was going, and about his safe return two years down the road. She hid her tears as best she could from her father, but there was no need. Sam knew how Ruth felt, and gently kept his arm around her for most of the ride back home. As much as he tried to comfort his youngest daughter, my husband too had his own doubts and fears for Ted's adventure. South America was a distant and dangerous place. Sam had recently read to me from a *National Geographic* article describing not only the beauty of the South American rainforests, but also of significant threats posed by disease, lack of medical care, and wild animals, including pythons, piranha, and panthers.

When Sam arrived home, he told me about the farewells at the airport and that Ruth seemed to be coping with this significant life change as well as could be expected. However, he also told me about a nagging feeling he couldn't seem to shake. "I don't know," he said prophetically. "I'm just afraid something might happen, and we won't see Teddy again." In the end, Ted did return to his beloved Minnesota, after two valorous, difficult years of service, but the return was bittersweet. His relationship with Ruth was as strong as ever, and they would marry one year later. However, Ted's heroes were all gone. John Kennedy had been struck by an assassin's bullet in November 1963, and a year earlier, my husband, Sam Travis, passed away prematurely from a heart attack in December.

Looking back now, the period immediately following Sam's death was surreal, as if it did not really happen. For God's sake, he was so young. How could he be dead? I'm not sure how we managed to arrange a funeral, run his businesses, and cope with the emotional burdens all at the same time. I surely had extraordinary help from friends and family alike, and I can only hope I thanked them all appropriately. I really can't recall. As with anyone, I suppose, you expect to see your grandparents and parents die before you, followed either by your spouse or you, but never your child. In the span of three years, my world had turned upside-down, and the proper order of death had cruelly not been followed. I had no role model to follow, since both of my parents were alive, and none of my siblings or friends had lost a spouse or child. I felt alone, scared, helpless, and lost. Being of proud one hundred percent German heritage living in a town of similarly descended northern Europeans, I also had the burden of not being able to show much emotion in public. Stoicism was the preferred remedy of the day, leaving me to sob in private until my daily flood of tears dampened every pillow I owned.

Thankfully, our children were raised, leaving me with simply my own emotional burdens to carry, though I did keep careful watch over Ruth, the only one of my kids yet to marry. She was especially close to Sam, and now she was the youngest in the family following Stella's early passing. I'm certain Ruth felt as lost as I did, wondering how and where to sail our ships forward now that our anchor had been so brutally ripped away. The days and months to come were indeed bleak, even for an enthusiastically positive person like me. I felt an indescribable sense of dread, of shadow, of death, and I couldn't help but think my life's best days were now behind me, and the candle of romantic love extinguished for all time. Quite often, the deafening silence of my now-empty home caused me to flee to where I could hear the faint murmur of human voices in a café, at the theater, or watching a game of ball in the park. Looking back, I suppose I should be thankful I did not reach for a comforting vice to dull my pain, but rather spent my remaining days reaching out for a hand of companionship and camaraderie with family and friends, so I could minimize my days spent alone. Yes, the loss of our husband, father, and grandfather took a tremendous toll on the Travis family. Sam was only fifty-three years of age, and really in the prime of his life. The hard work of youth had been done, the children were raised, and it was time for us to relax and enjoy summer evenings together on Lake Dunbar. Yet, those dreams were not meant to be. Many people lost their heroes in the 1960s. So, too, did the Travis family.

Grandma's Root Beer

With the passing of Grandpa Sam, I was now the official leader of the Travis family, and I did my best to play the role as matriarch and strict but fun-loving grandma to perfection. At first, we made very few trips to Lake Dunbar following my husband's death. My three adult children and I spent untold hours attempting to understand and run the businesses Sam had so skillfully managed with a tremendous memory, however, with very little paperwork trail or backup. Eventually, the businesses and properties were sold off one by one. The exceptions to this methodical divestiture were the family home, Travis Bus Service, and our properties on Lake Dunbar. The bus business was kept and managed under my leadership with significant help from my son, Jack. Almost everyone in the family, including some grandchildren, have driven rural school routes at one time or another for Travis Bus Service in Greenwood.

For myself, I navigated school bus routes for nearly fifty years before retiring begrudgingly at a youthful seventy years of age. It was a Minnesota State record. All of the kids in the countryside knew me. They also knew enough to behave while on my bus or pay a hefty price in verbal reprimands or reports to their parents. The Travis grandchildren loved to ride along with me on my routes, and then also to pretend they were driving their own routes in a stationary bus parked in our garage in Main Street in Greenwood. By the mid-1960s, I had plenty of grandkids for me to dote over. Eleanor, my eldest, had two kids, a boy named Walt and our sweet little Rose. My son Jack had just one child, Kate, whom he named after my mother. My youngest two grandsons, Eddie and Alex, belonged to my daughter Ruth. With

Sam gone, as Eleanor would say, "Grandma spent most of her time just being Grandma."

Walt was not only my eldest grandson, but also the most charismatic character of the Travis family, always good for a joke, a laugh, or a smile. Some say he was also my favorite, but I'll never tell. I must confess under my watchful eye, Walt likely got away with more than anyone. Like me, Lake Dunbar was undoubtedly Walt's favorite place in all the world. Later in life, despite fighting for life against a serious illness, Walt spent many a weekend at Whispering Pines. However, it was the early years of his life when Walt developed his deep love for Lake Dunbar. In the summer of 1964, fourteen-year-old Walt and I spent a wild weekend on Dunbar's shores. We completed the two-hundred-and-fifty-mile drive in record time, with Walt behind the wheel the last twenty miles aboard the good-looking Chrysler Imperial Sam had purchased for me a year before his death. The Imperial was a uniquely handsome car with taillight flares, big whitewall tires, and plenty of seating room inside. I guess it didn't occur to either Walt or me sixteen was the legal driving age in Minnesota.

"Grandma, we need to stop in Squaw Lake before we get to the cabin."

"What for? And watch your speed young man."

"Ah, we need some bait."

"It's cheaper up at Earl's Place. We'll get our minnows there."

"But Grandma, we also need cigarettes."

"Cigarettes? Cigarettes?"

"Yeah, cigarettes," he repeated, slightly embarrassed to have to ask his grandma.

"Walt, you know I don't smoke, and I'm sure your parents don't let you smoke either."

The Imperial had just crossed the Squaw Lake city limits. A few residents on the street watched in awe. They had probably never seen such a magnificent automobile, and were even more incredulous at the young boy behind the wheel. Squaw Lake, a booming metropolis of one hundred Native American and Caucasian inhabitants, remarkably had two general stores: Leino's and the Co-op. Mr. and Mrs. Leino, Scandinavian immigrants, operated a grand old grocery store across the river from their newer, more upscale competitor. Everyone in our family knew Mr. Leino. The grandkids would always beg to stop in his store for a bottle of root beer or an ice cream treat, and to hear the old man's funny Finnish accent.

Einar and Ellen Leino closed up shop in the early 1980s for any number of reasons: the economy, the competition, their age. The old store is still there, however. One can drive through town to this very day and still observe the empty, oak floor building on the banks of the Popple River. Nearly thirty years after going out of business, memories of the wonderful old general store are still revived as one drives past the building with the faded green awning whose sun-bleached letters still read "Leino's." In the two miles separating the city limits and Leino's, Walt's irresistible charm won me over. Walt steered the Imperial into the Co-op parking lot. I couldn't risk buying cigarettes from Mr. Leino. The transaction might come up in conversation at a later time when other family members were listening.

"Walt, park it over there near the gas pump, and come on in with me. We might as well get a few supplies."

Walt parked the Imperial with great care. He was on a roll, and wanted to stay in my good graces. We entered the Co-op and picked out a few grocery items before heading up front to check out.

"Oh, and we'll be needing a packet of cigarettes," I said nervously, speaking with the air of someone who did not want to reveal this was my first cigarette purchase—at age fifty-one.

"What brand, ma'am?" asked the burly clerk.

"What brand?" I replied curiously.

"Yes. Marlboro, Salem, Camel?"

Not wanting to reveal my naiveté in this moment of truth, I turned slightly toward Walt with a whispered inquiry from the pursed lips of my tense mouth. "Walt, what kind do we smoke?"

"Kools, Grandma. We smoke Kools."

I turned to the clerk and said confidently, "Kools, sir. Kools." Some would say I certainly am.

Walt and I eventually made our way to Whispering Pines. It was always good to come around the curve on the old dirt road and see our redwood-colored cabin with Lake Dunbar in the background. As usual,

I set to work getting all of the necessary tasks out of the way so there would be plenty of the weekend left to enjoy. I immediately persuaded Walt to mow the lawn, knowing without any chores to do, Walt would have the boat in the water and be long gone for an afternoon on the lake. I opened all of the windows, airing out the stuffy, musty cabin, and swept up the errant mouse tracks before going off in search of dead rodents. The Travis family rarely set mouse traps, either out of humane feelings for the innocent trespassers, or more likely because we didn't want to deal with the smell and mess of a three-week-old decomposed mouse. Still, we often found tiny mouse bodies in strange places, including the oven, the sink, or drowned in the toilet.

After finishing the inside chores, I joined Walt outdoors as he battled with the tall grass and millions of mosquitos whose lairs he had now disturbed.

"Walt, don't run over that *(crunch)* branch!" I yelled, but not loud enough to overcome the roaring motor and Walt's lightning speed. Walt looked up at my scowl, flashed his charming smile, and mowed on. In order to spare the lawn mower blade more destruction, I scoured the yard for any remaining fallen branches. With the few twigs I retrieved, and some old dried wood Walt and I retrieved later from the forest floor, we created a flaming bonfire in a sandy pit between the cabin and the lakefront. Despite the full dinner I prepared, Walt still had room for marshmallows, on a stick and burnt to a crisp over the open fire.

I just don't understand "burnt to a crisp." I like to roast my marshmallows slowly until they turn golden brown and melt in my mouth. Not Walt. He enjoyed the thrill of watching a puffy marshmallow turn black in a fiery inferno. Also, he could consume three charred marshmallows in the same amount of time it took me to make but one of my own golden brown. Eventually we had our fill; the fire was reduced to mere coals. "Oh, Grandma. I don't feel so good."

"So, how many of those marshmallows did you have after I told you to quit?"

"I don't know. Just a couple."

"Let's go on in and get you some bicarb and ready for bed. We're going out early for fishing tomorrow, right?"

"Yeah!" was the response from the swiftly improving Walt.

Lying in bed with a partial view of the nighttime sky through the outer room window, I was comforted by the red glow of the northern lights. "Boy," I thought, "I've never seen them stay one color for so long." Soon, curiosity got the better of me, and I rose to investigate.

"Walt!" I screamed. "Get up and help me outside. Our fire must have rekindled, and it's burning one of the trees in the front yard!"

For the next few moments we panicked as we assessed the magnitude of the fire before aiming the water hose and dousing the flare-up. We were exhausted but relieved, recounting and re-enacting our fire-fighting drama back in the comfort of the cozy, and now safe, cabin.

The following summer, Walt and I again trekked north to Dunbar's shores together. In order to avoid creating any more unnecessary trouble, we brought along two companions, my daughter Ruth, and Walt's little sister, Rose. Our crew sped north again in my brand new blue Chrysler Imperial. Upon reaching the end of a long stretch of Highway 65 just outside McGregor I asked, "The sign says left to Grand Rapids, right to Duluth. Which way are we going?"

"Duluth" was the standard and scripted reply from all three riders in unison, knowing full well despite their answer, I would *always* drive toward Grand Rapids, in the direction of Lake Dunbar.

"Okay, we're going to Duluth." And with their spontaneous reply, I turned right and headed down unknown highways toward Minnesota's northern port city. My passengers were stunned. None of them had ever been to Duluth, and they suspected down deep either I would turn the car around shortly, or take a secret road back to Whispering Pines. Two hours later, my car crested a large hill with Lake Superior in the distance, and entered the Duluth city limits.

"Mom, I can't believe you actually drove us to Duluth. But after all these years, I guess I can believe anything," said Ruth incredulously.

"Whoa, I better stop for some gas. We're pretty near empty," I noticed. "I see a Skelly station over there." I pulled into the full-service station and asked the attendant to fill 'er up with premium. After all, I only put top-notch gasoline into my classic American car. "Oh, by the way, how much is the gas here?"

"It runs twenty-five cents a gallon ma'am," the young man answered.

"Twenty-five cents?" I was justifiably appalled. Gas was only twenty-three cents back home. "Excuse me, sir, but I guess we'll just take fifty cents' worth." The station attendant looked at me, eyed my expensive Imperial, and was clearly a bit taken aback at my frugality. "*I am not* paying twenty-five cents a gallon. It's as simple as that! It's the principle." A short while later, as the car filled up with gas at the Standard Oil station down the street for twenty-three cents per gallon, I flashed a smug smile at my previously-embarrassed companions.

"Now, what should we get for supper?" I asked, ready to splurge with all of the money I had saved on petrol.

"A&W! A&W!" was the excited reply from Walt and Rose. I pulled into the A&W drive-in, and everyone crowded to the left side of the car to read the menu.

"I want a Papa Burger Basket," announced Walt, the self-proclaimed man of the trip.

"Son, are you sure you can eat it all?"

"Heck yeah. I'm also having a pineapple malt at the Dairy Queen for dessert, and it better be real pineapple."

"Are you ready to order?" came the voice through the new automated menu machines.

"Yes," I answered. "We'll take a Papa Burger Basket for Walt, a Mama Burger Basket for me, a Junior Burger Basket for Ruth, and a Baby Burger Basket for Rose." Upon hearing the order, little Rose burst into tears. She wasn't a baby anymore, she would turn eight soon. However, by the time Ruth and I deciphered what was wrong, the orders were already placed. To soften Rose's hurt feelings, I ended up eating her meal, and Rose was again wearing her stunning young smile as she gorged herself on the much-too-large Mama Burger Basket. And it tasted great.

When Sam died, I was only forty-nine. By the end of the decade, my daughters convinced me to try dating again. I was understandably frightened at the very thought. It had been nearly four decades since a man had courted me, and life had certainly changed since then. Heck, from the way my friend Nellie Johanssen tells it, today's men even expect a woman to pay for the date once in a while. And then there's all this talk about "free love" and sexual liberation for women in all the latest magazines. I wasn't so sure I'd be ready for this brand new world, or would even want to be. However, the girls eventually convinced me to at least give it a try. If dating ended up being a horrible disaster, I could always sell the house, move to Lake Dunbar full time, and never, ever show my face in Greenwood again.

While the pool of potential suitors in Greenwood was not very large, I didn't have to travel far before meeting my match. Down the embankment behind our house in Greenwood sat a small green house owned by a man named Gus Whitney. Gus was a divorcee only two years older than me. He was a very handsome man of average height with thinning brown hair, and actually quite similar to my Sam in temperament. Although rather quiet and modest, Gus was also an accomplished practical joker whose house was full of trick cards, trick statuettes, and trick candy. For the next twenty years, off and on, Gus and I would be an item.

Our relationship could best be described as spirited. We had great fun going out together for dinner and dancing, taking bus trips to Branson, Missouri, and playing cards until the wee hours of the morning. However, when we weren't laughing or having a good time, Gus and I were bickering. Sometimes it was over big things, but mostly it was insignificant. The fiery character of our bond was likely due to our individual fierce sense of competitiveness. Both Gus and I loved to win, and abhorred losing, especially at Five Hundred Rummy. On untold occasions, each of us swore never to play with the other again because of alleged cheating or unsportsmanlike conduct. Eventually, after a few days of cooling off, we'd be back together having supper down at the High Pointe Club amidst unending laughter.

After a solid year of dating, and when I felt sufficiently comfortable, I invited Gus to travel north with me to Lake Dunbar. Seeing as we were not married, and in an effort to avoid any hint of a town scandal that would end up the conversation of everyone at the café, I insisted we make this first trip in secret, and Gus kindly obliged.

Moreover, because I was not the kind of woman to shack up with a man in private (perhaps knowing I would need to admit my sin to Father Murphy at the next confession), Gus also agreed we'd sleep in separate quarters, me in the bunkroom, and Gus in the back bedroom. Despite all of these restrictions, Gus came to love Whispering Pines as much as anyone in the family, and probably did more repair work on it than anyone other than Jack and son-in-law Ted, before or since. He especially savored the ability to fish Dunbar's mysterious waters. Like many before him, Gus was also an excellent fisherman. And despite the peacefulness and solitude of Dunbar's paradise, Gus and I brought with us our competitive spirits. A perusal of the guest book entries over the years speaks volumes to our fierce fishing rivalry.

August 1, 1968.   Me: "I beat Gus getting his limit, then he tied me. Gus beat the tie, of course. Wait 'til next time."

July 28, 1969.   Me: "I had a *very* good time—I got the biggest fish."

September 4, 1971.   Me: "Fishing was not my best. But wait 'til you hear the *champ's* story."

Gus: "I got three big northerns, 9-1/2, 5-3/4, and 3-1/2 pounds. Also one big walleye, 6 lbs. 4 oz. I caught ten nice fish, and 25 overall."

Me: "I had a good time. Did you, Gus?"

Gus: "I sure did."

May 27, 1972.   Me: "I tied the champ in fishing!!!"

October 18, 1974.   Me: "I got 6 fish so far . . . now 7. Anyway, I beat Gus. Ha!!"

Gus: "I got 5, Isabelle got 7. I don't know how she did it."

In the end, Gus was indeed the champion as he pulled the largest fish out of Lake Dunbar in Travis family history. It was a thirty-eight inch, eleven-pound northern pike Walt and I struggled to land into the boat. In fact, the fish wouldn't even fit into the net; rather, it only lay across the metal rim. After that trip, the guest book was forever void of any crooning about who was the fishing champ. Nevertheless, it was after that very weekend that I bought an old wooden sign displayed proudly over the entryway of the cabin to this very day:

Women's faults are many but men have only two.
Everything they say, and everything they do.

The beginning of the 1970s brought a new round of grandchildren as visitors to the Travis family cabin. Walt and Rose still tagged along often, but now were joined by their younger cousins Eddie, Alex, and Kate. This next round of grandchildren enjoyed Whispering Pines as much as the older kids. However, the younger grandchildren were also subject to more reprimands than the others either because I had become increasingly strict, or because there was more to yell about. As two of these rascals wrote in the guest book as they arrived at Whispering Pines on July 4th, 1973: "We're gonna have a real good time getting grandma all wet with water balloons!" Trouble, indeed.

At Whispering Pines, the competitiveness between Gus and me must have rubbed off on the younger grandchildren as they soon became polarized into girls-versus-boys camps. The young guys hung out with Gus, and mostly went fishing, while the girls stayed back at the cabin with me, having fun on walks, trips to Squaw Lake, and making fun of the boys from shore. We girls would even sneak away from the boys now and then to see a movie at the theater in Blackduck. However, we enjoyed plenty of combined activities for both boys and girls alike. Every Fourth of July weekend, Gus and I would take the kids over to Bemidji for the annual summer carnival. The grandchildren would run around like wild animals between rides on the seaplanes, roller coaster, and carousel before gulping down caramel apples, cotton candy, and hot dogs. Gus and I would always plan for a few days back at the cabin before taking the kids home so as to avoid explaining to their parents why the kids looked so ill and worn out.

For Ruth's two boys, Eddie and Alex, vacationing at Whispering

Pines with us was a much-anticipated event, especially the prospect of fishing with Gus. As they cruised the lake one summer day in 1973, Gus and the boys thought of nothing but casting for northerns on the southern end of Lake Dunbar. About halfway there, grandson Eddie tried to get Gus's attention over the noise of the rushing wind.

"I said, do you think I could drive the boat the rest of the way?" seven-year-old Eddie yelled.

Gus slowed up a bit so he could hear the boy more clearly and think seriously about the request. After making Eddie repeat the question one more time, he answered, "I guess so. You know how to do it, don't you?" Gus knew darn well I had never let Eddie drive the boat, especially the new aluminum Crestliner Eleanor purchased for the cabin the year before. But the kid had to learn sometime, and there was no time like the present. They had a few rough spots where the engine killed, or where Eddie steered the boat a little too sharply, leading everyone else to think they would end up in the water. All in all, Eddie did a fine job, and surprised the heck out of me with his boat-captaining skills years later when I finally thought he was old enough to give driving the boat a try. This day, however, was just for the guys, and they spent it as they should: fishing. In fact, the fish were apparently so plentiful grandson Alex spent all of his time netting everyone else's fish, and barely had time for his own. Yet Alex didn't care, especially since he helped land the granddaddy of them all.

As they neared the cabin trolling along Dunbar's eastern shore, Gus got a strike. He knew he had snagged a big one from the way the fish fought. At first, Gus thought he had hooked a tough weed, but he soon became convinced it was a fish because of his progress reeling in the line. Gus yelled for Alex to get the net. This was going to be a biggie! Alex was the first to eye the famed catch, and appropriately withdrew the net. Gus didn't catch a fish. He caught a medium-sized log full of several frustrated fishermen's lost fishing hooks and lures. Or, as Gus exclaimed, "My God, I caught a Christmas tree!"

Understand I am by no means a feminist or a radical; however, I am independent and feminine. Nevertheless, it came as quite a shock to my neighbors and especially to my family in the summer of '72 when I painted Whispering Pines bright pink. With the family ties to Chrysler, I could not have a very popular pink Cadillac, so I procured the next best thing. Actually, pink was the color of the primer, not the paint itself. Once I completely covered Whispering Pines with a pink primer, I stood back, admired the hue of my handiwork, and decided no paint was necessary. The mixed reactions fell mostly along gender lines. But the cabin belonged to me first and foremost. And I would do what I wanted, no matter what the men said. As my Dunbar neighbors would say, "It was certainly unique. It was certainly daring. It was certainly Isabelle."

In addition to my sense of design and color, or lack thereof, I also had an ingrained sense of timing, as in mealtime. When I said it was time for dinner, it was time for dinner. Period. However, son-in-law Ted learned this lesson the hard way. Before taking off for an afternoon of fishing while the women stayed behind to paint, I reminded Ted dinner would be served at 7:00 p.m. sharp. And in the course of the afternoon, with help from Eleanor and Ruth, I was able to paint the entire cabin, clean up everything, and prepare a pot roast meal for eight. As luck would have it, Ted found a crappie hole at about 6:30, just as the sun was starting to fade in the southwestern sky. The crappies were biting like crazy on the small minnows on Ted's hook. He'd cast his line into the water, and bam! In thirty seconds another fish would bite. Of course, Ted forgot all about the time, and would have continued fishing for another hour had he not noticed a small fishing boat coming straight at him, full speed. I could have simply gone ahead with dinner, telling Ted later he had missed mealtime and was out of luck. But when I tell everyone dinner is at seven o'clock, by God, it means everyone. So poor Ted had to bite his tongue during my loud verbal reprimands all the way back to the dock, and on the hike up the hill with me to the freshly painted pink cabin.

As for the youngest of the Travis grandchildren, they knew a grandma slightly older in years but perhaps even younger at heart. Appropriately, the tireless threesome of Eddie, Kate, and Alex were responsible for initiating some of the more notorious Travis family traditions, centered of course on their grandma—me. On a cool southern Minnesota night in the summer of 1975, this threesome sat restless in my Greenwood living room watching *The Lawrence Welk Show* on my large RCA television. Having finished their evening baths, the grandchildren were anxious for one more adventure before they ebbed out into an ocean of nighttime dreams. Fresh from my own bath, and lounging in the Lazy Boy chair in nightgown and bathrobe, I hoped the mellow sounds of Lawrence Welk's voice and music would coax the heretofore-rambunctious youths into serenity and sleep. The plan was working until Katie noticed a slight tear in my tattered bathrobe.

"Grandma, you have a hole in your robe," said the six-year-old.

"Oh, this robe has seen its better days. I guess I need a new one," I replied, while nonchalantly ripping the hole a bit bigger just to prove the point. However, the action-seeking, polka-music-bored children apparently took my act as a cue, a prompting, and an invitation. They quickly stormed me in my chair and began ripping my bathrobe to shreds. Initially surprised, I soon joined in the revelry by running throughout the house, but always within reach of the marauding Travis grandchildren. For the next several years, whenever Travis grandchildren gathered for an overnight stay in Greenwood or at Lake Dunbar, all those present would anxiously wait for me to dramatically emerge from my evening bath wearing another ragged, threadbare nightgown or bathrobe bought at a used-clothing shop. Knowing I always wore an intact and proper nightgown underneath, the grandkids proceeded to tear at the outer rags with great delight, and much laughter.

This young threesome inaugurated a second Travis family tradition a few years later, a tradition affectionately known as "that damn celery dish." In the late 1970s, my mother sustained a broken hip during a fall in her Greenwood home. Due to the severity of the injury and her advancing age, she moved into a nursing care facility on the northern edge of town. My mother was a stern and proud German matriarch in whose image I would follow, and she was adamant about giving Christmas gifts despite her inability to leave the care facility for a shopping excursion due to her slowly healing hip. So Mom commissioned someone to make ceramic dishes in the shape and color of various fruits and vegetables she would then give away to her large community of family and friends. At Christmas, I received the soon-to-be notorious celery dish.

The ceramic dish was deep green and designed in the shape of a celery stalk, about a foot long, and rather heavy. At the time, I welcomed the gift, and even used it on a few occasions to hold, what else, but celery. Within a few years, however, my feelings toward the dish would change. Mom passed away in the winter of 1980, and following the often-typical post-mortem sibling rivalry, I felt as though my sisters had appropriated the vast majority of our mother's prized possessions. The celery dish came to epitomize how little of Mother's things I inherited. After hearing my apparently frequent complaints about this lackluster inheritance, my own family soon tired of attempts to placate my hurt feelings and instead tried a new tactic. Whenever I raised the subject, concluding with the familiar ". . . and all I got from Mother was this damn celery dish," my children praised the celery dish as a jewel to be cherished. I was playfully admonished not to overlook the dish's exquisite texture and linear features, not to mention its utility. My son and daughters even jokingly fought over which of them would inherit the treasured celery dish someday. The jesting approach was eventually successful in garnering a laugh from me, and the family never heard my pitiful inheritance story again.

Seizing the moment, and not realizing the permanent ritual they would create, one night Eddie, Kate, and Alex ferreted out the ceramic green creation from my colossal oak armoire and hid the dish where I was sure to find and appreciate it. As I lay down to sleep, I leapt from the bed after bumping my head against some unknown object underneath my feather pillow. It was, as I clamored and yelled, "That damn celery dish!" To this day, all members of the Travis family are required by unwritten rule to hide the celebrated creation under my pillow, and then blame the deed on someone else. Despite my protestations and verbal reprimands to the apprehended conspirator, the celery dish is easy to find, always in the exact same location in the lower left corner of my oak armoire. I myself finally got in on the act several years later, turning the tables and hiding the dish under the pillows of my children and grandchildren alike. As a result, the ceramic celery holder has traveled from the sleepy village of Greenwood to the bustling metropolis of Los Angeles and back again. None of the Travis family will publicly admit to wanting the ghastly dish, yet all will secretly confess a desire to feel its blunt edges as they unsuspectingly lay down to bed some cold winter night. Perhaps receiving the dish is a symbol that one truly belongs to our family's traditions. Perhaps there is exhilaration in clandestinely hiding the object under another Travis's pillow. Or, perhaps, it's just a damn dish. That damn celery dish, indeed.

For Eddie, Kate, and Alex, Lake Dunbar and Grandma Isabelle were synonymous, inseparable. As long as all necessary rules of conduct were followed (no feet on the couch and never, ever lose one of my lures while fishing), I tried my best to make Lake Dunbar memorable. The cabin had two sleeping rooms. Combined with the front living area, I had room for twelve slumbering bodies. Two in the back master bedroom, four on the rollout couches in the living room, and six sleepers in a bedroom measuring eight feet by six feet. This bedroom, with its two sets of bunk beds—one single and one full sized— was reserved for the grandkids and me. Parents slept elsewhere. My spot was always the lower, double-bed bunk. This bed, everyone's favorite, was an old steel-framed, one-piece double-bed bunk with sagging mattresses and deteriorating steel springs. As the doorway to this small room was a mere three feet wide, the bed arrived first; then the walls were built around it.

The grandkids alternated who slept with me, and who got their own bunk. Bedtime at the cabin was somewhere between nine and eleven. Actual sleep came much later. Showers taken and teeth brushed, everyone headed for bed. All was quiet, and hopefully, sleep was close. Then, the inevitable giggling began, initiated by me. For the ensuing thirty minutes, we'd tell stories and jokes, always followed by laughter, and an occasional "What's going on in there?" shouted from Eleanor or Ruth in the other room. When we felt real rambunctious, those of us in the lower two bunks would place our feet gently on the bottom of the top bunks and, on the whispered count of three, give a swift kick to our unsuspecting upper neighbor. Once asleep, though, there was no disturbance until morning, no lights except the moon, no noise except for the chirping crickets, and no more giggling except in the dreams of children.

The pinnacle of a Dunbar weekend visit for the youngest Travis grandkids was a trip out in the boat with their grandma. All suited up with life jacket, fishing gear, and youthful enthusiasm, I would then outfit the children with their fishing gear. These fishing trips were never spectacular in results. Some fish were caught on occasion, but very few, in comparison to the effort involved, and the inevitable complications, including snagging each other's life preserver with fishing hooks. No, the crowning glory for these children was the end of the boat trip. As the poles were brought into the boat, the cheers began.

"Root beer, Grandma. Make us some root beer!"

"I don't know," I would tease. "Are you sure?"

"Yes, yes. We want root beer!" was the unanimous reply.

As I steered the small motorboat in the direction of the Whispering Pines cabin, I pushed the little craft into full throttle, lifting the bow slightly above the water's surface. The lake water, usually reddish in color from the high concentration of iron in the northern Minnesota soil, was turned to a dark brown hue by the churning motor. A trail of cream-colored foam rested on the surface behind. As the children excitedly climbed over each other for the best view, they shouted with joy, "Grandma's making root beer! Look, it's Grandma's root beer!"

EARL'S PLACE

IF YOU KNEW EARL RITTER, OR HEARD ONE OF HIS EXTEMPO-
raneous tall tales, you had the experience of knowing a living legend.
Earl was not famous, nor did he invent anything, other than several
unbelievable hunting and fishing stories. But Earl made Lake Dunbar
come alive. Even in the dog days of summer when the fish lost their
teeth, and the mosquitos were feasting, people would come hundreds
of miles just for a few memorable evenings at Earl's Place. As it said
on the business card, Earl's Place was:

THE ONLY RESORT ON LAKE DUNBAR
IN THE HEART OF MINNESOTA'S LAKE COUNTRY

The term "resort" was certainly used in its most exaggerated
sense, in my humble opinion. Earl Ritter and his wife, Lucy, came to
Dunbar's shores in the late 1940s, having discovered it on a hunting
trip. Earl later said he had found the biggest fish and deer in all of
Minnesota right here at Dunbar. Earl and Lucy previously lived in
Minneapolis, where Earl worked as a used-car salesman. The accompanying stereotypical characteristics of those drawn to such a profession
seemed to prepare Earl well for his second career as a fisherman and
resort owner. One of Earl's favorite cabin plaques read something like,
do all fishermen lie, or do just liars fish? Will we ever know for sure?

Whatever the answer, Earl and Lake Dunbar were a perfect match.
Earl's Place was rustic, natural, and serene. It sat on the far northern
end of our lake on a gently sloping hill leading to a flat section of lakeshore. At first, Earl and Lucy built a charming log cabin, painted burnt
orange with brown trim, in the middle of the property. Later, they

constructed small, one- and two-bedroom cabins around the perimeter of the cleared land, all matching the main cabin in color and style. The resort had no clubhouse or cafeteria, but necessities were plentiful, like the outhouses labeled "Squaw" and "Chief," a large dock to hold fishing boats, and a small wooden building for cleaning and filleting the day's catch. The fishhouse sat in a low, shady grove not far from shore. It was a three-sided shack with the open side facing due north. Inside the fishhouse, Earl kept a large block of lake ice all summer long. He would cut the block from the lake in March or early April when the water was beginning to soften, then place it in the fish shack and cover it with sawdust. Protected as it was, the ice would always last well into September, keeping visitors' freshly caught fish cold until they were ready to leave for home. Earl's was a quiet place, nothing fancy, but the type of place attracting only a certain breed of people. Not too wealthy, not too picky, not too pampered. Earl's kind of people were those who didn't mind bringing their own light bulbs, as Earl outfitted the cabins with only twenty-watt bulbs, which were not always sufficient. And visitors received a glimpse of what was in store for them at the resort even before they arrived. On the back of the resort's business card, which Earl handed out generously with an insistence to pass them on to others, was a full description of Earl's Place, and what visitors could expect. The card was a gem, full of Earl's own unique one-liners.

Earl's Place

The perfect place to spend your summer vacation.

The prices are reasonable, only a bit beyond what you can afford, but equally beyond what it's worth.

If you love fishing, come on up though folks often find they came just one week too late for the big ones.

Our boats are certifiably safe when tied to the dock for some lakeshore fishing.

We offer one spectacular meal per day, though most folks who don't like grease prefer the diner in town.

Autumn is the best up here at Earl's Place. If hunting is your game, we'd be happy to show you where someone shot a deer three years ago.

*Our cabins contain all the luxuries of home, unless of course
your home has electricity, running water, and a roof. Those who
bring a tent say our cabins are perfect.*

*We have boxes full of thank you letters from folks, telling us
how grateful they were upon arriving home after staying a week
at Earl's Place*

Now, how about coming on up to see for yourself?

Everyone who visited or vacationed on Dunbar's shores knew
Earl Ritter. He made a point of monitoring the lake and its guests.
No one fished, hunted, or even swam in this lake without first being
seen by Earl. More often than not, visitors would also be subjected to
an earful of the latest lake gossip, and more than enough of Earl's tall
tales. But if guests could escape from Earl for five minutes, theirs was
an enjoyable, peaceful respite from civilization among the pristine
wilderness and rustic cabins. This peace would only be interrupted
by the sound of Earl's voice calling out for his pet deer and trusty
hunting dog. By the time we got to know Earl and Lucy, the Ritters
were in their late fifties, early sixties. No one seems to know how old
they really were, but everyone in our family seems to have the same
recollection of the Ritters.

Earl was a small, thin man, probably five foot six with crew-cut
hair and a wrinkled, well-tanned face. He wore round, framed glasses
with a semi-clean fishing cap, and he always had a lit stogie hanging from his lips—one of those medium-sized cigars with the rubber tip. Earl didn't even remove the cigar when he told his stories or
teased the Travis grandchildren. Lord only knows if it also stayed in
his mouth during meal times. In stature, Lucy was a tiny little thing,
but her oversized personality more than made up for what she lacked
in height. She reminded me of a small elf who lived in a mythical
forest. She was the typical grandma, even though she had no children or grandchildren of her own. Instead, Lucy adopted every small
child who came through the resort. She was a chain smoker, and had
a wonderfully raspy voice, which gave her much more authority than
her five-foot two-inch stature indicated. I also suspected from time to

time Lucy might have taken regular nips of firewater throughout the day, since no one was as perpetually happy as Lucy.

Earl and Lucy were certainly the most colorful characters on Dunbar's shores, but not necessarily the most notorious of the era. Sam's brother James bought some property on Lake Dunbar and eventually built his own cabin. James Travis built a place across the lake from our property, more than shouting distance, but in a spot clear enough to see him wave hello. James, as it turned out, was Earl Ritter's official understudy and loved the lake, especially keeping up to date with who's who and what's what. If there was ever a need for lake gossip or secret information, James Travis was the man to see. James gained real notoriety one summer day when he held a funeral service for his dog that had died rather suddenly. The dog had actually died the previous winter, but good old James knew his companion belonged on the shores of Lake Dunbar where it loved to run and play. So my brother-in-law simply kept the dog in his freezer all winter back home in the Twin Cities until the ground was soft enough for burial.

Next door to James Travis lived the inimitable Nellie Johanssen. Nellie undoubtedly became my very best friend on Lake Dunbar, following the death of her husband in the mid-1970s. Both of us widowed, Nellie and I were a perfect match for instigating trouble on the lake. We would entertain each other in our respective cabins until the wee hours of the morning, playing cards, laughing, and occasionally finishing off a bottle of Bailey's Irish Cream. Nellie and I also loved to harass Mr. Tucker, an old bachelor who lived down at the end of the lake. He never seemed to come out of doors much, unless it was to tell Nellie and me to carry our boisterous conversations farther on down the road.

In the 1970s, I met another fascinating character in the woods near Lake Dunbar. Helen Bryan is by no means a household name, and I doubt even many in all of the Chippewa National Forest would recognize her contributions to the cultural life of Minnesota, and particularly its Native Americans. As any student of American history knows, the "Indians" suffered unimaginable loss at the hands of white men over the course of three centuries. Before my European ancestors arrived in the New World, the Native Americans enjoyed unchecked freedom to thrive and develop their own rich culture. It just seems unfathomable to me now that my kind could so callously strip the Indians of their birthright, move them off of their land time and time again, and leave these amazing cultures so utterly decimated. In my lifetime, the new federal policy toward these native peoples seemed to be one of containment and ignorance. Tribes had been moved generations ago to reservation lands that were set aside for the Indians to practice self-government, and to allow continuation of their cultural ways as best they could. However, given the history of constant change, deprivation, and threats to their way of life, it is not surprising so many reservations are now home to chronic poverty and often feelings of hopelessness.

Perhaps it is because of this long, torturous history that I became so enamored with Helen Bryan. In my mind, she is as brave a soul as I have ever met, and yet another example of a strong woman who changed the world simply by trying to do what the mothering kind does best—fight for our families and for ourselves.

Helen grew up in Squaw Lake, Minnesota, in the heart of the Leech Lake Indian Reservation, a few scant miles from Lake Dunbar. Her Chippewa ancestors had lived, hunted, and fished in the woods and lakes near Whispering Pines for thousands of years, which makes the duration of my own family's history on Lake Dunbar seem quite small by comparison. Helen's husband, Russell, was also of Indian descent, though his family was from the White Earth Reservation several miles to the south. They lived together with their six children in a very modest house in Squaw Lake on the lands belonging to Helen's family for generations. The couple saved up money for years to afford this new family home, which they moved into in the summer of 1971. Helen was thirty-one, a couple of years older than my daughter, Ruth, and just as pretty. Perhaps it was that resemblance which drew my attention to Helen in the Squaw Lake Co-op, though her emerging and heroic life story really drew me in deeper with admiration for this blessed soul.

Like many Native Americans in the nearby area, Helen and Russell struggled just to get by, to keep a roof over their heads and food on the table. Jobs and other economic opportunities were by no means abundant in the area, and neither of them came from money. To their credit, they did what was necessary to thrive, perhaps even better than some of their neighbors since the Bryans were able to outfit their home with some essentials others could not: heat, electricity, and indoor plumbing. And because they lived on a self-governed reservation free from federal and state government intervention, they did not have to come up with the money for steep property taxes—at least until the watershed year of 1971. Someone from Itasca County showed up, took measurements, inventoried their property without permission, and sent the Bryans a $30 tax bill to cover the final two months of the prior year, followed by another invoice for nearly $120, covering all twelve months of 1972.

To Helen, this seemed just plain wrong. Living on a reservation meant neither the state nor federal government (and much less the county!) had any right to tell the people there how to live, and certainly couldn't bill them for it. Although her friends, and even her husband, tried to convince her just to pay the tax and not fight the government, Helen wouldn't hear of it. While she certainly would not be the first or last Native American to take on the government, and although she knew her people's horrendous track record for success, this was a matter of principle for Helen Bryan, and by God she was going to try. Her first call was to the Anishinabe Legal Aid office, a free legal service available to residents of the reservation. They seemed to think she just might have a good case, which was encouraging. Legal Aid agreed to investigate, and she promised to buy the kindly lawyer a beer, if he prevailed.

Months went by, and Helen heard nothing from the Legal Aid lawyer. However, she refused to pay the tax bill, and for the moment there seemed to be no adverse consequence. Unbeknownst to her, the case was indeed proceeding, and the arguments were quite complex. The case also seemed to take the local county attorney's office by surprise. Apparently no one had questioned their taxing authority before, and the county was keen to prove no one was exempt, not even the residents of the Leech Lake Indian Reservation. The county's efforts seemingly paid off as the Bryans lost their case in Itasca County Court, and yet again on appeal to the Minnesota State

Supreme Court. Facing this pair of losses, the Legal Aid lawyers seemingly gave up, moved on, and instructed the Bryans to just pay the tax bill. But the answer wasn't good enough for Helen Bryan. She knew she was right and was determined to prove it. Luckily and thankfully, she found a big city lawyer to take on her case, and try for the extremely remote possibility of a review by the highest court in the land. Their fancy metropolitan lawyer proved to be worth his salt, and sure enough, he secured an appeal to the U.S. Supreme Court. Though the government continued to fight them tooth and nail all the way to Washington D.C., the Bryans held their ground, literally and figuratively.

Soon enough, Helen's courageous fight paid off. On June 14, 1976, the U.S. Supreme Court issued a unanimous decision in her favor. The government was forbidden from taxing residents of treaty-protected reservations in any manner. Period. Newspapers from as far away as New York City hailed the landmark ruling, though few truly knew how far-reaching the effects of this simple judicial opinion would be. Within a decade, other smart lawyers had figured out that a tax-free zone in the middle of nowhere could yield a significant advantage in the form of Indian gaming. On the Leech Lake Reservation, and on similar protected lands across America, casinos soon rose like a blooming field of sunflowers, growing higher, bigger, and more fantastic than anyone ever dreamed. Soon enough, those same Native Americans who had lived in abject poverty and waning hope for generations had found an escape, and perhaps some degree of satisfying revenge. As each white man dropped a nickel in the slot machines, or left his wad of cash on the blackjack tables, the Indians with bloodlines to the local tribe racked up dollars by the boatload, and all of it tax-free.

At the center of it all was a kind, courageous woman named Helen Bryan. In fighting for herself and her family, she stuck to her principles and prevailed against all odds. However, somewhere along the way, everyone seemed to forget what this small woman had accomplished, both in terms of history and the unbelievable economic opportunity she created for Native Americans nationwide. As other tribes raked in millions, even billions of gambling money over the decades, Helen's share turned out to be roughly zero. Nada. Despite what she won for her people, they simply forgot about brave Helen Bryan. Yes, she won what she had set out to do, and never did have to pay the $150 or any future tax bill, but she deserved so much more, in my opinion. I guess she did receive one consolation from the Leech Lake tribe, though the honor went to her undeserving husband, rather than the woman who earned it. When Russell died in 1994, the tribe offered to pay for his funeral in exchange for their right to pick the wording on his headstone. I went out to visit Russell's gravesite near Squaw Lake one day, just to see it myself, and there it was: "Russell Bryan vs. Itasca County–Victory."[2]

On a warm summer day in the mid-1970s, I needed to do a thorough cleaning of the Whispering Pines cabin, so I sent my daughter Ruth and grandson Walt down the lakeshore road to check out the happenings at Earl's Place. From day one, Ruth and Walt had a special relationship. On paper, Walt was Ruth's nephew; in reality, he was more like her little brother. Ruth and Walt were only eight years apart, and Walt spent many of his summers living with Sam and me back in Greenwood because his parents each worked two jobs. Walt usually tagged along in Ruth's care, both at home and up at Lake Dunbar. Ruth was one of the few people in the Travis family who had my happy, playful, and celebratory demeanor. Walt, it seemed, got his own fun-loving approach to life from all of the time he spent with the two of us. Ruth was always full of energy, and tried to lighten other people's burdens through laughter. But she was also the family confidant. If there was ever a secret to be shared, Ruth's siblings, nieces, and nephew often went to her first. She especially relished her assumed role as Walt's mentor, and enjoyed giving him advice whenever he asked. This summer day on Lake Dunbar in 1971 was no different.

"You know, Ruth, I'm graduating next year, and I don't know what I should do next."

"Walt, what would you like to do?"

"I like working with people. I think I'm good at it. I want to make a big impact on the world, but I don't know if I'm smart enough to be president."

"First of all, you're real smart. I don't know what kind of grades you've gotten the last few years, but I've seen you talk your way out of some real trouble in the past. Maybe you should put your charm to use somehow."

"But I feel like I should do something really big, on a grand scale, or else it won't matter."

"Walt, do you remember last night when we snuck out onto the dock to look at the stars?"

"Yeah."

"And we noticed all those lightning bugs?"

"So?"

"Who do you think created the stars and the lightning bugs?"

"Paul Bunyan's forefathers?"

"Very funny, Walt. No, God made them. And in catechism they taught us that after creating the whole universe, God was happy with everything. If the puny light of a firefly makes God just as happy as the brilliant stars, I think you should just do your best, and it will be enough."

"When did you get to be so wise?"

"You'd be surprised how experienced and learned you get after having two kids. Especially when the first one is starting kindergarten but reading at a first-grade level. And the second one is already making his own meals at age two. I have to be on my toes when they start asking me tough questions."

Ruth and Walt turned up the short driveway leading to Earl's Place. Halfway to the house they were greeted by two huge dogs. The beasts barked like crazy, but were harmless and ultimately friendly. Soon, Earl came out of the house, hollering at the dogs and investigating what got them so riled up.

"If it ain't the Travis youngins. When did you kids get up here?"

"We drove up last night. It was too late to stop in and say hello," Ruth confessed.

"Oh, it's never too late," said Earl. "I'm a night owl, you know."

"Hell, you were in bed by nine thirty, you old fool," came a raspy voice from behind the screen door as Lucy came out to greet the Travis family. "Get over here and give your aunt Lucy a hug." Embracing each of them with her typical bear hug grip, Lucy tentatively released them, scanned them both head to toe, and asked, "So, how are you two rascals, anyway?"

"Couldn't be better, Lucy," said Walt. "Say Earl, Ruth and I were wondering if you wanted to go exploring some lakeshore with us over on the federal land."

"Sure. I got nothin' going on this morning that can't wait until afternoon."

Lucy Ritter raised her right eyebrow as she finished a long drag off her cigarette. "What about cleaning up the mess from fixing the truck, like you promised me?"

"Like I said," Earl said, turning back toward Ruth and Walt with a slight eye roll, "there's nothing that can't wait until later."

Lucy gave him one of her trademark scowls, then turned to hug Ruth and Walt once more before they ran off to meet Earl in his slick aluminum motorboat. The threesome sped across the bay and beached the boat by a grove of tall pines planted years ago by the U.S. Forest Service. Earl told them all he knew, and more than he knew, about the Native American settlements that used to be here, the fourteen-point deer he almost shot years back, and more previously untold fishing stories. Near the end of the federal lakeshore property, Walt noticed something in the water and took a closer look. Three feet out from shore he found a partially submerged dock that had either been abandoned or was lost by one of the nearby cabins in the last storm. It was in fairly good condition and Walt had an idea, which he kept to himself for the moment.

Later at dusk, Walt coerced Ruth into motoring with him across the lake to retrieve the wooden dock. They backed up to it, and Walt tied the end of the dock to two steel handles on the stern of the boat. Ruth motored back to Whispering Pines about half-speed to avoid both trouble and being noticed. However, the clandestine mission wasn't meant to be. Halfway across the lake the pair was spotted by old man Tucker who started cussing and yelling at Ruth and Walt to put the dock back where they found it. Mr. Tucker apparently thought he was the Lake Dunbar enforcer. He even ordered water skiers off the lake once. This was a fishing lake, not a playground, he argued. Eventually, the water skiers left. But on this day Ruth and Walt just couldn't take the dock back after they worked so hard. Besides, no one seemed to want it anyway. So they ignored him.

However, Mr. Tucker didn't ignore Ruth and Walt. He met them at the landing, and ordered them to put the dock back where they found it. Hearing all the commotion, I came storming out of the cabin to see what was the matter. I had little tolerance for Mr. Tucker. In my mind, he was anti-fun. With atypical restraint, I managed to calm Tucker down by compromising. Ruth and Walt would go over to all the nearby cabins in the morning asking if anyone wanted the dock, and return it if need be. Old man Tucker just grumbled as he walked back down the road to his cabin, threatening to call the sheriff. The younger grandkids had a rhyming nickname for Mr. Tucker, which I'm too polite to mention here.

Walt and Ruth thanked me for getting them out of trouble with Mr. Tucker, and went back down to the boat to unhook the dock, but I wasn't finished with them quite yet. I informed my daughter and grandson they would personally pay for any damage to my outboard Johnson motor caused by dragging the heavy dock behind the boat all the way across the lake. My rebuke was only half-hearted, however. Secretly, I loved the kids' antics, and only wished I had thought of it first. As Ruth and Walt untied the wooden dock from the back of the boat and dragged it up on land for restoration, we all heard the sputter of a passing motor not far off shore. It was Earl heading home following an afternoon of walleye fishing on the southern end of the lake. Earl sized up the situation, chuckled loudly, and tipped his hat to Ruth and Walt as he roared his boat toward home. Ruth and Walt looked at each other and smiled. They had received the respect and approval of the greatest prankster of them all.

Walt most assuredly thought about these events from the previous summer as he sat in a doctor's office with his parents in winter. His thoughts were suddenly refocused as he listened to the doctor explain Walt was being diagnosed with a rare form of childhood cancer. We all soon knew the details of his diagnosis, the painful and unpleasant treatments he'd face, and the corresponding low recovery rates for this wretched disease. If anything was in his favor, it was that his diagnosis came early, and Walt was young and strong enough to begin receiving strong chemotherapy. Walt's illness took a great toll on everyone, but the one person who helped our family through it all was Walt himself. It is said people in seriously ill situations develop a different perspective on life and coping. Yet, Walt transcended even the most stereotypically positive, hopeful patient. He believed fervently in God, in his family, and in his complete recovery. If this disease was meant to take his life, then so be it—but not without a fight. To Walt there was no question that he would always spend his summers on Lake Dunbar fishing, hiking, and hanging out at Earl's Place.

On a cool spring day in 1975, four years after Walt's initial diagnosis, I sat with his parents, Eleanor and Paul, once again in the hallway of Mercy Hospital. As Walt's doctor approached, we all looked to him with hopeful eyes. The stoic doctor announced further related tests needed to be undertaken, but Walt now appeared to be in complete remission. The cancer was gone. A miracle had been lived out among us. With his recovery, Walt did return to Lake Dunbar with me time and time again where he enjoyed many an afternoon at the resort shooting the breeze with Earl and Lucy, at least until the early 1980s. Like Mr. and Mrs. Leino in Squaw Lake, Earl and Lucy Ritter sold the resort in 1982 and moved to an apartment in nearby Deer River. They were each in their late seventies and wanted to enjoy their waning years in the more accessible surroundings of a small town with the friends and social events not available in the cold, silent winters on Lake Dunbar.

These were clearly evolving times. As we entered our fourth decade on Lake Dunbar, ownership changes were happening all around us. Soon enough, I could barely recognize the names on the mailboxes. Gone were the Saggisors, the Teichs, and even the annoying Mr. Tucker. While I certainly don't mind getting old (in fact, I feel better with every passing year), it is hard to say goodbye to neighbors we'd gotten to know through the years. Who knows if I'll ever see some of these old friends again as their visits become less and less often. I've even started to think about my own tenure on Dunbar, wondering whether it isn't time to pass the reigns and responsibilities of cabin ownership on to a new generation of the Travis family. You might think the prospect makes me sad. It doesn't. Whispering Pines is in my heart, and Lake Dunbar is in my blood. It doesn't matter whether the county recorder shows me as the owner of this beautiful spot or not. It will be mine in thought and memory until the day I die. Anyway, Earl and Lucy ultimately sold their property to a French-Canadian family named Dubois who decided not to maintain the site as a resort, but instead lived there for the enjoyment of their own large, extended family. Few reminders of Earl and Lucy still remain on Lake Dunbar, but they did leave their mark on folks like me who were lucky enough to have spent an evening or two at Earl's Place.

PART II

RUTH

St. Erhous's Day

Lake Dunbar entered my life when I was a mere ten years old, and it would never leave. No matter where I'm at or what my circumstance, I can summon thoughts of the lake at a moment's notice. I simply close my eyes, take a few deep breaths, and transport my mind northward. Within seconds I can hear her soft rippling lake waters, smell her thick pine needle scent, and taste the subtle iron flavor in a glass of her cool, deep well water. If I try just a bit harder, I can also envision the virgin land adjacent to Whispering Pines, and see my father and brother traipsing through our woods looking for deer tracks, arrowheads, and other random treasures of the forest floor. I see my sisters, especially little Stella, stationed in their usual places, reading magazines in the cabin's great room while Mom prepares a mouth-watering beef roast in the nearby kitchen. To me, Lake Dunbar is much more than a physical place. It is a state of mind. For the vast majority of my conscious life, the lake has been a presence deeply felt in my soul, and it is an escape to which I can flee whenever my real life is painful, or not all I'd dreamed.

I vividly recall the first time I laid eyes on those magical waters, racing with my brother, Jack, along the muddy, tree-fallen shoreline as my parents called frantically from far behind us with warnings of black bear, bobcat, coyotes, wolves, and other potential predators of the northern Minnesota forests. Alas, we did not care or feel the least bit threatened. To us, these woods held the treasures we had read about throughout our childhood. The castle of a prince-turned-beast, the hollowed-out tree house of seven dwarfed men, and the candy-sweet exterior of an evil witch's lair. Some sixty years later, as I look out across those same woods, I see my own grandchildren run with abandon and wide-eyed wonder as they chase each other, and their own childhood imaginings.

In my teenaged years, our voyages north held new adventure as I used the six-hour car rides to devour novel after new and exciting novel. Once there, I'd lie atop the cabin's bunk beds and across the wood dock, dreaming about how my life might someday be as exciting as the characters in my beloved books. There was Mikael in *The Adventurer* by Mika Waltari, who traveled freely across the kingdoms of Europe and met the most fascinating people as a student at the Sorbonne in Paris. I could truly see myself living in that magical City of Lights, listening to dashing young men woo me in French, and eating the most amazing and delicious food. Then there was *Marjorie Morningstar* by Herman Wouk. Now this young woman heroine *was to be admired*. The lead character was smart, exceedingly attractive, and very popular with the boys. Like me, Marjorie was the daughter of a successful businessman, and she dreamed of becoming an actress.

Yet perhaps the book with the greatest impact on me during those late teenaged years of the 1950s was *On the Road* by the inimitable Jack Kerouac. My older sister introduced me to the Kerouac books, but only quietly since anything from these Beat Generation writers was deemed off-limits in our house. My parents were fun-loving but morally strict people and they did not want their darling daughters to be influenced by the scandalous approach to drugs, sex, and irresponsibility Kerouac seemed to laud in his work. I, on the other hand, thought it liberating, not because I wanted to emulate the lifestyle of Dean Moriarty, but because living vicariously through these fictional adventures enabled me to see the world beyond our Rockwellian life in Minnesota. I specifically remember riding north to the cabin one Friday night with my father at the wheel and everyone else fast asleep in the post-sunset darkness. I sat in the backseat, holding *On the Road* up to catch the brilliant light from a full moon, perfectly placed in the western sky so as to illuminate the pages which I sped through as fast as Dad was driving. As much as I was amused at the antics of Sal and Dean, or the crazy adventures they embarked on at a moment's notice, I was also moved by Kerouac's powerful style, stringing together carefully-chosen words. Those words left me with imprinted images in my mind that would last for weeks, if not longer. I read and re-read certain captivating paragraphs ten times in a row, amazed at Kerouac's singular, flowing sentences that held so much in their literary grasp—a summation of the past, a snapshot of the present, and a promise of hope for the future. I could literally feel these written words flow softly off my tongue when reading along, to accompany the feelings of power, potential, and promise they generated somewhere deep inside me.

Perhaps Lake Dunbar has held such a tight bond on my soul because I am by nature a dreamer. Whether inspired by these books or the tall tales of my adventurous extended family, I've never lacked for imagination. And while some may deem my life to be as normal as the next person, they can't see inside my mind, or know I have been full of hope, wonder, and possibility throughout my long life. I also think of myself as a spiritual person, not in the sense of formal religion, but through my belief in a greater universal spirit and purpose for our lives. For me, such a spirit and purpose are inextricably intertwined with Whispering Pines and Lake Dunbar. It is of course my place of personal refuge, whether I am visiting her blessed shores, or very far away. At the risk of sounding crazy, I also believe I lived on Lake Dunbar once before, in a past life. Throughout my life, I've had a single recurring dream that comes to me unexpectedly while I sleep. In it, I am a young Native American girl running for her life from some unknown pursuer. I'm never caught, and always arrive safely home to Lake Dunbar. I've tried over the years to see the face of my elusive pursuer, without success. A hunter? A madman? The Grim Reaper? Perhaps, for I have feared tragic death, both for myself and my loved ones, throughout my life, and the one meditation that calms me is to picture myself along the shores of Lake Dunbar. With the passage of years, and the stinging loss of Dad and Stella far too soon in their lives and mine, as well as the painful losses soon to come, I cling to and savor the happy memories at Whispering Pines. Lake Dunbar entered my life as a young girl, and she is with me still.

After leaving home for college in 1960, and especially after marrying Ted a few years later, my own visits to Dunbar's shores became less frequent, perhaps one annual trip north at best. At first it was my studies, and then before I knew it, I was a young wife and mother. Less than a year after we married, Ted and I moved to Minneapolis and welcomed a baby boy into our midst. Theodore Jr., or "Eddie" as he was most often called, was a handful from day one, requiring my full attention, at least until I returned to work within a few months. Four years later, we were blessed with yet another son we bestowed with my proud family name: Alex Travis Walsch. Having one or more jobs to help support my own family was now routine, and those responsibilities took precedence over the more frequent Whispering Pines visits of my youth. The unforgettable 1960s and 70s flew by, and my love affair with Lake Dunbar was put on hold as I raised a family and made a life. Despite my neglect, she stuck with me, and even sustained me whenever the life I experienced wasn't all I'd dreamed. And I cherished the times I did see her, either on a trip with Mom or with my own new family of four (plus pets) in tow. Lake Dunbar is like a faithful old friend who welcomes you on every visit without judgment, ignoring the elapsed span of time between journeys to her bountiful shores.

By the middle of the 1980s, my two boys, Eddie and Alex, had grown to become fine young men, and each left the nest for college before I knew it, freeing me up to again pursue those things parents simply set aside for years, or even decades, without realizing it. As a mother, I've felt as if I were on an unstoppable train, watching my life move by far too quickly toward new destinations. It certainly feels as though we are reaching a time centered upon the completion of our lives as an intact family, moving from parent-child relationships to a new bond as four adults. Despite the occasional melancholy, it is indeed a most eventful and wonderful time in my life. The times and traditions from these years will be among my most precious memories as I move forward toward new visions for the future.

With the kids off at college or more interested in spending time with their friends, I found myself reminiscing more and more about Whispering Pines and yearning to spend quiet, peaceful nights wrapped up in its embrace. I also thought more intently during this time about my mother, Isabelle, and more specifically about her mortality. While she was a vibrant woman born in 1913, and in her late sixties was in excellent health, you just never know what will happen. Having been short-changed, even robbed of so many valuable years with my father, it dawned on me: I had better enjoy more time with my mom while it was still a possibility. And so it was in these early years of the 1980s I traveled with her frequently on the long road to Lake Dunbar. We fished together in our little green boat, laughed until we cried while recalling the many outlandish Travis stories over the years, and stopped for food or treats at all the usual places, including Leino's Store in Squaw Lake, M&H for snacks in Grand Rapids, and the unforgettable roast beef sandwich at The Sportsman's in Mora.

With each successive season as we entered the 1980s, I noticed much of the make-up of those living on Lake Dunbar was quietly but determinedly changing. Along with Earl and Lucy Ritter, several other neighbors had simply grown old and moved on. Nellie Johanssen, Mom's card-playing partner who lived year round in a small cabin down the road from Whispering Pines, died unexpectedly in the spring of '82. Even our arch-nemesis Leland Jensen moved off of the lake he had called home for thirty years. Whether due to all of these changes or her own desire to simplify her life, Mom too began to talk openly about selling the Travis property on Dunbar's shores. She retired from driving school buses in 1985, and while she had ample time to visit the cabin, she could no doubt use income from the sale to supplement her retirement. Besides, the drive was getting to be awfully long, and with the grandchildren nearly all grown up and beginning their own adult lives, fewer and fewer people seemed to accompany Mom on her trips north to help with the boat and other more strenuous chores required to maintain a lake home.

Mother's stormy relationship with Gus Whitney had also seemingly run its course around this time in her life. In 1985, the couple split up for what would be the last time, with no reconciliation for their long-running affair. All in all, 1985 seemed to be a watershed for Isabelle Travis. She retired, ended a lengthy romantic relationship, and moved out of the family home, all during one particular year. No specific reasons were given, but there seemed to be some link to the fact Mom was entering her eighth decade and, being the independent woman she had been all her life, she was bound and determined to make some change. The Travis family home, in which my parents raised four children, and where my mother had lived for the better part of forty years, was a large, midwestern, American Foursquare–style home, circa 1910s. The grand white structure with light blue trim stood at the pinnacle of Water Street, on Greenwood's highest hill. In addition to a sizable front porch and a detached single car garage, our family home had three bedrooms, a living room, dining room, kitchen, sitting room, basement, and meager back porch. However, it had only one bathroom for two parents, one son, and three of us girls.

Throughout the course of Isabelle and Gus's nearly twenty-year relationship, the commute between their respective homes was convenient insofar as Gus's modest brown ranch-style house sat directly down the embankment from Mom's house. With Isabelle looking over at him, Gus certainly never got away with any shenanigans. After their breakup, however, it was undoubtedly awkward, or even tense, when either of them wandered into their respective backyards, only to visually bump into one another. So with little notice to my siblings or me, Mom put the family home up for sale, and moved into a small green rambler on the opposite end of town. While the distance between her new residence and the old place was a mere nine-tenths of a mile, in small-town America the other end of town felt like light years away.

While saying goodbye to my childhood home was emotional enough, my sister, brother, and I had very mixed feelings when we heard of Mom's plans to leave Lake Dunbar as well. We had so much history in Whispering Pines, and everyone had worked so hard to build and improve it. We all had at least some fond memories from Dunbar, though my siblings had already established recreation routines of their own. My brother, Jack, in fact, had not returned to Lake Dunbar for more than one trip since my dad died in 1962. He seemed to hold the opinion that the strain of building the cabin may have contributed to our father's early death. Finally, after much hand-wringing, and before Mom could even approach a realtor to begin the process of offering the cabin for sale, she received a proposal from one of her children, a proposal to buy the cabin properties and keep Whispering Pines in the Travis family for yet another generation. It is no surprise to anyone: the offer came from me. My love for Lake Dunbar and the cabin was not materialistic but profound, deep, and based upon fond childhood memories. Lake Dunbar was the one enduring reminder to me of Dad, whom I loved so very much. In fact, when Dad passed away in the winter of '62, I was the last person to see and speak with him.

I was attending secretarial school in Minneapolis and had planned to spend a fun weekend in the big city with my new friends. However, by Friday afternoon, I sensed a strange feeling beckoning me home to see my parents. Without even calling first to see if anyone would be there, I packed a few necessities and drove south to Greenwood. Although Mom was away for the evening driving the bus carrying the basketball team to a local tournament, Dad was at home when I arrived. Actually, he was still at the shop, just where I expected him to be, and right where I looked first. I helped Dad close up shop and assisted with the evening bus-checking routine, a precise process he followed each night. Dad went over every one of the fourteen buses (although there were only twelve as Mom and my brother, Jack, were on a trip with the other two) and made sure everything was in order.

When Dad and I got home from the shop, we placed a big pan of barbecued ribs in the oven. Dad had purchased the ribs on his last grocery-shopping excursion with Mom. One of his trademarked tricks was to sneak a few special treats into the shopping cart while Mom wasn't paying attention. This time, it happened to be barbecued ribs. I put the chilled ribs into the oven, counting to make sure there would be enough for Mom and Jack when they returned from their bus trip. When I joined my father in the living room to watch the 10:00 p.m. news, I noticed Dad's body was limp in the chair, and he was breathing erratically. I immediately called the town doctor.

Dr. Burton, who had just returned from the same basketball game, rushed to the Travis home to see what he could do. Several minutes later, after the buses had both been put away, Mom and Jack also arrived at our family's grand two-story house. To their horror, Dad

lay on the living room floor with the doctor and me working fever-
ishly on his large frame to resuscitate him. Realizing the severity of
Dad's condition, Dr. Burton called for an ambulance. Soon, I was in
the back of the ambulance assisting the worried doctor in the archaic
method of modern-day cardiopulmonary resuscitation. As Dr. Burton
monitored Dad's pulse and pounded on his chest, I breathed air into
my father's lungs. Mom rode in the front of the ambulance while Jack
followed directly behind. From the hospital, we called Eleanor, who
immediately gathered her family into their Dodge station wagon for
the long trip to Greenwood, but they arrived too late. Dad was gone.

The home in which I grew up was occupied by someone else
once Mom moved to the other side of Greenwood in 1985. Travis
Sales and Service, to which my father dedicated his working life, was
sold long ago. What remained of his legacy, aside from pictures and
memorabilia, was Lake Dunbar. I had little difficulty in persuading
my husband, Ted, to purchase the cabin from Mom. Ted was equally
enamored with Lake Dunbar, and appreciated its history. For Ted,
too, had developed a relationship with my dad, albeit brief, and he
desired, much as I did, to carry on Sam Travis's dreams and visions
for this living sanctuary.

In 1985, Ted and I began our tenure as the stewards for Whispering Pines by following through on many of the plans Dad had made
for the cabin so long ago, and the cabin seemed to respond as though
awakening from a twenty-year rest. While cleaning out the tool shed,
we found screens for the kitchen windows missing all these years.
Once in place, the screens provided the cabin with its first constant,
refreshing northwest breeze in thirty-five years. Next, we replaced
several aging joists supporting the cabin floor, and the rusting pipes
connecting the well with the cabin. We also closed many of the secret
small openings to the cabin through which many a mouse had gained
unlawful entry over the years. Additional changes were made to the
outside of the cabin, including the installation of rain gutters and
cement block steps down to the lakeshore. The yard was also widened
to accommodate horseshoe pits and volleyball games. We even added
a new dock where we could moor our fishing boats.

But changes were not limited to the cabin itself. Ted and I spent countless hours in our dense forested land clearing brush and chopping downed logs into firewood. Many of the great jack pines were at the end of their natural lives, and were threatening to fall onto the cabin. The time for reforestation had come. Ted, it seemed, took great pleasure in collecting as much brush and wood as possible, and then setting it ablaze in a grand bonfire. Although fearful such flames might get out of control, I tolerated my pyro-maniacal mate. Nevertheless, my tolerance reached its limit one windy October afternoon as the flames from Ted's fire pyramid jumped to a pile of dry wood sitting adjacent the tool shed. We stayed up until the ungodly hour of 1:00 a.m. just to ensure the flames were properly doused. I promptly and clearly informed Ted he was not allowed to set any more fires at Whispering Pines unless it was in the middle of winter. As Ted wrote in the family guest book before departing at the end of the weekend, "Boy I hope she enjoys coming up in the cold." This sentiment was undoubtedly borrowed from one of Ted's favorite shirts he wore at least once on every cabin trip, much to my chagrin. The shirt reads: "My wife says I must give up fishing or she'll leave me. I'm sure going to miss her."

When Ted and I turned our attention toward refurbishing the interior of Whispering Pines, we tried to keep a balance of old and new in going about our work. Instead of replacing all of the existing furniture, we kept the charming pieces, merely outfitting them with new covers and pillows. However, we also furnished the cabin with several new items, including chairs, rugs, and tables. We even discussed, God forbid, replacing the old double bunk bed. The iron-barred bed with sagging mattress springs was well past its prime, and it took up a great deal of space in the already small second bedroom.

Upon returning home after the long weekend, our son Alex asked how the fishing was. He was incredulous upon hearing we had spent the entire trip working on the cabin, leaving us no time to fish. However, this news made him glad he had decided at the last minute not to accompany us. A weekend on Lake Dunbar without fishing? What a dreadful thought. Ted then shared with our son the idea of throwing out the double bunk bed and replacing it with a regular-sized one. Alex was furious.

"You can't get rid of that bed. It's my favorite. It's everybody's favorite."

"But it's getting to be an eyesore, and it really isn't very comfortable," Ted replied, somewhat defensively.

"Dad, the bed is an institution. If it goes, I go too!" After pondering our options for just a moment, it was decided the bed and Alex would stay. Needless to say, the sagging double bunk bed sat in the cabin's second bedroom for another thirty years, and whenever Alex would visit, he'd sleep quite comfortably on the old bed.

Alex was also instrumental in effecting one of the more significant technological advancements at Whispering Pines: the installation of a phone. My parents had always opposed it. Ted and I had no desire to allow such an invasion of our private palace, but our feelings changed quite radically in the fall of 1985 when Ted was stricken with a case of pneumonia while at home in Minneapolis. Ted was soon at our doctor's office after realizing he wasn't getting better with the standard remedy of plenty of rest and liquids. The doctor, who also had a lake home on Leech Lake, fifty miles south of Lake Dunbar, asked Ted if he had emptied his cabin's water pump yet. It was going to drop to near freezing, and because of a freak weather system, it would likely freeze in the Chippewa National Forest, causing water-filled pipes to burst. Because he had been sick, Ted had been paying no attention to the weather reports from northern Minnesota, and hadn't heard about an early season Alberta Clipper fast approaching the cabin. If Ted was ill before this news, he now felt even worse. Ted drove home quickly and told me about the problem.

"Ted, you cannot drive north in your condition. Let's call Krieger's Hardware store in Squaw Lake. They put in the new pump last spring, and they often remove them in the winter for several of the lake residents." I called, but several other cabin owners in the area were tracking the storm and had been calling Krieger's throughout the afternoon. The man at the hardware store told me it would be two days before they could get to our cabin on Lake Dunbar. I was in favor of taking a chance on the weather for two days until Krieger's could get to the task. However, Ted was troubled about the prospects of the freezing temperatures busting the new pump we had just installed in the spring, along with all of the water pipes and the water heater. So, my husband insisted we drive north immediately. I would not hear of it, given his condition, but he finally convinced me to call his doctor for an opinion. Now, the doctor had his own twenty-year love affair with the great northern forest, and he undoubtedly understood the dilemma. Reluctantly, with Ted's arm twisting and sudden enthusiasm over how much better he allegedly felt following the shot he'd received a mere hour ago, the good doctor gave his permission to go. Ted was only to supervise, however, and let me do all the work.

We quickly gathered some boxes of winter clothes and selected appropriate, heavy cold-weather gear. By seven p.m., we were ready to start the almost five-hour trek, driving through the gathering snow to Lake Dunbar. It simply had to be done. As Ted and I were ready to leave, we suddenly remembered Alex, our youngest son, a junior in high school. While Eddie was away at college in California, Alex still lived at home. We had to let him know we were leaving, but he was somewhere in Minneapolis at a basketball game and this was the age long before cell phones. Ted finally convinced me to write Alex a detailed note and leave it on the kitchen counter. We planned to stop along the way as often as necessary to call him until we connected and were assured he was okay. Despite my motherly instincts to the contrary, I reluctantly agreed to depart under this uncertainty, and we were soon on our way. While stopping to eat the traditional hot beef sandwiches and pie at the Sportsman's Cafe in Mora at nine p.m., we called home. No answer. I was a bit worried, but it was still early, and we would try again at the next stop.

At eleven o'clock we reached the M&H gas station in Grand Rapids, the customary fuel fill-up point. As Ted manned the pump, I raced inside the gas station to call home. I came back out to the car in a near panic as Alex was still not answering the phone. He was supposed to be back by ten o'clock at the latest, but he wasn't there and no message had been left on the answering machine. I was in favor of turning around and heading back immediately. With all the stress of getting this far, Ted felt it would be too much to drive another four hours back to Minneapolis. Given my husband's illness, I had already driven for the past several hours, and knew it would be very risky with the blowing snow and slippery roads to turn back now. I was justifiably nervous, but Ted assured me we would stop at the only public phone booth in Squaw Lake and wait there until we heard from our son. The storm was now in its full fury. Driving down the Avenue of the Pines on the last stretch of our long journey north, I had to slow down to only fifteen miles per hour just to see the road.

We finally crossed the Popple River connecting Squaw and Round lakes. The only public phone was across the river from Leino's old store, next to the Co-op. I pulled up to the phone booth, jumped out of my seat as if it were on fire, and quickly dialed home. Because of the poor road conditions from Grand Rapids, it was now one-thirty in the morning, and a brand new day. The phone rang and rang, but still no answer, and I was now in a sheer panic. We continued to call, to no avail. In the rush to leave for Dunbar, we forgot to bring our phone list with the number of Alex's girlfriend's house. We tried directory assistance, but the number was unlisted. We also tried to call two of our neighbors, but no luck getting an answer.

It was now 2:30 a.m., and both Ted and I were dog tired. I was also worried about Ted not having any rest and becoming dangerously ill, while I too had literally driven myself into exhaustion. There was little we could do; even the police would not respond to this non-emergency, and it was too late for us to turn back toward home. I tried to comfort myself with the knowledge that Alex was a good kid, with a great head on his shoulders. At three a.m., I turned the car back onto Highway 46 and drove the final five miles to Lake Dunbar. Ted agreed to set the alarm for seven in the morning and head back to the phone booth in Squaw Lake to try and call again. However, when we returned to Squaw Lake the next morning there was again no answer at home. We continued to call home until eight o'clock. At eight-thirty, I decided to call the high school. Classes had started and Alex could be summoned to the phone. Finally, the mystery and agony would be over. I dialed the school secretary.

"Yes, I would like to speak with student Alex Walsch."

"I'm sorry, ma'am, he isn't here. His mother called this morning and said he was sick."

His mother? After some discussion, Ted and I concluded Alex

must be okay. He was apparently alert enough to have his "mother" call in. However, he would surely have a lot of explaining to do when his "real" mother got back home. For now, all we could do was head back to Lake Dunbar and do what needed to be done. We would finish the job as soon as possible, and immediately make the long trek back home. Alex, the boy with two mothers, had some questions to answer.

As we arrived back at our Whispering Pines cabin, the snow was falling in large flakes on the unfrozen lake and hanging heavily on the great pines. It was a lovely sight I had never seen before, and it lifted my spirits greatly. I was sad we couldn't stay longer in such surrounding beauty.

As it turned out, Alex was indeed sick and home in bed fast asleep from the heavy flu medicine administered by his girlfriend. To ensure uninterrupted sleep, he had turned off the phone ringer. And it was his girlfriend who had made the call to school informing them he was ill. After all, neither she nor Alex could reach us at the cabin since we had no phone

Oh, yes, I reluctantly concluded while tradition means a lot to me, next spring, this cabin *will have* a phone.

In addition to changing the face of the cabin itself, Ted and I became true explorers of the forest surrounding Lake Dunbar in the early years of our ownership. We hiked for hours through the federal lands, to neighboring lakes, and along Dunbar's wooded shores. Not that we didn't enjoy fishing now and then, but Ted and I had a deep appreciation for the natural surroundings of our own small paradise. I particularly developed a special interest in bald eagles. While we frequently spotted this great bird among the high branches of Dunbar's trees, I acquired a keen sense for discovering eagle nests. An eagle will generally build its home on the very top of a tall red or white pine tree, less than a mile from the nearest lake. A typical eagle's nest is made of sticks and mud, and will weigh over two hundred pounds. This area has plenty of towering pine trees for eagles to use as material. In Ted's reforestation of the property, he wouldn't even think about hauling away any trees that stood proud and tall, even the dead ones. Those trees provided a home for the bugs the woodpeckers coveted. If an eagle had chosen to have his home in one of these trees, he would not have remained in hiding for long. The difficulty in spotting an eagle's nest is, looking up for the nest as you walk through the forest tends to result in injury as you plow into an immovable tree. After many walks and several good bumps, I spotted one not far from Whispering Pines in the adjacent federal forest.

Beyond eagles, Lake Dunbar teems with feathered wildlife. Loons, the Minnesota state bird, are often seen floating and fishing on Dunbar's waters. Another good fishing bird is the pelican. While loons are always joyfully welcomed on Lake Dunbar, their cousins, the pelicans, are not. Pelicans, you see, eat an extraordinary amount of fish. One lone pelican can easily consume fifteen to twenty pounds of fish per day. And the more the pelicans eat, the less there are for us to catch. Perhaps this explains why Ted and I were so apprehensive upon arriving at the cabin on summer day. We saw a squadron of 135 pelicans, ten rows across and thirteen rows deep, eating to their hearts' content as they circled the edge of the lake. If the pelican was an endangered species, it sure didn't seem like it here. With the exception of the always-hungry pelican, we enjoyed the variety of birds on Lake Dunbar: western tanagers, ruby-throated hummingbirds, wood ducks, mallards, woodpeckers, and Canada geese.

Besides simply watching these winged creatures in flight, we amateur ornithologists took it upon ourselves to feed the birds. After purchasing the cabin from my mother, Isabelle, I assembled a bird feeder to attract hummingbirds. Soon Ted noticed a particularly fat hummingbird that landed and sat drinking the sugar water for over five minutes. Normally, another tiny bird would buzz up to the feeder, take a quick drink, and then speed off into the distance, but this one just seemed to sit there without moving. Ted soon began to wonder if the poor bird had died or was inebriated. Perhaps, he suggested, I had been unable to find the sugar, and decided to mix the water with the sweet blackberry brandy I always kept handy at the cabin for emergencies. Ted approached the feeder and raised his hand to touch the hummingbird. As soon as he got within a foot of the creature, it suddenly took off, sending Ted diving for cover.

Canada geese were also the beneficiaries of our northwoods feeding efforts. I loved sitting on the end of the dock for hours throwing popcorn and breadcrumbs to a gaggle of these huge birds. While geese are not terribly friendly or trusting of humans, handing out generous helpings of feed allowed me to attract large flocks within a very few feet of the dock. One day while waiting for the geese to come around the lake, I witnessed one of the most fantastic natural encounters. Out in the middle of the bay was a lone Canada goose. This in itself was highly unusual. For safety and natural protection, these birds generally remain in large gaggles. Perhaps this lone bird was injured or lost. As I watched the magnificent goose, a great bald eagle suddenly appeared, approaching the goose along the water line, flying in from downwind. Its talons were set to grab the unsuspecting goose. At the very last second, the Canada goose dove under the water, averting the grasp of the eagle. I witnessed the battle between these two winged beasts for fifteen minutes as the eagle made half a dozen passes at the goose. Ted even returned from the forest in time to watch the struggle. We were in awe of the strength and skill of the eagle to even attempt to lift a twenty-pound fighting bird out of the water. In one last attempt, the great bird dove into the water, but the goose escaped yet again. The battle was now over, and the eagle took his leave. Ted and I agreed in all our years at Lake Dunbar, we had never witnessed such a sight.

On our frequent walks through the nearby forest, Ted and I would often find the delectable treat of wild raspberries, blueberries, and strawberries. While the raspberries can be difficult to pick because of their thorns, a few scratches on the arm is but a small price to pay. After an afternoon of berry picking, anyone visiting us could then enjoy raspberries and cream as a snack, strawberry cheesecake for dessert, and blueberry pancakes for breakfast. Yum! Yum!

As Ted and I returned to the cabin after an afternoon of berry picking in 1986, we noticed a big red cat following us ever so cautiously through the woods. We called to the cat, but it stayed ten feet behind. After walking a bit farther, the feline was still there, about ten feet behind. The cat followed us back to the cabin and spent the rest of the day hanging around, allowing herself to get closer and closer until someone quickly petted her. Soon it was getting dark, and the increasingly friendly cat did not appear to be going anywhere.

Surely she had an owner, so we left her outside and went inside for dinner. Although we both loved cats, and were thinking about the big cat just outside the door whom we affectionately named "Dunbar," neither one of us vocalized what we were both thinking. And since neither of us would say it, the heretofore uninvited Dunbar cat was left to speak for herself. Situating her big furry body keenly under the dining room window, Dunbar began incessantly meowing her request for food and love.

After just five and one-half meows, Ted was outside bringing our new visitor inside. After eating the fresh can of tuna I put down for her, Dunbar spent ten minutes perusing the cabin and marking her new territory by rubbing against anything and everything. Following a very short discussion, Ted and I eventually allowed Dunbar to stay the night, regrettably in our room. Our hospitality lasted about four hours before Dunbar was unceremoniously booted out of the cabin at two o'clock in the morning. For the previous hour and a half, the frisky cat ran through the cabin knocking items loudly to the floor and generally making a nuisance of herself. After darting back and forth across the bed where we were attempting to sleep, Dunbar had crossed the now clear guideline of conduct acceptable to us—Whispering Pines' new owners.

While Ted and I were serious about having it quiet when we slept, we used our stored-up energy to turn any family day on Lake Dunbar into a raucous occasion. Some would say I inherited this trait from my mother, and I'd probably have to agree. Instead of becoming sedentary, middle-aged parents, Ted and I saw ourselves as forever-young adults, and acted accordingly. Our sons, Eddie, now twenty, and Alex, sixteen, often brought friends along. Ted and I would then transform Dunbar into an energetic human playground. Typically, we ventured out after breakfast on a hike through the forest, at a good pace to be sure. And when I say hike, I mean hike in its most rigorous sense, and not along groomed, flat trails, but up and down hills, around swamps, and usually followed by a rousing game of volleyball on our makeshift court. And these games were not pretty. Many a competitor has left the game arguing, bruised, and battered. This was *serious* volleyball.

After the noon meal, we then accompanied our companions out

on the neighbor's floating dock doing cannonballs, back flips, and an occasional fancy dive. Of course, Ted was always obliged to make the first jump off the dock, as most of us were generally afraid of the unknown mammoth-sized fish lurking in the water below. Having seen a fish's jagged-edged teeth up close, our sons Eddie and Alex weren't about to trust their precious feet to my axiom that "the fish are more afraid of you than you are of them." The boys had heard far too many summer campfire stories to the contrary, including Ted's repeated tales of the piranha-infested Amazon. While the rest of the afternoon was usually free for fishing, reading, or lounging around the cabin, our family is typically ready for more action following dinner. After Mr. and Mrs. Leino retired and left town, there were no more weekly dances in Squaw Lake, so we had to entertain ourselves at Whispering Pines. First, someone would usually drag out Grandma Isabelle's old forty-five-speed record player, and we all sang along to Hank Williams, Patsy Cline, Merle Haggard, and my personal favorite, Roy Orbison.

With our voices now worn out, our attention turned to board games. Although from experience we know better than to play Pictionary®, this was often the chosen game. Pictionary, a board game version of charades, involves teams of two people where one person will draw an object name on the game card, while the partner attempts to guess what is being drawn. The guesser must compete with the other teams who are drawing and guessing the same thing. Inevitably, well-grounded allegations of cheating are heard, ranging from whispering the answer in a partner's ear to someone's eyes wandering onto the other teams' drawings. Worse yet, those paired with Ted always ended up regretting the match. While Ted is very bright, he is also quite analytical, and when his partner failed to correctly guess what Ted had drawn, he would berate the teammate for failing to "get it." Of course, what Ted had drawn seldom helped anyone get the right answer.

With both boys busy with other things, Ted and I inevitably spent most weekends up at Lake Dunbar alone, and we loved it. Both of us are voracious readers who enjoy the peace and quiet of having Whispering Pines all to ourselves, a bit contrary to my parents' approach of inviting everyone within a twenty-mile radius to join them. We would also wait with anticipation for *Prairie Home Companion* to air its weekly broadcast. While Ted and I could listen to Garrison Keillor's tales from home, there seemed to be something special about listening to Lake Wobegon stories on the edge of a northern Minnesota lake. For Ted, who was a classmate of Garrison's in the mid-1960s at the University of Minnesota, there was no question: like Lake Wobegon, at Dunbar "the men were handsome, the women were strong, and the children were above average."

On the second weekend of March in 1987, we traveled north unusually early to open the cabin for the season. Being too soon in the year to fish, Ted and I headed out on an adventure to explore our surroundings in the Chippewa National Forest. We traveled by car to see the Lost Forty where a lone forty-acre lot of ancient red and white pines stood tall in the forest. Ted and I picnicked at the Turtle Mound Monument over on Cut Foot Sioux, and we toured visitor centers and ranger stations in the Avenue of Pines and near the Third River Flowage. We also traveled farther to visit Lake Itasca and the headwaters of the Mississippi River near Bemidji. At its start, the mighty Mississippi is a mere ten feet wide, easily crossed by removing one's shoes and rolling up the pant legs. Having accomplished such a strenuous task, Ted and I bought big yellow ribbons in the gift shop commemorating the fact we had indeed crossed the Mighty Miss.

We also enjoyed perusing various neighboring towns to absorb the provincial culture, and to talk with the local folk. It was through these efforts our family first learned about St. Erhous and the day set in his honor. Now, our family has a deep Catholic heritage, but no one in our extended family had ever heard of St. Erhous before. In a very cold March, Ted and I drove north to Lake Dunbar for a long weekend and warmed up the cabin as best we could, spending the first afternoon snowshoeing atop three feet of compacted snow in the forest. Around three o'clock, we drove in to Squaw Lake to buy a flashlight, having forgotten how long a March night can be in northern Minnesota. When we reached the Co-op, the clerk informed us there was to be a twenty-float parade from Nelsen's garage to The Hill (a distance of one-quarter mile) at 3:30 p.m.

"A parade *in the middle of winter*?" Ted asked.

"Well, yes. St. Erhous's Day isn't in June, you know!" the clerk responded.

"St. Erhous's Day?" I inquired, not sure I should.

"You mean you've never heard of St. Erhous?" The clerk posed her question, giving us a look you might give someone who asks, "What color is the snow?" Actually, the answer to the latter question is subject to debate in the wider Travis family. An entire fishing expedition was once consumed with answering the following question: If snow is white and water is clear, what happens to the white when the snow melts? Admittedly, a warped family indeed.

The clerk explained. "St. Erhous was a hero, sainted after chasing all of the grasshoppers out of Finland." Our blank stares must have been a clue we were ignorant of our Finnish history. "As the story goes, once upon a time in the far northern reaches of Finland, there were multitudes of grape vineyards. The midnight sun of summertime Finland ensured plentiful crops of sweet and bountiful grapes. Anyway, an evil spirit named Saatana thought the people of Finland were too jolly, and he blamed it on the vineyards, which produced exceptionally good and mind-altering wine. As he plotted for ways to undo the unsuspecting Finns, Saatana sat atop a grassy knoll and spied a grasshopper moving across the rye fields. A light bulb flashed above his head, and Saatana quickly gathered all of the grasshoppers from the field and snuck them into the vineyards."

The clerk continued. "'The grasshoppers will have a feast eating all of those grapes,' Saatana mused conspiratorially, 'and they'll wipe the ugly smiles off the faces of those damn Finns!'" The Co-op clerk was seemingly into this story, so we continued listening with rapt attention. "Now, old Saatana was right: the grasshoppers found those grapes to be an irresistible delicacy, and they continued feasting right through those vineyards. The poor Finns didn't know what to do. Everything they tried failed to rid their land of the grasshoppers, and they watched in horror as the locusts devoured their livelihood right before their very eyes. Soon, a large, jovial local boy named Erhous came walking by the vineyard one afternoon as the town elders were at their wits' end in despair over their seemingly incurable plight. Charming young Erhous gave it some deep thought, and then surmised that by now these grasshoppers must have had their fill of fermented grapes, and might just be in a state of mind to be shooed away by his abnormally booming voice.

"Slowly and deliberately, loudly and clearly, Erhous began to shout: Heinairkka, heinairkka nene taalta hiiteen!" The Co-op clerk paused for dramatic effect as Ted and I stood there in honest disbelief. Was she making this all up? Did she even know what she was saying? Is the poor clerk as inebriated as the grasshoppers in her colorful story? When the dire meaning of these alleged Finnish words appeared not to register on our faces, the clerk continued. "In no uncertain terms, Erhous told those grasshoppers he expected them to skedaddle out of the vineyards and away from Finland forever. And they did, never to bother the Finns or their grapes ever again. Erhous was quickly sainted for his heroic efforts, and it's why we celebrate his holiday to this very day."

I didn't know whether to clap or burst out laughing.

"Of course, *that* St. Erhous," Ted said sarcastically under his breath, but loud enough for me to hear. I wondered to myself whether this woman was Swedish or Norwegian. After all, any time of year in northern Minnesota is the perfect time for the Swedes and Norwegians to tell Finnish jokes. Did you hear the one about Ole and Lena? As it was only three o'clock, Ted and I had time to kill and drove five miles to a coffee shop in the neighboring town of Max. We would be sure to hurry back to Squaw Lake, though, so we didn't miss the grand event. This, I had to see. At 3:45, Ted drove our silver truck into the Sportsman's Shop in Squaw Lake, strategically located between the Co-op and The Hill. Then the man at the Sportsman's informed us we had just missed the parade, and it was such a good one this year.

Ted and I began to wonder. How could we have arrived fifteen minutes late and missed a twenty-float parade through a one-road town? Surely, the townsfolk were just having fun with the winter tourists, since so few of us are in Squaw Lake. We headed over to The Hill for some drinks before making our way back to the cabin. The Hill was one of only two drinking establishments in town. It was a good-sized place fully stocked with every imaginable type of liquor, mounted antlers hanging on wooden walls, and a long sturdy bar with padded metal stools every two feet. The Hill went through a series of owners, and all were friendly and receptive to locals and tourists alike. The Hill also served an assortment of pub-style foods, had a booming pull-tab business, and housed numerous pinball machines and electronic games that went out of style years earlier in the big cities.

Upon entering the bar, Ted and I noticed the windows were completely covered with green paper cutouts in the shape of, what else, but grasshoppers. Passing up the daily drink special, grasshoppers, we went straight for the bull's-eye, ordering shots of bourbon. As we drove back to the cabin later that afternoon, Ted tuned in *Prairie Home Companion* on the truck radio. Garrison was broadcasting, as usual, from the Fitzgerald Theater in St. Paul. As we drove off into the dark, chilly night, I wondered aloud whether the people at Ralph's Pretty Good Grocery Store and Dorothy's Chatterbox Cafe in Lake Wobegon had ever celebrated St. Erhous's Day.

IN SEARCH OF THE BIG BLUE CAR

THE SUMMER OF 1988 BROUGHT WITH IT NEW HOPE AND OPTI-
mism for another good year of fishing and memorable journeys along
the shores of Lake Dunbar. It was, after all, a celebration of more than
thirty years at Whispering Pines for the extended Travis family. Like
most years, we made the usual trip north in mid-May coinciding with
Fishing Opener weekend. On the long car ride, this year's pioneers
(Grandma Isabelle, Ted, our son Alex, and me) stopped off to see my
niece Rose and her husband Patrick's new home, just north of the Twin
Cities. After the grand tour, Alex asked Rose an important question.

"So what's in the garage, Rose? Could it be the big blue car?"

"Oh my goodness. Won't you guys ever forget that?"

"Nope."

So a little backstory would help clear things up: for the past ten
years, Rose's younger cousins had teased her about the big blue car
on every possible occasion. And while Rose regretted telling them
about the big blue car in the first place, she in fact enjoyed the endless
needling. Rose, like her brother Walt, always seemed to have a grin
on her face, invariably laughing and happy. Rose, in particular, had a
wonderful smile and sparkling personality. Her curly brown hair and
petite frame were filled with boundless energy, enough even to with-
stand perpetual teasing about the big blue car. It all started in the
summer of 1975. Walt had just completed his miraculous recovery
from childhood cancer, bringing great joy to the family. Grandma had
promised to take Walt and anyone else who could come along north
to Lake Dunbar right after school let out for the summer. As much as
Mom enjoyed driving school buses, she loved her three-month summer hiatus even more.

The three youngest grandchildren—Eddie and Kate, both nine, and Alex, then five—begged to go along with Grandma and Walt to celebrate the end of the school year, and she was more than happy to take them. After all, it had been nine months since the last batch of Grandma's root beer. The young kids were ready to go as soon as possible. In fact, Kate traveled by Greyhound bus up to our house in the Twin Cities a few days in advance so the kids could get ready for a full week up north. To pre-teen children, getting ready generally consisted of a bike trip to the candy store, as well as fighting over which board games to take along to the cabin. While Eddie and Kate were the same age, and perhaps old enough to supervise my youngest son, Alex, I feared the destruction these pre-pubescent creatures left alone could cause in our house while Ted and I were both away at work. So, I enlisted Rose's help who, for a high wage, agreed to spend the day with her younger cousins. The kids loved Rose. She was cool, but didn't let them get too far out of hand. She wore all the great fashions of the mid-1970s, which naturally meant 100 percent authentic polyester. Rose was in high school, and she allowed the kids to listen to all the latest music: the Bee Gees, the Rolling Stones, and the Guess Who. Cool, way cool. After a full morning of music, laughter, and game playing, Rose suggested they go out to lunch at the golden arches. The kids screamed with delight. No tuna sandwiches and Campbell's tomato soup today. However, they had no way to get there since Rose didn't have a car. No problem. Rose got on the phone.

"Walt, come on over and we'll take you out for lunch." Rose's older brother had the morning off from his summer job. More importantly, he had a car. Although hanging out with one's younger cousins wasn't the hippest thing to do, Walt didn't care. He was an independent thinker, a free spirit. Soon, they were all sitting around a large booth feasting on their hamburgers, fries, and Coca-Cola.

"Wow, I didn't realize it was so late. I have to get to work. Are you guys ready?" Walt asked.

"I think so," said Rose. "You can drop us off on University Avenue, and we'll walk the rest of the way home. Besides, we might just have to stop at the park for a while, and then for ice cream cones." Eddie, Alex, and Kate heard the most important words: park and ice cream. Cool, way cool. Rose's younger cousins were soon exhausted from the slides, swings, and monkey bars, but not too tired to walk to Sandy's Sweet Shop for double-scooped ice cream cones.

Eddie and Kate noticed ever since they left McDonald's, Rose seemed as if she was constantly on the lookout for something or someone. Even at the park, she was frequently looking toward the road. And now as they walked along the busy street, Rose inconspicuously scanned the surrounding area.

"Hey, Rose," Kate asked, "what are you looking for?"

"What do you mean?"

"You keep looking around for something."

"Oh," Rose replied, trying to think of a way to explain herself with minimal embarrassment. She would never hear the end of it if she revealed the truth. Boy, was she ever right. "I'm looking for a big blue car."

"A big blue car?" the kids said in unison.

"Yeah, a friend of mine lives near here and he, I mean she, drives a big blue car." At first there was normal silence. Her cousins' inquiry had been satisfied. Kids' attention spans are short, after all. They would soon move on to some other topic, and this would end. No such luck.

"Which one is it?" an innocent and truth-seeking Katie asked. "A boy or a girl friend?"

Rose, while not perfect, had difficulty with lying. And it wasn't as if she had some big secret to hide. She merely had a crush on her cute classmate Patrick—a cute classmate with a big blue car. "Oh, it's a guy." Again, normal silence. Rose was in the clear, almost. Then the chants began.

"Rose has a boyfriend. Rose has a boyfriend."

"What's his name?" Eddie asked.

"His name is Patrick and he's *not* my boyfriend."

It was too late. The kids now made it their mission to assist Rose in her search for the big blue car, and to tease her incessantly.

"Rose and Patrick, sittin' in a tree, k-i-s-s-i-n-g . . ." Poor Rose. She had been so nice to her young cousins, and *this* was her reward. But she would get hers.

I would later pay very dearly through the pocketbook for this babysitting job.

Well, that was many years ago now. Needing to get back on the road for our inaugural trip of 1988, we thanked Rose for the tour and said how much we liked her new house. There were fish to be caught in this new year, following the dismal showing of 1987. Rose was envious.

"I sure wish I could go with you guys for opening fishing. The only time I've been up north this early in the summer was when I was in college."

Rose attended Bemidji State University and became one of the first Travis grandchildren to earn a four-year college degree. Rose had her choice of schools, but she opted to study on the serene lakeside campus of Bemidji State, a mere forty miles from Lake Dunbar. In truth, I must confess Rose wasn't the first member of the Travis family to attend B.S.U. In the fall of 1960, I selected Bemidji State from among several other campuses for my undergraduate studies. I also chose B.S.U. in order to be close to Lake Dunbar. However, my collegiate career at Bemidji State regrettably lasted but three days. Thankfully, Rose's tenure endured quite a bit longer.

After graduation from Bemidji State, Rose returned home to the Twin Cities and began a successful career in business. Having established her career, she again looked for the man in the big blue car, but Patrick no longer had the notorious vehicle, having traded it in at the end of the 1970s. Nevertheless, Rose and Patrick were soon together again, in love, and eventually married. In a few years, they would also have two handsome young sons. Perhaps Rose had found *her big blue car* after all.

As exciting as opening fishing weekend could be, it wasn't until the Fourth of July our summertime visits to Lake Dunbar became a weekly or bi-weekly occurrence. This year seemed to be no different as a growing number of the Travis clan made commitments to head north for a long holiday weekend. The lone exceptions were my brother, Jack, who was vacationing with his wife in Arizona, and their daughter, Kate, who had moved to southern California in the fall of 1986. After graduating from high school in May, Kate loaded her car to the rooftop and drove west in search of a job, California sunshine, and beach dudes. My niece, Kate, was likely the most free-spirited soul in the entire Travis family. She was the stereotypical young girl who giggled with friends about boys, dreamed of being a famous singer someday, and tried hard to grow up fast.

Kate fit well into the small-town atmosphere of my hometown of Greenwood, and she knew everyone. To her friends, a day was not complete without experiencing her laughter and pleasing smile. Kate was especially a hero to all the young girls in Greenwood, for she was a star athlete, honor student, and musician. But as much as she liked her hometown, Greenwood was just too limiting for Kate Travis. Like my mother, Isabelle, and perhaps me, too, in some respects, she wanted to explore the world, meet fascinating people, and live on the edge. As with my great uncle Frank and others in the extended Travis family, California called to Kate. She had always dreamed of traveling or moving there, and remembered the stories I told her about the excitement of Hollywood in the 1950s when we visited Uncle Frank and his wife, Ruby, who lived in Hollywood. These were the stories enhancing Kate's dreams of the golden coast.

Every summer, my boys Eddie and Alex spent their vacations in Greenwood with their cousin Kate. This fearless threesome would run wild all over town on their bicycles. One of the youths' favorite stops was of course at Travis Bus Service where they would tramp around Grandma Isabelle's bus garage exploring the buses, tools, and other unsafe childhood toys. In the corner of the bus garage was a 1964 Plymouth Valiant convertible, my very first car purchased with my own hard-earned money. Eddie, Alex, and Kate loved to climb inside the old car I was storing until we had time and money to fix it up. Each kid would take a turn "driving" as the others sat back with their arms out the window or the top, imagining the breeze blowing through their hair as they sped down nameless highways toward, where else, California. While two of the three kids actually did live in the Golden State one day, as a group they never did take their dream trip together across the open roads of America. And even though the kids never moved an inch in my old '64 Valiant, Eddie, Alex, and Kate knew a different reality. In their minds, they traversed Route 66 on its long and winding road from America's heartland all the way to Surf City, U.S.A.

In 1986, Kate settled into an apartment in Carlsbad, just north of San Diego. She took a job with an airline, which enabled her to make frequent trips home to her beloved Minnesota over the next two years. While she couldn't make it home for a long weekend at the cabin on July 4th, 1988, Kate hoped to bring some of her new California friends along to Minnesota in August to celebrate Harvest Days in our family's hometown of Greenwood.

Harvest Days was a grand occasion in our hometown, complete with parades, music, and free corn on the cob at the town picnic. The picnic was held in Tennison Park, rain or shine. We had country music bands, clowns, and rows of booths offering a variety of mouth-watering treats: pork sandwiches, homemade pies, grilled burgers, and locally brewed beer. You could participate in an assortment of games, including a softball tournament, balloon toss, and a water tank where you could sink the school principal with the proper aim of a softball. The ultimate event, however, was the Harvest Days parade. In contrast to the St. Erhous's Day parade in Squaw Lake, this procession lasted for over an hour, and included floats, restored collectors' cars, animals, and the town fire truck loaded up with all the local kids. One year, my brother Jack even served as the Grand Marshal of the parade, riding proudly through town in his restored red '57 Plymouth.

Greenwood's annual Harvest Days celebration followed in the tradition of several neighboring villages. Elgin had Cheese Days in June and Viola held the infamous Gopher Count every April, a festival culminating in a prize for the individual who captured and displayed the most gopher tails. Even tiny nearby Kellogg had its own special weekend set aside every autumn for its Watermelon Festival. Harvest Days was a hallowed event in the Travis family, not to be missed without an excellent excuse. But my dear, sweet Kate didn't make it to Harvest Days in 1988, and no one went to Lake Dunbar over the Fourth of July weekend. Returning from a long day at the beach in Oceanside along California's stunning and scenic Pacific Coast Highway, Kate's car was hit head-on by another whose driver shouldn't have been behind the wheel. He was swerving from side to side of the narrow two-lane road, passing other vehicles while unable to see what was coming in the opposite lane, and his blood alcohol level was well over the legal limit. My brother, Jack, and his wife immediately flew from their vacation spot in Arizona over to San Diego to be at the bedside for their only child. The torment they endured was certainly indescribable. Kate had been taken to a trauma center, but she was given no hope for recovery, considering the severity of the injuries to her young, vibrant body. Within a day, the unavoidable calls were made. Friends, family, and even strangers were stunned. We only knew Kate Travis as beautiful, spirited, happy, and alive. The shock hit and hurt everyone very deeply.

Ever since the first word of the tragic accident, people were praying and weeping, all in general disbelief. The immediate family experienced untold heartache and sorrow. My poor mother, Isabelle, who had already lost a young daughter and her husband, now felt the loss of her first grandchild. It had been almost twenty-five years since Sam and Stella's deaths, and Kate's passing brought back all of the old wounds and sorrows. Beyond her immediate family and grandmothers, another person who felt Kate's tragedy deeply was my son, Eddie. When not at home or at Lake Dunbar, he could usually be found in Greenwood where he and Kate were inseparable. Eddie thought of her as a sister, since she was the person most closely fulfilling that role in his life. Eddie and Kate were the same age. They were precocious children with wide-ranging interests, and both loved music. Even at an early age, they were a formidable combo when playing virtually every board or card game. No adults in the family had the courage to challenge them.

Eddie and his cousin Kate were kindred spirits, sharing every thought and dream as they were growing toward adulthood. I had the very sad duty of telling Eddie the tragic news of Kate's accident over the telephone while he was away at college. Though our call was somber and short, he told me later how he hung up the phone and pleaded with God to give Kate his own strength to live. Needless to say, his heart was broken upon hearing from me later in the day Kate had died. Gradually, Eddie's thoughts turned toward the wonderful memories of her life. He then sat down and poured out his anguish and love for Kate into a song that came to him apparently without effort, and he played it at her memorial service on a very sobering July 4, 1988.

No Time for Tears
We've all come for one purpose
To give life all we have
And if she at all was happy
Then we should not be sad.

For after that we belong to Him
To receive our well-earned rest
And of all the places she could be
That place is the best.

And there's no time for tears
Just remember with joy
All those happy, happy years.

Good times aren't forever
With God there is no end
So it's not one last goodbye
It's "See you later, friend."

For us these times are so bad
But we really have a choice
For what we've lost be very sad
Or for what she gave, rejoice.

And there's no time for tears
Just remember with joy
All those happy, happy years.

—Eddie Walsch

As my brother, Jack, embraced Eddie following the service, Jack thanked him for the music, and for caring so much about Kate. I then saw him hand Eddie an envelope addressed to "Eddie" in Kate's handwriting. Jack explained he had found it among Kate's belongings from her apartment in Carlsbad. I could tell immediately Eddie's heart sank as his eyes welled up with tears. He and Kate had written to each other frequently since she moved to California, and it was apparently her turn to write. He tucked the envelope into his coat pocket, saying he would read it later when he was alone.

Back at college for summer session a week later, Eddie searched his desk for a letter opener. He slowly opened a newly arrived letter from Uncle Jack. His enduring sadness was partially lifted with Jack's news: the transplant of Kate's organs into several very needy recipients had all been deemed a success.

"In the midst of her own tragedy," Alex explained to me over the phone, "Kate is still bringing great happiness into the world."

Eddie then moved toward the unpacked overnight bag at the foot of his bed and found a gently folded paper in his coat pocket. With a heavy heart, he opened the plain white envelope whose return address simply read "*Kate*."

Dear Eddie,   *June 22, 1988*

Summer is finally here and I am really enjoying it. The weather has been really nice. . . .

My job is going very well. I have a lot of fun and the benefits are great. I was planning on going to Puerto Vallarta this weekend but had to postpone my plans for a few weeks. My flight is going to be free because a girl I work with has a pass for two people, and asked me to go with her. I guess I can't complain about that!

I'm coming home in August (I think) so hopefully I will be able to see you. I'll be bringing our boss and a bunch of people from work home for "Harvest Days." I think that they will get a big kick out of it! Ha! Ha!

If you ever want to visit California, you have somewhere to stay. Don't forget that! I better get going. Some friends are coming over for a barbecue tonight and I've got to go get my laundry. Take care!

Love, Kate – your casual cuz!

At the bottom of the letter, Kate had drawn a nice-looking tree with a large heart on its trunk. In a postscript, she pointed to the tree and wrote, "This is the Love Tree, my trademark." Expressing and fostering love was indeed a quality that was uniquely Kate's. Earlier in the year, she had told Eddie how happy she was to have received a dozen long-stemmed red roses from her mom on Valentine's Day. "They were so pretty," she said. And it was classic Kate to add: "But I would have liked them even better if they were from a guy!" Although she died before experiencing her one romantic love-of-a-lifetime soul mate, those of us who knew her say Kate Travis spread more than her share of love and happiness throughout a brief life.

The following summer as we celebrated a happier, yet still somber, Fourth of July, Eddie joined his cousin Rose and me on a walk down by the boat landing to look for loons and skip stones across the surface of the lake.

"Rose, I see you and Patrick bought a new car," I said.

"Yeah, do you like it?"

"It looks nice and all, but it's certainly not big and blue," twenty-two-year-old Eddie added with a smirk.

"Are you ever going to forget that?" Rose laughed. We all did. "How about you, Eddie? Have you found your own big blue car?"

"Well, it depends on which big blue car we're talking about," he replied reflectively. "If you mean one specific person, then the answer is no. I'm still looking. But in the last year since Kate died, I've spent a lot of time working on happiness from within. The big blue car of inner peace and inner joy, I guess. I'm certain Kate found her big blue car before she died, and I know I'll find mine."

Rose looked over at her younger cousin as I nodded in agreement, watching my son as he skipped a rock five times along the surface before sinking. "So may we all, Eddie," Rose concluded. "So may we all."

The Treasures of Ted's Wood

My husband, Ted, and I lived most of our adult lives in urban or suburban settings, mainly in greater Minneapolis, but also a few years in Colorado and northern Oregon. During our time away in the west, we yearned for the relaxing days along Dunbar's shores, and relished the infrequent trips we were able to take back home. I especially noticed Ted's deep longing for his home state, and particularly the unfettered access to Minnesota's woodlands he so enjoyed. From his days on the farm outside of Greenwood, to our long-time suburban home near Minneapolis, Ted always lived within yards of a hardwood forest, and it seemed a natural place for him, the place he cosmically belonged. Though I grew up farther away from a big woods and spent my youth in the idyllic world of small-town 1950's America, my family's connection to the wilderness through our experiences on Lake Dunbar created in me a deep appreciation for the grandeur and importance of Minnesota's thick pine and hardwood forests from the time I was twelve years old.

When it came time for me to find a life partner a decade later, I must admit Ted's fondness for woodlands, both for work and leisure, was part of what drew me to him. The person I would share the majority of my life with had to possess a strong love of nature and commitment to shepherd the fantastic beauty of the thick pine forests surrounding my beloved Lake Dunbar. For this small piece of northern woodlands, the Travis clan was the first and only white settlers to ever foster the land and its resources. Ted took his role as steward of the Travis land very seriously, oftentimes too much so. Five years on, his vision of a grand reforestation of the Travis property on Lake Dunbar was now visible to those skeptics who questioned his sanity back at the time of planting. The Norway pines and seedling oak trees he provided such loving care to were now human-height and growing taller year by year. Ted rightly took great pride in this beautifully manicured forest which he aptly named "Ted's Wood." His pride in maintaining and enhancing our tiny patch of forest was palpable and inherent. As Ted wrote in our family's cabin journal at the end of one recent trip, "This has been a great and relaxing weekend. No one will ever recall we did not get out on the lake fishing, but someday when more and more of these young trees form a grandstand of towering pines, it will be our legacy, hopefully long-enjoyed and remembered by generations of the Travis family yet to come."

Our family's status as first stewards of this property arose from this fact: prior to the twentieth century, the land had always belonged to Native Americans who lived in this phenomenal forest for thousands of years. Though the area technically became part of the ever-expanding United States of America at the time of the Louisiana Purchase, and later subsumed within the newly formed state of Minnesota in 1852, this part of the Chippewa National Forest remained part and parcel of the Leech Lake Indian Reservation, land promised in perpetuity to the Chippewa descendants. However, as with most similar promises from the Federal government, this sacred vow was broken with very little hesitation and, in 1910, over thirty-three thousand acres of the vast forest areas surrounding Lake Dunbar and the rest of the Leech Lake Reservation were opened up to white settlers who competed for the right to homestead the land at the rate of $1.25 per acre.

The area's first homesteaders were principally interested in clearing the land and building farms. These first settlers were also mostly immigrants from Scandinavia, most notably those crazy Finns. As they apparently say back in the old country about the non-effusive and un-emotional Finnish people: "How can you tell if a Finn likes you? He'll stare at your shoes instead of his own." Drawn to a landscape reminding them of home, these hard-working immigrants tilled the land, planted wheat and corn, and raised all kinds of domesticated animals to satisfy their every survival need. Following the establishment of farms, other tradesmen and settlers would soon follow. By 1931, the Good Hope Consumers Co-operative Association Store was built a mile east of Lake Dunbar, supplying all area residents with a hearty supply of general goods and grocery items. True to their Finnish roots, the store was the creation of "The Suomalainen Tyovoen Yhtistys," or the Good Hope Finnish Workers Association. The store carried meats, feed, gas and oils, nuts and bolts, large five-cent candy bars, and virtually anything the local farmer or logger might need. The Good Hope store survived until 1958, shortly after the time when my parents arrived on Dunbar's shores to construct a cabin of their own.

Less than eighty miles from Lake Dunbar lay one of the richest natural forest areas in all the world. The Quetico National Forest of Canada, and the Boundary Waters Canoe Area (BWCA) across the border in Minnesota, combine to form a vast area of natural wonder. The BWCA is the largest federally protected area in the United States east of the Rocky Mountains. No motorized vehicles are allowed on, near, or above any of the hundreds of lakes and waterways in this area. No motorboats in summer, no snowmobiles in winter. The BWCA is a canoer's and backpacker's paradise. Groups or individuals set out for three-, five-, or seven-day—or even longer—trips into the wilderness without modern conveniences and with very few people around. Early in the season one can go several days without seeing another human. But you are guaranteed to experience wildlife: black bears, beavers, loons, moose, otters, fox, fish, Canada geese, and more.

In the spring of 1989, our sons were both home from university and the family took a five-day detour from Whispering Pines over to the BWCA. We loaded our canoes with tents, packs, fishing gear, and other necessities, including the family dog, Daisy, for a trek down the Kawishiwi River near Ely, Minnesota. As it was springtime, the river was high, affording us an opportunity to run some rapids. Later in the season, with a diminished water flow, one must haul canoes and packs over land around the dangerous rocks.

Following a full day of canoeing and portaging, we found a campsite on a small island in the middle of the Kawishiwi River.

Once on shore, everyone except Daisy had a job to do. Eddie and Alex set up tents and rolled out sleeping bags. I unloaded the supply pack and organized food, cookware, and other camp necessities. Ted chopped wood and hung the bear rope. Black bears also inhabit the BWCA, and are generally no danger to humans. The opposite, unfortunately, is not always true. However, black bears do have one great love: camp food. So, after the day's final meal, we loaded all food, candy, gum, or other edible items into one of the packs and hoisted it high up into the air over the branch of a tree. The pack must hang at least ten feet high, since most bears can reach to eight feet. The pack must also hang two to three feet down from the branch and the same distance out from the tree insofar as black bears are excellent climbers.

The important rule, however, is everyone must place all food products in the pack without exception. No gum, candy wrappers, or any other tasty elements can be left to litter the campsite, and especially not in one's tent. Bears have a superb sense of smell. As the Dunbar gang finished their long day's adventure, we filled up our food pack and hoisted it into the air. On the first night of a BWCA trek, this is no easy task as the food pack can be quite heavy. We were finally successful with Eddie, Alex, and me pulling on the rope, and Ted pushing the hefty pack up with a canoe paddle. After a relaxing few minutes by a waning fire, we headed to our tents one by one. Ted and I were in one tent, with Alex and Eddie in the other. Nothing feels quite like sleeping on the firm wilderness ground after a long day out of doors. As Ted readied himself for sleep and piled up his weathered clothes, he made a frustrating discovery.

"For cripes sakes," boomed his voice from our small green tent.

"What is it, Ted?"

"I've got a full packet of Sweet-N-Low® in my pocket. I must have put it in there when we made coffee. But I guess a bear won't bother us with this tiny packet."

"The heck he won't. Go out and get rid of it!" I protested over the barely muffled laughter from the other tent where Eddie and Alex knew that in the event a black bear did come into our camp, they would not be bothered in their unsweetened tent.

Ted begrudgingly got dressed, walked out into the dark, fast-cooling night, and dumped the contents of his small pink packet into the river. After dousing the wrapper with water, he placed it in the ashes of the fire pit and returned to our tent. All of us weary adventurers were now ready for sleep. Everything outside was silent, broken only by the chirping crickets and an occasional loon's plaintive call. Having said our goodnights, each rolled over in his or her sleeping bag consuming deep breaths of fresh forest air. No more interruptions, except for one last question from my smart-mouthed son, Alex, breaking the night's cool silence.

"Equal®, anyone?"

I was recalling a similar trick Ted had pulled a few years back while camping in another part of the BWCA, up on the Sawbill Trail. He had hidden a leather pouch filled with blackberry brandy in the bottom of the food pack for the two of us to share once the kids were fast asleep. However, he failed to consider the weight of the pack's contents which, when dropped, caused the pouch's lid to come off, and blackberry brandy penetrated everything, including the lining of the backpack itself. Blackberries are to bears what nectar is to bees. No way can you hide it, because they can smell it from miles away. I remember sitting up that night on the Sawbill Trail holding a flashlight at the edge of the lake, entertained by a swarm of mosquitos while Ted washed out every item in the food pack, which we then tied extra high in the tree.

Yes, we survived our Boundary Waters adventure and soon found ourselves back in the comfortable surroundings of Lake Dunbar. People might well call me crazy for describing a rustic cabin as comfortable, but compared to sleeping outdoors with minimal protection from the harsh environment, a night's sleep at Whispering Pines was pure and simple heaven. As our boat pulled up to the Travis dock after a first foray of fishing, our stringer was empty. Inasmuch as I had truly planned on fresh-caught fish for dinner, I informed my companions someone would have to visit the Co-op in Squaw lake for some supplies—namely, food. Eddie and Alex were soon on their way. At the Co-op, they began scanning the aisles for the items on my cryptic list. However, the boys were keenly aware everyone was staring at them—the cashier, the man behind the meat counter, and nearly all of the customers in the store.

"Do we smell?" Alex wondered aloud to Eddie.

"Hmmm, I don't," he replied, receiving a swift jab to his gut in return. "Maybe it's these," Eddie said, motioning toward his own head. Eddie and Alex were sporting white cloth headwraps resembling bandannas but with tie straps and long tails covering their necks. The product was Ted's creation, following his idea he could make money by designing and selling a lightweight cloth head covering that protected the skin, especially the neck, from the burning summer sun. Although the idea was eventually transformed into a successful small family business, it was still in the planning stages while Eddie and Alex modeled them in front of the fashionably conservative world of northern Minnesota. It would be unfair to say the people of Squaw Lake were not open to new, avant-garde ideas. Yet they were clearly curious, if not suspicious of the two young hoodlums in the middle-eastern-looking garb. The source of the people's stares was confirmed when I called the Squaw Lake Co-op hoping to catch the boys so as to add a few items to their shopping list.

"Good afternoon, Squaw Lake Co-op," answered the burly clerk into the rotary-dialed phone. It took all I had not to giggle upon hearing this greeting, for my boys routinely made fun of the clerk with the heavy Finnish accent who invariably pronounced "Co-op" as if it were a one syllable word, spelled "kwap."

"Yes, I'm calling from over here on Lake Dunbar and I'm looking for my sons. I sent them up there for some groceries, and I just remembered a few additional things I'd like them to get."

"What do they look like?"

"The older one's about 5'7", average build, and light brown hair. He should be there with his younger brother, who's actually the taller of the two."

"I don't remember seeing anybody like that. Maybe they're not here yet."

"If you do see them in your store, could you please have one call me at our cabin? They should be easy to spot. They're wearing white bandanna-type things on their heads."

"Oh, those two," he said quite slowly, followed by a long pause. "Yeah, they're here. Hold on." Eddie was startled as the big Finnish man in the faded red clerk's apron came down the aisle, obviously toward him.

The boys eventually got all the items they needed and raced back toward Lake Dunbar, constantly looking over their shoulders for the lynch mob.

The summer days on Lake Dunbar are nearly endless. The sun bursts into the eastern sky as early as 5:00 a.m. and doesn't set until after 10:00 p.m. The sky never does become totally black in the long days of summer. Winter, on the other hand, is a dark and solemn season in the northwoods with as little as six hours of daylight. Winter can also be a lonely time on Lake Dunbar. Gone are the birds, the leaves, and the people. Occasionally, one hears the roar of a snowmobile. But the air is generally dominated by the sound of a cold, blustery breeze sweeping across the Chippewa National Forest. Deer huddle together on south-facing slopes, hoping for some shield from the bitter winds. While most of the wildlife is gone or fast asleep for the season, the fish remain. They remain, that is, for those willing to find them.

Ice fishing seems to attract only a certain breed of people. One must be patient and have good ways to keep your feet warm. After the strenuous task of clearing the several feet of snow from the lake top, a dedicated fisherman must begin the arduous drilling of an ice hole. While there are automated means of accomplishing this task, for a purist, the hole must be carved by hand. Piercing the air with a motor-driven ice drill would be sacrilegious, imperfect, unworthy.

Alex is the closest to being a real ice fishermen in the Travis family. He has the patience and, presumably, the warm feet. During the winter of 1989, we ventured north with our sons for a few peaceful days on Dunbar's icy shores. Early in the day, Alex began clearing away snow from the lake to do a bit of ice fishing. After shoveling an area nearly five feet in diameter, his brother, Eddie, came along to help with the drilling.

"Hey, Alex, this is gonna take all day."

"What do you mean? We'll have this hole finished in ten minutes."

"I'm wondering how you're going to fit the boat in such a tiny hole," said Eddie, surely thinking about how incredibly funny he was.

"Boy, you sure got me. It's going to take a whole week just to thaw the grin from my face after laughing so hard." A good comeback. He had out-one-lined his older brother, as usual.

"But picture this," Eddie tried again. "After we catch a fish, we could hold it halfway in and out of the water until the hole freezes up, and then we'd have a fish with its head sticking out of the ice," Eddie exclaimed, taking pride in his vast imagination.

"Oh my," an exasperated Alex whispered to himself. His older brother was home on break from his first year of law school. "I sure worry about the future of the legal system in this country."

So should we all. My younger son Alex had more penchant for fun than his older brother and loved practical jokes, puns, and riddles. But he really excelled at comical drama, a genre of acting he perfected. And his impromptu performances seemed best when played out on Dunbar's shores. The previous summer, while taking video footage of a lazy Dunbar afternoon, I caught a glimpse of something in the left-side view of my lens. So I panned the camera in the direction of the cabin. There, standing tall, was Alex in full uniform as a deranged killer. He wore Grandma Isabelle's sturdy red fishing hat, Ted's woodcutting goggles, and a surgeon's mask. Oh, and he was armed with a BB gun.

Back at the cabin, Alex aimed the unloaded gun at the camera, then quickly lowered the pointed gun and dove into the bushes behind the cabin. I followed this strange sight, this strange son, while trying to balance the camera and avoid tripping in the tall grass. Rounding the cabin corner, he was gone. Had I looked with my eyes instead of through the viewfinder, I may have seen him sneak behind the tool shed. Instead, I panned the yard looking for Alex the Ripper. Suddenly, he jumped in front of the camera with the now loaded gun, slammed the barrel against his fishing hat, and shot. While the BB ricocheted off the hard hat and into the woods, the psychopath played out his apparent suicide. Alex grabbed at his uninjured head, staggered from side to side, and fell violently to the ground. After a few convincing and over-acted body quivers, he was gone. The camera jiggled up and down as I applauded enthusiastically.

But Alex did not desire mere acting alone. In fact, he was probably best behind the camera directing and providing narration for his self-made Dunbar documentaries. Alex's classic documentary film was created during the winter of 1989. After a full morning of ice fishing with ne'er a bite, he joined the rest of us on a hike through Dunbar's winter woods. Although it was high noon, the sun sat low in the southern sky, and in a few hours would fade behind the frigid pines. We headed out from the cabin toward the western shore where we would then turn up the old, rarely used Teich road, which would certainly be covered by pristine snowdrifts. In order to record our arctic journey, the video camera was brought along, operated by the master himself. Alex followed behind Ted, Eddie, and me, recording our every movement, the cold scenery, and his narrated version of whatever came into view. First, a large German shepherd came bounding through the snow toward our small hiking party. Although usually afraid of such large dogs, the brave director pointed the camera at the canine creature, simply commenting, "Man's best friend."

We continued along and soon happened upon an old tractor, circa 1930s, parked near a neighbor's cabin. It was stored for the winter, but not very well. As the vintage tractor entered Alex's scope, the sarcastic narration continued, recalling his father's endless tales of how much harder things were *back then.* "Here's how Dad used to get to and from school as a boy on the farm."

Nearing the cabin after a long walk through the quiet, snow-filled woods, our group noticed a lone downed spruce tree on the edge of the Travis property. It was probably run over by a passing snowmobile. After a brief investigation and severe mocking of Ted's suggestion the sheriff be summoned, Alex focused in on the small tree. "Admit this as Exhibit A. What a shame. You can't even own property anymore without it being vandalized!" Perhaps we could sue someone after Eddie finished law school.

After the long, cold walk, we all settled inside the cabin for the evening. The temperature fell to a crisp five degrees below zero. Because of the wind, it seemed even colder inside the cabin at first. The thermometer in the back bedroom registered a cool minus ten degrees Fahrenheit. By morning, a pan of water left out for the dog in the entryway was frozen solid. But thanks to the warmth of the wood-burning stove Ted and I installed, we had relief from old man winter. The mere sound of dried wood snapping back at the slowly warming flames comforted our frigid bodies huddled in sleeping bags around the fire. The cabin was also filled with the aroma of Walt's famous corn chowder warming on the old wood stove. I had made another of my nephew Walt's famous recipes, and it needed none of Walt's special commentary. Just to smell it cooking was enough to make one's mouth water.

WALT'S CORN CHOWDER

This chowder can be frozen, but is best when first made or reheated. The recipe is the base, so add to it what you like. I sometimes add garlic, carrots, or whole kernel corn for more substance. The more corn used (cream or whole kernel), the larger the volume. Enjoy! (A note from Ruth, the editor: This chowder has kept us warm and fed on several occasions in the northwoods. Thanks, Walt!)

½ lb. bacon
2 cans creamed corn
1 onion, chopped
½ stick butter
1 ½ c. hot water
1 can evaporated milk
Pepper
2 c. diced raw potato

Chop bacon and onion coarsely and put in soup kettle. Add water and cook 'til done. Add potatoes and corn and simmer 'til potatoes are tender. At this point the chowder will have a tendency to stick.

Stir occasionally and try not to scrape too much off the bottom.
Add butter, milk, and seasonings. Reheat to simmer and serve.

Our collective cold bodies were warmed simply by the anticipation of eating the chowder still simmering on the black iron stove, a perfect addition to Whispering Pines. Ted had found the stove out in the tool shed under several boxes and plenty of dust. The last person to touch the stove was my dad, Sam Travis, who brought the stove here to Dunbar in 1962. Dad had retrieved the black iron fire pot from his parents' homestead after they had both died. Following my father's own passing, no one seemingly had the ambition to install it for the next thirty years. In the summer of 1990, during my mother's now once-annual trip to the cabin, she stood in amazement at the first sight of the old wood stove. She had forgotten it had been in the shed for all these years, and immediately talked about my father and how he would have loved seeing it all cleaned up, shiny, and installed in the cabin.

Mother also thought about the first time she ever saw the stove as a young woman visiting my grandparents' homestead outside of Greenwood. She had been sitting nervously as Sam told his parents he and Isabelle were to be married. While both Sam and Isabelle were bright individuals with upstanding reputations, they had reason to be nervous in communicating the *good* news to their parents. In small-town America of 1931, this was not a marriage made in heaven, so to speak. My mother was Catholic, my dad a Lutheran. Both sets of parents reluctantly acquiesced to this significant obstacle, with one common condition: the offspring of this mixed-blessed union must attend church in the grandparents' respective denominations. So, from the birth of Eleanor in 1934 until I left the house in 1960, my parents faithfully honored their own parents' wishes. Mom brought us kids to Saturday evening Mass at St. Bernard's while Dad accompanied us the next day to Sunday morning services at First Lutheran. When the grown children were given the eventual independence to choose their denomination, the results were strikingly balanced. Eleanor attends a Lutheran church while Jack's family attended Catholic Mass. As for my family and me, perhaps due to Ted's eccentricities, we provided the only oddity by attending an Evangelical Covenant church. We were indeed the black sheep of the family.

During my mother's 1990 trip to Lake Dunbar, Ted and I, and also my brother, Jack, and his wife, Evelyn, accompanied her. It had been quite some time since my beloved brother had made the trip north to Whispering Pines, and this long Fourth of July weekend constituted a reunion of sorts for the cabin's founders. They enjoyed a full weekend of eating, hiking, eating, fishing, and, of course, eating. As Mom, Evelyn, and I are each excellent cooks, we really tried to outdo one another. Ted and Jack were the happy, stuffed benefactors of this culinary madness. Mom and my brother also relished their respective returns to Lake Dunbar, enjoying it in their own individual ways. Mom took the green Crestliner boat out for a tour of the lake. She noted places that had special meaning so long ago, and she studied the various lake cabins where she spent hours with neighbors who had long since left. Jack spent his Dunbar reunion days walking through the forested lakeshore and doing some work on the cabin wherever needed. He was a handyman at heart; not even a vacation would stop him. Both Mom and Jack noticed the changes Ted and I had made to the cabin, but were glad to see that, along with the newness, the cabin's essential character remained. The iron double bunk bed, some of the same wall hangings, a virtually unchanged workbench, and Dad's old green rocking chair were still in the same old places. In some odd sense, time always stood still at Whispering Pines.

Sadly, our group left Lake Dunbar on our 1990 weekend with bad news. A neighbor stopped by to let us know Lucy Ritter passed away the previous weekend. She had been living alone in an apartment after Earl died several years ago. My family had kept in touch with Earl and Lucy after the Ritters left Lake Dunbar, but telephone calls and letters became less and less frequent once Earl died. And then, after my mother left the lake in the early 1980s, contact became virtually nonexistent. Such things happen, even here on Lake Dunbar, and time marches on.

My husband was a typical outdoorsman father. He chose his winter wardrobe with great care, and his sense of fashion had priorities. Clothes must be warm, comfortable, and mostly clean. Color coordination was a secondary consideration, if it was one at all. As he strode down the hill to join his sons on the frozen lake for some ice fishing the next morning of our family's 1990 winter stay, Ted was in top form. Warm, comfortable, and mostly clean. Based upon the standards of most fathers, his outfit was a colorful, fashionable masterpiece. Faded blue jeans with a gray cotton sweatshirt partially covered with a tan down-filled vest. Oversized black leather gloves with green and white stripes, stocking cap pulled down to eyebrow level. And, of course, bright red moon boots. What Ted lacked in fashion, he made up for as the consummate outdoorsman. Ted loved fishing, camping, and especially cutting wood. He would spend hours in the Travis's forested lakeshore chopping down trees, surveying his recently planted seedlings, and clearing underbrush. Over the years, Eddie and Alex came to see the humorous side of Ted's warped rural logic. They no longer questioned the old adage, "You can take the boy out of the country, but you can't take the country out of the boy." It was absolute truth in their minds.

Beginning in 1991, Ted and I initiated a second round of major tree planting in the Travis woods. We cleared the land of all the old-growth jack pines, which in a good windstorm might have toppled onto the cabin. We set to work planting pine, spruce, and fir seedlings every three to four feet apart in the near-barren grove. We coerced nephew Walt into accompanying us on this tree-planting trip. Actually, it took very little persuasion to solicit Walt's help. An afternoon of tree planting was a small price to pay, in his eyes, for two days of unlimited fishing. Walt, you see, is the family sportsman. If it swims, Walt will fish for it. If it runs on all fours, Walt will hunt it. Given his love for the northwoods and all of its offerings, it was obvious Walt was a Travis to the core. He tried city living once, but it was a short-lived experiment. Leaving behind a good job in the Minneapolis area, Walt returned to his roots near Greenwood and bought, what else, a farm. While he could have built or purchased a good-sized home in town, Walt preferred the countryside. There, he could be a gentleman farmer with his coonhounds, two pigs, and a cow named Henry.

On occasion, others in the Travis clan would gently challenge Ted on his reverence for trees. Cultivating an excellent forest was one thing, but keeping shoreline foliage intact at the expense of a decent view of the lake from the cabin was another. For years, our sons would badger Ted about the arguably excessive amount of scrubby trees and unnecessary brush along the lakeshore, obstructing an otherwise picturesque view of the lake from the large cabin windows up the hill. As Alex explained in the cabin journal, "If those two pine trees don't come down soon, I'm just going to have to buy a place in the middle of a cornfield so I can have the exact same view—nothing but green."

Ted, Walt, and I awoke early on a cloudy, overcast Saturday morning following a late night's arrival at Whispering Pines. It was the third weekend in May, which meant only one thing: opening day of fishing season. Needless to say, Walt requested the early morning start and worked diligently to get the job done so he could move on to something important: angling. The work was divided as evenly as possible. Ted dug holes in the sandy soil, every five to six feet. I then placed one pine, fir, or spruce seedling in the hole and surrounded it gently with dirt. Finally, Walt would come along with buckets of water providing the new trees with their first moist nourishment. By noon, over six hundred seedlings had been planted: three hundred black spruce, one hundred and fifty white pine, one hundred Norway pines, and fifty silver maple. By three o'clock, we amateur arborists were tired and hunchbacked, with only a few seedlings left. Walt was the first to notice my attempt to expedite the remainder of the job, but with an afternoon of fishing ahead of him, he kept silent about his discovery. As long as Ted didn't come around for inspection, it would not be a problem, and no additional work. No such luck.

"Uh, guys. Is this a new planting scheme I'm not aware of?"

"What do you mean?" Walt asked in return, as if he didn't know.

"The idea is generally to put one seedling in each hole, not two or three."

Planting the last remaining seedling, I looked up at Walt as if to say, "Thanks, we tried."

Ted naturally sensed the exhaustion of his companions, and he, too, was tired from the day's work. "But who am I to question new ideas? Who knows, maybe we'll have a drought this summer, and at least one of each pair will survive."

Within minutes, Walt returned the water buckets to the shed and was out in the boat, racing toward some secret fishing hole. He'd had enough green thumbing for one lifetime. As Ted walked up the hillside toward the road to see exactly how many sets of "twin trees" had been planted, I found a small open space in the woods to sit down and rest my aching muscles. I sat for a few moments looking around at the nearly nine hundred trees we had planted. It was quite an accomplishment. I pictured how attractive and thick the forest would be several years from now, just like it was when I first came here almost forty years ago as a young girl. When I lay back, wondering how many others had ever stopped at this very spot just to sit and enjoy nature, I felt a sharp pain in my lower back. Shifting over a few inches, my hand searched the ground beneath me for the twig, rock, or other pointed object. What I found was an amazing discovery, a fluke, and a piece of history. I had found an actual arrowhead, the tip of a spear probably left here by a Native American hunter after striking an unsuspecting deer hundreds of years ago. I searched the ground for more, but found none. This lone arrowhead had survived across the ages without discovery, and without being touched by human hands. I tried to picture the ancient hunter who carved and created this object, and thought about how he must have walked through these woods hundreds of times, right through the land where I now stood. Climbing the small hill to tell Ted of my improbable discovery, I was both humbled and excited to know I was actually retracing others' footsteps among these whispering pines. Today the arrowhead stands mounted, framed, and hanging at the Travis family cabin, with a special commemoration as follows:

"The Arrowhead from Lake Dunbar"

This arrowhead was found by Ruth Travis Walsch in May of 1991 while replanting trees in the old pine grove above Lake Dunbar in the Chippewa National Forest. It was discovered approximately a hundred yards to the northwest from a point on a line parallel with the lake-facing side of the original cabin on Lake Dunbar constructed in the 1950s by the Sam and Isabelle Travis family, in Good Hope Township, Itasca County, Minnesota.

The small hill sloping to the lake where the discovery was made is still today a favorite spot for deer to gather in the winter for protection from the bitter northwest winds. This arrowhead symbolizes the presence of Native Americans who also knew the secrets of Lake Dunbar in ancient times when this arrowhead found its resting spot among the pines of this great forest.

THE GARDEN OF DELIGHTS

THOSE WHO KNOW HIM WILL AGREE MY HUSBAND, TED, IS A true propeller head like many of his brethren in the computer industry. If anything ever seems a little out of place or kinky at Dunbar, it could more than likely be attributed to Ted. For example, he never talked of catching "northern pike" or reeling in a nice "walleye." Instead, he will tell stories of successfully landing an *esox lucius* or a *stizostedium vitreum,* their Latin equivalents. I guess he paid more attention to the Latin-speaking Catholic priests during the pre-Vatican II era *than I did.* Certainly, no one in the family will forget the day Ted came racing in from the lake boasting of a prize *pomoxis nigromaculatus* (black crappie) he caught down near the Round Lake *canalis* (canal), which he planned to take into *Anes Rubripes* (the nearby town of Blackduck) for *metiri* (a measurement). We sent him merrily on his way, not knowing or caring what in the hell he was talking about.

The oddities did not end there. While others stored their hunting rifles at the lake, Ted kept a set of Bolos he acquired in Argentina. Though the Bolos make less noise than guns, and are therefore arguably more effective in silently felling a deer, Ted never did bring in a deer or any other creature for the evening meal. From what I could tell, he mainly caught the pine trees. Ted was in accord with one of the Travis traditions, however. He agreed the cabin's master bedroom was made for the adults. In my parents' era, the handsome knotty pine walls and ceiling were tastefully decorated with appropriate pictures of the flora and fauna of the forest. A year or so after acquiring the cabin from my mother, however, a non-descript lake country painting in the bedroom was silently and inconspicuously removed. In its place, Ted hung up Hieronymus Bosch's 1450 A.D. painting,

The Garden of Delights. This great masterpiece depicts flowers, fruit, men, and animals living in joyous community. The work represents the road taken by a man who does not seek salvation, but abandons himself to pleasure and gives free reign to his fantasies. Its triptych depicts the journey from the Garden of Eden to Hell. In between these two extreme ends lies Bosch's fervid portrayal of all creatures passing through a season of love. True to the painting, Ted believed the oxygen of the Travis forest produced more than peaceful rest. It was the ultimate source of love, fantasy, and adult delights.

As Scandinavian descendants, Minnesotans are polite and proper souls. Consequently, no one ever spoke of the true delights of the northern forests. Nevertheless, several rumored sightings were made of amorous affairs in the Travis woods, on the floating dock, and in rocking boats among the weeds. But unlike our southern European contemporaries, we were good stoic northerners who did not kiss and tell. While we never elicited any confessions of Dunbar delights, it is interesting to note that all of my parents' eleven children, grandchildren, and great grandchildren were born in the months of February, March, April, and May, nine months after the warm-weather visits to Lake Dunbar in May, June, July, and August.

The secret of northern Minnesota lovemaking was, however, exposed to the world in 1991 by the "Screamer from Squaw Lake." The following article appeared in a weekly syndicated advice column in the *Bemidji Telegraph*, and eventually numerous other papers and magazines across the country. This week's column was entitled "Screamers Need Privacy Too."

> *Dear Betty:*
> *My wife and I have been married for almost fifteen years, and our sex life is still fantastic. Maybe not quite as exciting as when we were first married, but just about as often. The problem, Betty, is we can only have sex when no one else is in the house. You see, my wife has an excruciating time keeping her ecstasy under wraps. To be rather frank, she grunts, cries, and outright screams the closer we get to a climax. The truth is, Betty, I wouldn't have it any other way because it really turns me on!*

But here's the problem. We have four children—ages eleven, nine, five, and two. They can't help but hear what's going on, and once the five-year-old came running into our room in the middle of the night to see what was so terribly wrong. We've tried different accommodations, but it gets so frustrating having to wait sometimes. Most of the time, we make love over the noon hour on my break from work, or any other time we manage to be alone. Summertime is the best because we sneak off before dinner to a secret little spot way off in the woods over near Round Lake and really let things loose.

Winter is a little harder, but we rev up the truck, drive off to a remote spot, and my wife screams to her (and my) delight in the back of the cab. But Betty, we're a little afraid of getting caught. I think the county sheriff is onto us, having driven up behind my pickup twice now at the boat landing on Bowstring Lake, thankfully after the screaming was over. Betty, we need your advice. I'm afraid my fishing buddies will soon figure out who the "Screamer from Squaw Lake" is and I'll never hear the end of it. "She's screaming from the agony of having sex with you," they'll all say. Betty, what should we do?

Looking for Privacy in Squaw Lake

Dear Privacy,
You make love with screaming delight in your house at noon, you continue such passion in the local woods and at boat landings in the heart of Minnesota's prime fishing and hunting lands, and you've been doing this for fifteen years? I'd say your fishing buddies (and everyone else within ten square miles) already know who the "Screamer from Squaw Lake" is.

Betty

The eyes of a nation were suddenly focused on the little town of Squaw Lake. Rumors flew hot and heavy. Was it the secretary at the local school or the waitress down at The Hill? Of course, the guessing went on only in private. The town had but a few hundred people. How many women could possibly fit the profile given to Betty, the advice columnist? As my dad used to say, nothing much happens in a small town, but the rumors certainly make up for it. Inquiries poured in from across the country. The gathering spot for gossip in Squaw Lake was the Hoot & Holler where Ted and I have dined on many occasions. The telephone did not stop ringing there for weeks.

No tourist could pass up stopping at the Hoot & Holler over the years since the incident to enjoy a cup of coffee and inquire as to whether any disclosure was ever made. Apparently even the "Screamer" herself was in a quandary about what to do. She also sought advice from Dear Betty about two months later. Her plea for help was as follows:

Dear Betty,
I'm not sure what to do. My husband wrote to you recently, explaining the difficult situation with our sex life. As you've probably guessed, I'm the "Screamer from Squaw Lake," though it does make me sound rather tawdry. I think of myself as quite shy. Anyway, I'm mortified that you printed his letter, and I just know everybody has figured out it's me, including our next door neighbor, Sister Alberta. At first I punished my husband by refusing to sleep with him for a week, which only made matters worse. He's such a good lover and with my pent-up needs, the minute we got back in the same bed I was screaming my head off! Betty, what can I do?

Shy Girl in Squaw Lake.

Dear Shy Girl,

I think your problem is the best one I've ever read, and you should not change a thing. But if this sex-driven screaming is truly a challenge or embarrassment, you might try sneaking off to a cheap motel room in another town. I hear the one in Climax, MN is quite nice. And as for Sister Alberta, she took a vow of chastity, not you. So go have your fun, and forget about the nun.

Betty

Climax is a small town near Duluth, not far from Embarrass. Yet some incorrectly say we Minnesotans have no sense of humor. Embarrass has its own unique national reputation as the coldest little town in America. Many a morning, in the dead of winter, the town's name is prominently flashed across TV sets and in newspapers for its sub-zero temperatures. Obviously, it would be an appropriate place for a "Screamer." Now, the good people of Squaw Lake did not want to end up with a reputation like the town of Embarrass. In any event, it seems the "Screamer" is destined to become, like many other tall tales in the forest, little more than a legend or local myth.

After reading these entertaining advice column exchanges, everyone who visited Lake Dunbar had a new appreciation for the "Garden of Delights" painting. When several of our friends and relatives asked Ted if such moans were ever heard on the distant shores of Lake Dunbar, he indiscreetly responded: "The deeper you go into the forest, the louder the howl of the wolf."

Our youngest son Alex is the baseball pride of the Travis family. Alex was a Little League star and an All-State player in high school, the pride of Roosevelt High. In 1987, he set a state high school record by striking out twenty-one batters in a nine-inning game. Alex later went on to play baseball in college, and he even played in the Junior College World Series. Thus, 1991 was a memorable year for Alex and all of us Minnesota baseball fans because it marked the return of the Minnesota Twins to the World Series. Four years earlier, in 1987, the

Twins astonished the sports world, and many of their fans, by capturing the American League pennant from the favored Detroit Tigers. Then they went on to beat the St. Louis Cardinals in a dramatic seven-game World Series.

The core members of the 1987 team, names that will live forever in the hearts of Twins fans, were back in 1991: Kirby Puckett, Kent Hrbek, Greg Gagne, Dan Gladden, Gene Larkin, and coach Tom Kelly. The opponent this time, the Atlanta Braves, was new. Aside from the excitement of the series, in which all but one game was to be decided by less than three runs in the winning team's final at-bat, the games received some notoriety from the protests of Native Americans. For some time, these people have rightfully objected to the use by professional sports teams of names that they contend degrade the image and reality of native cultures: the Braves, Redskins, Warriors, Blackhawks, and more. In 1991, they finally had a national forum in which to voice their opinion and protest against "The Braves." Ted, Alex, and I drove north in early October 1991 and heard about this as we traveled to Lake Dunbar, in the heart of the Leech Lake Indian Reservation, on the first weekend of the World Series. We were going to shut down the cabin for the season. We listened intently as the Twins won a close match in game one. By Sunday evening, none of us had any fingernails left as the Twins pulled out another victory, 5-1.

"Boy," said Ted, "these games have sure been exciting. Can you imagine actually attending one?"

"There's nothing like it, Dad. Watching a World Series game in person is a real rush," said Alex who had attended one of the Twins' victories in the equally nail-biting World Series of 1987. At this particular moment, however, Alex was not very excited. To miss at least watching a World Series game on television was an unfathomable sacrifice for him. Alex was the ultimate Twins' fan. Why had he consented to come north to assist his parents in shutting down the cabin? Granted, he had been playing league baseball all summer, and this was his first trip north all year. We had no television in the cabin. The nearest stations were in Duluth or Alexandria, both more than two hundred miles away, making any TV reception even questionable. The cabin had an antenna my brother Jack put up in the 1960s.

It seemed the cable broke in a storm in the 1970s, and no one had the courage or ambition to climb up and fix it since.

You see, Ted and I have the old-fashioned idea that the cabin is for reading, fishing, and sleeping. Praise the Lord, Alex thought, at least someone had invented the VCR. In the last few years when Eddie and Alex came to the cabin, they always brought the VCR and portable television along. On the first trip north with the VCR in the late 1980s, we discovered a new video rental shop had opened in Deer River. When making the drive north to the cabin, principal routes can be taken. The first is the eastern route up Highway 65 through Grand Rapids past old Calijah, the wooden Indian. The second is the western route up Highway 169 along the shores of the striking Mille Lacs Lake and the big statue of Wally the Walleye. Mille Lacs was purported to be the best walleye fishing lake in the world. Either way, travelers had to pass through Cohasset and Deer River, the gateway to the Chippewa National Forest.

Stopping at the new Deer River video rental shop, our kids struck gold because they learned the shop also had an outlet in Squaw Lake. Amazing, they thought, videos only five miles from the cabin. If this were not enough, the video shop was also offering a limited number of lifetime memberships as part of its grand opening promotion—on a first-come, first-served basis. This was too good to be true. A membership was not cheap, but when you traveled this far, you want to have the best. So, of course we bought one. Everyone had his or her preferred videos. For me, the top pick was *A Trip to Bountiful* with the late Geraldine Page, who won an Oscar for her role as Mother Watts. Perhaps I identified with Mother Watts's quest to make one last trip to her beloved hometown of Bountiful, Texas, which had become abandoned as the original residents departed over the years. Mother Watts's only obstacle was Jessie Mae, the daughter-in-law with whom Mother Watts lived.

Eddie and Alex would have to bear my watching the movie for the hundredth time. However, they often reminded me I had better keep my retirement plan updated, or they would marry mean-spirited spouses like Jessie Mae and there would be no more trips back to Lake Dunbar.

Ted's favorite videos were the Steve Martin stand-up comedies. For days, we would all put up with Ted's claims of being a wild-and-crazy guy. Everyone's agreed-upon favorite was Bill Cosby's *Himself*, in which he describes the humor of parenting, drug use, and visiting the dentist. To counter Ted's Steve Martin routines, Eddie and Alex would relentlessly mimic the Cos by screaming, "Stop touching me," and demanding chocolate cake for breakfast. When we traveled north again the following summer, the Deer River video shop was closed, for good. The sign said, "Gone out of business." So much for the life-time membership.

In the absence of television for the 1991 World Series, Alex tried to tune in the game on the cabin radio. Better yet, when we didn't work him into total exhaustion by evening, Alex took the truck by himself to The Hill in Squaw Lake. It was Saturday night and, Twins or no Twins, Ted and I surely would want to stay home and listen to *Prairie Home Companion* on the radio. Although he was not yet of age, Alex's imposing physical stature made him look a few years older. He would have no trouble getting into the bar at The Hill in order to watch the game on their big screen TV fed by the large satellite dish out back.

People at The Hill were used to seeing big men in this country. Only fifty miles up the road in International Falls on the Canadian border lived the legendary Bronko Nagurski. Bronko was selected as the NFL's greatest football player in the first half-century for his great exploits with the Chicago Bears. Bronko's championship ring, a size twenty-six, was the largest ever made. In college, Bronko was the only player ever selected as an All-American at two positions, fullback and tackle-in, the same season.

On the following Saturday, after returning from Lake Dunbar, Ted's question about how exciting it must be to attend a World Series game was answered. There sat Ted, Walt, my sister Eleanor, and me in the Hubert H. Humphrey Metrodome for game six of the 1991 World Series. Walt had acquired the tickets at the last moment. The Atlanta Braves had triumphed in three straight games down at Fulton County Stadium in Georgia, and were one victory away from winning it all. The Twins, on the other hand, needed to win both remaining games in Minnesota to avoid a series loss. Game six turned out to be as exciting, if not more so, than the rest. At the end of nine innings, the score was tied 3-3. The game, and possibly the series, would be decided in extra innings. At the end of the tenth inning, the score remained 3-3. As it turned out, the game would be decided in the eleventh inning. First up for the Braves in the top of the eleventh was the veteran Sid Bream. He faced the Twins ace reliever, Rick Aguillera. Sid promptly hit a hard line drive into the right field corner for a base hit. Because Sid was not a speedster around the base paths, Keith Mitchell came in as a pinch runner. One on, no outs.

Next to bat for the Braves was Brian Hunter, only the second rookie in baseball history to hit home runs in both the League Championship and World Series. As Hunter watched the first pitch from Aguillera whiz past for a strike, Mitchell took off from first base attempting to steal his way to second. Throughout the Series, the Braves stole bases with relative ease against the Twins and their catcher, Brian Harper. But not on this night; not on this attempt. Harper made a perfect throw to the second baseman who tagged out Mitchell a split second before reaching second base. Nobody on, one out. Soon, the Braves' hopes in the eleventh inning were dashed as both Hunter and the next batter, Greg Olson, hit easy pop-fly balls that were caught by the Twins infielders. No runs, one hit, no errors. Score tied, 3-3.

It was now past 11:00 p.m. and the game entered the bottom of the eleventh inning. Due up for the Twins was the heart of our batting order: Kirby Puckett, Chili Davis, and Shane Mack. Even though the match was nearly four hours old, the crowd roared with enthusiasm as our hometown hero stepped up to the plate. Already Kirby had a single, triple, and a stolen base, a run batted in, and a run scored. But now he was facing a fresh pitcher, Charlie Liebrandt. Kirby eyed the pitcher's first offering and listened as the umpire bellowed out his decision: "Strike!" A few seconds later, Kirby watched again as a ball whizzed past him about eye level. "Ball!" The count was even, one and one. The crowd soon began to nervously wonder as Kirby, normally a first-ball hitter, watched a third pitch fly past him, a bit outside the strike zone. "Ball!" The count was now two balls and a strike.

What ensued next was miraculous. Kirby sent a hanging curve ball deep over the left field fence for the game-winning home run. The crowd erupted with excitement as Kirby, a stocky guy, ran the bases thrusting his fist into the air amidst sheer pandemonium. Along with fifty thousand others, Ted, Walt, Eleanor, and I danced, hugged, and screamed with exhilaration, our hearts pounding with adrenaline. The television commentator announced the noise level inside the Metrodome measured 120 decibels after the home run, and it did not abate for several minutes. The blue-collar guys from Minnesota had pulled even with the feisty Braves. It was to be the first time the World Series had lasted for seven full games since 1987, the last time the Twins played in the championship.

Game seven was nearly as exciting as game six, perhaps even more so. This one was a pitcher's duel between the Braves' John Smoltz and the Twins' Jack Morris. Morris, a Minnesota native, typified the hard-working, tough guy image of the Twins. With his long, gruff mustache, he stared down batters for nine full innings. At the end of regulation play, the score was again tied, 0-0. The 1991 World Series was to be decided in extra innings, perhaps by just one swing of the bat as the night before. As the Twins took to the field for the tenth inning, Morris was back on the mound throwing as hard as ever. Although the Twins had plenty of pitching firepower available in the bullpen as relief, and although Morris was pitching on just three days' rest, coach Tom Kelly stayed with his main man, Jack. "After all," Tom would say later, "it's only a game." Jack met the challenge head-on, sending the Braves down in order in the top of the tenth inning. And although Jack could probably have pitched another ten innings on sheer emotion alone, there would be no need. The Twins got a bases-loaded single from Gene Larkin in the bottom of the tenth to send the team on to a 1-0 victory. As summarized by Fay Vincent, the last independent baseball commissioner, "It was, I think, probably the greatest World Series ever. I was proud to be here, and I think all of the fans appreciate the effort you made and the effort of the Braves—two superb teams."

The hometown boys had done it, and everyone savored the victory—a victory for Alex's heroes, a victory for our state, and a victory for those whose Native American protesting voices were heard. On this night, it was a full-out celebration.

Returning to Lake Dunbar early the next spring, we were relieved as always to be back in the comfortable surroundings of Whispering Pines. We were also pleased to have our elder son, Eddie, join us for the weekend, visiting from California. On the last afternoon of the trip, Eddie, Ted, and I set out in the boat to do some fishing. After only half an hour on the lake, Eddie reeled in his line (which was being completely ignored by the lake's scaly inhabitants), set up a few boat cushions, and spread himself out for a brief nap. A weathered baseball cap covered his eyes, and his feet dangled carelessly over the edge of the boat. I decided sleep was not in the cards for Eddie, however, at least not right away. Instead, I wanted to talk. Actually, I wanted to conduct a psychological analysis. How could this young man with a long lineage of Travis fisherman's blood pull in his pole and sleep away an afternoon on the boat? I should have known better than to interrogate my law school student son, for I received an answer all right, and more. In fact, the following exchange was forever after known in our family as the Story of Truth, Honesty, and Bitterness.

"Hey Eddie, are you sleeping?"

"Planning on it."

"How can you sleep? It's a perfect day out, and you sure can't catch anything with your pole in the boat. I've never seen any flying fish on this lake!"

Eddie had two options. He could certainly just ignore me. Of course, he would then have no opportunity to sleep because I would inevitably keep him awake with constant reminders of the gorgeous day at hand, the gorgeous last day of our trip. Besides, I would tell him, I had nothing else in the cabin to eat for dinner. It was either fish or nothing. This was a veiled threat I used at least once on every trip. A bit overused, perhaps, but an effective part of my repertoire of guilt. Eddie chose option two. He would answer my question, reverse the direction of induced guilt, and create an atmosphere conducive to sleep. My son cunningly planned to silence his parents on the topic of fishing versus sleeping, for good. With feigned seriousness, Eddie lifted the cap from his eyes, peered out over the lake, and poured forth his saga of truthful events and highly exaggerated emotions.

"Well, it's a difficult question, and the answer is not pretty. In fact, it's rather tragic. I'm not sure I can really put it into words."

"Why don't you give it a try," I said, sensing my creative son was about to come up with something good.

"It's a long story, but here goes. Are you sure you want to hear this? It might be painful."

"I wouldn't miss this for the world," I replied, gently nudging Ted who was heretofore oblivious to the conversation. How silly of him, he thought he was out here on the lake for some quiet and serious fishing.

"Okay. You see, I was a good fisherman once. Right up until the age of about thirteen. I used to come up here to Lake Dunbar with Grandma Isabelle, and I'd catch the biggest and most fish of any-one—four-, five-, and six-pound northern pikes every time. And I always caught them with my old black-and-white Zebco, the best-ever rod and reel. I loved my old pole, even slept with it next to me in the cabin at night to protect it. It meant more to me than life itself!" So far, all true. Now, if only Eddie could force some tears, I might see an Academy Award™ nomination in his future

"Then, it all fell apart. The meaning in my life was brutally stripped away at the tender age of thirteen. Do you remember our family canoe trip in northern Wisconsin? Remember how I got into the canoe, and entrusted my life and that of my precious Zebco to you and Dad who were paddling? Remember what happened as you switched your paddle from the left to the right side of the boat, and 'unintentionally' knocked my Zebco into the muddy river water? Yes, I think you remember quite well! The Zebco sank before I could even reach my young, innocent arms to save it. Within an instant it was gone, never to be seen again. Ever since, I have never been able to catch a fish bigger than two pounds, if I even catch one at all. You were so jealous of my pole. You just couldn't stand to see us happy together." His hands now covered his face to hide the absent tears. And the Oscar® goes to . . .

I was torn. While I certainly enjoyed the performance, I had a slight feeling of guilt since the story I just heard was mostly true.

With respect to alleged jealously and intent to harm the pole, I can neither confirm nor deny those assertions, however.

"And do you feel bitter?" I inquired.

"Oh yes, I'm very bitter. My childhood was taken from me prematurely. I have attempted fishing since, but it just isn't the same. I sure miss my old pole. But that isn't even the end of the story. Besides my Zebco pole, I also owned a tiny orange tackle box. It held only a few lures, but it was mine, and I loved it. Some years after the loss of the Zebco, my little orange tackle box mysteriously disappeared. Gone. I have my suspicions, and they center upon three certain individuals in my immediate family. But I'm not naming names, of course."

"You can be sure I didn't take it," I said. "Your dad bought me my own tackle box. Besides, do you think I'd dare take your little tackle box after the episode with your pole?"

"I don't know. We've already established you have a prior record." Eddie then turned his attention to Ted. "What about you, Dad? Do you recall seeing my little orange tackle holder around the house or the cabin?"

"No," was Ted's short answer. He seemed to be preoccupied with steering the boat and watching his fishing line, yet revealing a nervous grin on his face.

"So, Dad, let's just look here in your tackle box for good measure."

"Come on, you're going to mess up the inside of the box or drop it or something," Ted replied nervously. "Give it here." Although he truly did not like anyone snooping in his tackle box, Ted was also now vying for best supporting actor honors. As Eddie opened up Ted's three-layer, expandable green fishing box, he admired his father's well-organized trays of fancy lures and hooks, including real Daredevils, Little Joe's, Lazy Ikes, and a few Red Eyes. Quite a collection. Few if any people were ever allowed to see or even touch this hallowed treasure. Ted was protective of his fishing gear, and often kept it under lock and key. Digging through the bottom of the box, Eddie found it. His long-lost orange tackle holder, filled with Ted's fishing weights, or sinkers.

"I can't believe it. You actually had it all along!" Eddie's exclamation was full of sincere shock and surprise. He had not expected to uncover such a dramatic revelation in telling his story. The guilt inducement was now fully in reverse.

"Ted! How could you do such a thing to your own son?" I was now making my own late bid for an acting award, and hoping the role of villain had been transferred to my husband, taking me off the hook. Not so.

"You see, the trauma continues. It's why I can't fish, but must simply lie back and rest," Eddie concluded. And so he did for the remainder of the afternoon on the boat, without interruption.

Truth be told, Eddie did not catch a keeper again until an autumn trip to Dunbar many years later. The landing of a twenty-one-inch northern pike ended an eight-year drought for him. As Ted concluded in the guest book on our glorious trip: "Now we believe he will come back again." This much certainly was never in doubt. Even without the prized catch, Eddie was enjoying a wonderful four-day respite, one of the few he'd been able to enjoy away from his life in California, and Dunbar was a most accommodating host. The leaves were in full bloom with explosive shades of crimson, gold, and burnt orange, and had fallen onto a backdrop of green grass. Eddie would indeed return to Lake Dunbar, again and again.

My husband Ted's love for pets, while not fanatical, was as steadfast as mine. We had a dog (Daisy), two cats (Ralph and Boots), and a large tank full of tropical fish (variously named). Lest anyone should doubt, these creatures were the favorite children in the family. Eddie often recalled how the only curfew in the house was for the pets. He and Alex could stay out until all hours of the night while Ted and I slumbered away, but if a cat did not return home by ten o'clock, a search party would be assembled to seek out the missing pet. Our love for these pets reflected an emotion evolved over time. Ted did not approve when the boys brought home a black ball of fur named Daisy from the pet store on a summer afternoon bike ride. I later repeatedly said "no" to pleas for keeping the stray kitten, Ralph, and neither of us was delighted when Alex presented us with Boots after discovering he was not allowed to keep pets in his college apartment. Eventually, we gave in to each pet acquisition, provided the boys pledged to feed, exercise, and clean up after the beasts. When the boys' promises failed to last but two weeks, Ted and I soon found ourselves acting as parents to the ever-increasingly likable pets. Soon, the creatures were even sharing sleeping quarters with us at night, each mammal and animal fighting for its share of the queen-sized waterbed.

While we took exceptional care of our pets, including walking the dog twice a day for several blocks or miles, at times our patience was put to the test. On a Labor Day weekend at Lake Dunbar, Ted and I took a daytrip to Baudette, entry point to Lake of the Woods, the most northern point in the continental United States, heading toward Canada's Quetico National Park. At the entry checkpoint, however, we encountered a few difficulties. The guard went through the litany of standard questions, which seemed to last forever. Any drugs? Alcohol? Tobacco? Ted began whispering to himself, though loud enough for me to hear, "Where do they get these nitwit border guards? What do they think we are going to Canada for anyway?"

The list went on for five minutes with Ted answering no each time, until the border guard reached the final question.

"Any pets?"

Seeing as he couldn't conceal the obvious dog sitting on his lap in the driver's seat, Ted truthfully responded, "Yes." After all this, we were informed that while we could take Daisy into Canada, we could have problems re-entering the United States without proper documentation on the dog's medical status, including rabies shots. Consequently, this mangy, $25 investment called Daisy was preventing us from entering Canada and Lake of the Woods after a two-hour drive north to get there. Ted pondered the possibilities. Perhaps Daisy and the border guard deserved each other. As he later wrote in the cabin guest book, "This was our chance to leave her after she kept us up all night last night, trembling from the lightning and thunderstorm." Alas, Ted and I had no choice but to turn around and drive two hours back to the cabin, with Daisy sitting proudly and contentedly in the front seat between us.

In all our years as stewards of the Whispering Pines cabin, Ted and I rarely ventured north without one or more of our now-beloved pets. While the cats were brought along on two or three occasions, they proved a bit more worrisome for us as the felines wandered off into the woods, far from the cabin, and required great coaxing to return. The constant cabin companion, however, was Daisy. On her first trip to Dunbar as a puppy, Daisy learned the lesson of cautious curiosity. Running wildly through the Travis woods, Daisy happened upon a box turtle and carefully sniffed the odd-looking reptile for identification and inspection. Apparently, the turtle had no interest in joining the canine ritual of orifice smelling, and proceeded to snap Daisy right on the snout. Hearing Daisy's wails of pain, Ted and our boys ran to Daisy only to find the feisty box turtle hanging on for dear life to Daisy's nose with his powerful jaw. Ted grabbed the turtle's mid-section with one hand and Daisy's face with the other. With one good yank, he pulled them apart, setting the turtle back into the woods and watching Daisy run off with a whimper and a scar she would carry with her to the end of her days. Ultimately, Daisy's long life of 105 dog years came full circle. We laid her to rest in a marked grave among newly planted pines in the Travis forest, not far from the site of her battle royale with the wily tortoise.

It has been said that one person's folly is another person's pleasure. During the thirty years my great-uncle Frank lived in California, one thing he mentioned missing the most was a great midwestern thunderstorm. The fury of a low-pressure cell, laden with warm water from the Gulf of Mexico, tangling with a fast-moving, cold, high-pressure cell out of the arctic over the great pine forests, is a spectacle never to be forgotten. Nothing of man's creation, not even the fury of Pickett's charge on July 3, 1863, at the battle of Gettysburg, comes close. The mighty pines do battle, boldly swaying and rebounding to the force of the wind. The battle is lost many times by both the older and younger trees as they crash to the forest floor. The tremendous electrical force and energized particles in the air light the darkened night sky with brilliance comparable to the sun at high noon. One can never fully erase the resulting images painted on one's consciousness. Such storms have become a major source of mysticism and wonder of untold cultures, passed from generation to generation as archetypes of the Jungian mind. If this is the effect on the human mind, imagine the horror striking the mind of a pint-sized dog. For Daisy, the only place of safety and refuge during a storm is at the head of the master bed under the pillows between Ted and me. The dog's intense shaking reminded us of our years in Oregon and the occasional earthquakes. However, this trembling and shaking was only the first of the problems during one of the great storms at Whispering Pines in the late summer of 1992.

Some say I had a lot of my mother's toughness, except as it relates to small crawling creatures. The sight of a spider, a June bug, or any of the other myriad insects from the forest floor would send me into a near panic. By eleven o'clock in the evening during this late summer visit, both the rolling thunder over Lake Dunbar and the dog's shaking had subsided. The chirping of the crickets took over. Their wonderful melodies celebrated the freshness of the forest floor and the night air from the newly fallen rain. At last, peacefulness had come to Lake Dunbar. Suddenly, the songs of the crickets and the movements of all the creatures of the forest stopped. The silence of the night had been pierced by a tremendous scream from the bedroom. Mine.

"BUG! BUG!" Before Ted could realize what was happening, I had jumped out of the bed and stripped myself of all nightclothes, imploring him to "SEARCH ME! SEARCH ME!"

As Ted rubbed the sleep from his eyes, he was probably thinking, "Wow, is this another of Ruth's crazy dreams? If it is, I definitely hope this nightmare occurs more often!" Finally, Ted realized my keen sense of creepy crawling creatures had awakened me.

"For God's sake, do I need to get an anatomy book for you?" I yelled because it was taking him forever for his hands to finally search the spot where I felt the crawling sensation. I was *so irritated* at him.

"No, I think I've got it located, I just want to be thorough," Ted replied as he soon discovered the source of the anxiety. I was right. Nestled in the small of my back was a tiny wood tick.

"Gee, isn't it late in the year for these things?" I demanded to know once it was removed, almost breathless.

"I've never seen them this close to autumn," Ted answered. "But then again, we picked strawberries and raspberries just a couple of weeks ago. Everything is a full month to six weeks behind schedule because of the early spring drought. Maybe the ticks are late, too."

The crisis had been solved. It must have been a late-season straggler that crept up my sock and hid in this inconspicuous place. With the renegade appropriately drowned in the toilet, we turned toward sleep once more. Peace and quiet returned to the forest. All the creatures of the night returned to whatever adventure consumed them before this strange interruption. Tranquility prevailed at last. The freshness of the rain-cleansed early fall air created a deep slumber. The dog, after all the excitement, reclaimed its position close to my pillow. This lasted for all of an hour.

Once again I sprang from the bed with the same screams of something invading my physical privacy. And yet again, Ted performed his faithful duty of a full anatomical scan done with both willing hands. All the while, I was interrogating him as to whether this was some kinky ritual he had concocted. After all, since I had conceded to letting him put up his *Garden of Delights* picture, his bedroom mannerisms had become a little kinky. Needless to say, it was another wood tick. In fact, it was two ticks this time. This was all too much for me, and I demanded a full search. Off came all the clothes and the bedding. Every inch of the place was searched, including under the bed with a flashlight. Nothing. It was now well after two o'clock in the morning, and suddenly it dawned on me.

"You don't suppose they're on the dog, do you?"

Ted, with a look of reservation, admitted he had let Daisy off the leash for a while in the woods during the afternoon. I was not amused. We moved into the living room to search for the dog who had bolted from the bedroom during all of the excitement. Sure enough, it was Daisy. For the next hour, I held my canine companion as Ted proceeded to remove fifty ticks from Daisy's wooly fur.

No one really knew what type of dog Daisy was. The pet shop said she was a Pomeranian Poodle mix. According to Stan Coren in his book *The Intelligence of Dogs* (The Free Press, April 1994), out of 133 pure breeds of dogs, only the Border Collie is more intelligent than the poodle, while the Pomeranian ranks twenty-third on the list.

Given the events of this night, I let Daisy know repeatedly during the tick extraction ceremony she had no more brains than a Bulldog, Basenji, or Borzoi. These three were considered the dumbest dogs in God's creation. They were to be out-done only by the Afghan hound, which Coren describes as "nothing more than a fashion accessory." After cutting away large chunks of hair to get at all of the ticks, Daisy was not going to score any points for some time in the fashion world either. By three in the morning, the job was complete. I gave Daisy the choice of sleeping either outside or on the living room floor with Ted, the man now banished from the bedroom because he let Daisy off-leash in the woods. After all of the drama he had subjected me to, I made it quite clear: there was to be *no delight in the garden this particular night.*

I.W.T.S.L.

AS THE TRAVIS CLAN ENTERED THE MID-NINETIES, OUR FIFTH decade on Lake Dunbar, visits to Whispering Pines were again dominated by two of the cabin's original founders: my nephew Walt and me. For Walt, the trips to Lake Dunbar became even more frequent following his diagnosis with a recurrence of cancer in 1992. The relapse caught everyone by surprise. Since doctors said he was in remission back in 1975, Walt had lived such a wonderfully full and normal life. He married in 1980 and almost immediately brought his bride to Lake Dunbar in order to share his secret hideaway. Walt's wife wasn't too sure about the cabin experience at first, but soon became as dedicated as anyone else in the family to fishing, card playing, and hiking. Despite the renewed bout with cancer, the Travis family had great hope Walt would again pull through and overcome yet another battle.

In this second round of the disease, the standard treatments didn't seem as effective as years ago. Walt struggled through the discomfort of radiation and chemotherapy, but with minimally successful results. Finally, the doctors told him he had but one choice: a bone-marrow transplant. First the doctors would need to face the tremendous odds of finding a perfect donor match. Then, if the obstacle could be overcome, Walt had even greater odds for permanent recovery. Yet, my ever-persistent nephew pushed on. He was still the same old Walt—funny, caring, and youthful. Soon after potential donors were tested, he received miraculous news. His sister, Rose, was a perfect match. Rose did not think twice about it. She donated her marrow without hesitation. The only limitation was that she was currently pregnant, and they would have to wait to perform the procedure until after the birth of her first child. Only one week after that blessed event, Rose underwent the painful procedure of extracting a fraction of her bone marrow.

The bone marrow transplant took place in the spring. Throughout the summer, everyone in the Travis family was constantly checking with Walt and Sophie on his progress. How was he feeling? What was the prognosis on the leukemia? Was the transplant a success? The news was always seemingly mixed, but hopeful. As far as the doctors could tell, the cancer was gone, but they had continuing problems with the rejection of the new marrow by Walt's organs. These problems would remain with him for some time, but did not limit his ability to live life to its fullest. While continually fighting for new treatments and improvements, Walt spent most of his energy and time concentrating on loving his family, and on living as normal a life as possible. Soon, Walt was well enough to resume regular trips to Whispering Pines. If anything served as a motivation for Walt to go on living, it was the thought of spending summer evenings with his wife on the shores of Lake Dunbar. While he still was limited in a way that prevented him from serious fishing, hiking, or other strenuous activities, this did not deter Walt. Instead, Walt just invented new ways to entertain himself and others.

The first form of entertainment he devised was a card game called, appropriately, "Walt's Game." It was similar to 500 or Rummy, but the rules were uniquely Walt's, and uniquely known to Walt. Most importantly, it was called Walt's Game because Walt always won. No one let him win; he just simply always won. His winning streak continued until he traveled to the cabin one weekend in 1993 with Ted and me. I did the unthinkable, the improbable, the unacceptable. I won a round of Walt's Game, but it didn't stop there. Feeling emboldened with the victory, I proudly announced since it was called Walt's Game inasmuch as Walt always won, it should now be referred to as Ruth's Game. Walt was not pleased. He simply challenged me to another round of—he could barely say it—Ruth's Game and trounced me fair and square, according to Walt's rules, naturally.

On a long weekend trip north in 1993, Walt and his wife again enjoyed several spirited rounds of Walt's Game with Ted, me, Rose, and her husband, Patrick. Between rounds of Walt's Game, the winners would casually refill their glasses with Crown Royal whiskey. The group had retrieved several bottles of the potent elixir on a daylong trip to St. Francis, Canada. There, we took advantage of bargains on liquor, jewelry, and more. And it soon became apparent who was winning most of the rounds of Walt's Game.

"Honey, it's your deal," Walt announced to his wife.

"I can't."

"What do you mean, you can't?"

"It's my arms. I've got heavy arms." Indeed, the Crown Royal had gone right through her system and straight to her arms, which were no longer mobile. The more she and the group laughed about it, the less she was able to control anything from shoulder to fingertips. So by this point in the evening, one player had heavy arms, I was arguing the game should be called Ruth's Game, and Patrick was becoming very protective of the remaining Crown Royal. For his part, Walt was becoming a bit irritated with the whole group. It seemed only he and Ted were still serious about the game. Walt ultimately decided to terminate Walt's Game for the evening, once his uncle Ted dealt the final blow.

"Go ahead and play your card, Teddy," Walt said. "Everyone else has played theirs."

Ted looked up at Walt and asked, "By the way, what suit was led?"

Walt looked at the pile of cards in the center of the table. They were all hearts. Walt thought, "I know he's not stupid, but he doesn't seem to be making a joke." Everyone else, however, broke out into laughter. Whatever remained of Ted's thought process had obviously been reduced to zero. Walt was now disgusted with the whole gang. He looked over at his brother-in-law Patrick and demanded, "Give me the Crown Royal now. I'm going to bed!" It seems we'd have no more heavy arms, except for Walt who would sleep comfortably with the firewater wrapped in his warm embrace. Poor Rose, she didn't win a single round of Walt's Game, and apparently was also passed over when the Crown Royal was distributed. As she wrote in the cabin guest book, "Next time I want heavy arms, too!"

During the first few years of the nineties, Walt spent many a weekend at Whispering Pines with various members of the extended Travis family. Seeing as Walt was now spending most of his Dunbar vacations inside the cabin, he took more time than ever before to notice the nuances and subtleties of the structure that had been his most consistent home for almost forty years. He sat in the living room observing the fantastic views out of each picture window. He perused the kitchen, remembering the wonderful, large meals Grandma used to prepare. He stood in the back bedroom carefully noticing the fine carpentry work accomplished so long ago, while chuckling at Ted's new addition, *The Garden of Delights*. And he lay in the bunkroom remembering the laughter he had shared with his cousins, while from the other room we parents begged them to go to sleep. Walt scanned the entry room and its walls filled with old hooks, rods-n-reels, and tools. He also sat in Grandpa Sam's tattered green rocking chair, gazing for hours at the Schlitz Light. The Schlitz Light was a blue ball of glass covering a light bulb, surrounded by a red stripe with the name and emblem of Schlitz Brewing Company. Walt especially loved to turn the light on at night after everyone went to bed, and watch it whirl around in the midst of complete darkness. On each trip to the cabin, Walt would threaten to take it home, and then deny knowing its whereabouts whenever I might finally notice it missing. I guess it became an obsession for Walt, if only to generate laughs and more jokes. But drifting off to sleep on a cool Dunbar night with the glow of the Schlitz Light was the closest thing to heaven here on earth Walt could hope for.

Between Walt, Ted, and I, someone was at Whispering Pines nearly every weekend in 1993. And each time a group prepared to leave those hallowed halls, someone was appointed to write in the guest book, to leave a record of the journey, telling all. Part of the fun in keeping this book was to read what the previous visitors had done. However, in the summer of 1993, one thing puzzled me as I read Walt's cabin summaries. They always ended with the initials I.W.T.S.L. What could it mean? Ted and I spent hours deriving formulas, searching the dictionary, and looking around the cabin for clues to this unidentifiable phrase. We asked everyone, but those who knew its meaning refused to reveal the secret. One night, very late, the answer came to me and I called Walt right away. Granted it was late, but hadn't he put me through untold agony trying to figure this out?

"Walt, this is Ruth. Did I wake you?"

"No, not at all. What makes you think I'd be in bed at half past midnight?"

"I just had to call to see if I was right."

"What do you mean?"

"I.W.T.S.L. I figured it out."

"You did, did you?"

"Yes. It stands for 'I Went to Squaw Lake.'"

"Goodnight, Ruth. Try again."

Late that summer, we all attended a reunion of Isabelle Travis's extended family. It was quite a large affair since my mother had five sisters and four brothers with each of them having large extended families of their own. Given such a sizable family, it was inevitable some members would not be able to attend because they lived so far away. However, all of the surviving members of Sam Travis's family were there. It had been some time since my mother's extended family gathered together in one place all at the same time, but our combined presence is also indicative of the uniqueness of this group, and our commitment to the common bond of blood relationships.

After one trip through the bountiful potluck buffet line, I found Walt and Ted discussing two cookbooks assembled in time for the reunion. The idea for the books was my inspiration, thank you very much. Even Mom, the venerable cook, conceded I was the family gourmet. Each book was filled with homemade creations, and the *Travis Family Cookbook* in particular had some real gems by these names: Spiced Pecans, Hot Broccoli Dip, and Cocktail Rye Bread Canapes for a sampling of appetizers; Beer Cheese Soup, Pink Party Salad, and Crunchy Carrot Mold as soups and salads. The main course recipes were Piquant Pork Chops, Fejoada, and Creamed Chip Beef. Of course, in this cookbook the largest section was reserved for desserts: Pistachio Chocolate Cake, Fudge Meltaways, and Rhubarb Custard Pie, just to name a few. Some of the recipes were innovative, most were delicious, and all of them would fail to qualify as part of any reputable diet. While most of the family submitted their recipes by simply writing down the ingredients and instructions, for some reason those Walt submitted also contained commentary.

GRASSHOPPER

Mix vanilla ice cream and milk to a thick malt mixture. Add shot of creme de menthe (clear or green—green adds color). Another delicious after-dinner drink, but be careful.

Note: If concerned about gaining weight, I suggest doing this with a partner: take off all clothes and watch for any kind of enlargement or body changes.

P.S. Send children to bed first.

BOURBON BALLS

2 ½ c. finely crushed vanilla wafers
1 c. chopped walnuts (or 1 c. coconut)
2 tbsp. cocoa
3 tbsp. corn syrup
1 c. powdered sugar (less if using coconut)
¾ c. bourbon
Extra powdered sugar to roll in

Mix all ingredients together and form small balls. Roll in powdered sugar. These are best if placed in a sealed canister and left for three to seven days. Fantastic!

Note: This is a holiday favorite of mine, and one year our dog, Moses, found them delightful. I returned home to find him passed out in an empty water dish and next to an empty canister holding approximately twenty bourbon balls. We revived him with water, and then the sickness began. We called the vet and were told not to let him drink or he'll be throwing up all night. I was so ticked off I picked him up and threw him in the snow bank. He staggered and went to sleep. It was about an hour before he was ready to come back in. Keep these bourbon balls away from pets.

It became readily apparent upon reading Walt's recipes he had learned his culinary and commentary skills as a young lad from hanging around Mom and me. Ted could not help but see the humor in it all.

"Walt, I wish I had your charisma and charm."

"What do you mean, Teddy?"

"Just look at this *Travis Family Cookbook* that your mom, Ruth, Evelyn, and Isabelle put together, at your insistence and constant prodding."

"So?"

"So, who else could have convinced all the headstrong women in the family to assemble a cookbook and have it dedicated to himself?" Indeed, the cookbook was dedicated to Walt for his "persistence and dedication in making this book a reality for everyone to enjoy and cherish as a family treasure and memento."

Walt laughed. "Keep watching me, Teddy—maybe you'll pick up a few pointers."

"Oh, Walt," I interjected, "I forgot to tell you we finally figured out what I.W.T.S.L. stands for. It means 'I Will Taste Some Lutefisk.' Your wife's family is Scandinavian, so you were probably making some big joke about it, right?" Lutefisk is, of course, a "unique" Minnesota tradition handed down from its Scandinavian ancestry. The meal consists of white fish filets left to soak in lye, then sealed and buried in the cold ground for several days before eating. For some reason, no recipe for lutefisk appeared anywhere in the Travis's cookbook.

"Great guess, Ruth. But keep trying."

In the fall, Walt's physical condition became increasingly worse. Since his bone marrow transplant, Walt had regularly been in hospitals for extended periods of time. Sadly, his body was still rejecting the transplant. He underwent two subsequent major operations, one to remove his gall bladder, and one to remove a large section of his colon. He also spent untold hours in chemotherapy. During Walt's first bout with cancer in the 1970s as a teenager, he lost most of his hair, and he resorted to wearing cleverly disguised wigs. During this second bout with the disease, he disposed of all such vanity and resorted to setting a trend with caps. Because Walt loved sports, his family bought him every type of sports hat they could find.

With the radiation treatments wreaking havoc on his sweat glands, Walt's skin had tremendous difficulty breathing and producing hair follicles. But he just accepted this in his normal jovial fashion and said, "What the hell, just call me chrome dome." The doctors had informed Walt there was little more they could do, but such news did not deter him. "We're all going to die," he would say, "so why should we waste time worrying about the day or the hour when it will happen?" Walt didn't waste much time. Instead, he spent it with his family. In September, Walt made one more trip to Lake Dunbar, which he knew would be his last. Although probably too ill to go, he went anyway, along with his wife; his parents, Eleanor and Paul; and his sister Rose's family. Walt spent his last Dunbar days simply enjoying the cabin, the woods, and the lake, while reminiscing about his nearly forty years at Whispering Pines. He also had to inspect the fire pit he had demanded Ted and I build.

Earlier in the summer, Walt had scoured the back roads of the Chippewa National Forest looking for an old rock quarry he had been to years ago with Grandpa Sam Travis. Walt knew the quarry would have rocks suitable for building a fire pit back at Lake Dunbar. He eventually found the quarry down near Lake Winibigoshish, but was not strong enough to move the rocks himself. So he left a detailed, penciled map at the cabin for Ted and me to follow on our next trip. Ted and I did drive up in July, along with our sons and their significant others. We followed his map, but I couldn't help but think how it was as illegible as the one drawn by Louis and Frank so long ago when my parents first tried to locate Lake Dunbar. Yet, the map was sufficient to lead us to the abandoned quarry where we loaded up the truck with several rocks of varying sizes. Back at Whispering Pines, we broke ground, hauled in sand, and arranged the heavy rocks in a semi-perfect circle. In the evening, we were enjoying a roaring fire all thanks to Walt's dreams. Reflecting on the same rocky circle later in fall, the eldest Travis grandson inspected the pit and was pleased with our efforts. "This place is now complete," he confided in me upon his return home. After a few evenings of Walt's Game and sleeping under the Schlitz Light, Walt and his family left Lake Dunbar with no regrets—and no dry eyes.

In early November 1993, my son Alex and I were driving together toward downtown Minneapolis where Walt had been admitted into a hospital for the last time. "I guess it doesn't sound too good," said Alex.

"Yeah, but you know Walt. He could recover and be out running around again tomorrow."

"I wanted to bring him something to cheer him up. Hospitals are so dry and colorless. But I didn't know what to bring," said Alex forlornly.

"Flowers are always nice, son."

"I wish I could bring him the Schlitz Light."

"Why the *Schlitz Light*?"

"You know, the one from the cabin."

"Yes, but why would you want to bring him the light?"

"Because he loves it. He's always talking about it when I come up to visit him. Last time, he brought out a photo album of pictures he took this year at the cabin, and he had seven or eight pictures of the Schlitz Light. Walt under the Schlitz Light, him holding the Schlitz Light, and more."

"I had no idea. Does he really want it?"

"I'm not sure. He recently gave me one of the pictures of him with the Schlitz Light telling me to show it to you and convince you to give it to him. But you know Walt is the family comedian. It's probably all a big joke, a way to generate laughs."

We walked into the hospital and eventually found Walt's room. The rest of the family was all there and in fairly good spirits. They greeted us warmly as Walt was awakening from a brief nap.

"Ruth! I didn't know you were coming or else I would have dressed up a bit."

"I could come back later if you want time to go out and get some new clothes." As usual, we laughed together over our mutual silliness.

"Walt, I feel so bad. I finally figured out what I.W.T.S.L. stands for: I Want the Schlitz Light. Why didn't you tell me?"

"I thought you'd try and charge me for it." More laughter.

"Walt, I've wanted to say this for a long time, and I have to tell you now. You've been a great inspiration in my life."

"I have?"

"Yes. I think it's amazing how you can maintain such a loving, comforting personality after all you've endured."

"I don't know," he said too humbly, "but if I've been an inspiration to you, then I want you to go out and be one for somebody else."

Within days, my dearest friend and nephew Walter Samuel Travis Hudson, the eldest member of the third generation of our family on Lake Dunbar, passed from the earthly midst of his family into the peace, calm, and rebirth of mortal death. It was likely no accident Walt was called home in the Christmas season, for he was a man of deep Christian faith. Not a self-righteous religious zealot, but a person who aimed for the example of love-filled living set forth by Jesus Christ. Advent season was also timely for Walt's death because he represented the eternal child present in every human being, the child with whom many identify at Christmas. Walt lived to be a man of barely forty years, but in his heart and in everyone's mind (especially mine), he was always a kid. One who made you laugh, lightened your burdens, and encouraged you to live your life in the here and now.

To the end, Walt maintained his childlike humor. He was not buried in a traditional suit. He chose, rather, baggy Minnesota Gopher workout pants, his favorite baseball cap with a large orange "W," and a blue Notre Dame sweatshirt with a green-and-gold leprechaun on the front atop the words "Fighting Irish." An eclectic collection, to say the least. The image of Walt as an ageless youth can only be set in one place, on the shores of Lake Dunbar. And for Walt, the cabin defined his whole life. Nearly every year of his life he spent at least one weekend there. No one other than my mom or me had spent more time at Whispering Pines than he did. Walt shared the hallowed cabin and pristine lake with those he cared about most in life—Grandpa and Grandma Travis; his parents, Eleanor and Paul; his sister Rose; and his lovely wife, Sophie.

I will never forget the chilling call I received late in the evening on the night Walt died. In the waning hours of his life, Walt cried out in near delirium to Sophie, asking her to call me immediately.

"Tell Ruth to get the truck ready because we need to go to the cabin."

No one knows for sure where the journey to heaven leads, but for me one thing is certain. Walt's journey to the afterlife included a long stop along the shores of Lake Dunbar. Not to be lost among these stories is this. He was not exceptional because of his tragic illness and early death. Walt was exceptional because of his God-given charm, and his wonderfully full life. As holocaust survivor and evangelist Corrie Ten Boom said, "The measure of one's life is not its duration but its donation." Walt gave all who knew him an important lesson on life: living it to the fullest, in the present. He was not preoccupied with the past or the future. Despite his tremendous suffering, especially in the last days, his spirit never faltered. His love for family and friends was generous and uplifting, beyond our mere mortal ability to understand. Walt's mission and purpose in both life and death had no bounds, no limits, no prejudices, and no judgment. It only knew abundance, understanding, and love.

Walt showed no anxiety over his imminent death. And why should he? Helen Keller once said that death is nothing more than passing from one room into the next. But there was a difference for Walt. In the next room, he would be able to sing, dance, laugh, and enjoy his eternal youth without the infirmities of a body limited by disease. Walt knew this, and therefore had little trepidation over the heavenly journey on which he was about to embark. Rather, he talked of being reunited with Grandpa Travis, Aunt Stella, Cousin Kate, and his paternal grandparents. Even more, Walt looked forward to his passing into the heavenly realm to meet God. Shortly before his death, he wrote these words: "When I die, I want to have an Irish wake and funeral, even though I'm not Irish. You can cry for half an hour, then you can party. I want you to be happy for me because I am with my Father. Dance and sing and celebrate for I will be in heaven."

Few, if anyone, who knew Walt would doubt he is indeed in heaven watching over his family in our daily lives, and especially on our journeys to Lake Dunbar. And all of us too will be reminded of him as we fish the murky Dunbar waters, hike her thick wooded shoreline, and sleep under her calm, starry skies. As a permanent memorial honoring Walt's contributions to Whispering Pines and to the Travis family's lives, we eventually dedicated a memorial bench in our woods above Dunbar's shores where anyone can now sit and enjoy the serene setting of Walt's favorite place on Earth. On the bench it reads, in part:

Walt Samuel Travis Hudson
1950 – 1993
I.W.T.S.L.

THE MOUSE HOUSE

THE FINAL DECADE OF THE TWENTIETH CENTURY WAS LIFE changing for both Ted and me. We each turned fifty and were empty nesters. We also had the constant nagging feeling our time on Earth was passing too quickly, and it was high time to pursue our respective lifelong dreams. For Ted, it meant a focus on writing and nature, so he was happiest on our frequent sojourns to Lake Dunbar. There, he relished in his early-morning wood chopping and planting routines before settling in for an afternoon of creative writing from his perch at the Whispering Pines kitchen table, looking out across Dunbar's waters for inspiration. While I, too, love our time up north, my life-long passion has focused on a different outlet for creativity: cooking. And though creating meals for my family and friends was certainly among life's greatest joys, I needed more. I needed to pursue this passion in a career, where I could experiment in a professional kitchen and produce award-winning meals for the general public. In short, I wanted to own and operate my own restaurant, which is exactly what I set out to accomplish.

Whether it be fate or coincidence, a very interesting prospect arose for us just as these thoughts were at their apex in my daily dreams. In Greenwood where Ted and I grew up, and where our mothers and several siblings still reside, there were always two or three cafés and coffee shops, but only one true restaurant: the supper club along pristine Carver Lake on the south edge of town. We of course had eaten there a hundred times over the years, and knew the original owners well, though they had long ago moved on to other pursuits. The current owners proved to have more enthusiasm than skill when it came to running a restaurant, and they soon abandoned town without notice, leaving the bank holding the bag. We contacted the bank, negotiated a fair price, scraped up enough for the down payment, and soon found ourselves the owners of Greenwood's finest and only full-service restaurant. What did Ted and I know about running a restaurant? Absolutely nothing. Did anything stop us from pursuing my dreams? Absolutely not.

Yet, as with most middle-class Americans who pursue dreams that require an initial investment of cash, we were faced with some hard choices in figuring out how to pay for my deep desire to purchase and operate this new restaurant. Should we raid our retirement accounts? The idea certainly didn't seem prudent. Deplete our savings? Another uncomfortable choice. Ted meekly raised the idea of selling Whispering Pines, but I quickly shot it down. Sell my childhood and lifelong family treasure? Unthinkable. However, in fairness to our situation, I was forced to at least contemplate the possibility. After all, this was my life's passion we were pursuing. Ted had no strong interest in opening a supper club and starting a new career as a bartender. Nevertheless, selling Whispering Pines just seemed too far beyond where I was willing to go. The only chance I would even pursue that option would be if we sold the place to our sons, under the promise it be kept it in the family and we be allowed continued visits, of course.

For the time being, selling Whispering Pines became a moot issue when Ted and I decided to take a much less drastic and emotional path: we sold our family home instead. We were the original owners of a modest four-bedroom home in Minneapolis, but if we were going to buy a restaurant a hundred miles away, what was the sense in keeping the house we wouldn't see much anyway? Besides, we felt something more daring and permanent about selling our house and going all-in on the restaurant. We were not doing this half-hearted with a backup plan of returning home; rather, we would enter this new venture and new phase of our lives with every ounce of our commitment. God help us.

Even though we decided to remain owners of the Whispering Pines cabin, we fully acknowledged our number of trips north would be significantly reduced in the short-term, as we spent every waking hour working in our new business. In fact, the number of annual visits dropped precipitously once we bought the restaurant, from eight or ten down to a mere one or two. Who, then, would check in on things at Lake Dunbar, including keeping the lawn trimmed and the cabin in continued tip-top shape? Alex was certainly willing, and made a few trips north during these years with his long-time girlfriend and their friends, although Alex now had two consuming time commitments of his own: working at his own job in finance for a local small business, and maintaining the new home in Minneapolis he had just bought *from us*! Ultimately, our concern about Lake Dunbar was for naught since the members of our extended Travis family eagerly stepped forward and took turns spending weekends up north.

In fact, it was during these years my sister initiated a wonderful new tradition at Whispering Pines: women's weekend. In late September of 1994, the Travis family women (my sister Eleanor and her daughter Rose, along with Jack's wife, Evelyn) embarked on an extended male-free cabin weekend, their first visit since losing Walt in the fall of '93. Oh, how I wish I could have joined them, but I couldn't exactly trust Ted to properly grill the New York strips and jumbo shrimp, now crowd-favorite menu items at my supper club on those busy Friday nights. I was able to experience the group's joy vicariously, however, upon reading their cabin journal entries later in fall.

September 25, 1994
Dear Ruth & Ted,
As always, it was very peaceful and relaxing here. Thank you! Many, many memories of Walt came flooding back this weekend. I needed this. It was hard to be here without him here physically, but I know he was with us in spirit. Was it his influence that resulted in us catching no fish, so none needed to be cleaned? Anyway, the leaves are gorgeous and the weather perfect. Thanks for letting us be here. I.D.W.T.S.L.!
Love, Eleanor

Hi Ruth & Ted,
It was definitely the "girls' weekend" here at the cabin. Maybe we should make it an annual tradition, but ONLY if Ruth comes next

year! As always, it was fun and relaxing. Even though I missed my boys, it feels great when every bit of stress leaves your body. On our walk, in addition to seeing a bear, I simply enjoyed the great, pure "fall scent" in the air along with the wonderful wind rustling through the trees. We caught no fish, but it was just fun riding in the green boat seeing the stunning fall colors. Despite all of our fun, we still feel a void, an empty feeling that comes and goes. I feel Walt, I see Walt, and of course I hear Walt up here. Most of all, I miss Walt. Thank you so much.
Love, Rose

Hi Ruth & Ted,
It was a picture-perfect, beautiful weekend with not a minute of inactivity. Sooo relaxing on the lake. I could see Walt running the motor, and the wind blowing through the cowlick in his hair at the age of fifteen. We shared lots of Walt stories, and I think he was the extra bright shimmering star we observed last night. He is definitely a presence here. It felt great to be at the cabin and I hope to be back soon.
Love, Evelyn

However, the idea of a women's weekend lost traction after the following year. While the same group of Travis women ventured north in the fall of 1995, and undoubtedly had a terrific time, they were mostly confined to the interior of the cabin due to a weeklong torrential rainstorm. The women of course again reflected upon their beloved Walt, and literally "heard" him during the weekend when they sang along to some cassette tapes of him singing cabin songs recorded years ago. I guess the skies did finally clear up on the very last day of their stay, and the gals were able to take their annual autumn walk through the adjacent woods. Each of them again wrote appreciative, heart-warming sentiments in the cabin book before they left, and it always makes me happy knowing the magic of Whispering Pines lives on in the hearts, minds, and memories of the extended family. As my niece Rose so aptly summarized, "I have so many wonderful thoughts and reflections sitting here on the dock. This is heaven and peace, and what being alive is all about. Thanks to Grandma Isabelle. Just look at what she started!"

My sister Eleanor visited the cabin again later in summer, along with her husband, Paul, and our mother, Isabelle. It had been a few years since Mom had traveled north to Whispering Pines, and she certainly enjoyed being back at Lake Dunbar. She resumed her favorite spot in the cabin kitchen, whipping up a scrumptious beef roast with vegetables, and she fondly took in the sights of the cabin and surrounding property she and Dad first laid eyes on some forty years ago. And of course they spent those days fishing the shores of the lake, followed by non-stop games of 500 Rummy long into the night. While their luck with fishing was less than stellar on this particular trip, Mom commandeered her old position at the stern of our little green fishing boat, producing Grandma's root beer in the wide-open channels of Lake Dunbar. My sister even commented in the journal how Mother "still runs the boat like she used to!" It makes me happy looking back and reading about the wonderful weekend Eleanor and Mom had together. It seemed so complete, so perfect, especially considering what I know now—the trip would be Isabelle's last journey to Lake Dunbar in this lifetime.

The other person to pick up the slack as a steward of Whispering Pines during these years when Ted and I were so occupied with the supper club was my son Eddie. For the past dozen years, he had loved Lake Dunbar from afar, seeing her only once per year, at most, during infrequent trips home from his life in California. He flew in for a long weekend visit in the late fall of '95, and after picking him up at the airport, we immediately drove north. It was mid-November and hardwood trees were already bare. As we drove farther and farther north, you could feel the temperatures drop like a balloon slowly leaking its helium, and the oncoming wintry landscape seemed ever more barren. It was well past 10:00 in the evening when we finally arrived at the cabin. All three of us bristled at the thirty-degree temps upon exiting the truck and visibly watched our warm, misty breath with every utterance into the cold, dark night. Ted and Eddie unloaded our gear while I started a fire in the old wood stove and rounded up electric blankets for the long, cold night ahead.

The warming effects of the fire and those cozy blankets surely did the trick, and none of us crawled out of bed until eleven the next morning. In fact, we were awakened by a ringing telephone, a wrong number. Thank goodness for the caller's error, or we all might have slept past noon. What little daylight we had left, given our late start, was filled with activity relating to our annual ritual of closing up the cabin for another season. Ted reignited a fire in the wood stove, and we kept it tended all through the day and into the night. The first task was to remove my sister Eleanor's green boat and the dock from the lake. Under even normal conditions, this task is arduous, given the hefty weight of our steel-framed dock. Atop our dock rests a series of wooden pallets made of six or seven two-by-fours held together by nails and metal staples. While they serve as sturdy platforms upon which to fish and launch our angling expeditions all summer, these beasts seemingly weigh a ton as we lift them one by one and carry each pallet up the steep embankment to rest against a strong pine tree throughout the winter. While I never shy away from that work when it's just Ted and me closing up the cabin, I certainly appreciated deferring my job to Eddie this time around. I then took on the equally challenging task of deep cleaning the cabin's interior and securing each of the single-paned windows with storm covers.

Because we had no snow yet covering the grounds of our property, we three spent the entire afternoon on outside work, including raking leaves from the yard then piling them into the forest, and also clearing those same leaves from the cabin's gutters (those never making it the final eight feet to the ground). Although some find raking tedious, I enjoy it thoroughly. If you've never experienced a good autumnal raking in the northern Minnesota forests, you really cannot appreciate the unique aroma of stirred-up earth and the refreshing feeling of working up a great sweat in cool, forty-degree breezes, looking out occasionally to the shimmering lake waters in the distance. Yes, I admit it involves a bit of work, but this routine brings me peace, serenity, and a sense of earthen spirituality I wish all could enjoy.

With a hard day's work complete and the sunlight fading, we retreated to our wonderful Whispering Pines cabin where I started to prepare a sumptuous dinner. You'd think perhaps one of my companions would offer to cook the evening meal, seeing as I was on a three-day respite from the restaurant where I had to cook every night. However, even if they had offered, I would've declined. Cooking is in my blood and brings me such joy I never consider it labor. Given all we accomplished today, and the thousands of calories burned, I decided we had earned a full-and-filling supper. From the old Norge refrigerator I took out the rib-eye steaks I'd purchased at the market in Grand Rapids on our voyage north. I marinated them in a secret recipe before broiling them in the oven until they sizzled with flavor and heat. I also served baked potatoes, a special green salad, and my signature corn cake side dish Ted and Eddie consumed in about a tenth of the time it took me to prepare it. For dessert we had Isabelle's favorite: coconut cream pie. Now lest you be too impressed, I should admit the dessert was nothing more than a pre-made graham cracker pie crust filled with stove-top coconut cream pudding, courtesy of the folks at Jell-O. While it may not be as fancy or truly homemade as the desserts I served back at the restaurant, this is a treasured family favorite, and a must-eat at Lake Dunbar.

We awoke the next morning at a much more respectable hour and immediately began the principal task of the day: removing all trace of water from the cabin's pipes and plumbing so as to avoid frozen, broken pipes over the winter. This was always our least-favorite task, not only because it took so much time, but also because it involved such unpleasant work. First, we'd shut off the pump to stop water flowing up from the well; then we'd turn on all faucets to let the remaining water empty out of the pipes. We next had to drain the gargantuan water heater sitting in the cabin's bathroom by affixing a garden hose to its base and letting the water flow freely out into the yard and on toward the lake. Next, I usually undertook the time-consuming task of removing all water from both the back of the toilet and from its bowl, which can become rather tricky when you get down to the very bottom of the toilet in a small, narrow space at the water's exit point. Meanwhile, Ted and Eddie spent an hour or so under the cabin in the dirt-floored crawl space, removing all water from the holding tank by lifting bucket after bucket filled with water and dumping it out in the woods. When that backbreaking task was complete, the two of them had to crawl back on their knees and backs to reach the remaining pipes, valves, and spigots to make sure every liquid drop was drained from the plumbing.

With the work now complete, it was time to close the door to the cabin both literally and figuratively on another season here at Lake Dunbar. It is always a melancholy time for me, thinking not only of the past year's journeys here, but also reflecting back to years gone by, and to all of those who have crossed this same threshold and created so many special memories in this sacred place. As we drove the two-hundred-plus miles back south, I had a great conversation with my son about his own planned journey of returning to Minnesota permanently the following spring. For the past five years, he was working in a small law firm in Los Angeles, and though he enjoyed the work, the people, and the warm California weather, he was on the verge of turning thirty, and felt as though life was calling him in a different direction.

When Eddie finally did arrive back in the midwest, he seemed to have two primary centers of activity: finding a new job, and spending as much time as possible along the shores of Lake Dunbar. Indeed he timed his arrival back in the Heartland to coincide with the opening of Whispering Pines for the 1996 season. Between his arrival in May and the start of a new job in mid-July, he and his brother, Alex, visited the cabin four times together and initiated several long-overdue projects. They mowed, trimmed the trees, reorganized the front entry, painted the bathroom, hung curtains in the kitchen and living area, stacked piles of wood, removed a huge stump from the middle of the front yard, stained the wooden pallets on the dock, painted the front door and exterior cabin trim, laid new carpet in the bunk and living rooms, and put several fine finishing touches in various nooks and crannies of the cabin. I was amazed on my next visit to see antique milk cans in each living room corner filled with brilliant birch branches from the forest floor, pine needle-scented potpourri in tin cups adorned with fishing-related stickers, and cabin-themed slipcovers over all of the living room pillows.

Alex and Eddie barely had time to fish on these first few journeys north, but they didn't seem to mind. In fact, they felt all the hard work justified their decision to forego down-home cabin cooking in favor of dinners out at some of the area's finest eateries. They enjoyed Swiss mushroom chicken sandwiches at The Hill in Squaw Lake, pizza at the Trail's End in Blackduck, and their favorite, steaks at The Dockside on the edge of Island Lake. The Dockside served the best food around, in our opinion, in a picture-perfect setting that justified their higher prices. From the vantage point of any seat in the restaurant, a patron could look out across expansive Island Lake to watch birds in flight, fishermen in pursuit of a catch, and vivid sunsets to remember forever. Ted and I even spent an anniversary or two dining there. This northern Minnesota culinary hideaway burned down at the beginning of the twenty-first century, and now we can only reminisce fondly of those special evenings at The Dockside.

During these mid-1990s journeys north, Alex and Eddie often brought along their infamous friend, Mike, a character to say the least. We too enjoyed it when Mike accompanied our whole group on trips to the cabin, for he worked as hard or harder than anyone else, and could always be counted on for an unexpected one-liner, some fabulous grilled dinners, and a tasty cocktail. Mike was also instrumental in steering the boys away from work once in a while and back onto the water to do what we came up here so many years ago to do: go fishing. Mike grew up in southern Missouri where the Mighty Mississippi is wide and the rivers of the hill country plentiful, fast flowing, and full of fish. He gladly joined Eddie and Alex on numerous "men's weekends" at Lake Dunbar where these boys would fish all morning, work all afternoon, and sit around the fire pit shooting the breeze 'til the wee hours of the night. As for the fishing, Mike clearly took it more seriously than the rest. Though he could laugh and joke with the best of them around the evening fire pit, a morning fishing outing was meant for one thing and one thing only: earnest fishing.

At the start of each men's weekend, Mike would volunteer to drive into town to commandeer the requisite bait: minnows for crappies, wax worms for large-mouth bass, and leeches to catch the feisty and elusive walleye pike. Mike also made sure his fishing companions always embarked with sufficient gear for a long morning outing, including spinners and hooks, plenty of replacement fishing line, and a huge hot mug of black coffee to carry them through until lunch. And while Mike was certainly hopeful the entire group would catch their limit of fish so he'd have plenty to grill for dinner at Whispering Pines, I always had the sense Mike preferred to come out on top in the macho competition to see who caught the biggest and greatest number of fish. In addition to my own few experiences with Mike on Lake Dunbar, I specifically recall an outing he had with my sons in the fall of '96.

Alex was off to a fast start, catching his limit of northern pike before anyone else could catch a thing. Mike apparently became a bit testy when asked to pass along a fourth fathead minnow for Alex to bait his hot fishing hook. In fairness, as I was later told, Mike's irritability may also have been due in part to the fact that his companions had indulged in a few too many of Mike's potent Long Island iced teas around the fire the night before, and thus their near-inability to arise from bed at the appropriate fishing hour the following morning. When Mike did finally rouse them from their slumber, he basically had to cook their breakfast and do all of the boat prep work because the others could barely dress themselves and get to the dock. So it is quite understandable what transpired when, within minutes of baiting his hook for the fourth time, Alex yelled, "I got one."

"Geez, dude, do you have to yell and scare away all the fish for the rest of us?" Mike replied gruffly as he began reeling in his own line in order to hold the net for Alex's fish. Yes, in addition to running the motor and trying to troll for a keeper-sized walleye of his own, Mike had to man the net since his bleary-eyed companions had enough trouble just keeping their heads up.

"Yeah, man, it's a monster. This one is definitely bigger than my first three," Alex asserted, again much too loud for Mike's liking. Besides, Mike probably thought, did he really need to mention his three-to-nothing lead in fish again? "Here she comes, oh man, she's a fighter. This one might just be for the record books!" Alex was gaining in excitement by the moment. Apparently the prospect of finally besting Mike at fishing was the tonic he needed to overcome the headache from last night's activities. All eyes were darting back and forth between the severely bent end of Alex's pole and the surface of the water. Each man wanted to catch the first glimpse of the fish that just might finally top the record-sized catch proudly landed by Grandma Isabelle's boyfriend Gus so many years ago. A picture of Gus holding his prized fish still hangs above the kitchen sink at the cabin, in honor of his achievement and as an incentive to Travis fishermen ever since.

The excitement of the moment evaporated more quickly than a raindrop in Death Valley as soon as Alex's record-breaking catch showed itself just below the surface of Dunbar's waters. Alex must have had his fishing line out a very far distance, long enough to reach the weedy edges of the nearest shoreline, for attached to his hook with the minnow buried somewhere inside was the largest patch of lake vegetation any of them had ever seen. No one knew what to say. Alex felt obligated to say nothing, seeing as he'd already caught his limit of northern pike. Though Eddie admitted an inclination to laugh, he was behind in the count by three fish already, so he didn't really have the moral or competitive standing to mock his younger brother.

Thus all eyes drifted toward Mike, who had by now put up with about all he could stand from these two clowns and was ready to throw them both into the lake. Turning with a sneer toward Alex who had just proudly forecast a "monster-sized fish" on his line, Mike fixed his gaze back toward the lake in disgust, uttering his thoughts just barely loud enough for Alex to hear. "It's a fucking weed. . . ."

While I normally am not fond of such language in any setting, I could certainly feel Mike's frustration. And given all that he's done to help around Whispering Pines, he continues to be a valued guest, and he can return to Dunbar's shores any time he pleases.

Regret to say, but not all of the guests at Whispering Pines in the mid-1990s could be considered welcome. There were a number of visitors who left their mark, not by writing in the cabin journal but rather by depositing tiny tracks of excrement on my handsome cabin floors. Now, many people have questioned the sincerity of my love for the outdoors, given my extremely strong aversion to creatures smaller than a baseball. Admittedly, I dislike bugs, spiders, flying insects, and every other creepy, crawly piece of God's creation. Even more, I detest most anything in the rodent family, particularly mice. As far as I'm concerned, they are pointless rather than cute, and the thought of a mouse crawling across my foot sends shivers up my spine. Nevertheless, I'll put up with all of these critters as long as they keep to their natural space; namely, outdoors. I well understand that when I'm in the woods or on the lake I am invading their natural habitat, but I want them out of mine. Don't dare set foot, paw, or whisker inside my cabin.

Apparently these furry vermin can read neither my mind, body language, nor screams to "keep out," for we've had many an uninvited whisker-nosed guest at Whispering Pines over the years. And whether it can be blamed on global warming or some other unintelligible reason, the mice of Lake Dunbar were especially active in burrowing their way into our cabin in the middle of the 1990s. We tried every imaginable effort to keep them out, mostly without success. We covered up the basement air vents with mesh screens that they promptly chewed to pieces. We set traps with delicious morsels of cheese that they somehow stole without getting themselves sliced in half. And we placed boxes of sweet-smelling rodent poison at strategic locations around the cabin, only to have them sit uneaten week after week all season. You may question the intelligence of the local Finnish descendants that live around Lake Dunbar, but you cannot debate the caginess of its mouse population. They lived the high life at Whispering Pines during these pivotal years of my cabin stewardship, and I couldn't stand it one bit.

Dead or alive, these mice showed up everywhere. Eleanor found a tiny rotting corpse in the kitchen sink, Eddie discovered a pair floating in the bathroom toilet, Alex aromatically detected a long-dead mouse at the bottom of an antique decorative vinegar jug in the living room, and Rose arrived at the cabin late one night to the horrific scene of a triple rodent murder-suicide right in the front entryway. Why can't they take their fatal activities outdoors as God intended? What is this driving need to spend their final minutes curled up inside the cabin? We named it Whispering Pines, not "The Mouse House." It is especially disturbing for me to think about these nasty creatures decomposing on my cabin floor, or worse yet, in the sink or atop any furniture. Yuck.

And yet, it could be worse, for me that is. Dying in the cabin is one thing; making Whispering Pines a mouse's personal playground in quite another. Over the years, we've witnessed some crazy sights from the Lake Dunbar mouse community, particularly one mischievous, acrobatic, and death-defying critter in the summer of '98. My sister Eleanor was the first to detect this little bugger as she described so well in the journal at the end of her stay:

What a great week we've had, though not without a bit of drama. First, we encountered a leaky pipe, and quickly called a plumber who drove all the way from Squaw Lake to help us out. Shortly after he left, our next crisis began. We heard a creature in the attic above the refrigerator, and assumed it was a mouse, so we set a trap and went fishing. While we were gone, it stole the bait without setting off the trap. That night while everyone else was sleeping, I heard the dang thing again in the ceiling, and pulled the covers up over my head, though in retrospect I'm not sure what good that did! My grandson Pete was in the opposite bunk and must have heard it as well, because a few minutes later when we both heard the creature running down the hall toward the bunk room, he screamed "Grandma, there's a mouse!" Bravely, we each jumped up out of our beds and reached for the closest defensive (though likely useless) weapons: a flashlight and a pair of pants. We slowly and cautiously made our way toward the hall and eventually the main room, but could see nothing in the dim glow of the flashlight. What a sight we must have been, looking for the mouse in the living room at four in the morning. Not seeing the mouse anywhere, we then devised a homemade trap involving three brown bags to protect us. Not surprisingly, it didn't work, but it gave us sufficient false comfort to go back to bed.

The next day, our mouse saga continued. We purchased some sticky paper and more professional traps at the Max Store, which we set with cheese before heading out again for more fishing. I knew these traps worked since I even snapped my own finger in the process of placing the cheese in the optimal spot. Ouch. Yet again, the critter stole the cheese without setting off the spring-loaded trap. This was one smart mouse! Later that night while playing Scrabble, we spotted him running across the living room floor. We immediately and unsuccessfully tried to catch him, but he evaded capture. Now we were just plain mad, so I loaded the trap with both peanut butter and cheese and set it in the middle of the floor surrounded by the store-bought sticky paper that "guaranteed results." Apparently, the only guarantee was to the mouse himself, because he got the results he wanted: he ate the cheese and somehow avoided both the trap and the paper.

It was late in the evening on our last day, and we were determined to get this mouse (hoping, of course, that there was only one). This time, I loaded the trap with more cheese (which by now we'd proven he likes) and set the whole thing right on top of the sticky paper, leaving no navigable trail for the mouse to get to or from that trap. We packed up the Scrabble game and started to make our way toward bed when we finally heard the delightful sound for which we'd all been waiting: "snap!" Racing eagerly into the kitchen we were soon face to face with our death-defying mouse, and yet again he'd avoided fate, almost. While the poor creature's tail was firmly trapped by the mechanical spring, the rest of the mouse sat looking up at us pleadingly, his paws stuck in place on the sticky paper. He was still alive! Paul finally did the deed, putting the mouse out of his misery (or perhaps putting him out of our misery). I had mixed feelings, though, about the mouse's demise. I was proud and relieved that man had finally conquered mouse, but just a tad bit sad that such a seemingly smart, clever, and persistent critter had been killed.

I adore my sister Eleanor, of course, but cannot for the life of me relate to her feeling bad for that darn mouse. And apparently her expressed hope that there was "only one" turned out to be far from reality. In fact, this clever, persistent mouse had an identical twin who showed himself barely a month later when my niece Rose traveled north to Lake Dunbar with her husband, Patrick, and their two boys. As she explained in the cabin journal:

We've had a perfect few days here at Lake Dunbar, with sunny days and clear, cool evenings. We saw a lot of wildlife on this trip—deer, fox, skunks, bald eagles, loons, and unfortunately mice. We were visited each night by these furry little critters. They were quite wise as they did not come out at night until the boys were in their beds. Each night between eleven and midnight, they would scamper about wildly. At one point, a particularly fearsome-looking one sat behind the wood stove staring at us for a minute or so before taking off like a mad man, running a zigzag path between the stove and the kitchen table. We think they may be coming in from behind the refrigerator since that is where the scratching sounds are. Those rascals are quite good at licking the peanut butter off of the traps without getting caught, but we did manage to capture two of them. Anyway, we had a wonderful time as always as we feel so fortunate to be part of this Travis clan. Thanks to Ruth and Ted for letting us stay and to Grandpa and Grandma Travis for starting it all!

By far my favorite cabin mouse adventure involved my special mouse-hunting hero: the boys' weed-hating friend, Mike. He traveled north for a late-season visit with Alex and Eddie that year and put an end to the mouse shenanigans for good. Indeed, we saw few if any mice at Whispering Pines ever again following that landmark trip. As Eddie explained in the cabin journal:

An absolutely wonderful weekend here. We arrived late in the evening, started up the old wood stove, and soon went to bed. We all heard mice in the night. In the morning we chopped wood and finished a successful first round of fishing before setting off into the woods for a long walk. Knowing there were deer hunters about, I ran back into the cabin to grab some bright orange-colored hats from the bunkroom dresser. Upon opening the top drawer, I saw a little gray mouse jump down the back of it and into the drawer below. I yelled for Mike, who came racing into the cabin with his hand-held BB gun. He eagerly tracked the mouse down to the very bottom drawer where he discovered two more.

With one shot he gutted the first mouse, then wounded a second before the third got away.

We took all of the dresser drawers outside, finished off the wounded mouse, and realized that these guys had been building a well-stocked condominium shelter for the long winter: acorns for food in one drawer, chewed-up clothing as bedding in another, a bathroom in the third (as evidenced by the numerous mouse tracks), and a lounge area in the fourth. Despite our scrubbing, you can still see the bloodstains from Mike's kill in the bottom drawer, though we resisted his desire to also leave a chalk out-lined imprint of where the body came to its final rest.

The thought of that third escapee mouse was clearly on Mike's mind the rest of the day, and he even made a sighting of it in the front entry toward evening. Mike immediately set to work creating the perfect mousetrap from his educated and practical mechanical background. He then strategically placed the trap in the hallway and chose to sleep in the lower single bunk in order to have a first-hand view of the potential murder scene. Within two minutes of getting into bed and turning out the lights, we heard the proverbial "snap!" and indeed the final mouse was done.

Truth be told, Whispering Pines was not the only family resi-dence to experience the mysterious sounds of creepy, crawling crit-ters in this last decade of the twentieth century. During a late-season trip to Lake Dunbar, Ted and I were unexpectedly called upon to counsel our youngest son through an ordeal at his own home that involved squeaking that sounded awfully similar to a mouse. Sleeping soundly in the cabin that night, we were suddenly awakened by the ring of the telephone as Alex called us in a panic. He and his fiancé had spent the last two days with the family at Whispering Pines, but returned early so Alex could play in a summer baseball league game. As they entered the dark house, Alex heard a strange noise coming from the kitchen. With baseball bat in hand, my son's fiancé climbed the stairs, with brave Alex close behind. The loud, squeaking noise was in the kitchen and they approached it cautiously. The unidentifiable sound could only be coming from one of two places: the refrigerator or broom closet, which stood side by side.

The most likely candidate was the broom closet. Alex figured that Ralph the cat had dragged in some small rodent which was hiding, albeit noisily, in the closet. Alex got on the phone and called the cabin. He wasn't looking for advice; rather, he wanted a witness in case he and his fiancé were struck down in cold blood by the mysterious intruder. With trepidation, Alex opened the closet door while she waited with the baseball bat over her head ready to strike down the intruding animal. Whoosh! The door swung open, but nothing jumped out. I listened on the other end, relaying information to Ted, interpreting the events from back home. Alex returned to the phone.

"Well, there's nothing in the closet and the noise is getting louder. It must be the refrigerator," Alex reported.

"What in the world could it be?" I asked, confounded by the riddle.

With complete seriousness, Alex offered a possibility. "Do you think that it could be coming from an egg that hatched in the fridge?" Anti-climactically, the mysterious noise turned out to be a broken refrigerator motor. For years to come, Alex would endure endless teasing about his heroism in attempting to rescue a lonely chick that had beaten the odds and hatched in the family icebox.

As difficult as it was, living so much farther from Lake Dunbar and unable to see her often given our non-stop duties at the restaurant, there was a significant advantage in moving back to our hometown of Greenwood in southern Minnesota. Both Ted and I were able to see our mothers several times each week as these two strong women entered their eighties. I was especially fond of living once again within minutes of my mother, Isabelle Travis, the matriarch of our family. Over the prior decade, Ted and I had spent a year living in northern Oregon then another in Colorado, chasing after the high-tech jobs of Ted's career path and experiencing more of America. As exciting as those years were and despite all the new sights we saw and friends we made, a corner of my heart always yearned to come home to Greenwood and be nearer to my lone remaining parent. It's funny, of course, to say these things out loud, especially given how fast I wanted to get out of town after graduating high school forty-plus years ago. Yet I hope it is somewhat normal to have felt a re-ignited flame of love and appreciation for my own mother, now that the primary years of my own mothering were fading into the distance.

Thankfully, Isabelle was still in very good health as we moved to Greenwood in the mid-1990s. Notwithstanding her advancing age, she was arguably the picture of health for an eighty-two-year-old. My mother walked several miles a day around town, rain or shine, in all four seasons. Every day I would see her, either during breakfast down at the café or out at our restaurant where she drove for lunch or dinner several times each week simply to enjoy a good meal and proudly tell all the patrons that her daughter Ruth was the head chef and owner. On my relatively few days off, we would also drive over to Winona together for some shopping or to meet other friends and relatives for lunch. I relished every moment of these days, given all the time with Mom that I'd missed over the decades and not knowing how many more years that we might yet have together. That uncertainty came racing to my mind one morning in late October when I received a call from the lady at the town coffee shop informing me that Mom had collapsed during breakfast and was on her way to the hospital in an ambulance.

I jumped in the car and sped off to Winona, without even telling Ted where I was headed since I didn't have time to wait for him to return from his morning walk in the wooded Bass River Valley. I met my sister and brother in the hospital's emergency room and we were quickly assured by the EMTs that Mom had experienced some type of blood sugar event; either she forgot to take her morning medication or did not ingest the right combination of food. She was released that same day and we returned her home and back to her routine without much trouble. Now, Isabelle Travis has always been a strong-willed, independent woman and this little "episode" was not going to slow her down, no matter what her children said. We did our best to reassure ourselves that she would take it easy and remember to take her medicine, but I must admit that I didn't sleep too well that night or for many of the nights that followed. Perhaps my mothering duties weren't over after all.

Mom indeed picked up right where she left off, refusing to let a simple case of public unconsciousness either slow her down or embarrass her. She continued to appear at the café for coffee and a light breakfast each morning and we resumed our frequent dinners and shopping excursions as if nothing had ever happened. I admire that about my mother, to be honest. Her tenacity and zest for living in the moment are qualities that I strive to emulate when I reach her station in life. Well, the busyness of running our restaurant continued and the days often flew by in the passage of hours that seemed like minutes, weeks that felt like days. Throughout this time, I often noticed in Mom a slightly faltering memory, but I simply chalked it up to the fact that she was now closing in on eight-four years of age.

Quite frankly, I also couldn't very well criticize my mother's memory when my own was often in doubt as I ran through the restaurant kitchen wondering where I last left my spatula. So it came as a strong shock but little surprise a year later when I received yet another jarring phone call, informing me that Mom was in the hospital with what they suspected to be a minor heart or vascular event. She stayed at the hospital in Winona for several days, as her children and health professionals tried our very best to assess exactly what was going on and then how to move forward. After being released from St. Luke's, we all agreed to let her return home on the condition that she assent to have a nursing service monitor her around the clock. That plan lasted about a week, as my strong-willed and independent mother was not about to have her life and home overtaken by a stranger. My siblings and I agonized over what to do next, as I'm sure so many in our situation have done as well. Ultimately, we concluded that the only realistic plan was to move mother to a very safe, loving, and comfortable full-time nursing facility in nearby Rollingstone where she would still be close to home and also surrounded by people she knew and loved.

As with the first plan, this second one lasted about a week. Mother was apoplectic with anger at the whole situation and repeatedly demanded to see her grandson the lawyer (my son, Eddie) who would assuredly get her out. Right or wrong, we acceded to her request, but with a compromise that we deemed in her own best interest: Mother moved into a home with five other adults in our hometown of Greenwood, all of whom needed only minor but constant care and assisted living. Being back in her hometown surroundings seemed to relax her a bit for a while, though she often looked longingly out the front window, aching to traverse the winding paths of her previous daily walks. One day, to no one's surprise, mother apparently decided enough was enough and she snuck out the back door and walked straight for the nearest pay phone, demanding to go home.

Everything about this ordeal was emotionally draining. There's no manual on how to deal with your aging parent and his or her unique circumstances. Everyone offers advice and varying opinions, but ultimately it comes down to making very difficult decisions for the person who brought you into this world. Our difficult decision was eventually to move Mom back to the calm surroundings of the nursing care in Rollingstone where we knew that she'd be safe, kept healthy, and had friends. Certainly, my siblings and I had been through a harrowing ordeal with my father's unexpected and early death so many years ago, but that was something that happened to me and my family. These new challenges with Mother were happening with us, where we had some degree of control over the situation, and I prayed to God that our decisions were for the best.

Indeed, over time, I think our decision was right. Despite an expected period of adjustment, Mom eventually settled in and calmed down. We all visited Mom as often as possible and frequently took her out for lunch or other appropriate adventures. Within a year, it actually got to the point of seeming normal, as odd as that may sound, and I was confident that Isabelle Travis had fully entered the next stage of her life and was exactly where she needed to be. Yet there was still an important and emotional decision left un-made: what to do with Mom's quaint rambler house on the southeast edge of town in Greenwood. I remember vividly how thrilled she was when this modest home came up for sale in the winter of 1985, for it sat on a dead-end street and adjacent to the town ball fields and public pool.

Mom loved baseball, especially the amateur variety, and I don't think she missed a single game on those beloved fields, except when she was up at the cabin on Lake Dunbar or off on one of her many coach bus tours to Nashville, Branson, or other distant destinations.

In the autumn of 1998, my siblings and I had yet another tough call to make: what to do with the small home that Mom certainly adored, but in which she had not lived for a year, and to which she would never conceivably return. It couldn't sit unoccupied forever, and Mom eventually would need the money sitting in her home's equity to pay for the rest of her life. I suppose, intellectually, we all know that a day like this will come, but that doesn't make it any easier emotionally on the day such reckoning arrives. I certainly wasn't ready for it and I don't think my brother or sister were either. While I knew in my head that selling Isabelle Travis's home was the right thing to do for Mom, I couldn't help but feel deep in my heart that I was betraying her.

After many discussions and much hand-wringing, the eventual sale of Mom's home was set in motion and we then began the gut-wrenching process of sifting through her belongings to determine what mementos would be kept in the family and what items would be auctioned off along with her home. On the last weekend in September 1998, the entire Travis family gathered around the modest tan rambler and listened as the auctioneer began his solemn duty to methodically yet caringly go about his work. Even though I had already laid claim to photos and any other family memorabilia of personal value, I still found myself bidding on a number of items, perhaps in a subconsciously silly attempt to keep as much of my mother with me as possible. I was careful not to bid when others in the family seemed intent on an item and I have to say that it all just seemed to work out amongst us, unscripted. I bought Mom's sofa, the brass bed from her guest room, an old red AM radio that sat in her kitchen, and the wooden desk chair that once supported my father at his desk at Travis Sales & Service down on Main Street.

As much as obtaining these items brought me comfort, it all fell away as the auctioneer began taking bids on the house itself. I remember standing alongside my niece Rose and sister Eleanor as two bidders kept ratcheting the price higher and higher. Feeling wet tears race down my cheeks, I offered the girls a handkerchief to help wipe theirs. I sensed strongly that none of us wanted it to be over, for when the auctioneer's final gavel hit the podium, a wonderful chapter would then be written and my mother's story of full independence would seemingly and finally come to its end.

PART III

EDDIE

Travis Cabin Company

TEN MILES SOUTH OF GRAND RAPIDS, MINNESOTA, ALONG PIC-
turesque Itasca County Road 10, sits a nice-looking dairy farm owned
by Herbert Beer. The setting is a both a farmer's and outdoorsman's
dream, for its pasture and cropland are surrounded by a thick pine
forest, and three hundred yards to the east flows the Mississippi
River. This adolescent stage of the Mighty Miss defies the grandeur
of her wider girth from St. Paul down to New Orleans, for this stretch
of the river in Itasca County meanders quietly and narrowly like an
overgrown stream, with little inkling of what she will become in a
matter of miles farther south. Herb Beer's farm itself might be just
as understated, for it would be difficult to distinguish from others
across Minnesota. Dozens of cattle, a few hundred acres of plantable
land, and several blue-green outbuildings dot the landscape within
her boundaries. It's hardly any quainter than its neighbors. Yet an
image of the Beer farm is burnished into my mind and never to be forgotten, for I've laid eyes on this farm more times than I can possibly
count, on every trip north to Whispering Pines these past forty-some
years. I never met the man, truth be told, and never once set foot on
his land, but Herb Beer was an integral part of my childhood, thanks
to the woman who made the wonder years of my youth so magical.

In my mind as a child, and still to this day, I consider myself to be
one of the luckiest people on earth—a grandchild of Isabelle Travis.
She was a force of nature and nurture, a unique presence and voice in
my life as long as I can remember. If you weren't having fun while with
this wild and wonderful woman, then you either weren't paying attention or didn't truly know how to live. Spending time with Grandma
Isabelle at her home in Greenwood was a special treat, and I began

traveling there frequently on a Greyhound bus from Minneapolis, all by myself, as soon as my parents would allow it. I continued doing so all the way through college, the tradition ending only when I moved to California and switched to air travel instead. Grandma Isabelle always welcomed me with open arms, a hearty laugh, and a bear hug. She was a true people person, choosing to spend time with family or friends rather than sitting home alone. Isabelle would take me down to the town café for morning coffee, riding along as she drove her twice-daily school bus route, and then out to dinner for either jumbo shrimp and hamburger steak at the Rockwell House, or an all-you-can-eat fish fry at Trout Camp along the Mississippi River. During the many years she dated Gus, we'd bring him along on our eating adventures. Because I never knew my Grandpa Sam, who died before I was born, Gus was a grandfather figure to me, and a person who almost equaled the antics and fun of my grandmother. After dinner, we'd all head back to Isabelle's house and fire up the turntable on her mammoth-sized stereo console in order to tap our toes and occasionally dance a few steps to the beat of her favorite country-western artists, including Mo Bandy, Patsy Cline, Frank Jones, and Tammy Wynette.

However, as much fun as we had at Grandma's house in Greenwood, my best memories of growing up with her took place at our cabin on Lake Dunbar, as well as on the long ride to get there. Whether alone or with others, the routine was always the same—and I loved every minute of it. After stopping at Aunt Eleanor's to say hello and pick up some tasty baked treats, we'd head north along Minnesota 65, about as straight and northbound a road as you can imagine, curving only slightly and infrequently to navigate around some of Minnesota's infamous ten thousand lakes. At Mora we'd stop for a hot beef sandwich or piece of sour cream raison pie, depending on the time of day, then keep striving northward toward our personal Polaris in the heart of the Chippewa National Forest. To break up the long drive, Grandma would always point out landmarks as a way of proving our progress, and these landmarks became a tradition. Failing to spot one would be considered sacrilegious, unthinkable, and Isabelle never missed any of them. The little red cabin sitting on a lonely but visible island in the middle of Big Sandy Lake, the

Continental Divide alongside Highway 46 in the Avenue of Pines, the café in Deer River where Aunt Eleanor once found a fly in her tomato soup, and of course the sprawling farm of Herb Beer south of Grand Rapids. Spotting these mileposts in fact became a contest, and the first person to see them earned the cashless prize of immense pride in knowing he or she cleverly saw the marker before anyone else.

We only knew the farmer's name from the lettering on his mailbox, which hung precariously close to the graveled shoulder of County Road 10 as we flew past in one of Grandma's successive Chryslers. It was enough for us to leave the real story of the farmer with the funny-sounding last name shrouded in mystery, for it allowed us to focus on the most important part of his existence for us: being the first person to shout, "I see Herb Beer's farm!" as we sped past without stopping. Curiosity eventually got the better of me as 1999 turned over to 2000. My grandmother was increasingly frail and living in a nursing home in Rollingstone, her days of traveling with me to our family cabin long gone, never to happen again. I decided to see what I could find out about old Herb Beer, this mythical man who unknowingly provided us with so much pleasure over the years. As it turns out, he and Isabelle Travis had much more in common than we could have ever imagined. They were the same age, and both drove school buses for over twenty years. Herb was born on the eve of World War I to parents named Mary and Joseph. Apparently "Jesus Beer" didn't sound like a good enough name to them. In addition to driving school buses, he was an Army veteran, a miner, and a farmer.

Herb passed away in 1998, just a year before I started my search for him, and about the same time Grandma Isabelle moved out of her home in Greenwood. The Beer farm is still in the family, thankfully, as Herb's sons Marvin and Edward live on the homesteaded property. Who knows, maybe I'll stop in sometime and introduce myself, though it may be slightly awkward because I feel as though I've known them for forty years, and they have no clue about the Travis's existence. Actually, such a visit may not be necessary, for I am comforted to know that just as Grandma and I made a contest out of who could be the first to spot the name of "Herb Beer" on his hanging mailbox, so too will I play the same game with my children, as they may someday play it with theirs. After his passing, and due to his long-standing service to Itasca County as a member of the Township and Conservation boards, Herb Beer's legacy lives on as the namesake of a boat landing along the shore of the Mississippi River, just yards from his lifelong farm. There's an engraved wooden sign posted along County Road 10 to prove it, and forevermore on every single journey northward, the first person in the Travis family car to spot it and shout the name of "Herb Beer" is the champion for that particular milepost.

I was born in the middle of the tumultuous 1960s, and given the baptized name Thomas. I'm told my first out-of-town trip was, naturally, to Lake Dunbar. Needless to say I cannot recall the journey, but after so many years of making this wonderful northward trek, they all blend into one constantly flowing memory, interspersed with specific recollections of my immediate and extended families. In 1968, when I was two and just beginning to experience some stability and routine from the first two years of life, and relying upon the rock-solid trust of my parents, they pulled the rug out from underneath me by changing my name from Thomas to Theodore Jr., or "Eddie" for short. Their version of an explanation is always a bit sketchy and often changes. The way I see it, this was the summer of love when so much in the world was changing, for better or for worse, and I got swept up in my parents' atmosphere of "anything goes." Whatever the truth, one thing is for certain: Lake Dunbar has been an integral part of my life for longer than I've carried my legal first name. Regardless of what I'm called, I'm blessed to be part of this ongoing life experiment with them on the shores of Lake Dunbar—the place where relationships are forged and cemented, tested, and rewarded. It is the place where I still feel the physical presence of those in the family who are no longer with us. I tend to be a spiritually minded person, and Whispering Pines is definitely mystical to me. I have a reverence for its inhabitants and its history, even to the point of feeling reluctant to make any significant changes to the cabin, for fear it would no longer be quite the same for me as it was for them.

Nevertheless, the beginning of a new millennium seemed an appropriate time for an inevitable major change at Whispering Pines: passing the torch of cabin ownership to a new generation of the Travis family. While my parents continued their summertime visits, the frequency diminished once they had moved back to their hometown of Greenwood to run the restaurant. Responsibility for cabin maintenance therefore fell mostly to my brother, Alex, and me, as we were both able to make more frequent trips north than our overworked parents. Still, our parents, Ted and Ruth, were not ready to fully relinquish the reigns of cabin stewardship, and even thought about living more full-time on Lake Dunbar if and when they ever retired. For our part, Alex and I too were not ready to take on the financial and handyman burdens of lake-home ownership since both of us were starting families of our own.

As the unofficial and unpaid family lawyer, I eventually stumbled upon a solution to which everyone agreed. We would form a family limited liability company under Minnesota law, and each member would own a given percentage share based upon our individual capital contributions. At some point in the future, Ted and Ruth will likely sell more or even all of their shares when we're all good and ready. In the meantime, this change in legal ownership accomplished many objectives—keeping the cabin in the family, sharing the financial burdens and work, protecting this treasured family asset from a frivolous personal injury lawsuit, and allowing for a managed process of eventually passing the cabin on to future generations more fully. The only true challenge with this arrangement was devising a name for the company, as required by Minnesota law. After some degree of brainstorming, the light bulbs went off, and a perhaps obvious choice was made. Our company, whose sole purpose was to own and operate the Whispering Pines cabin on the shores of Lake Dunbar, was officially registered as "The Travis Cabin Company, LLC."

We inaugurated this period of Travis Cabin Company (TCC) cabin ownership with a men's weekend in late 1999. I journeyed north on a crisp October weekend with my father, Ted, and brother, Alex, hoping for a few days of rest, relaxation, and fishing, as well as an evening at The Hill in Squaw Lake. My father, of course, had work for us to do as soon as we arrived, including raking the yard before winter, transplanting a few of his beloved pine trees, and the required tasks of closing down Whispering Pines for another year. My father eloquently summarized our time in the Whispering Pines journal upon concluding our fine weekend journey:

Well, here we are at the end of another year, as well as the end of a thousand-year millennium. I wonder who if anyone was here at the end of the prior one. It was a fantastic weekend, sixty-five degrees and gorgeous. We trimmed trees around the yard and deep into Ted's Wood. A large jack pine tree went down at the far end of our property near the new neighbors, so I used my chain saw and saved four growing Norway Pines in the process. I'm happy to see so many of our trees doing so well. The stars last night were spectacular as we watched them from the dock, and then listened as a pack of wolves or coyotes started howling. After a lone animal then sang an amazing solo, we all headed to bed, lest we become his supper. Speaking of canines, we also enjoyed smoking Wolf Brothers cigars soaked in rum. The store clerk in Squaw Lake warned me that after finishing one of these cigars, we'd probably all look like the old, weathered Native American guy in aisle three. Oh well, the cigars were definitely worth it.

Things at the cabin are looking great as we close out yet another season. It is unbelievable to see how the trees have grown. Some are nearly twice my height. We caught six good-sized northerns between us, which is not bad for not having a fishing license. They tasted great. The past two days have been absolutely perfect. To borrow a phrase from Ruth's great-aunt Ruby, could heaven be any nicer than this?

Closing the cabin this year, as with the last, made me especially mindful of my grandma Isabelle. For obvious reasons, I think of her often on trips to Whispering Pines, remembering our journeys north together so many years ago. She lives in a nursing home now, and with her travels to Lake Dunbar all in the past, my feelings are a melancholy mix of wanting her here with me, and moving on with life to create my own new memories and legacy here as she would wish. I visited her a few weeks before this season-ending trip, and it is difficult to see Grandma become so frail and forgetful. It is strange to see her in such a subdued state, after the highly energetic and enthusiastic life she led for most of my existence. I feel so fulfilled by her presence in my life, and just hope (unrealistically) it never ends. It sounds selfish to want and expect more and more life from someone who is nearing ninety years of age, especially when others die so young and deserve more time, but I think her role and influence in my life were so great I simply always wanted more. Anyway, we finally closed up the cabin for the season, and despite all of the work involved, I sense a definite spiritual aspect to the process. We are truly shepherds of this wonderful place, and it has deep meaning for me to be part of its preparation for winter's hibernation and eventual rebirth in the spring. Closing up Whispering Pines feels eerily like the closing down of my grandmother's long life. While I'm reasonably confident I'll see Lake Dunbar again once the spring equinox warms our northern climate in March, I can enjoy only as many more seasons with my beloved grandma as God permits.

Along with a change in cabin ownership, the new millennium brought other updates to Whispering Pines. We all decided the interior of the cabin was long overdue for a refreshing upgrade. In particular, the cabin's flooring and sleeping quarters remained unchanged since my grandparents built Whispering Pines more than forty years earlier. With our parents running the restaurant, my brother, Alex, and I decided to take the lead in a grand remodel effort in the summer of 2001. Leaving our spouses and children behind, we started gathering materials and making our way northward. The first stop was to rent a truck and trailer large enough to hold the new flooring and other supplies we would collect along the way. Next, we visited a discount home goods warehouse, carefully selecting new rolls of carpet for the cabin's main room and bunkrooms, as well as linoleum for the kitchen and main hall.

After loading the hefty carpet and linoleum rolls onto the trailer and gently strapping the razor-sharp edging strips to the top of each roll, we headed for a second large home improvement store where Alex made the one arguably extravagant, or at least non-essential, purchase for the weekend project work. He bought a kit so he could create a faux-rock wall behind the cabin's antique wood stove, providing a more cozy and rustic feel in the main room. Little did he know how difficult and time-consuming his little extra project would be, especially given that all of the remodeling work this particular weekend would essentially be undertaken by Alex alone, without any meaningful assistance from me.

Our next stop was at a major brand warehouse in search of new mattresses. We desperately hoped this would be the last stop. The heat of this mid-summer day was rising with each passing hour, and we wanted to get to Lake Dunbar as fast as possible in order to begin our work. Besides, my faithful hunting dog, Max, was with us, and I couldn't leave him in the warm truck for any extended period of time. Despite the relatively small size of the Whispering Pines cabin on Lake Dunbar, a mere seven hundred square feet, it slept as many as a dozen souls on a combination of seven twin and full-sized beds. And though each of the bed's mattresses was still comfortable for sleeping on after an active day on the lake, the mattresses were in desperate need of replacement. In particular, the full-sized mattress atop the old iron bed's upper bunk was a sorry, sagging sight, no doubt from Grandma Isabelle's endless playful kicking of her neighbors up above. At the mattress store, we quickly chose the mid-priced products we would then need to secure tightly on the soon-to-be-full trailer.

Before heading to the loading dock to collect our purchases, Alex and I repositioned the carpet rolls off to one side of the trailer in order to make room for the new mattresses. Reaching down for a good grip, I counted to three, and then lifted the roll upward with both hands and all of the strength I could muster. Too bad I completely forgot about the shark-toothed carpet edging attached (teeth outward) to the unseen bottom of the roll. Not noticing at first any pain from the edging as it entered the flesh of my right hand, I lifted and moved the carpet roll before feeling a warm sensation surrounding my right index finger. Looking down, I nearly fainted as bright red blood pooled in my hand and squirted intermittently skyward with each rapidly increasing heartbeat.

Alex quickly noticed what had happened, grabbed a nearby rag, and applied full pressure to my gaping wound. Soon the rag turned red with blood. With a trailer full of remodeling materials, a panting dog inside the truck, and a brother whose now-white face contrasted starkly with his red-blood hand, Alex pondered his sudden emergency. Turning back to a familiar hospital was no option, so he called 911 asking for the nearest urgent or emergency care. Thankfully, or so we thought, Caring Hands Urgent Care was a mere ten-minute drive away, and we headed there with lightning speed. Arriving at Caring Hands in a strip mall on the northern edge of the Twin Cities, the day's temperatures had reached into the eighties, and Alex couldn't in good faith leave my beloved dog Max in the truck alone, so I headed into the clinic by myself. After all, I likely only needed a couple of stitches and would be back outside within twenty minutes so we could get on the road and headed north.

On this particular Saturday afternoon, the clinic was moderately busy, with a collection of people whose maladies either weren't serious enough for an emergency room, or couldn't wait for their regular physicians on Monday morning. I registered my name, provided the requested information, submitted my co-pay, and waited to be seen. It took no more than ten minutes for my name to be called, and I dutifully followed the nurse down a sterile white hallway and into a standard examination room. As instructed, I placed myself atop the ever-familiar examination room table, in a sitting position four feet above the floor. The kind nurse routinely asked why I was being seen today, though she could clearly see the blood-soaked rag wrapped around my throbbing right hand. I explained how the accident happened, and very reluctantly relinquished my hand over to the nurse who gently removed the makeshift bandage. Instantly, blood again resumed its pulsing flow from the inch-long wound into my flesh. For a seeming eternity, the nurse viewed my hand, frequently wiping away the blood in order to better see the gash. Turning her back to me, the nurse then fumbled through the adjacent cupboards, retrieving a small metal bowl. She filled it with water and some form of astringent, and carefully placed my injured hand into it.

"There," she said with a kind smile. "We'll just let that soak for ten minutes or so until the doctor comes in to stitch you up, and then send you on your way."

"Ten minutes?" I asked incredulously. "I think I may bleed out in five!"

Admittedly, I am not the best patient, especially if it involves the sight of blood. The nurse assured me I'd survive, and asked me to just relax and wait for the doctor to arrive. Nodding my head, I told myself I would be fine, just as long as I didn't look anywhere near my hand resting in the metal bowl sitting atop a portable medical tray the nurse had rolled over next to the examination table. That strategy lasted roughly three minutes. Like a passing motorist who cannot resist looking over at an automobile accident on the other side of the road, my eyes were magnetically drawn to the metal bowl. After all, I wasn't even sure I could feel it anymore. Had my finger actually been severed? Was my arm (and soon my entire body) now devoid of precious blood? Would I ever leave this room alive?

The last thing I remember before it all went black was peering down at the metal bowl, unable to see my injured hand because the water was all dark red, and confirming my fear. Goodbye cruel world. With that, I promptly fainted. I would have been fine had I fallen backward, landing my upper body onto the cushioned padding of the exam table. My body instead chose the path of most resistance. In my temporary comatose state, I fell forward, crashing through the medical tray and sending the contents of the blood-filled metal bowl flying across the room as my body went head-first toward the ceramic tile floor of the doctor's office. I remembered none of it, and lay there for an indeterminate amount of time, until I eventually heard strange voices, asking seemingly strange questions.

"Get everyone in here!" A man's serious voice barked orders before turning to his limp patient lying on the floor. "Robert, are you with us, Robert?" The voice was faint and unrecognizable, but the question was clear. "Nancy, for God's sake, what happened? How did he end up on the floor?"

"I don't know, doctor. When I left him a minute ago he was fine, other than his cut right hand, of course."

"Let's get something with a strong smell to see if we can revive him. And check his pulse. His color looks horrible, and I'm concerned he's had a heart attack." This was far more excitement than the doctor had bargained for on this random Saturday shift. He tried once more to get my attention.

"Robert, do you know where you are? What are you feeling?" The good doctor's hopes rose as I began to open my eyes ever so slightly, moaning undecipherable words, and trying to reach for my head. "Nancy, get me a pillow and some gauze. He's bleeding from his head. Good Lord, what happened?"

I was indeed coming around, slowly becoming aware of my unfamiliar surroundings, but with so many more questions than answers. Where was I? And more importantly, *who* was I? Why was this stranger holding my arm and calling me Robert? With help from the two worried clinic personnel, I sat up slowly, opened my eyes, and began to speak sensibly.

"Am I still in the clinic? What happened? And who is Robert?"

"You are, son." Apparently in the midst of rushing to discover what or who had crashed so loudly in exam room number seven, the doctor never checked my chart and simply relied upon information from the nurse who, after seeing dozens of patients already, picked the first name she thought of; I was now on my third official first name.

"My name is Eddie," I said weakly, either due to having fainted or perhaps because I was not 100 percent certain. The doctor, who now looked as confused as his recently blacked-out patient, stared at the nurse and nodded for her to check the records.

"Alright, son. Let's get you up into this chair, okay? Everything will be fine. How do you feel?"

"Do you mean other than my throbbing finger and pounding headache?"

"Yes, of course we know about your finger. I'm just concerned about why you fell unconscious to the floor, and whether there's something more serious going on. Do you have any chest pains?"

"No, just my finger and head. And my neck is pretty sore, too. I can't seem to move it too far left or right without some pain. I probably blacked out since I get a little weak at the sight of blood."

Indeed, I had fainted, and was not experiencing a more serious health crisis. However, I did now have another one-inch gash on my body, this time atop my head. Together, the doctor and nurse got me back up on the examination table and began to work on my two flesh wounds, never taking their eyes or hands off of me, fearing a repeat performance of my acrobatic dismount. After stitching up both injuries and feeling assured I was indeed fine to go, and that I had a ride home, the doctor and nurse sent me on my way. As a gesture of goodwill for my troubles, or perhaps an olive branch offering in the hopes I would not sue, they generously waived my $22 clinic co-payment. Yes, the entire $22.

Meanwhile, Alex waited impatiently in the car as the minutes, and then more than an hour passed, with no sign of his brother. What in the world could be taking so long? After all, it was just *a little stitch.* Parked in the only nearby shade he could find, Alex kept alternating his eyes between the front door of Caring Hands Urgent Care and the clock on the truck radio, lamenting the passing daylight being wasted in this wretched parking lot, and eating away at the time remaining to drive north and get started on our work. Finally, he saw someone exit the clinic doors. He resembled me, except for the bloodstained shirt, disheveled and discolored hair, and obviously painful gait. "Eddie? How could it be?" Alex thought to himself. As I approached the truck and finally stepped through the passenger door, I explained what had happened. Alex didn't know whether to laugh or cry. The story was sufficiently strange to defy belief, but the clear mess of a human being sitting next to him matched the almost incomprehensible tale.

Ultimately, Alex would be the last to laugh at this situation because of what it meant for him over the next two days. With me experiencing searing pain every time I moved my head too far left or right, I was limited in how much I could do in terms of lifting furniture, laying carpet, putting up a rock wall, or replacing heavy mattresses. I also could not drive the truck, given I couldn't even turn my head. While I am not the most handy person to begin with, and would often look for ways to get out of this type of physical labor, it is doubtful my multiple injuries were a worthwhile trade-off for avoiding the weekend's heavy work.

As the old saying goes, the more things change, the more they stay the same. In the midst of these generational changes, we still encountered reminders of Dunbar's history and the many characters whose paths we've crossed in this beloved place over the years. In the late summer of 2001, my parents were enjoying a long weekend break from their restaurant business in southern Minnesota to relax and celebrate their thirty-eighth wedding anniversary on the shores of Lake Dunbar. While enjoying a peaceful afternoon fishing off the dock, they were alarmed by the arrival of a rather official-looking vehicle. Worried about the possibility of bad news from back home, they hustled up the shore to meet a sheriff's deputy halfway across the lawn.

"Good day, ma'am. Hello, sir. I'm from the Itasca County Sheriff's office. How are you folks doing today?"

"Fine," my parents answered nervously and in unison. "Can we help you with something?"

"Yes, I'm looking for someone who owns a large tract of land up behind your cabin here. It seems it has overdue property taxes going back several years. We don't have a current address, and are trying to track down the registered owner. Her name is Lucy Ritter. Have you heard of her?"

Relieved no one in the family had died, my mother quickly replied she knew of Lucy Ritter. Lucy and her husband, Earl, owned the old resort over on the northern shore of the lake many years ago.

"Thank you, ma'am. Can you tell me where she is now?"

"Well, that depends, officer, on whether you mean her body or her soul. You see, she's been dead for almost ten years." My mother later relayed this story to me over the phone, including a description of the deputy sheriff's less-than-enamored reaction to my mother's sarcastic humor. The names of Earl and Lucy Ritter hadn't crossed our lips in more than a decade. They had moved from Lake Dunbar back in the late 1970s, and each of them died soon after. Knowing just what a trickster old Earl Ritter was in life left us all wondering how he had managed to keep his and Lucy's names on the public record books as property owners long after they were both dead and gone. It also gave us an opportunity to reminisce about the Ritters' presence on Lake Dunbar and in our lives, and to retell once again the many stories originating from a stay at Earl's Place.

Later that summer, our cabin needed some repair work done on the bathroom floor, a project far too involved for one of us in the family to undertake. We called up JT Dubois, whose family bought the old resort property from the Ritters when Earl and Lucy pulled up stakes and moved to Deer River. JT was a handyman, a jack-of-all-trades, and he did terrific work on all the neighboring cabins. He's an affable guy, always armed with a story, and nearly reminds me of a much-younger Earl Ritter. JT came over to Whispering Pines one Saturday morning during our extended weekend stay late in the season and sized up the project, talking us through the various options for flooring, a replacement toilet, and other finishings. Along the way, he regaled us with some local stories and tall tales, then looked up at us as if in a moment of epiphany.

"Say," he said, "if you're Ted and Ruth's son, then you'd be Isabelle Travis's grandson, right?"

"Yes, indeed," I replied proudly.

"I haven't seen her in years. How's she doing?" he asked with some visible discomfort, likely from the inevitable internal conflict we all experience when asking about someone's elderly relative, not knowing whether they are living or deceased.

"She's doing pretty well, for eighty-eight years old, but she's slowed down significantly and now lives in a nursing home down in Rollingstone. I'm afraid her days of visiting Lake Dunbar are all behind her, but she sure loved this place."

"Please give her my best when you see her. Isabelle was always such a great neighbor and a fun lady to talk with. I remember driving home along Highway 46 one afternoon, probably twenty years ago now, and I came across your grandma's car stuck in the ditch. When I stopped to see if I could help, she explained a deer had forced her to swerve, causing the right front and back tires of her Chrysler to get stuck in the steep embankment. I think she was a little sheepish about her predicament, yet very happy to see a friendly face stop to assist."

"I imagine she was thrilled," I added. "Knowing what a proud woman she always was, I'm guessing she would have sat in the front seat of her fine-looking car waiting for a gallant rescuer like you to come along, rather than subject herself to waving down a passing car for help, much less hitch-hiking her way back into town."

"Oh yeah," JT went on, "she was pleased as punch to have me pull her out of the ditch with my truck. In fact, she didn't seem to want to let go of my hand as she thanked me profusely once she was freed. Isabelle even promised to bring me a bag of her hometown's finest corn on the cob during her next trip north in a couple of weeks. At the time, I figured she was sincere, and I told her not to worry about it, because I didn't expect her to get me a thing. We parted ways and I didn't see her again during the weekend. Anyway, a couple of weeks passed by and sure enough, a sparkling blue Chrysler came rumbling down our gravel driveway around one o'clock on a Saturday afternoon. As I walked toward Isabelle's easily recognizable car, she was already opening up the trunk. Upon rounding the corner to give her a welcome hug, I was stunned at the sight. She had a virtual trunkful of delicious-looking sweet corn, and said it was all for me. I'll never forget it, and I'll never forget her."

Isabelle Travis, unforgettable? Yes, indeed.

Despite the significant changes taking place at Whispering Pines at the dawn of a new millennium, both in terms of ownership and the cabin's interior, I have to say my parents took it in stride and embraced all the new things. You might even say they welcomed these changes with open arms, knowing it was an important transition from one relay racer to the next, and a foretelling of yet another generational change in the nearly half-century of Travis stewardship along the shores of Lake Dunbar. Thankfully these changes did little to quell my parents' enthusiasm, both for trips north to the family cabin and also for their love of participating in Whispering Pines' constant improvement. They continued to re-forest our woods with coniferous and deciduous seedlings, restore the eroding shoreline, and replace aging equipment on the property. I often felt guilty about my own lazy inactivity at Lake Dunbar, at least compared to my parents who were a quarter-century older than me, but certainly appreciated watching them work so diligently as I spied them from my own perch lounging in the hammock.

With my parents entering their sixties, I was especially inspired by their active lifestyle, combining a healthy amount of physical labor with sufficient time for relaxation as well. They continued to fish Dunbar's depths for all of our long-time favorites—walleye, northerns, and crappies. The cabin journals clearly attest to their accomplishments in those endeavors. They also developed a knack for spotting birds of every variety, and undertook successful efforts to attract hummingbirds to a sugary feeder outside the dining room window. Perhaps most satisfying of all was their love of sharing Whispering Pines' experiences with their grandchildren on as many trips as possible. Alex's daughter, Savannah, became an excellent swimmer following numerous trips to myriad lakes of the Chippewa National Forest with Ted and Ruth, while my son, Tyler, learned how to make fancy desserts with my mother, the expert cook, from their joint perch in the cabin's rustic kitchen. Tyler also took great joy in spending time fishing alone with Grandpa Ted where they could conquer the beasts below Dunbar's silvery surface, and engage in deep discussions on topics of mutual and oftentimes surprising interest, including religion, politics, and the American Revolutionary War.

As the 2003 summer cabin season careened toward its inevitable close, my parents spent a long autumn weekend at Whispering Pines and seemed to enjoy it as much, if not more than ever before. As Ted wrote in the cabin journal:

> Ruth and I decided to spend a few unexpected days here at Dunbar, and the weather is simply gorgeous. We've had plenty of rain this year and the trees seem to love it for they are growing so tall. On our first day we accomplished a bit of trimming, and what a discovery we found. Less than fifty feet from the north end of the cabin, Ruth stumbled upon a bouquet of yellow moccasins, or

lady slipper flowers, as they are also known. We've been coming here for forty years and searched for these rarities high and low without ever finding a single one. Yet we must have some cosmic divining rod guiding us, because we have recently found five back in Trout Valley in addition to these two here at Lake Dunbar. It is an incredible coincidence, and I wonder if God is sending us a message. Ruth always said she wanted to find a yellow lady slipper in the wild before she died. I sure hope impending death is not the message! Whatever the deeper meaning, if there is one, being here at Whispering Pines is truly symbolic of our recent and complete escape from the tavern and the restaurant business that has wholly dominated our lives for far too long. This weekend truly represents the most relaxed either of us has been in recent memory, and reminds us what a wonderful place Lake Dunbar can be for relaxation and completely getting away from life in the fast lane. We are so blessed to have this special place.

The Journey at Fifty

THE YEAR 2004 MARKED A SIGNIFICANT MILESTONE IN THE lives of the Travis family, our fiftieth year along the shores of Lake Dunbar. As the new year dawned, my parents and I brainstormed about a proper way to celebrate this joyous occasion. We eventually decided to hold a fifty-year Whispering Pines family reunion, at the cabin of course. We set the date for June 12, and sent a "save the date" to all children, grandchildren, and great-grandchildren of Sam and Isabelle Travis. However, we had much work to do and preparations to make before the event came. Also, an auspicious, momentous, and unexpected intervening event would change the tone and importance of the reunion in ways we couldn't foresee as spring arrived to northern Minnesota.

Thanks to very favorable and unseasonal weather patterns, we actually opened the Whispering Pines cabin early, heading north in late April. My parents joined my brother Alex's family and mine for a long weekend to begin surveying the cabin and entire property for any and all project work we could or should complete before the fiftieth reunion two months away. The very first item on our agenda was an unexpected one: as we went to put the dock in the water for the year, we discovered one of its tires went flat over the winter. This required a trip into town for tire repair, and Mom quickly volunteered. She relished any opportunity to hit the Emporium or other nearby craft stores along with a stop at the Max Store in Squaw Lake for an ice cream cone. She came back to the cabin a bit disappointed, however, upon discovering the infamous ice cream machine wasn't scheduled to be up and running until May, another six days away.

Because her ice cream adventure did not pan out, Ruth insisted

Ted take her out for an early dinner, and she would get a tasty treat in Squaw Lake one way or another. At five o'clock, we all piled into my truck and drove the seven miles into town, anticipating the delicious array of choices at our favorite nearby eatery, The Hill. Our "usuals" included their barbecued ribs, a Swiss mushroom chicken sandwich with fried onions, and The Hill's delectable wild rice soup. However, as we neared the restaurant, it quickly became apparent Mom would be experiencing her second food disappointment of the day. The Hill was under renovation, an expansion plan designed for completion by the time the Fishing Opener rolled around in a few weeks. In its place, the owners erected a large white tent with outdoor grills and cooking stations from which they were offering a single menu choice: "The Hill's first-annual Sauerkraut and Meat Feed." At least the journey into town was not a total loss, for we arrived in time to watch the much-anticipated egg toss in the yard adjacent the restaurant, followed by the yellow rubber ducky races down the street on the Popple River.

I always enjoyed our early-season cabin trips as a kid, and even more as an adult. The crowds of campers were yet to arrive, fishing season was a few weeks away, and best of all, the pesky mosquitos and black flies were still incubating. The downside was an absence of green foliage, as the northern Minnesota trees were just beginning to shows their buds, and the springtime Dunbar nights could truly be quite chilly. It was on one of these brisk nights I regrettably learned how my strange parents chose to stay warm while sleeping in the cold back bedroom. As Mom and Dad awoke from a satisfying night of Dunbar slumber, they staggered out to the kitchen in order to start the morning coffee maker. Spying them from my perch atop the rolled-out hide-a-bed in the cabin's front room, I saw them both wearing long johns. Now, I have nothing against thermal underwear, and admittedly wear them myself on an occasional cold Minnesota winter night. However, I put them on feet first, pulled up to my waist, rather than my parents' unique method of placing the long johns' wide opening over the tops of their heads for warmth, like an old-fashioned nightcap. As Alex too awoke to the dawning morning light and saw our parents' attire from across the room, he turned back toward his pillow, murmuring something about the sauerkraut and meat feed, the egg toss, and the unsightly hooded thermal underwear before concluding just barely audible for the rest of us to hear, "Everyone up here is clearly smoking something funny."

With our work complete, we spent one final evening of the early-season trip enjoying Mom's famous pot roast, baked in the aging electric oven, and also sitting around the roaring wood stove listening to a crackly broadcast of Garrison Keillor's *Prairie Home Companion* on the radio. After the show ended, I climbed up into the attic and brought down Grandma Isabelle's antique portable turntable. It played nothing but 45s, and I don't think any new records had been purchased in over thirty years, based upon the selection of songs available inside the holding case of Grandma's record player. I reached for my very favorite, a single Grandma Isabelle and I had listened and danced to with deep, soulful laughter on virtually every trip north in my childhood—"Hey Good Lookin'," a 1951 classic by the iconic Hank Williams.

Perhaps everyone feels this way about their own grandmothers, or other special older adults in their lives, but this woman simply made life more fun and colorful for me, both as a child and on into adulthood. As a boy, I would look forward to my annual weeklong summer visit to Greenwood where I played from dawn 'til dusk with my cousins, interrupted only for meals with my beloved grandma: breakfast at the café, lunch at Grandma's big white house at the top of the town's biggest hill, and dinner at Trout Camp or the Rockwell House down in the valley. Then, after coyly hiding the infamous green celery dish under Grandma's pillow, I'd anxiously go to bed in the spare room and await her unique shriek of joyful feigned surprise followed by a yell of "Eddie, you rascal!" Today, if I close my eyes and block out all noise, I can still vividly hear those three words as if Grandma Isabelle were in the very next room.

I especially treasure the multitude of letters I received over the years from my grandmother. Living two hours away, our personal visits were often few and far between, but we made up for it in phone calls and frequent short notes. I've kept every single one. Grandma's letters sustained me as I went away to college and later moved to California. She was a sweet connection to home in those years of my young adulthood, and a constant, gentle reminder that I was loved by a woman who had a lot of it to give. What struck me about Isabelle's correspondence was the breadth of content she could fit onto two sides of a five-by-five piece of parchment paper, including a report on the local weather, the latest gossip from the town coffee shop, and a description of her dinner from the night before. Even more, my grandma helped me to stay focused on others in the family who were struggling, and to keep alive the memories of those who were no longer with us. From February 1979, she wrote to me at home:

Dear Eddie,

I hope you have a real nice birthday! Yesterday was a real big day for me as I was driving the school bus all day long. First there were the normal routes and then I took the high school girls to a basketball game in Stewartville. I just got back from the café and had soup, a sandwich, and graham cracker pie. It was delicious! I went to church this morning at nine o'clock as it is Ash Wednesday. We buried Stella twenty-one years ago today. It doesn't seem fair. She was so nice and so very pretty. I hope you have a very nice birthday.

    Love, Grandma Isabelle

Then in July 1988 she sent a comforting letter to my college dorm room:

Dear Eddie,

I hope everything is going well with you. I've been trying to keep busy so I don't have time to dwell on our very sad time now with your cousin Kate's passing. It is unbelievable how well Jack and Evelyn have dealt with this tragic situation. I guess it is the only way. They are so strong and very good Christians which helps. I'm sure we will all remember Kate for a very long time. I know how close you and Alex were with Kate. When I stopped down to Jack's house today, I saw how many cards they've received—must have been over six hundred. I guess it shows how many friends and loved ones they have, as well as how many Kate had. Hope to see you soon.

Love, Grandma Isabelle

A letter from November 1993 continued the tradition even when I lived far away in California:

Dear Eddie,

I apologize for being so slow at answering your very nice letter. I've had a difficult time lately as you probably know. Walt is very, very ill and in the hospital. Evelyn took me up to see him a few days ago, and Jack drove me up there yesterday. Walt is on his last days, and I can hardly stand it. He is so special to me and worked so hard on transferring my pictures to video. He's done so much for me and was with me when I really needed somebody. I couldn't possibly love him more than I already do. I just don't understand why he has to suffer so much. He is one of the best, and never hurt anyone. We all love him so much. Eleanor and Paul were there, as were all the rest. They all seem to handle it better than me because I'm a nervous wreck. I'm sure looking forward to seeing you when you get back to Minnesota. God bless you, Eddie, and thanks again for the wonderful story about your trip. I loved it.

Love, Grandma Isabelle

And perhaps my favorite letter was the last one she ever sent me, arriving late in 1995, just a few months before I moved back to Minnesota. In the final years of my relationship with Grandma Isabelle, our communications were all in person or by telephone, for we lived much closer together as she approached ninety years of life:

Dear Eddie,

I just received the nicest treat. I can't tell you how happy I feel and how much I appreciate you! You are so special to send me a beautiful flower arrangement. It is so pretty and not even my birthday! I love you so much for it, but I loved you anyway. Thanks from the bottom of my heart. I even cried because I was so thrilled. When you get back, I will have to think of something to do for you—maybe I'll make you a quilt or whatever you like. I wrote you a letter last week and didn't get it mailed quickly but hope you get this one sooner. I just got back from Winona and stopped for dinner at your mom and dad's restaurant. Your mom sat down to eat with me, and I sure enjoy her dinners and just being out there. I can't wait until you are back here and I can treat you to a meal there. Thanks again for the special bouquet, and I will try to write more often until your return. I miss you and think of you OFTEN.

Love, Grandma Isabelle

Indeed one of the greatest things about moving home to Minnesota in the spring of 1996 was being able to visit with Grandma Isabelle much more frequently. Those visits quickly changed, of course, when she moved to the nursing home a couple of years later, and then again as she slowly succumbed to the effects of old age. Yet, every time I visited with her was special to me because this woman was such a significant part of my life from the day I was born. This is why it was so difficult for me as the realities of time became apparent, and Grandma Isabelle's journey here on Earth neared its inevitable conclusion.

Mom drove down to Rollingstone late one morning in May 2004 to visit with her mother, Isabelle. Grandma had not eaten for three days and seemed to be near the end of her long life. I often wonder whether people have some say in determining the exact hour when they leave the rest of us behind. One of Grandma's brothers died just the Friday prior. Did Grandma somehow sense the loss of this brother, who was probably her favorite and closest sibling? As Joseph Campbell writes, "The dark night of the soul comes just before revelation. When everything is lost and all seems darkest, there comes new life and all that is needed." At 9:45 p.m. Mom called to tell me my beloved grandma Isabelle had passed away. Mom was by Grandma's side all day, then stepped out for some fresh air and to buy a small cone at The Creamery down the street. In those few minutes of absence, Grandma took the opportunity to take her proverbial next step toward the great beyond.

My mother was the only one in her family to be at Isabelle's side in her waning moments, just as she had been the only one with Sam Travis when he died forty-some years earlier. I was heartbroken to learn Grandma had passed, but so very proud to know she lived her ninety-one years to the fullest. Her life might well have been lonely in some respects, seeing she was widowed for so many years. Yet she was a very strong, outgoing person who made the most of all life had dealt to her. She was the strength of our family and loved by so many, both in the family and beyond, who appreciated her undying spirit and energy. She was the queen of bus drivers, and a beacon of hope and safety to generations of schoolchildren who will always remember her fondly.

Despite our collective sadness, for Grandma's funeral we celebrated her life with as much gusto as she celebrated her own life for all those years. Perhaps the most fitting tribute of the blessed funeral service was when my Aunt Eleanor walked to the St. Bernard's Parish organ and played the rousing Greenwood High School fight song, a song Isabelle Travis stood to and sang along with on hundreds or even thousands of occasions. For in addition to driving generations of Greenwood schoolchildren to every imaginable sporting event, she was also their most loyal and vocal supporter. No one cheered on the Greenwood Warriors in so many different sports for so many years than our family's matriarch.

For me, the other memorable moment from those funeral events was when my cousin Rose stood and recounted a story that really epitomized the life of this wonderful woman, Isabelle Travis. Naturally, the story takes place near the shores of Lake Dunbar. It seems as though during the infamous Women's Weekend trip to Whispering Pines back in 1994, my Aunt Eleanor was driving the last stretch of Itasca County Highway 32 before the final turn-off on Dunbar Beach Road. Highway 32 is blacktopped for only two miles before transitioning quite suddenly to a gravel road. Like most of us, Eleanor anticipated where the blacktop ended, and soon slowed the car from sixty down to thirty so as to lessen the impact when hitting the gravel surface. Her daughter Rose, sensing this slow-down, asked a question that for me crystallizes my grandmother's approach to life. "Mom," she implored, "why are you slowing down? Grandma Isabelle never did!" Indeed, Isabelle Travis took the gravel road and her entire life at a full sixty miles per hour. Those of us lucky enough to be in her actual and metaphorical car over the years were treated to the ride of a lifetime.

We celebrated the fiftieth anniversary of the Whispering Pines cabin on June 12, 2004, and were thrilled to have so many members of the Travis clan in attendance, including Aunt Eleanor and Uncle Paul; Uncle Jack and Aunt Evelyn; Cousin Rose along with her husband, Patrick, and their boys, Pete and Andrew; my parents, Ted and Ruth; and of course my brother, Alex, and our two small families. We had an entire day full of activities planned, starting with festivities right there on Lake Dunbar at noon. The morning's overcast clouds soon gave way to sparkling blue skies and seventy-some degrees of pure sunshine. We set up the patio with a dozen or more chairs assembled in a large circle near the fire pit for food and conversation, two boats ready for a fishing contest, and yard games scattered in front of and behind the cabin. Family members kept arriving one by one, car by car, and the party soon began.

First was a potluck midday dinner with every family bringing their individual favorite dishes. Next, everyone went off for their own choice of activities, with some engaging in a competitive game of croquet, others in an even more competitive fishing contest, and still others taking time to enjoy the surroundings of Whispering Pines and the wider shores of Lake Dunbar, which several had not visited for many years. Around mid-afternoon we gathered again 'round the fire pit and shared stories from the entirety of our fifty years on this blessed land. This led to a pre-arranged trivia contest, where questions ranged the full spectrum of our Dunbar tenure and involved virtually every family member to visit these hallowed shores, along with many friends and extended family as well.

Next up were two ceremonial activities, one symbolic and one made of solid rock. For each person present, we crafted a Certificate of Honorary Membership in the Travis Cabin Company. Whether you officially owned a share of the TCC was irrelevant; all in the family were welcome to visit and stay under Whispering Pines' sturdy roof any time they pleased. Then we walked a few yards toward the lake for the much-anticipated dedication of a memorial bench in the woods just beyond the cabin's fire pit along a grassy path. It was a low, decorative, two-person concrete bench with a spectacular view of our own special Lake Dunbar and beyond to the northern bay of this beloved lake. Atop the bench appears an engraved plaque honoring Whispering Pines' two founders. Their names would stand for all time as a testament to each of these special people's key contributions both to this phenomenal place of serenity and to each of our lives. The plaque reads:

50th Anniversary of the
Travis Cabin
June 12, 2004

In memory of
Sam Travis   Isabelle Travis
1909–1962   1913–2004

Those assembled for this hallowed event shared so many wonderful memories created over the past five decades, and it was especially heartening for me to hear so many new tales from times before I was born. My dad commented it felt very much like the ending of a phase in the life of the Travis family on Lake Dunbar, and the passing of the torch to a new generation. Perhaps that is an unstated purpose of these kinds of gatherings and commemorations. I also wondered whether any of the original cabin founders, aside from Ruth, would ever venture this far north again. Time will tell, as it marches forward unceasingly, and without interruption.

June 12 was simply a spectacularly sunny day. I also like to think Grandma Isabelle was smiling down on us a mere eight days after her death and providing this wonderful gift of light to celebrate fifty years of the Travis family on Lake Dunbar. Quite ironically, and for the first time in our collective memories, upon plugging the infamous Schlitz Light into the wall, it spun around like usual, but the bulb did not light up. What could it mean? In my mind, Grandma Isabelle and cousin Walt were here for the party in full spirit, playing one last trick on us all. Or perhaps it was just Grandma stopping by Whispering Pines on her way to heaven so she could bring Walt the fantastic Schlitz Light he always so desperately wanted.

The rest of 2004 brought several more wonderful cabin trips, all contributing to an exceptionally magical year on Lake Dunbar. Immediately following the fiftieth reunion, Rose's sons, Pete and Andrew, stayed on at Whispering Pines for some serious fishing. Pete was indeed rewarded for the extended journey by catching a seven-pound, thirty-three-inch northern pike, and both boys caught a stringer full of nice-looking bass. While fishing the lower end of the lake, they even spotted a sizeable black bear, and kept their hands on the throttle of the motor just in case they needed a fast getaway. We also took the guys, including my five-year-old son, Tyler, on what we thought would be a brief bike ride through the Chippewa National Forest near the Deer River Ranger Station. Two hours and many miles later, having portaged over fallen logs, bushwhacked through an overgrown dirt trail, and survived the horrendous stench of a massive illegal dump of fish guts, we made our way back to the van and quickly bought everyone an ice cream cone at the Max Store in an effort to win back their exhausted affections.

Pete and Andrew must have recovered from this traumatic bicycle adventure, for they joined us on another trip north later in the summer, along with their parents, Rose and Patrick. Together, we packed more into one week at Whispering Pines than I had done in the past three seasons combined. We visited the local attractions of Itasca State Park and the Lost Forty, caught or hunted various critters, collected forest berries, and constructed bluebird houses and a debris shelter in our woods. Rather than recount these adventures myself, here are the cabin journal entries from our guests:

It has been a great week here at the cabin. The northwoods are so quiet and peaceful! We've laughed, had so much fun, and created many lasting memories. We visited Itasca State Park on Monday then drove into Grand Rapids on Tuesday where we found some old historic blueprints of the Dunbar and Squaw Lake area. Wednesday we hiked the Lost Forty. We fit so many things in this week, but the best times were just in creating memories and laughing non-stop.

Rose

I just loved our full week at the cabin. We drove up on Saturday and had a ball! On Sunday we went to the Emporium where I got several fishing lures. Back at the cabin, Tyler, Pete, and I hunted for snails and went on a boat ride around the lake with everyone. On Monday we went to Itasca, had a picnic, and swam at the beach. We even found a mini-catfish. Then we walked across the Mississippi River and climbed a fire tower. On Tuesday we picked three full buckets of raspberries. We also went fishing and visited some baby kittens at the neighbors'. On Wednesday we built bluebird houses at the Chippewa National Forest Station followed by a picnic at the Lost Forty. I had a great time at the cabin and hope I can come back again soon!

Andrew

We had some nice, cool weather for most of the trip and even fired up the old wood stove one night for warmth. I caught a twenty-one-inch walleye pike, and the little kids had fun hunting for snails in the lake. On our last full day we looked down to the dock, only to see Tyler clinging to it with the lower half of his body immersed in the lake. He didn't seem too distraught so we all had a good laugh. Before leaving, everyone pitched in to build a debris shelter in the woods. We gathered logs and sticks of every size, and I think it will stand for a very long time.

Patrick

Our final trip north for the 2004 season provided a spectacular bookend to another memorable season on the shores of Lake Dunbar. It was mid-October, and we of course performed all of the necessary year-end closing tasks, including removal of the dock from the lake and draining all of the water lines in the cabin. Yet we still had time to enjoy the quintessential quiet solitude that is October in the northwoods. Gone are the tourists and fishermen, as well as many of the lake's seasonal residents. Summertime toys and machinery are all stored away, and one can enjoy peaceful, mosquito-free walks through the virtually leafless and seemingly endless woods.

As my son gets slowly older and quickly more independent, it is heartwarming to observe him exploring the woods and shoreline of our property and engaging in activities a boy should be doing at his age, the same activities I enjoyed here thirty-some years ago. Soon after arriving, Tyler already had a small metal pail full of lake water into which he began to place snails, frogs, minnows, and other critters from the shoreline. Determining quickly his new amphibious and watery pets needed more space, Tyler devised an ingenious method to get water from the surface of the lake thirty inches below the dock on up to a large blue bucket sitting on it. My son positioned himself down in the green fishing boat where he scooped small pails full of "sea water," as he called it, handing them up to me stationed on top of the dock in assembly-line fashion where I was then instructed to dump the pail's contents into the larger container over and over again until it filled.

The remainder of our weekend brought even more antics from five-year-old Tyler. This child has been a climber from even before he learned how to walk, but on this particular trip, he literally took his ascension skills to an even higher level. While my wife and I were distracted with disassembling the dock, Tyler wandered down the shoreline and found an irresistibly appealing dead tree that was tipped at a forty-five-degree angle hanging over the lake. Apparently he had been troubled by the number of basswood trees unjustly felled by the obvious gnawing of a beaver along our shoreline. Upon seeing a beaver swimming past the cabin earlier, Tyler was bound and determined to keep an eye out for those darn over-sized rodents and shoo them off our property. Upon hearing my son's gleeful cry of "Hey Daddy, look at me," it took me a full minute of scouring the ground before lifting my eyes thirty feet into the air to witness Tyler waving to me with one hand and hanging on for dear life with the other. Though feeling incredibly panicked inside, I did my best to calmly congratulate him on his climb, but then immediately coax him safely back down to earth.

Earlier in the afternoon, we had taken one last boat ride around the lake, surveying all of our favorite landmarks, including the Mona Bell Hill cabin, the Ronning Forest, and the triple-decker cabin, which was the envy of all local inhabitants. The lake water was unusually high for October, allowing us to take the little green motorboat quite a ways down the Dunbar River as it meanders its way for miles through dense pine forest, and eventually flowing into the much larger Round Lake. It was my son's first-ever boat trip back in this remote marshy stream, now teeming with wildlife of all varieties—beavers, egrets, otters, porcupines, and the occasional bald eagle. Tyler was visibly elated as he spied animal after animal, and while peering over the edge of the boat, he even spotted a fish or two beneath the surface of the clear water. When I asked him whether he liked it back here in the Dunbar River, Tyler exhaled a long sigh, broke into an incredibly wide smile, and simply said, "Yeah, Dad, my heart is just glowing!"

Before leaving for home, we spent one more glorious afternoon in Aunt Eleanor's little green fishing boat where I again tried to impart the knowledge and art of fishing to my son, just as Grandma Isabelle had taught me. Any sane person might rightly ask why we do it, sitting out in the elements, dangling a line and bait in the water for hours on end simply in the hopes (oftentimes unfulfilled) of catching a solitary, slimy creature from the lake's murky depths. Is it to enjoy the fishy taste of these beasts? For the annoying mosquito bites? For the messy job of cleaning the fish for cooking? No, most certainly none of these reasons explains it. Rather, fishing alone or with a friend or loved one in a remote northern lake is truly a spiritual and peaceful experience. It is about enjoying the solitude of others, listening to the call of the loon and the wind-rippled waters, just waiting with calm anticipation for a mighty fish to show himself, tug on your line, and then to hear the soft, excited voice of your son exclaim, "I've got one, Daddy!"

That evening, we decided to treat ourselves to dinner in town at The Hill, a long-time Travis family favorite. My wife and I ordered our usual, a chicken Swiss mushroom sandwich, while Tyler devoured a bowl of wild rice soup with breadsticks. Tyler was his usually well-behaved self, and it got the attention of our waitperson, who must have been accustomed to screaming children in booster chairs. As Tyler said a heartfelt and unprompted "thank you" upon receiving his bowl of piping hot soup, the young woman server commented, "Your son is such a polite young gentleman, he deserves a special treat," with a hearty emphasis on the word "polite." She proceeded to bring him a bag of M&M candies once he finished his dinner.

This lesson clearly stuck in my son's mind, as evidenced when we stopped for dinner at the Sportsman's Café in Mora on our journey home. Taking seats in a booth near the front window, we were greeted by a server who had been working here virtually her entire adult life and was a friendly soul who wanted to know her customers. "Where you comin' from?" and "Where you headed to?" she asked us, before turning specifically toward Tyler and asking, "And who is this fine-looking young man?"

My son's immediate and perhaps well-rehearsed reply? "I'm Tyler, just a *polite* young boy." The waitress laughed heartily, and said, "Yes, you certainly are!" However, as pleased as my son was with the kind waitress' friendliness, he was disappointed not to be awarded another bag of candy.

Yes, it was indeed a remarkable year, and our October journey north provided a fitting end to it. As I wrote in the cabin journal toward the conclusion of our wonderful weekend, the very last entry in the journal for 2004:

I had a perfect cabin moment on Friday morning. I awoke at seven, looked out the front window to the sunny morning, and saw steam evaporating off of the sixty-some degree lake into the thirty-five degree air. Then, just to the left of the cabin I saw them in the mist, a family of five loons with a couple of them doing their loon dance on the water. Perfection. It was another melancholy end to a wonderful cabin season. We left home on Wednesday afternoon and stayed the first night at the Sawmill Inn of Grand Rapids. After a lazy start on Thursday, we arrived at the cabin around three in the afternoon. All of the leaves are gone and the air is crisp and cool. We mowed, raked, and had a bonfire.

We checked on our debris shelter deep in the woods and caught the last snails of the season. We took the dock out of the water on Friday and closed out the water lines before departing on Sunday morning. We took some fabulous walks through the barren woods and even ran into a wandering grouse hunter. We also made one last trip of the season to Ida's Emporium and found some true bargains, including a hardcover train book for Tyler, a 1940s pie plate, and two used baseball mitts. Our dog Max also took in her last run through the deep woods and got plum worn out. All in all, it was a great cabin season, 2004. We enjoyed two two-week trips here, and celebrated the fiftieth anniversary of this blessed place. We have so many good memories to sustain us through the winter as we look forward to 2005. After all, Fishing Opener is only seven months away!

ALL GOD'S CREATURES,
GREAT AND SMALL

NOW, I'M THE FIRST TO ADMIT THE TRAVIS FAMILY HAS A FULL kaleidoscope of personality types (mostly good, of course). We possess a fully diverse set of human quirks, frailties, or idiosyncrasies, and we embrace each and every one. However, all of these traits put together pale in comparison to the fascinating array of characters inhabiting Lake Dunbar in the first decade of this new millennium. Certainly, my extended family met its fair share of colorful personalities during our first fifty years on Lake Dunbar, as my mother and grandmother have already written about extensively, but I contend the most interesting and infamous local residents came out of the woodwork once 1999 turned over to 2000. They say truth is stranger than fiction, and I couldn't agree more. Just when you think you've seen and heard it all in life, pleasant and unexpected surprises will catch you off guard as they did for our family in the far northern woods of Minnesota at the dawn of this great new century.

First, there was our dear neighbor Jeremiah Cauley who owned the closest cabin to ours, the same one my grandpa Sam bought from Leland Jensen back in the 1960s just to calm my grandmother's nerves. Jeremiah was the sweetest soul imaginable, and a fully committed evangelist. I spent many an evening down by the dock listening to Jeremiah extol the virtues of evangelism, and the need for all of us to become missionaries to the world. While I consider myself a spiritual-though-flawed person, evangelizing is not in my DNA, and so I happily leave that task to the Jeremiah Cauleys of the world. Jeremiah suffered from several serious health issues, including diabetes, and this significantly limited the distances he could travel, and therefore, how far his godly mission could be carried out. Still, I admired this man's fervent passion and attempts to win me over. "Jesus was a fisherman too, you know," Jeremiah told me more than once. "He fished for the souls of men like you and me. And so we too must carry out his mission and save the souls of the lost."

Then there was the youngest of the Dubois boys who bought the old resort from Earl Ritter in the late 1970s. The rest of the Dubois kids made their way off of Dunbar eventually, but "Tiny" remained. Like Jeremiah Cauley, Tiny was a kind man who generously allowed us to use his personal boat landing to launch and land our pontoon boat each spring and fall, rather than navigate the treacherous, graveled, and steep public landing closer to the cabin. Tiny also put on an explosive and fantastic fireworks display directly across the lake from us every Fourth of July. Most of all, Tiny earned the love and respect of everyone living in the Chippewa National Forest, due to his accomplished skills as a bull rider. Tiny could outlast anyone in the nearest five counties, and even placed tenth in all of Minnesota in 2010. As aptly characterized by our cabin neighbor Elias Hinck, "Seeing Tiny in those contests is like watching a wood tick ride a bull!"

Another colorful local character was Ida Ojanen, proprietor of the world-renown Ida's Emporium over in Alvwood. Operated in nothing more than a large pole shed, Ida's magical Emporium was filled to the rim with both practical and desirable goods ranging from fishing gear to dinner plates, videotapes to locally made jams, table linens to toys for children, and handyman tools to used books. On every journey north for our family, we stopped at Ida's Emporium, not only to peruse the latest offerings, but more importantly for a chance to shoot the breeze with the inimitable Ida, and to learn about all the latest local news. Ida and her husband, Charlie, were lifelong residents of the area, with Charlie working in the mining industry seemingly forever. Ida tried her hand at a few different careers over the years, but finally determined she wanted to open and run her own business. Taking a gigantic leap of faith, Ida convinced Charlie to construct the large pole shed, banking on her prediction that her upscale Emporium would meet the needs of three presently underserved groups—local cabin owners looking for equipment locally rather than driving all the way to Bemidji, the wives of visiting fishermen, and Ida's fellow housewives of area lumbermen looking for a place to sell their homemade goods and hand-me-downs.

Ida's business gamble paid off in spades, for the fledgling Emporium she opened in the 1980s is still going strong thirty years later. It is always an immense delight to pull our truck into her grassy lawn-turned-parking lot, then walk into the Emporium as Ida chats away with another customer. We patiently wait for the wonderful moment when she notices us, calls us each out by name, and says with great enthusiasm and sincerity how good it is to see us. Ida has taken a particular interest in my son, Tyler, over the years, always walking him over to the toy area to show him the latest arrival. Of course, her strong interest in Tyler also led Ida to issue me her one and only reprimand. In the summer of 2005 when Tyler was a mere six years old, Ida was trying to show him a batch of unused yellow yo-yos and gently demonstrate how they worked. Though Tyler watched with rapt attention and indicated his interest in acquiring this exciting toy, he hung his head in disappointment, telling Ida he would have to pass.

"Why?" she inquired. "Doesn't it look like a lot of fun? You could even teach your cousin how to do it once you get back to Lake Dunbar. Why, maybe you even need two of them."

"Yeah, right," was young Tyler's downtrodden reply, "like I'd ever be allowed to get two. I don't think my dad will go for it."

"Oh, they only cost a dollar apiece," Ida replied. "I'll tell your dad this is a bargain."

"Good luck," was Tyler's closing admonition. "He's so tight with our money!"

Yes, Tyler did say, "*our* money." True, I am often called tightfisted or miserly by my family; however, I prefer the word "judicious."

And in terms of Ida's Emporium, I've spent my fair share of the family budget at her fine establishment over the years, and am especially excited when we find a bargain. A few years ago, my brother Alex and his wife uncovered a box of antique Fire King coffee mugs and assorted dishware at one of the tables, so they quickly put down their measly fifteen dollars to secure the purchase. However, the deal of the century was uncovered by no less than Tyler in the fishermen's section along the far left wall of the Emporium one spring morning. He was searching for a new tackle box, something to hold the numerous lures, spinners, and other equipment he had received the prior Christmas as a gift from his grandparents. Tyler honed in on some antique-looking fish boxes whose metallic latches and hinges creaked with the sound of sturdy construction. As he opened the fading brown box, he couldn't believe his eyes, for inside what he thought was an empty box was actually a treasure trove of old tackle, left behind by some aging fisherman who either had given up the sport or decided to have his own new box full of brand new supplies. For a meager ten dollars, my son now owned at least fifty dollars' worth of new tackle, including several never-before-used Daredevil brand lures. For the remainder of our trip, we couldn't keep him off of the water because he was intent to try virtually every newly acquired piece of fishing equipment. Ultimately, Tyler's success matched his effort as he reeled in a stringer full of northerns, crappies, and bass.

Beyond this endearing cast of vibrant local characters, we also spent many an evening shooting the breeze with neighbors Elias and Clara Hinck who lived just down the way. These were two of the finest human beings you could meet, and they became our dearest and closest friends in our entire history on the shores of Lake Dunbar. They moved to the lake in the late 90s and were related to the Hinck family on a nearby farm. We learned quickly these two souls were not only wonderful friends and neighbors, but also immensely talented in their respective careers. Clara became Dunbar's resident chef extraordinaire, ultimately feeding us all too well over the next decade with meals and baked goods rivaling the fanciest places in the Twin Cities several hundred miles away. Like Ida at the Emporium, Clara too became quite fond of Tyler and my niece, Savannah, inviting them over to cook or bake with her many times over the years.

As for Elias, it is no exaggeration to say he is the finest master craftsman anyone in our family has ever met. He built the couple's log home on the property across the lake from ours, and he did it virtually all by himself, from the plumbing to the heating to the wood construction to all the finishes, and it is a home of incredible stature and beauty. Luckily for us, Elias Hinck had some spare time in which to undertake a few projects at Whispering Pines, and our property's value and enjoyment increased significantly as a result. Elias built a deck on the front of our cabin, installed dormer windows for an amazing lakefront view, constructed a work shed at the edge of our woods, rewired Whispering Pines top to bottom, rebuilt the wood floors and support joists following an unexpected water incident, and consulted with us far more times than he probably desired on various projects both actualized and those yet to be done. Though we paid him what was asked for each of these endeavors, I'm certain we'll never fully repay Elias for the incredible work he accomplished at our treasured family lake home.

Even more than these appreciated talents, however, was the friendship we developed with Elias and Clara Hinck over the years, and the incredibly good humor our family enjoyed in their presence. We never failed to have a deep, hearty chuckle over the playful repartee between Elias and his wife during each of our trips to Lake Dunbar. On our very first visit to the couple's newly built log cabin, we admired the stuffed black bear standing adjacent their good-looking rock wall fireplace.

"Wow," I said on the verge of an assumed and sexist statement, "what an amazing-looking bear, Elias. Where did you get him?"

"I didn't," Elias replied. "Clara did. She shot him straight through the heart with one bullet on her first attempt. My woman is deadly accurate."

Clara then added without missing a beat, "Yeah, Elias, and let my skill be a reminder to you in case you are ever tempted to get out of line!"

Then there was the time Clara Hinck walked down to our cabin on a particularly hot summer day, delivering a freshly made sour cream raisin pie. We were immensely grateful, and enjoyed the pie thoroughly after an afternoon of reshingling our roof. Clara observed our amateur work, tactfully not pointing out our flaws or the places where Elias might have performed better. She did mention, however, that her husband was off working on a project in Grand Rapids for the day, and had already called her three times before noon on her cell phone, all for something rather minor. Upon answering his fourth call in a span of ten minutes, we couldn't help but overhear.

"Elias Hinck, if you're not injured or dying, hang up right now!" He did.

Hearing this from his perch atop the roof, my father Ted couldn't help but inquire. "What if Elias was just lonely for you and wanted to hear the sound of your voice?"

"Well, then he can just get a girlfriend to chat with, now can't he?"

However, the most regrettably unforgettable character on Lake Dunbar was affectionately known to his neighbors as "the willow man," so named because he made a living crafting beautiful furniture out of stripped and lacquered willow branches, which he sold in local bazaars and eventually over the Internet. The willow man was a life-long bachelor who inherited his modest midcentury cabin from his mother, another truly memorable lake resident. The mother, Dorothy, who originally inhabited the place, was a rather quiet and strange character who lived meagerly on a pension that her deceased husband had earned from a long insurance career. Though we rarely encountered Dorothy over the years, my dad had a particularly startling run-in with her one afternoon as Dad was tending to the spruce trees in his beloved forest adjacent Whispering Pines. As Dad rounded the corner of a small spruce tree grove, a voice reached out to him.

"Afternoon, sir," said the gravely toned, haggard-looking Dorothy who was leaning against a large jack pine with a hunting rifle resting on her shoulder.

"Oh," my father replied with a start and a rapidly increasing heartbeat. "I didn't see you standing there in *our* woods. How're you doin'?"

"Fine, fine. Just out surveying the local woodlands, seeing who and what is about." Dorothy's dark eyes never focused on my dad or on anything else for more than a second. She seemed a bit frazzled, possibly even affected by something inside of or around her.

"Looks to me like you might be hunting something, though I'm not sure what's in season here in mid-summer." My dad decided to choose his words carefully and opted not to remind the bedraggled northwoods woman she was also trespassing on our land.

"Oh, this?" Dorothy barely even gazed at the rifle as she lifted the barrel slightly skyward. "Nah, I'm not huntin' today. I just carry it with me for safety. You never know who or what might be after ya. A single woman's gotta protect herself up here in the deep forest. Had a friend who went missin' a few years ago over by Kelliher. No one's seen her since. Probably got attacked and eaten by a bear, a cougar, or by one of those drunk natives." Interesting theory, thought Ted, assuming Dorothy even had a friend who went missing, much less a friend of any kind in the first place. In the end, my dad simply wished Dorothy well and returned to the cabin, hoping his strange neighbor would simply make her way back home soon. Dad warned my mother not to go into the woods alone under any circumstance.

Anyway, the willow man moved in shortly after his mother died in a midnight boating accident a few years after the encounter with my father. Though none of us knew him, all of us were hopeful the new resident would be closer to normal, in the scheme of things. Perhaps we should have been *more specific* in our collective wish. Although the son was far less strange in his interpersonal interactions with others, he was also a bit compulsive and particular about how to maintain lake property, and not just his own. In the span of less than five years, the place went from a modest, perhaps tattered little cabin with an overgrown lawn to a candidate for a potential reality show called *Outdoor Perfectionists* with not so much as a blade of grass out of place.

The willow man was also in a constant mode of construction and expansion from day one. He built a garage, a fish house, and a tool shed to house his growing willow business and ever-expanded array of lawn care instruments. For the Travis family, the man's dedication to his cabin's pristine appearance was a joy to behold on every trip to Whispering Pines, for we passed the willow man's pleasant homestead on every drive into town. However, the unexpected burden of living with this compulsive cleaner fell upon the willow man's immediate neighbors, Elias and Clara Hinck, who did not enjoy a very sociable relationship with the willow man, and not for lack of effort. Their attempts at friendliness were accepted but not reciprocated. Like his mother, Dorothy, before him, the willow man simply wished to be left alone to shape his branches into stunning furniture and live the life of a hermit. And so the Hincks and others left the willow man to himself, at least until the arrival and then mysterious disappearance of Roxy, the Hinck's imposing yet affectionate German shepherd.

Given her breed, Roxy was a large dog, and to the unknowing eye, she looked like something straight out of Africa—half lion, half hyena with the speed of a gazelle and the strength of a water buffalo. Her bark was definitely worse than her non-existent bite, and she had a healthy curiosity in every passing creature, both human and animal. For those of us who frequented Lake Dunbar in those years, we got to know and appreciate Roxy, all one-hundred-plus pounds. I even spotted the dog swimming across the entire width of the northern-most bay one summer day, presumably returning from some canine curiosity in the heavily wooded property across the bay.

The unthinkable turn of events seemingly had its start when the willow man complained about the wandering Roxy and pointed with horror at the trampled hostas all along the front of his cabin. The willow man screamed and hollered whenever Roxy approached, and given how close they lived and Roxy's penchant for adventure, this happened several times each day. The willow man brusquely informed the Hincks they needed to keep Roxy tied up on the other side of their property, far away from his precious, sensitive plants. However, Lake Dunbar sits in Minnesota's remote and far northern forests, and Roxy had enjoyed free reign for years, a freedom she routinely respected by never venturing farther than yelling distance from the Hinck log cabin, and then only to meet another canine or human visitor with wagging tail and panting tongue. The tension between the willow man and the Hincks concerning Roxy increased, without an acceptable res-olution, so Roxy's unbounded roaming continued for a while longer.

"Roxy, Roxy." One afternoon in early May, Clara Hinck called for Roxy to come into the house—but the large and faithful dog was nowhere to be found. She called and called, to no avail. She then strode up and down the dirt road in search of Roxy, even traipsing through all of the neighbors' woods. Nothing. No sign of Roxy any-where. After an hour, the poor lady became downright frantic, for the seven-year-old Roxy had never wandered off for this length of time before. Where could she be? Mrs. Hinck called her husband at work, and together they again searched every corner of Lake Dunbar, but still no luck. As daylight faded, so did their hopes, fearing the worst for a dog that never missed a meal in her entire life. Before reluctantly giving up their search and going to bed for the night, they called everyone in the neighborhood, including the willow man, in the misplaced hope Roxy had been spotted by someone on the lake. They even tried the Itasca County Sheriff, but came up empty-handed. By morning, the Hincks were in a full panic. At daybreak, with still no sight of Roxy, Mrs. Hinck drew up several flyers she posted all over the area, showing a picture of Roxy and asking anyone with information about her disappearance or whereabouts to call them immediately. They even offered a modest reward. However, minutes painfully turned into hours, hours into days, then days into weeks. No one called, and Roxy did not come home. Soon, the Hincks reluctantly resigned themselves to the obvious. Something horrible, unthinkable had happened to their beloved Roxy, and more than likely they would never know exactly what happened.

From day one of this ordeal, the Hincks cast a suspicious eye toward their neighbor, the willow man, given his strident dislike of Roxy for the way she incessantly trampled on his flowers. However, their allegation was only a gut feeling with no actual fact the reclusive willow man had something to do with Roxy's fate. Nevertheless, after less than a week, the local rumor mill was aflutter with talk surrounding one suspect and one suspect only—the willow man. Local gossip reached fever pitch when a hunter from the neighboring town of Alvwood reported he'd overheard the willow man asking around Bluegill Bar whether anyone was willing to make a discreet delivery for him a few weeks earlier. Upon hearing this news, many in Squaw Lake had drawn their own conclusion—the willow man took Roxy, and hired someone else to drive her (or her body) some distance. Still, there was absolutely no proof, nothing beyond circumstantial supposition and speculation. Weeks passed, and the chill of a late northern spring soon turned into the dog days of summer. Just as everyone had given up hope of ever solving Roxy's mysterious disappearance, the regional beverage distributor rolled through town and made an obligatory stop at the Max Store in order to replenish its stock of sodas, iced teas, and over-priced bottled waters.

The deliveryman lingered in the store, shooting the breeze with the familiar cashier clerk and sipping a cup of the Max Store's unusually fine brewed coffee. Perusing the message board adjacent the store's exit, which was covered in all variety of signs, the deliveryman paused at the "Missing Dog" poster and the seemingly familiar photo of Roxy. "Huh," he said while gazing at the poster, his mind several miles away. "Sure looks like the stray they showed me up at Red Lake." Although talking mostly to himself, the deliveryman was the only patron in the store, and thus was overheard by Sara Cauley at the cashier's post.

"You've seen that dog?" she inquired with a mix of circumspection and cautious hope.

"Well, I think so. It sure looks like her. I was up at Red Lake last month, and they were regaling me with a story of the magical dog who wandered into their resort seemingly out of nowhere."

"Red Lake?" Sara asked with a start. "That's seventy miles north of here as the loon flies. It can't be the same dog. Did you actually see her?"

"Yeah, I did. Just as the Red Lake clerk was telling me the story, into the store walked a woman from Grand Forks, North Dakota, along with the stray dog she'd been housing in her rental cabin. I guess when the dog walked into the resort off the main road, the owner wanted nothing to do with it. He's already got enough responsibility as it is. Anyway, this lady from Grand Forks was staying at the resort and was a real dog lover, so she insisted on taking the poor thing in." Then, with a chuckle he added, "I guess when the resort owner reminded the lady about the 'No Pets' policy, she right told him either the dog would be welcomed with her, or she'd find a new place for the both of them to stay for the rest of the month. So, the guest got her way, and the dog stayed in the visiting woman's cabin. By the end of her extended stay, if no one claimed the stray, and it had nowhere else to go, the lady said she'd pack up the dog with her stuff and drive back home to North Dakota."

"Are you sure about this?" Sara asked rather skeptically.

"I can't say for 100 percent certain, but if it ain't the same looking dog, it's a pretty close impersonator."

"What's the name of the resort again?" Sara was bound and determined to follow up on this lead, the only one they'd had on Roxy's disappearance at all, other than the hunter's story about the willow man looking for a hit man/driver. She took down all of the deliveryman's details and quickly called the Hincks. They in turn called up to Red Lake, and soon had the phone number for the guest from North Dakota. A few days later, the Hincks drove several hundred miles west to Grand Forks and retrieved their beloved dog, Roxy, returning her home where she belonged at Lake Dunbar.

When confronted some time later, the willow man expressed as much shock as anyone else, both at the fact Roxy was alive, and she had found her way home. To this day, no one has solved the case of the missing German shepherd that ended up so far from home, but nearly everyone rejoiced in her homecoming. The Hincks keep a close watch on Roxy these days, and even tie her up on a long chain on their property when they can't watch her every single second. And the willow man? He's still there too, perhaps plotting the next way to vex his neighbors, or possibly just cursing the beverage deliveryman and the incredible luck, against all odds. This unexpected and unwitting stooge foiled the possibility of the willow man from ever living in peace next door to the inimitable Roxy.

As entertaining and varied as the neighbors could be, they ultimately paled in comparison to the even more exciting array of wildlife encounters our family experienced on Lake Dunbar. Our stories involve every imaginable form of feathered and four-legged forager, virtually everything other than a Sasquatch, and most of these tales were witnessed by only two people: my parents, Ted and Ruth. Now, my brother and I speculated from time to time how the never-ending, never-resting life of restaurateurs led my parents to become rather crazed, or at least more so than they already were. Nowhere was this more evident than in their stories and Whispering Pines journal entries from the early years of this decade. It all started innocently enough with a very early trip north in mid-April. With ice still covering half of the lake, my parents were forced to focus on the woods, which is precisely where their long line of strange or exaggerated animal encounters began. From my mother's entry in the cabin journal:

I took Friday off from work and we drove north, arriving at Whispering Pines around one in the afternoon. Ted and I spent most of the afternoon cutting, chopping, and dragging logs and small trees. Physically exhausted, we headed to The Hill for dinner and the Co-op to select a movie for the VHS. Inside the cabin was a bit chilly, but outside it was in the mid-60s. Both Saturday and Sunday were spectacular days, sunny and warm. Ted spent hours clearing paths in the forest for the grandchildren to traverse while I picked up and stacked all of the sticks left in the wake of Ted's chain saw. This went on all weekend, at least until Sunday morning when I was deep in the woods and a giant snake appeared. I swear it stared directly at me, and I did what any sane person would do in that situation. I screamed. Needless to say, Ted could not convince me to return to the woods for the remainder of our stay. Before retreating nearer the cabin, I also witnessed a large loon nest and two trees recently felled by those pesky beavers. As usual, we worked far too hard and relaxed far too little, but the eagles are here, the loons are here, and life is good.

The action continued a few weeks later when Ted and Ruth ventured north on the eve of the blessed event every Minnesota sportsman anticipates through our dreadfully long winters: Fishing Opener. An entry from Ted during a trip in early May:

Wow, a four-day break from the prison/restaurant! Incomprehensible. For early May, the weather was delightful, though Sunday's was a little bleak. We took long walks on the road toward the south end of the lake, and moved a dozen or more pine trees to a more hospitable place. Ruth saw a couple of interesting fauna episodes. First, a hawk or owl snatched another good-sized bird off a tree. It was large and looked like a turkey, or possibly some form of hawk or eagle. It had a long red beak with white on its tail. Then we saw what we think was a pair of canvasbacks down in the Lake. Ruth thought it was an albino loon at first.

Now, tree-nesting turkeys and the first-time-in-recorded-history albino loon were surely something to behold, but it wasn't until a few years later my brother and I started contemplating a psychiatric intervention for our parents, the Doctors Doolittle, upon reading our mother's animal-antics journal entry in the summer of 2005:

I can't believe we had five full days here at Whispering Pines. We had really nice weather with some scattered rain, but not too much. While replacing rotting boards on the shed, Ted got attacked by killer bees as he must have disturbed their nest under the eaves of the shed. He got three stings. We also saw a moose swim across the lake right out front of the cabin, coming from the south end of the lake and continuing on toward the Hunting Lodge on the northern end (Editorial note: a two-mile swim). We then saw a deer on the road near the cabin and the funniest-looking fish, a dolphin pike, bobbing in the water near our boat and sticking his mouth up as if gasping for air. He disappeared under the boat, and when I caught a real northern shortly after, I threw him back toward the bobbing dolphin-pike in case he was looking for his friend. Later, when we went to sit on the deck chairs on the dock, Ted noticed a snake curled up alongside the coiled boat rope, and it didn't move as we walked slowly past, though he eventually wriggled his way back down the dock toward shore. Last but not least, we saw an eight-inch fish at the base of the tree roots next to our dock, just sitting there in a half-inch of water.

Killer bees, backstroking moose, a dolphin pike, rope-imitating snakes, a deer, and a fish trying to survive in water that does not even reach its gills. In the entire fifty-year history of the Travis presence on Lake Dunbar, the rest of our extended family combined has witnessed exactly one of these same events, usually at the end of a rifle during deer hunting season. As fantastical as this may sound, I made none of it up. These were their experiences, real or imagined, and they were just the tip of the iceberg. Over the ensuing three years, they would witness and experience every imaginable (and unimaginable) form of northwoods creature, recorded in excruciating detail.

Given what happened at the end of their July cabin trip, combined with the unwelcome anaconda/garter snake incident earlier in spring, it is surprising my mother would continue to subject herself to the numerous and inevitable scary creatures of the forest. Nevertheless, Ruth would do just about anything for her grandchildren, and when we joined my parents at the end of their fateful time at the cabin, the opportunity for more creepy, crawly terror once again presented itself. We had arrived at the peak season for berry picking, and you could literally see the plump, deep-red raspberries hanging from the bushes adjacent the road as we made our slow and final approach to Whispering Pines.

"Grandma, we saw berries down the road. Let's go pick 'em!" yelled Tyler. He was halfway out of the truck racing toward his beloved grandma Ruth practically before I had brought the truck to a complete stop.

"Sure," she joyfully replied. "Get some buckets from the shed and we'll go picking. Maybe we can even make a pie if we gather enough." I must admit the thought of fresh-picked northern raspberries appealed to me as well, and I joined them after unloading our weekend gear. By the time my wife and I caught up with them, Mom and Tyler had plucked enough juicy berries from their unsuspecting branches for two or three pies and nine jars of fresh jam. I had barely picked a handful myself (deposited into my mouth, rather than my bucket) when I heard the most painful and gut-wrenching scream imaginable. It came from twenty yards away where my mother stood motionless in shock before racing toward me in the deep brush, shouting, "Get it off! Get it off!"

Mom had lifted her blouse halfway up, not exactly the sight adult men wish to see on their mothers. However, there was no mistaking the source of her screams, for next to her belly button was firmly affixed the largest wolf spider I'd ever seen, and at least five times as large as her navel. I safely positioned myself behind my wife, so she'd reach Mom first. After all, I'm no greater fan of large arachnids than my screaming mother. Neither one of us could ever touch the nasty things. Thankfully my wife whisked it away with one brush of the back of her hand before Mom nearly collapsed in exhaustion and appreciation. The only thing keeping her from a full collapse, in fact, was the knowledge the ugly, horrible wolf spider was now lurking somewhere on the ground in the immediate vicinity. Needless to say, berry picking ended for the day, though I'm certain Mom had numerous painful flashbacks with every last bite of those scrumptious raspberry pies.

Things settled down for my parents in the ensuing years, but the parade of animal encounters continued for the rest of us unabated. Tyler picked up right where his grandparents left off, divining stories of the fantastical creatures of the local lakes and woodlands. Upon arriving at Lake Dunbar for our inaugural trip of 2006, neighbor Clara Hinck informed us one of the residents on the opposite side of the lake had blown up the beaver dam on Dunbar River over the winter in order to free up a path along the meandering creek all the way over to Round Lake. It also had the unwelcome side effect of lowering our lake water and making our dock stick out high above the water line and virtually impossible to use for casting a line or launching a boat. Tyler listened intently to Clara's tale of the heartless neighbor's use of dynamite to completely destroy the home of the Lake Dunbar's truly busy beaver. And while Tyler felt no great affection for those beavers that had unceremoniously gnawed down several tall aspens on our own property, he also did not wish any harm upon one of God's creation.

These thoughts occupied his seven-year-old mind for the rest of the day and into the night, for he emerged from the bunkroom far after his normal bedtime, asking rather directly, "Were there any beavers inside when the neighbor blew up their dam?"

I answered as best and as ignorantly as I could, saying, "I don't know for sure, but I don't think so. Clara is sure she spotted the beavers swimming down here and looking for new trees to rebuild their home." And I added for good measure, "She also said they stopped to pee all over that neighbor's yard in revenge."

My answer seemed to assure him no foul play had been committed, even though he continued to hold a grudge against the TNT-happy neighbor for destroying the beaver's well-built house. Tyler returned to his perch in the uppermost bunk, seemingly at peace with the beaver's fate, at least until his mind followed a long path of logical segue jolting him again out of his bed and marching right back into the living room where I was trying to watch a movie.

"Now I know why we didn't catch any fish today, after trying all afternoon. Big Ed and all of the other fish must have swum out of the lake, down the river, and into the next lake!"

Ah yes, Big Ed. I'm certain every lake has one, though perhaps by a different name. Big Ed was the name I gave to the mythical, huge, elusive walleye pike living in Lake Dunbar. He was both the envy of all other fish in the lake, and the target of every fisherman above its surface. From the time my son was old enough to understand, I told him stories of Big Ed, how the fish would tauntingly surface near our boat, eyeing us with his steely, cold gaze, and how he had out-strategized and out-lived many a fisherman, including several in our own family. I had Tyler convinced Big Ed was a prize worth seeking, a catch worth long hours of dedicated fishing in the rain and wind, and how a glimpse of him was a sight worth beholding. He devoured those stories with rapt attention and hunger, even to the point of occasionally convincing himself on occasion Big Ed had tugged on his fishing lines before spitting out the hook and slinking off into Dunbar's depths. I consider those stories to be anything other than deception, for who's to say there isn't a Big Ed in our lake? After all, there have been more plausible sightings of that giant fish than there have been of the monster in Loch Ness. Regardless, I think my stories were inhaled by my son more deeply than Big Ed ever swallowed a shiny silver hook, for Tyler still believes in his existence today, far longer than he held onto a belief in Santa. Apparently I convinced my parents of this hidden creature's existence as well, for in the cabin journal on June 10, 2007, my mother wrote:

Ted and I drove up for a short trip with granddaughter Savannah who caught her first fish. I also felt a huge hit on my line and something in the water swirled back and forth causing quite a wave near the boat before—boom—my line broke. I think it was Big Ed.

True to my stories over the years, Big Ed proved craftier than any of us above the surface, and to this day he has avoided capture. However, this reality has not discouraged my fisherman son, for he continued his quest and has taken great solace in the creatures he has landed into our small green fishing boat. One week after Mom's brush with Big Ed, Tyler caught a stringer full of walleyes in addition to a sizeable "northern python," known to everyone else as a "northern pike," or just plain "northern." A few weeks later our focus was on pan-fish, and we landed plenty of sunfish, crappies, and pumpkinseeds. At dinner Tyler proclaimed, "This is the best fish I've ever tasted!" Soon, this seasoned, expert fisherman was feeling rather confident in his angling abilities, and rightly so, given the volume and variety of his catch. Tyler's confidence showed up in spades during a 2008 fishing trip with my parents and son. As Dad wrote in the journal:

On Saturday the clouds parted to reveal a glorious sunshine. We took Tyler out for a trip around the lake in Eleanor's old green boat, and it turned into quite a contest. To this point in our journey, none of us had caught a thing, but a change in the weather brought a change in our luck. As we backed out into the Lake, I caught a tremendous bass on my very first cast. Tyler barely looked at my prize, obviously intent on either catching something more grand or hauling in more fish than me by the end of our outing. Within an hour, together we'd caught ten northerns. I specifically recall catching six of them, though one did not make it fully into the boat, according to Tyler, announcing new rules on the spot for counting fish, and another of mine did not count because it was allegedly the same fish I had caught and released five minutes earlier. Although under protest, I eventually agreed our contest ended in a tie at four fish apiece. Adding insult to injury, Tyler called me at home two days after our trip, asking me to pay him ten dollars for the fishing lesson.

My niece, Savannah, Alex and his wife's only daughter, also enjoyed this same playfulness with my parents. Such a pretty young girl, she was a natural heir to the jovial, fun-loving spirit of my grandmother and mother. She exuded an abundant love of life, and shared her joyfulness with everyone she met. This earned her an endearing nickname early on, with a double entendre to reflect both her happy disposition and her favorite Dunbar fish, Sunny. Seven-year-old Sunny would eventually spend many a weekend with her grandparents on Lake Dunbar, and perhaps more than anyone else in her generation of Travis family, she would become the most prolific catcher of fish. What's more, Sunny succeeded in discovering a species of fish none in the family had ever seen or heard of before. It was the ugliest and strangest-looking beast you can imagine, and no one other than Sunny would even dare to touch the wretched fish, so poor Sunny had to remove them from her hook one by one as she caught scores of these creatures right off the dock. Not recognizing the species, and determining quickly it was neither pike nor panfish, we asked around the lake and later in town what this odd creature might be. The oldest-known fisherman in Squaw Lake solved our quest when we finally shared a photo of the fish around town one day.

"That there's a lawyer fish. We call it a lawyer because it's an ugly, nasty, and unwelcome old catch." Of course, the conversation quickly took a turn for the worse for me once my father shared that I was a lawyer. The old fisherman's reply? "Like I said, those lawyers are ugly, nasty, and unwelcome." Everyone present had a great laugh at my expense. As it turns out, the "lawyer" fish is officially known as the bowfin or dogfish (again, because of its unsightly, mongrel-like appearance) and is actually Minnesota's most ancient fish, a species dating back to the time of the dinosaurs. These medium-sized, greenish-looking fish thrive in murky, oxygen-depleted waters of lakes and streams, and have been known to survive quite a long time out of water, at least compared to other fish. A Department of Natural Resources publication says it is the male bowfin who primarily tends to the young, so I suddenly felt less offended about them being nicknamed "the lawyer fish," at least until I read further and learned the baby bowfin's primary predator is none other than adult bowfin. The lawyer fish apparently eats its young.

As these middle years of the twenty-first century's first decade came toward a close, we continued to experience the vast diversity of Dunbar's wildlife. In 2007, our neighbor Elias Hinck caught a fifty-pound snapping turtle near the shore out front of his cabin. He took the reptile down to St. Paul where he displayed her at the State Fair, and even won a blue ribbon, before driving her all the way back home and releasing the turtle back into the wild waters. Neighbor JT Dubois reported seeing a large cougar just across the lake from our cabin, a fine-looking cat he estimated at 140 or more pounds. While I would not care to meet face to face with either of these wild animals, perhaps the scariest encounter was experienced on a long family walk deep into the heart of the Chippewa National Forest. Mom and Dad joined my family and me for a long cabin weekend, and together we all headed out one morning after breakfast to walk the length of Lake Dunbar before turning inland through some deer paths in the forest. It was a gorgeous summer day, with minimal bugs and maximum sunshine. Carrying an ample supply of water and picnic snacks, we ventured farther into the woods than we ever had before and everyone pushed forward in anticipation of what lay around the next corner, and the next one and the next one.

Leading the charge was none other than my faithful yellow Labrador retriever, Max, who ran with limitless energy and inexhaustible curiosity over the innumerable smells of nature flooding his senses. He would run back toward us every so often to check in, and always when called, but otherwise sprinted like the wind, dodging trees and diving into the bushes perhaps in the hopes of flushing out some wild game. Well, Max got all he asked for and then some when he ran into a wild animal he had never before experienced, and likely never will want to again. We all heard him yelping with pain in the distance, and Tyler jogged faster ahead than the rest of us, reaching Max in a matter of seconds and then yelling for my assistance. The very worst crossed my mind. Was Max caught in a metal trap, in the mouth of a mother black bear, or in the grip of a puma? What I saw as I rounded the corner hidden by some tall brush was far less threatening, but likely for Max just as painful. Tyler had succeeded in pulling Max back from the brush and onto the trail, preventing him from diving back into the woods for round two. As my faithful dog turned his head at my approach, I quickly saw the problem—a dozen or more quills sticking straight out of his face and snout.

We were miles from our cabin, or from anyone else's, so we couldn't yell or run for more help. We also couldn't expect Max to walk all the way back to Whispering Pines in this condition, for he would surely try to impatiently rub out the quills, making matters worse. So we did the only thing we could think of, and I held Max tight while Dad plucked out the quills, one by excruciating one. As for the porcupine that inflicted this damage, we saw him perched in a nearby tree, likely feeling whatever sense of victory a wild animal can feel.

Undoubtedly, for our family, fishing and hiking are the first and second most favorite recreational activities at Whispering Pines, not necessarily in that order. A close third, however, is venturing to the Squaw Lake Dump. Yes, the dump, as in trash, junk, garbage. Every generation of the Travis family has spent untold evenings watching the sun set over the mighty pine trees, amidst the aroma of human refuse. Almost exactly at sundown, with the sky still well lit, the show begins. Everyone in the car pushes his or her way as far forward as possible, hoping for the first sighting and the best view of bears. Northern Minnesota's black bears are generally shy, and will see you long before, if ever, you see them. But when it comes to the food free-for-all at the Squaw Lake Dump, a bear's reticence vanishes as he forages for food to the delight of the onlookers.

The younger members of the Travis family have mixed feelings of fear and excitement as bears rumble through the trash pickings. Then, of course, occasionally a macho male member of the family gets out of the car for a closer look, much to the chagrin and protests of those still in the vehicle. Uncle Jack tried such a maneuver once, only to be scared back into the car upon sighting a previously unnoticed, fast-approaching, and curious bear. Black bears are impressive, strong animals, even human-like in their curiosity and meaningful stares. As black bears rummage through the dump, they effortlessly move aside rusted stoves and broken refrigerators in order to forage delicately through bags of discarded food scraps. Watching these creatures in action is truly breathtaking, and dreaming about them can be frightening.

If I were to survey my extended family, however, I think there would be near unanimity in our vote for favorite wildlife at Lake Dunbar. Faster than an eagle, more stealth than a cougar, smaller than a squirrel, and hungrier than a bear, this particular creature is also relatively easy to lure into sight from the cabin's kitchen table. One of the very first tasks we undertake upon arrival at Whispering Pines on every visit is to fill a large pitcher with water at room temperature, mixed with several cups of refined white sugar. We then fill two red plastic feeders with this super sweet mixture, hang them from a nail in the facia board in front of the cabin's two picture windows, and await the arrival of a hummingbird. Experts report these tiny beings migrate annually from as far away as Argentina, all the way north to the middle of Canada, and back. Their tiny wings flutter an incredible fifty-five times per second at top throttle, and their miniscule hearts beat far more rapidly than ours, as many as twelve hundred beats per minute.

I never tire of peering out our cabin's main window, gazing toward the lake, only to have my visual focal point reorient itself to a spot a few feet from where I stand. I am watching a ruby-throated hummingbird fly gingerly close to the feeder, appear to look around for predators, then perch itself along the red rim of the plastic contraption, and stick its relatively long nose into the pencil-lead-sized holes, drawing deeply from the sugary manmade nectar. Regrettably, they never remain for more than a moment, flying off instantly to some far-off nest or temporary perch. They will appear again and again over the course of an entire weekend, perhaps knowing they must drink their fill before this group of humans departs, forcing them to look for feeders at other cabins around the lake.

An Ojibwe legend says hummingbirds symbolize timeless joy and the nectar of life. These tiny creatures accomplish what seems impossible and represent energy, wonder, and swift graceful action. I like that image, for these spectacular birds teach us that joy is simple, life is a miracle, and that happiness in life can be found when we simply flutter our wings and dance.

SISTERHOOD

I GREW UP WITH A BROTHER. COUSINS KATE AND ROSE WERE the closest thing I had to sisters in my formative years. Later I would have very close female friends both in college and then in law school, but I can't say I truly know what it means to enjoy the bonds of sisterhood. My mother, on the other hand, lived with two of them so I've heard tales about the benefits (and detriments) of having sisters. Mom's eldest sibling, Aunt Eleanor, is certainly the sweetest soul you could ever know, the kind of person who truly places the happiness of others above her own. Eleanor often showed her love for others through cooking, and boy was she good at it. My aunt was particularly known for turning out multiple pans of a single dish all at once, and sending a batch home with anyone within reach who would accept it. Everyone did. Her specialties included manicotti, enchiladas, and all varieties of sweet desserts. Eleanor's banana bread was my all-time favorite. She also created a unique, homemade sandwich consisting of ground-up bologna, mayonnaise, and dill pickles served between two slices of soft, white Wonder bread. It may or may not sound appetizing to you, but our family could never get enough of the delectable treat we famously named "Ellie's Sandwich."

When Eleanor and her husband, Paul, left their hometown of Greenwood in the mid-1950s following Paul's naval service in the Pacific, they settled in Colombia Heights where they would raise two children and live out the rest of their lives. Luckily for everyone else in the wider Travis family, Colombia Heights sits strategically along the route from our homes in the southern part of the state onward to Lake Dunbar in the north. On virtually every trip to the Whispering Pines cabin, the family would stop by to visit with Aunt Eleanor for the opportunity to spend some quality time with this wonderful lady, knowing also she would invariably send us off with enough pans of delicious homemade creations to last us through the weekend. Her only request: bring back her baking dish when you were through, hopefully washed and clean. I recall one particularly cold and windy weekend late in the season when Eleanor outfitted us with a pan of her signature dish, lasagna with spicy Italian sausage, complete with grated Parmesan cheese, a loaf of French bread, and even a stick of butter. We rarely missed a stop at Eleanor and Paul's as we sped north toward Whispering Pines, and our stomachs were always rewarded as a result.

My brother, Alex, was no exception to this routine, though he also succeeded in causing me a bit of trouble with my beloved aunt. It was an early May trip north for Alex's family, and they too were treated to a freshly made pan of Eleanor's delicious lasagna with all of the fixings. Although they heated and consumed most of the Italian delight upon arrival at Dunbar that chilly Friday night, the last four pieces were snatched off of the countertop by their hungry, industrious dog, Pixie. As the canine slyly dove for the very last piece, she succeeded in bringing Eleanor's thirteen-by-nine-inch glass baking dish crashing down on the floor, split in half. Alex was beside himself with worry, not so much for the number of times he would likely now need to let Pixie outside during the night to relieve herself following four servings of lasagna, but rather in trying to figure out what to say to our dear Aunt Eleanor. Alex's wife devised a potential plan to make everything right. Perusing the offerings at Ida's Emporium the next morning, she came across and purchased a same-sized glass baking dish, though not with the exact same design as Eleanor's original dish. However, it was close enough and, more importantly, served the same purpose.

Coincidentally (or not), Alex was forced to drive a different route home after this dish-breaking trip to the cabin, due to a detour on the normal route through Colombia Heights. Knowing I would see our aunt two weeks later, Alex asked me to return the dish on his behalf, offering whatever apology seemed appropriate. Sure enough, I appeared at my aunt and uncle's door later in the month to "return" the new glass baking dish, and gleefully accept whatever edible delight Eleanor might offer. I also made the intentional though not-well-thought-out decision to save my brother some embarrassment and not mention the broken original, but rather simply hand over the purchased replacement. What was I thinking? Just like the proverbial parents who replace their child's dead goldfish or hamster with a new "look-alike" in the hopes of saving the child some unnecessary grief, it never works. Just as a child can tell the difference between a beloved pet and an imposter, Aunt Eleanor immediately knew this was not her baking dish.

"Thanks, Eddie, but this is not my dish. Perhaps you mixed it with one at home before you left?"

The dilemma was about to take off in a new direction, toward the gravitational pull of my idiocy. In addition to not wanting to hurt Eleanor's feelings about a favorite baking dish, I also did not want to appear to be making excuses by pointing the finger of blame at Alex in his absence. Under pressure to say something, anything, without telling an outright lie, I blurted, "Well, the original had a crack, so we got you a new one in its place."

"Funny, it wasn't cracked when I baked lasagna for your brother. Oh well," she said forlornly, "I guess this will do, even if it isn't quite as nice as mine. Thanks, Eddie."

What could I say other than "You're welcome" and move on? Somehow, I was likely tagged with blame for the broken dish, and would have to live with it. Thanks, brother, I owe you one. Luckily, I had built up years of goodwill with Aunt Eleanor, having spent many days in her and Uncle Paul's quaint cedar-shake rambler home. I really enjoyed hanging out with my older cousins, and they patiently tolerated me. I specifically remember staying with Aunt Eleanor and her family back in the winter of 1974, when I was almost eight. I had just been summarily dropped off at Eleanor and Paul's house by my parents who were racing to the airport for a three-week trip to the tropics. I'm not even sure they slowed the car down as I jumped out and navigated my way across Central Boulevard, holding my sleeping bag and H.R. Puff-n-Stuff lunch box. Staying with my aunt, uncle, and cousins was truly a vacation for me; however, I still had to attend school every weekday during my visit. We played card games non-stop, ate an abundance of delectable food cooked by my culinary-expert aunt, and inexplicably did a lot of typing, presumably because my scholarly cousin Rose had just taken a typing class and was anxious to teach me as well. All in all, I thought my older cousins were the coolest people on the planet (I still do). I thought Uncle Paul was a shrewd but fair card player (he always made sure we each won the same number of games), and my dear Aunt Eleanor was of course an excellent cook (I got dessert every night). But rather than retell the story with a revisionist perspective, I've included some journal entries from my wonderful three-week stay, as told through the eyes of my seven-year-old self.

Tues., Jan. 29, 1974
Today I got up and went to school. During the day my mom and dad went to Brizzill and I had gym. My uncle Paul gave me a ride home and then I played cards with my cousin Walt. We told jokes and riddles, then watched Gilligan's Island. Then cousin Rose made me do some typing. Aunt Eleanor made us hamburgers, beans, pickles, onions, and cottage cheese then we watched Marcus Welby and went to bed.

Thurs., Jan. 31, 1974
I woke up and had hot chocolate and went to school and I had music. Then when I went home my cousin Walt gave me a ride and we went to the library. Then we went home, played cards, and watched The Waltons before dinner. We had hot dish, then we played more cards and went to bed.

Fri., Feb. 1, 1974
I woke up and had hot chocolate and toast, then I played cards and went to school. In school I had show and tell, then I went home. Earlier we changed our desks around, and this was the last day for Jody! When I got home we played cards and had pretzels and water, then Rose and I typed a little. Then for supper we had beans mixed with hamburger, then I watched Snoopy and Six Million Dollar Man.

Groundhog Day, Sat., Feb. 2, 1974

I woke up and typed a little with Rose, then we had scrambled eggs, toast, and elderberry jelly, then I typed a little more. I went to my friend Troy's birthday party and had a cupcake, ice cream, and a dish of M&M's. Then for supper we had hamburger and potato hash. After a while we had pizza, then I went to bed.

Mon., Feb. 4, 1974

I woke up and went to Country Kitchen. I had orange juice, hot chocolate, and French toast with butter and syrup. It was maple. And today is my cousin Walt's birthday. We danced the jitterbug, and then I had to learn to type the "f" and "j" from Rose. We had barbecue ribs and my cousin played cards, then we all went to bed.

In fairness to cousin Rose, I should acknowledge, while typing may or may not have been my favorite activity as a seven-year-old, she clearly was an excellent teacher then, as she is now professionally. I recently uncovered a handwritten letter to me in a box of old papers from Great-Grandma Katherine, Isabelle's mom, dated February 3, 1974. The first two sentences sum it up well. "Dear Eddie, you are pretty smart typing a letter, and you did a good job. You did better than I would as I never have learned to type."

Perhaps Rose is the one to blame, then, for inspiring me to write, because ever since staying with her family, I have kept a personal journal, and yearned to write books. Yet, I should also credit Aunt Eleanor for encouraging me along the way. She was always supportive of my endeavors, whatever they might be, and she often wrote notes of thoughtful praise. It was especially heartening to receive her letter a few years back after I had sent her the first manuscript of a novel in progress. "I wanted to let you know I read your book," she wrote. "I really enjoyed it, and am very proud of you. How many of us really do things we dream of? Who knows, maybe someday you can be a writer along with being a lawyer."

And so it was especially sad to receive a call from my cousin Rose one day in 2009, telling me her mom, Eleanor, was experiencing some sudden, unexpected health challenges related to the removal of a cancerous bile duct a decade earlier. Over the course of several weeks, she had become ashen-looking, rather weak, and experienced pains in her abdomen. It seemed her liver was slowly failing, a long-term side effect of the decade-old surgery. Soon, Eleanor was moved to a hospice where she could be under constant nursing care. As much as it surely pained her to be away from Uncle Paul and unable to bake her daily meals for the entire family, I think she knew it was the right place to be, and she did not put up a fuss. My parents and I, along with my brother, Alex, went to visit Eleanor and bring a gift basket of fruit. She welcomed us with weak though open arms from her bedside, and we had as nice a visit as ever. Of course, Eleanor wanted to hear all about our busy lives, and not dwell for a minute on hers. She apologized for missing Tyler's recent birthday as she did not have a chance to buy a card. Just like his cousin Savannah, Tyler received a birthday card from Eleanor and Paul every single year, and it contained a gift of money. One year we reciprocated, sending her a birthday card containing a crisp one-dollar bill. She never spent it because "it was too precious," she said, and it hangs to this day on the family office wall along with the card and drawings from my son. This will forever be my enduring image of Aunt Eleanor—always spending her time and talents on others, while rarely spending anything on herself.

As we left the hospice, wondering whether we'd ever see our beloved Eleanor again in this lifetime, our hearts were heavy with silent sadness. My cousin Rose followed close behind, and thankfully lightened the air by changing the subject as we all moved toward our cars in the parking lot. "Hey guys, check out my newest tattoo." Rose had carefully and methodically chosen tasteful, artistic henna designs over the years, focused on elements of nature, love, and spirituality. Her latest marking was of an eagle, with dramatic flowing wings spread delicately across her right shoulder.

"Wow," I said. "Amazing. Though I'm not sure tattoos are for me."

"Well, I'm going to get one," my mother chimed in. "I've always wanted one, but just never knew what to choose. Any ideas?"

"Oh, you have so many options today," Rose replied. "Anything's possible. You could get a cross, a flower, or an eagle like mine. Heck, maybe you want to tattoo Ted's name across each of your arms," Rose teased, before chuckling her unique and infectious laugh. My cousin had also noticed my father's increasing discomfort with this conversation. Body art was not something Ted desired, much less approved.

"You're not getting a tattoo," Dad offered up to my mother in a slightly quieter tone, trying to end this talk of nonsense with enough verbal force to reflect the seriousness of his conviction.

"Oh, I'm not?" Mom retorted without any attempt to match Dad's hushed tone. Closing in on seventy years of age, my mother was intent on doing whatever she wanted to her body, no matter what anyone said.

Sensing her defiance, Dad did his best to diffuse the situation while subtly maintaining the earnestness of his perspective. "Well, if you do get one, I just may not sleep with you any more."

"Really?" Mom said, without missing a beat. "Is that all it would take?"

Game, set, and match to Mom. Well played. We all soon dispersed to our cars, making our way back to our respective homes. And as I drove away from the hospice, the sadness about my dear Aunt Eleanor's declining health was slightly offset by a growing smile as I thought of my mother's quick wit, and by my curiosity over what kind of tattoo she would inevitably soon get.

Within a few weeks, Eleanor Travis Hudson passed away following seventy-six years of a humble and love-filled life. The day we heard of Aunt Eleanor's death, my brother and I headed north along with my parents to what has been an annual tradition at Whispering Pines for the past fifty-five years. It was time to close the cabin for the winter and to store Eleanor's old green boat until spring. It is always nostalgic for me to be at Lake Dunbar at this time of year, where I palpably feel the spirit and presence of those in the family who have gone before me, including Grandma and Grandpa Travis; my aunt Stella; Eleanor's son, my cousin Walt; and of course my beloved cousin Kate. As we all sat at the large walnut dining room table the first night, looking out over the changing colors of the fall leaves and still waters on Lake Dunbar, I thought about Eleanor. I'm sure we all did. As we shared our own reflections on Eleanor, we all agreed we knew of few people who not only lived with such dignity, but who also died with dignity in the manner of Eleanor, and also the manner of death expressed by her son Walt. This was a tremendous testimony not only to Eleanor, but also Paul and their wonderful family, demonstrating the kind of love and caring Eleanor had so well taught them.

For those of us privileged to have had Eleanor's presence in our lives, we know her life was not about contradiction or motives; she truly lived her life from the heart. Hers was a joy of endless happiness. During her final visit with Eleanor, Mom asked her about the good times, and also possible regrets in her life. Eleanor looked at Mom and gave her a generous smile as she always did for everyone before saying, "I have absolutely no regrets, only happy memories."

I barely had time to recover from my dear aunt's passing when another jolt of news hit me like the proverbial ton of bricks. This time, the news was good. I remember the day so vividly. It was a special Saturday morning in March 2010, the time of year when we in Minnesota wake with new anticipation every morning as the temperatures climb with each passing sunrise and the hours of daylight increase ever so gradually with each fresh new spring day. I eagerly answered the phone upon seeing Mom's number on the caller ID, wondering what new and creative meal she had planned to serve at my parents' restaurant that Saturday night. Instead, Mom told me that she and Dad had just closed a deal to sell their restaurant in Greenwood. They had given their best efforts to my mother's life dream for more than a decade, and it was time to "hang up the spatula," according to my mother who laughed quite heartily at her own little joke. Within weeks they sold the restaurant to a younger couple, and happily moved back to Minneapolis where they would be closer to my brother, Alex, their grandchildren, and me. The challenge for my parents, however, was that the restaurant was far less profitable than they initially had hoped. In fact, a number of unexpected building repairs, along with the national recession, meant dipping far into their reserve savings. Rather than retire from the working life when they sold the restaurant, my parents went in search of new jobs at a rather late stage in their working lives.

Soon after closing that sale, my parents deservedly took off a few days for the most restful refuge they knew—the shores of Lake Dunbar. Yet, the term "rest" is not exactly in my parents' vocabulary when it comes to northwoods visits. In their minds, they always have one more project to tackle. This late spring of 2010 was no different. They sped out of town before dawn on a fresh June morning, stopping briefly for a coffee and cinnamon roll in Elk River and later purchasing a bucket of chub minnows in Squaw Lake for fishing. They spent the long weekend seeding the yard at Whispering Pines, and supervised our always-helpful neighbor, Elias Hinck, who had agreed to remove the large poplar tree whose ominous dead branches hung threateningly over the cabin's eastern roof.

Dad and Mom also tackled their long-desired plan to clear a portion of the adjacent woods to make way for planting new varieties of pine and hardwood trees that would mature in the generations to come. To do so, they commandeered a bobcat from Elias to level off the near-acre full of stumps left behind when they felled giant jack pines several years before. They also raked, trimmed, and seeded before a most wonderful slow rainfall arrived almost perfectly on schedule. When the skies cleared, they hauled out their new, gently used Snapper riding lawnmower, and Mom was in her glory driving it around the expansive cabin yard. Alex and I agreed to this lawnmower purchase with great trepidation, thinking about the frequently uneven lawns at Whispering Pines, as well as the very steep bank falling down to the lakefront. The first effort with the Snapper took Mom about four hours to completely mow the back and front yards, mainly because she was learning its navigation and limitations, and kept going in circles while missing spots of grass. Perhaps my fears for her safety were half justified, for I later learned Mom "only jumped off the Snapper once," when she felt it tipping over the edge of the embankment.

Regrettably I was not there to see this acrobatic sight, though I did arrive a day later to begin a weeklong stay at Whispering Pines. Tyler and I overlapped with my parents for one night, affording us the luxury of a sumptuous cabin-cooked meal from my mother, the master chef. Beef roast with potatoes, carrots, and onions, accompanied by a fresh-made coconut cream pie for dessert. Tyler served the role of sous chef alongside his grandma, and their efforts were roundly appreciated. Mom told me the next morning she had a vivid dream that made her feel confident about their decision to leave the restaurant business and seek new jobs. Fittingly, the dream was set at Lake Dunbar, and in it, my parents were adding a one-thousand-square-foot basement underneath Whispering Pines, along with other upgrades and amenities. In her dream, she sensed the presence of throngs of people, many of whom she did not know. One group was washing clothes belonging to a child, though she did not recall seeing a child with them. Then, in the dramatic moment of the dream, Mom walked down to the dock where she noticed a large woman casting a line using Mom's favorite fishing pole. My mother asked the stranger what she was doing there. When the woman ignored Mom as though she didn't belong, Mom, in not so kind words, told her to "get off my dock!" My cousin Rose was there too along with her husband, Patrick, talking about all the weekends they would now be spending at the cabin, and all of the fun they would have at Lake Dunbar this coming summer. When Mom later conveyed the details of this dream to me, she wondered aloud as to its meaning, and exactly what it was that made her feel more comfortable about their recent life change.

"That's easy," I replied. "You are a relatively private person, especially when it comes to issues of your personal finances. The cabin improvements in your dream represent your life, and in particular, your restaurant business, including your constant quest to make it grow in new and better directions. With the unfortunate economic situation, and the unexpected building problems, you feel as though all sorts of new people are invading your life and your personal well-being. The woman on the dock casting with your pole is one of your investors. She has invaded your beloved Lake Dunbar dock, and she is ignoring your pleas to get the hell out, which is how you feel about the dominating investors who pressured you guys into selling the place before it really made a profit." I concluded by saying that the part about my cousin Rose must represent the hopeful presence of a supportive family and that this concluding portion of the dream was what lifted her subconscious spirits and awakened her with fresh hope. Reflecting on this almost four years later, I think in fact my mother's dream was profoundly and eerily knowing, foretelling Rose Travis Hudson's return to Lake Dunbar in the future in a way none of us could have predicted in the spring of 2010.

LAKE DUNBAR DRAMA CLUB

THEY SAY THE TWO HAPPIEST DAYS IN A MAN'S LIFE OCCUR ON the day he buys a boat, and then on the day he sells it. If that's true, then one of the happiest days of my brother Alex's life took place in October of 2008 when he purchased a pontoon. I must admit he seemed to have struck a great deal with the outgoing members of the Lake Dunbar Fishing Club (LDFC). The LDFC was a group of four families who had pooled their money to build a very nice lake home on the northern end of Dunbar several years earlier. The place was the envy of so many on the lake with its long private driveway, expansive wooded property, and finely furnished interior. They even had an attached screened-in porch in which to escape marauding mosquitos on hot summer nights. The LDFC lasted for about a decade before its members decided to call it quits and sell their nice house and property to new owners. They also rid themselves of other cabin amenities, including a twenty-foot pontoon sitting on their property mostly unused for the past two seasons.

Now, for the record, I was not as enthusiastic about this purchase as my beloved brother, but I was convinced to go along with the deal, seeing as he reached such a favorable price, and all we had to do was move it several hundred yards down the road to Whispering Pines. My principal objection was a practical one; namely, I didn't want one more thing to take care of and repair while up at the lake. But, as part of the Travis Cabin Company democracy, my vote was duly noted and promptly defeated. Besides, my father pointed out, in the event of any trouble, we could always rely upon the expert service of local handyman Nate Peters who owned and operated a repair shop for all varieties of motorized vehicles in the nearby town of Alvwood. Not the most reassuring endorsement, in my judgment, given our prior dealings with old Nate. While he may have been a skilled motor craftsman in his heyday, I think he made his money nowadays by nickel and diming the seasonal sportsmen, and even swindling them on occasion. Years ago, Alex's car had broken down a few miles from Whispering Pines, and he pulled it into Nate's service station for an evaluation.

"Yep, just as I suspected," Nate concluded with a bit of dramatic flair that included sucking air through his clenched teeth and shaking his greasy head from side to side. "She'll need new rotors, belts, and front suspension at a minimum. Who knows what we'll find when we open her up for a closer look. I could probably have her done and running smooth again in eight to ten days tops, if all the parts arrive from Bemidji on time."

"Geez, I can't be up for ten days," Alex acknowledged innocently, not knowing Nate took every fact and admission into account as the estimated repair price in his head ratcheted up dollar signs faster than a Las Vegas slot machine. "I've got to get back to work, and Savannah has a soccer games she can't miss."

Nate Peters just scratched his head in apparent deep thought, straining to find a solution for the fast-wearying travelers. "I guess I could trade you even up for that fine station wagon over there in the yard. It don't look like much, but I bought it on a trade from Mrs. Nesbitt. She drove it with the utmost care for eight years. Not a scratch on it, and she runs like a gem. You'd be getting a heck of a deal given all the problems with your car, but I guess I could take a small loss just this once."

Alex depressingly considered his options. The station wagon seemed as though it arrived right off the set of the movie *Family Vacation*, with its faux-wood side paneling, steel roof rack, and uglier-than-sin yellow paint job. An even trade between his five-year-old Honda Accord and the late-model Ford wagon hardly seemed fair, but he had little choice. It's not as if he could hitchhike two hundred and fifty miles back home with a dog, a young daughter, and all of the family's belongings. The only other option was Greyhound, but the nearest bus service was an hour away in Grand Rapids. So, after a minimal test drive along the Avenue of Pines on Highway 46, Alex packed up his family and gear into their new wagon, driving off into the day's fading sunlight, gazing up in the rearview mirror every once in a while to see Clark Griswold staring right back at him.

At the time of the 2008 boat purchase, it was late in the season and time to close the cabin up for the year. Alex and my parents were able to test drive the boat extensively, ensuring it ran fine enough before loading it back up on the trailer, buttoning down the cover hatches for the long winter ahead and parking their new treasure on the far edge of our Whispering Pines property. I can't say for certain whether they each said a little prayer over this newly purchased toy or not, but I offered one up from afar:

> *May our outboard be saved after hitting that rock*
> *May our bow be rebuilt after ramming the dock*
> *May we find Dad's new watch that fell overboard*
> *May the neighbors quit stealing our slip's powercord*
> *May air freshener mask the musty smell under the berth*
> *May we someday owe less than the damn boat is worth.*

As I feared, our boat troubles began as soon as we first opened up the cabin for the season in early May of 2009. Dad and Mom ventured north for this inaugural trip, as usual, filled with the excitement we all feel during these initial cool days of spring, and ready for more months along the shores of Lake Dunbar. Once they hooked up the water pump and planted sixty trees around the property, they eagerly turned their attention to the waterfront, and with the help of neighbor Elias Hinck, soon had the new pontoon into the water and ready for a journey around the lake. Not so fast. After innumerable attempts and countless inappropriate words, they determined the boat's battery was dead. Resigning themselves to only fishing from the dock, my parents nevertheless still caught plenty of fish. Their return trip one week later with a brand new battery solved the problem, and it now was time for the next one, as recorded in Mom's cabin journal entry dated June 7, 2009:

The major project for the weekend was to get the pontoon boat functioning. Earlier it was the battery, and now it appears to be the engine. Last weekend, Alex could only get it to go backwards, a very tough way to fish. Ted checked various things, made some minor adjustments, but had no luck. He ended up removing the entire engine and taking it into Nate's Garage in Alvwood. I'm not sure what else to do as Ted suspects it has repair needs beyond his limited abilities. Nate's initial assessment said the motor was of 1970s vintage, much older than we were led to believe when we purchased a five-year-old pontoon just last season.

If that were not enough, we also could not locate the pontoon engine's gas can. Ted specifically recalled Alex telling him it was left under the blue boat tarp when Alex's family left for home the weekend before. But when Ted moved the blue tarp, the gas can was nowhere to be found. Ted was beside himself and ready to call upon the Itasca County Sherriff to begin an investigation. Well, the problem turned out to be Ted's selective hearing (shocking). Alex indeed had referenced the blue boat tarp, but meant the one in the back of the shed, rather than the one adjacent the boat landing. I naturally found the gas can within minutes of him conscripting me for missing-gas-can-finding duties, which probably frustrated Ted even more.

Now, I do not wish bad luck on anyone, but did feel a twinge of "I told you so" with these stories of pontoon boat woes. However, as long as those maladies did not directly impact my enjoyment of a Whispering Pines weekend, I had no problem. That reality lasted roughly one full season, for when I went north for my inaugural Dunbar trip of 2010, Ted casually mentioned I should really stop by Nate's Garage to retrieve the pontoon engine he had left with the wily mechanic for reconditioning over the winter. I begrudgingly drove over to Alvwood on my first Dunbar morning and was less than pleased to discover I was also required to hand over $211 before Nate would release the freshly tuned motor he declared to be "good as new." I should have asked for his guarantee in writing. The only writing to console me at the end of the day was Dad's cabin journal entry on the next trip in early June 2010.

> *Eddie picked up the two motors from Nate's Garage last month, but all was not well. I had left both the pontoon and fishing boat motors with Nate for different reasons. I asked him to check the spark plugs on the pontoon motor as well as give it a proper tune-up. Despite replacing two spark plugs and replacing a fuel line, it still did not work properly. As for the boat motor, it is nearly thirty years old and in need of just a simple tune up, in addition to a new shifter knob to replace the one that broke sheer off. However, he ended up replacing the propeller, water pump, and fuel line, whether it needed it or not. Like the pontoon motor, this one too failed to work 100 percent after we got it back from Nate. So, we took both motors back into Nate's Garage on this trip and the scruffy, greasy old repairman was truly perplexed and "pulling his hair out" over these troublesome engines and the plethora of other work stacked up in his meager garage. Of course, this is the same guy who told us last fall he was desperate for business. Anyway, he promised to give them both another look, and we left his shop less than fully confident.*

With great apprehension, I drove into Nate's Garage on my next visit to Alvwood at the end of June 2010 and timidly inquired as to the state of our motor maladies. Nate assured me they were fixed once and for all. Sure enough, when affixed to the boats back on Lake Dunbar, the little engines seemed to work as they should, and all was solved, at least from a mechanical perspective. My brother, Alex, did have some additional difficulty on his first trip of the season just one week later. It seems as though he ran out of gas with the pontoon halfway down the lake, and facing a strong wind from the direction of Whispering Pines. He was able to negotiate a tow from Mr. Hinck across the bay and eventually made his way home to our cabin. Since then, our boat troubles have been thankfully few and far between. My parents spent an entire weekend reupholstering the pontoon's leather seats, and had a bit of an unexpected challenge when they attempted to land the pontoon at the public access on the very last outing of the season, only to have the shifting lever break in half right at the moment Ted needed to downshift and land the ship with grace. Oh, the unending joy of boat ownership.

We continued to occasionally drop off our boat motors in the fall with Nate for checkups and tuning. Early one year, Dad also asked him to put a new shifting handle on the fishing boat motor, which we had been throttling with a vice grip for far too long. "No problem," Nate said back in June before proceeding to complain about the slow season it had been thus far, and how bad business was. Inexplicably, then, when Mom and Dad stopped in, he apparently could not even remember which motor was ours, although according to Dad it was right there in plain sight. The good news was the motors were apparently ready to go; the bad news was it cost another $200, and Nate was not particularly clear on his invoice what work he had performed on which motor. The other bad news was the fishing boat motor didn't work when Mom and Dad arrived back at the lake. Yes, shocking.

When attempting to accelerate the motor, it simply clanged, banged, hissed, and stopped. Upon returning to the garage in Alvwood, Nate swore he had run the small engine in a tub of water and it had worked just fine. After spending yet another $200 on Nate's lack of expertise, Dad and Mom picked up the fishing boat motor, and this time it seemed to perform like it should. Apparently a ball's worth of string was wrapped around the propeller, which somehow Nate did not notice the first time when he declared it to be "running fine," and the gear that drives the propeller had a couple of teeth knocked out of it. This was indeed strange as the motor ran fine when we first took it in, and if Nate indeed ran it in a tub of water after making repairs the first time, he would have surely found this problem. Given the fact a couple of teeth blades were missing, it's highly likely he ran it but forgot the tub of water, and instead the propeller hit the cement floor of the repair shop. Perhaps the last straw came a year or so later when Dad's journal entry revealed the end of his extended patience with Nate Peters.

So, we took the pontoon motor into Nate the bandit in Alvwood as we simply could not get it to start. It is a serious one-man job just to remove the heavy engine from the back of such a large boat. Of course, we picked the busiest day of the year to visit the quaint small village, which was overrun with hundreds of tourists for the annual Rhubarb Rumble. At least we were able to get out of town before 5:30 for the extremely competitive "rhubarb bake-off." While awaiting the motor repair, Ruth was in seventh heaven visiting two flea markets and one local craft store. We left our cell phone number with Nate who was supposed to call us when his repairs were finished.

Having not heard from him by five o'clock, we stopped by Nate's Garage only to find the motor to be sitting outside. Would he have ever called us? I doubt it. Nate informed us the lower gears were shot, and it would cost four to five hundred dollars to fix. Of course, it was Nate who put those gears into the pontoon motor two years ago. We told him to forget it. On my last trip, I saw a sign at the Northome Hardware store indicating they have a professional repair service. I think Nate Peters has received his last business from us, unless our need is something absolutely dire.

Despite his expressed frustrations, Dad left the pontoon motor with Nate for "one last try," and Nate must have sensed this was his last opportunity to impress for he finally succeeded in fixing the elusive engine, as my parents and brother discovered in early July. Apparently the third attempt at the very same repair was indeed the charm. Once attached to the back of the behemoth pontoon, the old motor with the new propeller, new shifter, new gears, new cables, and new accelerator worked just like, well, new, and probably for only one or two hundred dollars more in repairs than we would have spent for a brand new motor in the first place.

Mom and Dad went north in 2011 for their annual anniversary weekend, a tradition dating back to when they spent their honeymoon at my mother's favorite spot on earth, along the shores of Lake Dunbar. Rumor has it the 1965 honeymoon included some activities beyond the usual fishing and boating, for the neighbors later told Grandma Isabelle her daughter and "some strange man" appeared to be skinny-dipping "in the nude." Is there any other way to skinny-dip? When questioned about it over the years, my mother's adamant denials are always followed by a playful smirk. In anticipation of a tasty dinner at The Hill on the evening of their forty-seventh anniversary, Mom decided to have her hair done up special, so she made an appointment at the only beauty parlor in town, owned and operated by the wife of infamous boat motor non-repairman Nate Peters. None of us had ever met Mrs. Peters, come to think of it, but we'd all been into Nate's Garage more than a few times. Yet, Mom decided to give it a try, and left a voicemail message for Mrs. Peters in the morning.

Mom never heard back from Nate's wife, Sally the hairdresser, for her request for an appointment, so she tried calling once more. This time she heard the saddest outgoing phone message in the most forlorn tone a customer had ever heard.

"Hi, this is Sally. I will be closing my business on July 3 due to a personal matter at home. I will be starting a new job at Nip Clips in Grand Rapids, so if you want me to cut your hair, I can do it there." This message was delivered by an automated voicemail message with a delivery tone to make you think one of her children had just been eaten by a deranged wolf.

The saga took on an even stranger twist when Mom and Dad stopped down the road at the Co-op. They apparently thought it best not to poke their heads in and discuss the matter with Nate. When Ted and Ruth entered the store, a sign on the wall said Sally would be closing her store on July 3 for good. It was now several hours since Mom had left a message, well into the middle of the business day, and it was only the twenty-seventh of June not the third of July, so why was the salon not open for business? Mom then asked the clerk if the salon might still be open, but the clerk cautiously replied, "Oh I don't know, but it is so sad." What was so sad? Who died? The next day, my parents drove down for some shopping in Grand Rapids, and a haircut was high on Mom's list of priorities, but somehow in all the excitement of lunch at a local northwoods pub and one or two too many black and tans, or the thrill of shopping at a different Wal-Mart and Home Depot, the haircut completely slipped her mind before leaving town. Yet, they were in luck upon discovering a quaint little beauty shop in the neighboring town of Deer River. As Mom was getting her hair cut by a local beautician, she mentioned how she had tried to have her hair done in Alvwood but the salon was closed. The attentive beautician proceeded to also repeat exactly the words used by the store clerk back at the Co-op. "Yes," the lady from Deer River said to Mom. "It is so sad!" Here, twenty-five miles away from Alvwood, it was still "so sad." Generally the most you get from any of these Finlanders up here is "ya" or "sure." No one wanted to come right out and say what was going on because it would take way too much effort, so all Mom got from the hairdresser was simply the story was just "so sad!"

The Deer River beautician did add one more sentence to the burgeoning mystery, which clarified nothing but increased the drama. She proceeded to say, "It was probably all due to the bad accident Mr. Peters sustained a few years back." The whole affair did indeed seem to smack of possible marital discord at home, seeing Sally was apparently moving to Grand Rapids and it was universally "so sad." Naturally these cryptic clues led to a mirage of wild thoughts on what the discord might be. Dad and Mom eventually left Deer River totally perplexed on the meaning of the "so sad" story.

Thankfully, this northwoods mystery was solved the very next day back at The Hill Restaurant and Lodge in Squaw Lake, the place where white lightning and John Barleycorn eventually loosens all tongues and truth reveals itself. My parents entered The Hill to use the coin-operated laundry services to wash some bedding and clothes before their anticipated guests were to arrive the following day at Whispering Pines. Mom diligently applied herself to the task, and felt she would complete it more efficiently if Dad just stayed out of the way. Instead, he found himself a good seat on the steps to the upper loft of the apartments overlooking the laundry, lit up a Dom Diego cigar, and proceeded to crack open a new book.

Though enraptured by his reading and sensing exhilaration from the Dom Diego, the "so sad" northwoods mystery, like the ending of his book itself, was soon to be revealed. It was six p.m. or so and time for some of the local happy-hour clientele to start filtering out of The Hill. The first stumbling patron climbed up into his rusted-out pickup but stopped as another local fellow came waltzing out the door and hailed down the pickup driver to share some more gossip. They were speaking through the pickup window and throwing their cigarette butts in the back of the truck which contained a couple of old gas cans as rusted as the truck itself. For a moment, Dad anticipated a giant explosion and pondered whether he ought not extinguish his Dom Diego cigar.

While the two aging lumberjacks continued their low-murmured gossiping through the pickup window, a rather large lady came out of the tavern door and stopped several yards away from the truck. Apparently she had a range of hearing that would challenge the best hunting dogs in the northwoods, and she seemed to fully hear the conversation from the driver's side pickup window. As the woman continued toward the truck, she belted out in a voice that would have drowned out a Toscanini opera at the Metropolitan, "HELL, HE'S BEEN BANGING HER FOR THE PAST TWO YEARS!" The remainder of the locals' animated conversation revealed Nate had been consorting with some twenty-five-year-old beauty from the local village, and the ruthless repairman had promptly shown Sally the door. Now the "so sad" mystery had been solved. Apparently Nate had more firepower burning in his own internal engine than in all of the broken-down motors of his customers combined.

To be fair, not all of the Lake Dunbar Area Drama Club events involved the infamous Nate Peters. The extended Travis family created plenty of its own, and I must admit to playing a contributing role. In the summer of 2009, I enjoyed a weeklong trip to Whispering Pines with my brother, Alex, and our kids as soon as they were done with school for the year. The journey north started with such promise—another new cabin season, and two new Zebco fishing poles from Joe's Sporting Goods store. The fact my parents were just ending their own week's vacation at the cabin also meant the grass would be mowed, and I could simply relax.

My relaxation lasted until approximately 4:30 a.m. on the second morning of our stay. I was sound asleep in the upper single bunk bed, having been displaced by a sixty-five-pound yellow Labrador retriever from my normal spot in the back bedroom. I awoke sort of abruptly from a very peaceful slumber by a constant gnawing sound emanating from the far corner of the bunkroom. I could barely make out a small rodent-like shadowy figure. Great, another mouse. Hadn't we fixed the mouse problem a few years back? I wondered.

Then, at the very moment the dreaded mouse "jumped" four feet vertically from the floor to the screen window, I began to question whether I was awake or dreaming, and concluded I must be dreaming after rubbing my eyes thoroughly and seeing the mouse-like creature now chewing on the screen like crazy in an attempt to get out. Finding no exit, what I thought was a mouse then flew around the bunkroom in search of some other avenue to freedom. That was the last thing I saw before diving under my covers, and yelling for Alex to come to my aid. Now normally, I wouldn't be frightened of such a small critter, but this thing was flying around as blind as a, well, a bat in the dark, and I was concerned it just might get its mythical sticky wings caught in what remained of my receding hair.

After several desperate cries for help, Alex jolted out of his bed and came to see what all the excitement was about. When the gravity of the situation, or the lack thereof, dawned on him, Alex scoffed at my refusal to get out of bed, and he grunted I should simply shoo the beast away myself. It was precisely at such bravado moment the bat turned on a dime in the air, flew straight at my groggy brother, and chased Alex all the way back down the hall screaming and diving under his covers. Bat: two; humans: zero. We then decided upon a joint strategy. I timidly reached my arm out of the covers, reached for the light-bulb pull chain, and illuminated the room while Alex more bravely emerged from the safety of his bed, grabbed a broom from the hall, and chased the bat down with vigor. He eventually cornered the poor, confused flying forager, and brought our middle-of-the-night drama to its fatal finale. It was there the poor creature met his demise as Alex's prodding with the broom either scared the bat to its death or crushed him with the same result. I am able to accurately report these events as an eyewitness to the action. In fact, my eyes were the only thing visible from under my bed covers as Alex took care of the bat.

Alex also played a starring role in the Dunbar Drama Club during these years, despite his normally shy, stoic, and staid demeanor. In truth, it was not my brother who sought out drama, but drama found my brother. In early 2011, he bravely ventured north with Savannah, his ten-year-old daughter, and two of her friends, but without the help of his wife who stayed behind to begin a new home-based gardening business. Thankfully, all three girls were quite compliant with my gentle-natured brother, doing their share of chores and keeping their pre-teen troubles to a minimum, at least until they all ventured into Squaw Lake for a visit to the Max Store. Alex decided it best to enter the store with only one girl at a time, so as to better manage the chaos of all three kids' demands for various treats. Good plan, at least until halfway through the first rotation when Alex was inside the store with one of his daughter's friends. The girl quickly scoured the shelves for a favorite snack, knowing her time was running short, and soon she must trade places with the other girls. Alex gathered the few groceries he needed, and then waited patiently at the checkout counter, mingling innocently with the long line of fellow patrons. Savannah burst through the front door and announced full-throated the reason for her unexpected and early entrance into the Max Store.

"Daaaaad, Emma farted and the whole truck stinks!"

If you know my brother, you can easily envision the deep red color quickly engulfing his face, reflecting the utter embarrassment now consuming him. Yet, it was only the first of several maladies to befall my brother on that trip. Alex also took the girls swimming at a sandy beach over on Cut Foot Sioux, a very pretty lake with a gentle entry beach many miles off the main road, deep in the heart of the Chippewa National Forest. However, they shared the lake with some particularly irritating and incredibly small bugs called chiggers. On the drive back to Lake Dunbar, everyone in Alex's vehicle had a similar discomfort, and the kids' constant scratching of their legs and abdomens only made matters worse. Alex spent the rest of the day applying calamine lotion to the girls' skin, over and over again.

Then Alex took the girls on a daytrip to Washkish, roughly fifty miles to the north where the girls could swim in Minnesota's largest pair of connected lakes, the mammoth 288,000-acre Upper and Lower Red Lakes. The vista from Red Lake's shores is almost oceanic, for the horizon seems endless and the lake ever expanding. A unique feature that has drawn many in our family to visit this spot over the years is the incredible and unexpected shallowness of this massive lake. Like others before him, Alex watched from the shore with the family dog as the girls walked over one hundred yards out into Upper Red Lake, never finding a spot more than waist deep. Soon Alex and the girls were chased from the lake by a ferocious onslaught of biting deer flies, and they spent the evening once again back at Whispering Pines practically bathing in soothing, antiseptic aloe lotion.

To add final insult to these literal injuries, Alex was foiled in his lone attempt at fishing with his companions when the infamous pontoon boat stalled and would not restart, just as the little group reached the far end of our lake. After a frantic and frustrating hour of failed engine engagement and ineffective paddling of the far-too-heavy pontoon, Alex finally caught a break when a neighbor came roaring past and offered them a tow-ride back home. Despite all of these challenges, my inherently happy and optimistic brother retained both his well-known sense of humor and seemingly endless sense of gratitude, as reflected in his cabin journal entry at the end of his disastrous northwoods weekend.

> It was sure nice to reconnect with the cabin and more importantly each other this weekend. Life at home gets so busy with work, housework, friends, soccer, school, etc. and it's easy to lose touch. So, a week spent in this special place was perfect. I cannot explain how good the girls were, and how much fun they had. They absolutely love this cabin and I'm pretty impressed by that. I owe so much thanks to Mom and Dad for all they do to keep up this place as it should be. I won't list all of the things they have done to produce an amazing experience for all who come here, but I do hope they know how much we recognize and appreciate it.

Notwithstanding its occasional northwoods drama, Whispering Pines indeed remains a peaceful refuge for me, and for so many others in the extended Travis family. As we close in now on the end of our sixth decade along these hallowed shores, it is difficult to be anything but thankful for all we've experienced, for all we've shared. Dunbar is the shining star deep in the darkest heavens of the night, calling to us, beckoning us home. My brother and I answer her call as best we can, assuming the stewardship mantle established by our grandparents, and then carried forward through time so tenderly and caringly by our parents, Ted and Ruth. It is comforting too, knowing Uncle Jack and Aunt Evelyn hear the call as well. Despite having no heirs with the tragic passing of beloved cousin Kate so long ago now, my aunt and uncle still make annual treks north, and continue to share in the endless, repetitive stories from our years on Lake Dunbar, the magical place of our childhood brought back to life with every visit to her sacred shores.

As my recording of our family's sixty-year cabin journey comes to its necessary yet melancholy close here in the summer of 2014, a pleasantly surprising moment of hope has sprung forth among us. It is the amazing fulfillment of my mother's prescient dream back in 2010 when she and Dad had just sold their restaurant. My cousin Rose and her husband, Patrick, just purchased a neighboring cabin along Dunbar's western shore. Like Whispering Pines, it is a modest structure, but with a slightly more expansive green lawn, sloping gently to the water's edge, looking out across the lake's largest bay and onward to the Ronning Forest. It will be rejuvenating to see the Travis family presence on Lake Dunbar yet again touch new lives as the children and grandchildren of Rose and Patrick create their own memories along the shores of this great lake. With a bit more luck and hard work, the deep laughter of our grandparents, Sam and Isabelle Travis, and all who have followed in their playful footsteps, will echo forth across the cool dark waters of Lake Dunbar for generations yet to come.

The End of the World

It is important that I include one more letter from Grandma Isabelle, for it brings the story of my family's sixty-year experience at Lake Dunbar full circle. Her letter was dated September 16, 1993, and was written from her home in Greenwood, Minnesota.

Dear Eddie,

Thank you so much for the pretty birthday card. My kitchen table is full of cards, all so pretty and nice. Jack and Evelyn took me up to the Edgewater Café last night where everyone met for my party. Your mom, dad, and Alex came, as well as Paul and Eleanor. Walt and Rose made it, and we all had a grand time! The food was excellent and I really enjoyed it. I received so many presents and it was so very enjoyable. There were even three bouquets of beautiful flowers. My kitchen table is covered with cards and flowers.

I dreaded my birthday because I turned eighty. I never wanted to hear that number! Your grandma Trudy sent me an eightieth birthday card a week ago, and I hid it because I wasn't ready! Thank you again for your wonderful card. I'm going for coffee now but I'll write again soon. Take good care of yourself.

    Love, Grandma Isabelle

And so this story ends where it began, on September 15, 1993, in Cannon Falls, Minnesota. According to the old round clock hanging slightly askew near the door, it was now 11:30 p.m., and all other patrons had left the Edgewood restaurant nearly an hour before. The aging, unshaven cook leaned halfway out the back door taking two last drags of a cigarette before calling it a night. The busboy finished clearing tables from the dinner rush, and waited impatiently for the Travis family to get out. The skinny teenage waitress sat in the corner booth studying for an upcoming exam, and hoping the group would leave her a hefty gratuity.

"Come on everybody, only four pieces of cake left," announced Eleanor. "Walt, Alex, you guys get over here and finish it up. It looks like they're closing up in the other room. They'll be kicking us out any minute now."

"Grandma, we have time for one more story," said Walt. "Tell us about The End of the World."

"Oh boy," Isabelle exclaimed with slight surprise. "I almost forgot about that. It's been a long time since I was back there. Well, give me one of those last pieces of birthday cake, and I'll see what I can remember." Isabelle's children quickly obliged. At eighty years of age, one can never have too much birthday cake. "It was one of the first summers your grandpa and I were up at Lake Dunbar. I just couldn't get over how lovely and peaceful it was. Anyway, we had spent most of the day doing hard work around the cabin. Sam put a door on the bathroom, and I hung shades on all the windows.

"After lunch, we decided to take a walk down the old Beane road from the cabin to see how far it went. We must have walked for half an hour when the road narrowed and became more or less a horse path. Pretty soon we came upon two signs. The first was made of metal and said in bold black writing: End County Road 3. About one hundred feet farther a faded wooden sign said: The End of the World. Sam and I looked around a bit, and decided it probably was. We finally turned around and walked back home. Boy, were my feet tired. Over the years we've heard strange tales about the place, though. Ruth claims she and Teddy were snooping somewhere past the sign once, and all of a sudden some men with long hair and rifles came running toward them shouting to get the heck out."

"It's true, they did!" shouted Ruth. "We were scared to death."

"Oh, I wasn't scared, you were," said Ted.

"Then how come you ran back to the car and tore out of there like a bat out of hell?" Ruth retorted. Isabelle flashed a scowl at Ruth for interrupting this important story.

"Teddy's brother Harold was up at the cabin one fall doing some deer hunting," Isabelle continued. "He was looking for Jack's deer stand over by the federal land, and somehow ended up at The End of the World. Harold said he walked straight down the road trying to get out, but he ended up right back at the exact same spot from where he started, staring at the very same sign, and he got real spooked."

"Well, you know those Walsch boys. They'll make up any story if there's a crowd willing to listen," Eleanor added, noticing another stern look from Isabelle. This was her birthday, her moment in the spotlight.

"You know," Isabelle concluded with a far-off look and a deep feeling of misty recollection, "I've been back to The End of the World a few times over the years with Sam, Walt, and Gus, but we've never gone far enough past the sign to see who or what is back there. We've speculated over the years about the hippies, recluses, or other characters who might live there. But to tell you the truth, none of us can really explain it. None of us has seen what lies beyond The End of the World. Who knows, maybe the sign speaks for itself."

Reaching The End of the World has indeed been an initiation rite for the Travis family. Everyone has made the trek at one time or another. And despite what some might perceive as insignificant, the Lake Dunbar property seems to have a deeper meaning for our family, a reminder that it is truly our last refuge, The End of the World. If society collapsed and chaos ensued, the Travis family would have a metaphorical and literal place of safety. We would be strong. We would have what so many others seek: a sense of connection to family, the ability to laugh through great trials, and an undying commitment to move forward together in joy, peace, and strength of spirit. Even more than that, our family has something no one, not even death, will ever take away from our collective, common memories of life, love, and laughter from sixty years of soul-affirming experiences at a small, non-descript cabin on a scenic, hidden lake in the midst of a vast pine forest. And perhaps it is comforting for readers to know the tales and characters my mother, grandmother, and I have brought to life in these pages live not only in the past, but continue on anew, into the future.

I left my beloved Minnesota in 1984 on a journey like those of great uncle Frank and cousin Kate so many years ago, one that would take me to live along the shores of the Pacific Ocean in southern California. My journey no doubt involved the same internal feelings of angst every young person experiences upon leaving home for a far-off adventure. I was excited beyond belief at the thought of new landscapes, new people, and new possibilities, while also feeling the strong tug of home, and of all the people I must leave behind.

In times like these of leaving home once and for all, as we each take the phenomenal, transformative, and calculated risk in temporarily letting go of all we know and hold dear, we just might be able to grab on to something new and permanently worthwhile. As I said an emotional goodbye to my frequent visits on Lake Dunbar during a final trip north during August of 1984, I received a gift from my parents and brother: a picture book of Minnesota's northern forests. In it were inscribed these words:

One of the most wonderful gifts God gives us is our relationship with others. When we spend time with friends and family, memories are etched into our minds that will always be special. As you go away now, a deep sense of sadness and loss remains. Also, however, there is the realization time brings change and, although you are leaving, a part of you will always remain. You may not be close in miles, but you will always be close in our hearts.

Our world has many spectacular places, and we believe you have had the opportunity to grow up in a region with some of the most diverse and changing beauty imaginable. We hope you have enjoyed your youth in this land. Its majesty, wholesomeness, and pureness will hopefully serve to inspire you throughout your life to seek to preserve the fantastic world that has been created for us. We are merely shepherds of the land and, therefore, appreciate and serve it as it serves us.

As you journey forth into a new land now, may God fill your days with rewarding experiences as you touch the lives of others. We have enjoyed our journey together in this land and will cherish its remembrances with you. Let it be a source of strength and fond memories to you wherever life takes you on your own unique journey.

Love, Dad, Mom, and Alex
August 1984

My life's journey indeed took me far away from Lake Dunbar's shores, and for well more than a decade of my life, I saw her on only a few occasions. Still, no matter how far I traveled or how remote my destination, the constant thoughts, which sustained me throughout those formative years of my young adulthood, were the vivid images of Lake Dunbar and everyone in the Travis family who made her so unique, so memorable. This is the place, and these are the people who not only formed the stories in this book, but also shaped the story of my life.

I eventually did return to the land of ten thousand lakes one day, and to one in particular. Whispering Pines on the shores of Lake Dunbar is my heritage and my home. Together with the memories of all those who created and sustain her, it is the journey we remember. May God bless each and every one of you with a similar journey to call your own.

Eddie Travis Walsch
Whispering Pines
September 1, 2014

Acknowledgments

So many people contributed to this book, in so many wonderful ways. Special thanks go to a pair of great storytellers, Don Binder and Howard Holst, and also to Bernie Feils for his videotaped footage of a special birthday party, which first inspired me to write this story. Thanks also to the late Glenn Goetz who sat down with me one afternoon just before his ninetieth birthday and reminisced about his days fishing on a northern Minnesota lake. I would be remiss if I did not also acknowledge the tremendous input and encouragement I received from my father, Ken Fliés. He contributed mightily to these wonderful stories, and especially gave me great lift and ideas in the early stages of this writing, which began so long ago. And, of course, I'm so very grateful for JB, Millie, Linda, Art, Anne, Arlene, Jean and Rachel. Without you, there would be no story. I appreciate very much the time and dedication given by Mary Kate Boylan and Patty Stigen who each read through early drafts of this novel and gently pushed me in better directions. Sincere gratitude also goes out to my editor, Connie Anderson, and the wonderful, creative people at Wise Ink, including Amy Quale and Laura Zats. Connie's honest, critical advice and direction on this novel have undoubtedly made me a better writer, and the expert guidance from Amy and Laura was invaluable. Equal thanks go to Ryan Scheife for his amazing design work, both on the cover and throughout this book. Last but certainly not least, my heart is also full of thanks and love for three very special people who sustain and empower me every single day. Rand, Isaac, and Jason, thank you for your love and support. I appreciate you more than you know.

ENDNOTES

1   *A Woman Alone* by John A. Harrison, p. 127.
2   *Rez Life* by David Treuer, p. 228–237.

BOOK CLUB QUESTIONS

1. The Travis family encountered one neighbor who did not share their love of boisterous cabin weekends. Would you want a cabin next door to Whispering Pines? Why or why not?

2. Both Isabelle and Ruth reflect back upon the death of Sam Travis. How were their individual experiences and reactions different from one another?

3. The Travis family has various encounters with the Native American culture surrounding Whispering Pines. How did they act in those situations? Was it the way you would expect?

4. Isabelle, Ruth, and Eddie all describe places the family visited on the way to or near their cabin. Which of those places stuck out most in your mind, and why?

5. The narrators tell many stories about their infamous neighbors. Which ones were most memorable to you? Most hilarious? Most notorious?

6. Both Walt and Eddie had a close relationship with their grandmother, Isabelle. Does it remind you of a relationship in your life with an older relative or family friend? How and why?

7. Owning the cabin was both challenging and rewarding for the Travis Family. Do you think it was worth all the effort?

8. These stories span from 1929 to 2014. Which era was your favorite, and why?

9. Do you remember what I.W.T.S.L. stands for? What significance does it hold for you?

10. Whispering Pines brings together many different cultures, including Finnish, Native American, German-American, and more. Did you learn anything new about people who come from those backgrounds?

11. In her concluding chapter, Ruth addresses the challenges facing adult children with aging parents. Did those challenges resonate with you? Should Ruth and her siblings have acted differently?

12. Which family member had the greatest positive impact in these stories?

13. Both Mona Bell Hill and Helen Bryan are real people. Did either woman's story speak to you? Why? Which woman do you consider to be a better role model?

14. Have you had a personal experience with the Upper Midwest's so-called "cabin culture"? Besides the presence of many lakes, why do you think it is so prominent there compared to other areas of the country?

15. Which member of the Travis family would you like to talk with over a cup of coffee? Why?